The Devil's Heart

A Nick Randall Novel

Robert Rapoza

THE DEVIL'S HEART
by
Robert Rapoza
Copyright © Robert Rapoza 2020

Robert Rapoza
Rancho Palos Verdes, CA 90275
http://www.robertrapoza.com
Email: authorrobertrapoza@gmail.com

First Printing December 2020

Printed in the United States of America

ISBN: 978-1-7323912-3-9

To Rob and Jonathan Lait for helping to get the details right.

Chapter 1

Southern Argentinian Jungle
July 18, 1:07 p.m.

Professor Jim Grady skidded his bright yellow Jeep to a stop near his team's camp. He stared out his window through a small opening in a nearly impenetrable wall of Argentinian jungle. To the untrained eye, it appeared to be nothing more than a small break in the foliage but the opening fed into his team's remote archeological site.

The camp was a twenty-five-meter circle hacked from the jungle brush, which radiated outward for miles in all directions. A small group of tents were arranged in a neat row near the left side of the clearing, dwarfed by the huge Camboata trees towering above and behind them. To the right of the tents was the pit his team had excavated, and beyond that were the team's trucks. The only thing missing were the people.

Grady slid his six-foot, 185-pound frame from the vehicle, a wall of humidity blistering him as he scanned for signs of life. He found none. No one working in the main pit, no one getting lunch in the mess tent, no one walking around the camp. There wasn't a single colleague or worker from the university on the site. The

1

flaps of their empty tents fluttered in the afternoon breeze and their equipment lay haphazardly scattered on the ground, like they had been there one moment and gone the next.

Grady's pulse quickened.

He had called and texted many times over the past two days, trying desperately to reach his team. No one had answered or returned his messages and his concern had grown with each failed attempt.

The locals had warned him about the dangers of searching for the underground chamber and mysterious stone. They told stories about explorers disappearing into the jungle, and of armed men knocking on doors in the middle of the night, dragging away screaming villagers. Grady had dismissed them as folklore meant to scare children. He had set his mind on finding the fabled stone with mysterious properties and making a name for himself in the archeology field, but now, seeing his site turned into a ghost town, fear ripped through him. Had he condemned his team to some gruesome fate?

A humming sound rose from the center of the camp. Grady tensed, then spun in the direction of the unfamiliar noise. It pitched up, increasing in intensity, like a crystal glass humming before exploding, then it stopped.

"Jennifer is that you?" he called timidly to his team leader.

No reply.

"Is anyone there?"

Only silence.

Grady closed the Jeep's door and took a few tentative steps toward the main tent, which served as the dining hall and meeting area for the camp. He paused, scanned the area again, took a deep breath and marched to the tent, covering the span in several tense minutes while his heart strummed loudly in his chest.

The canvas structure loomed larger up close than it appeared from the distance, its tall sides casting a shadow on the forest floor. Grady stopped at the entrance, wiped his sweaty palms on his shirt, and gingerly lifted the flap to look inside. The dining hall was empty, but the stench of rotting food spilled out, causing Grady to recoil in disgust.

He looked back at his Jeep, overwhelmed by the urge to sprint to it and get away. But he couldn't leave. Not without looking for his team. Their safety was his responsibility.

Get it together and find your damn people.

The sun shone brightly against a cobalt blue sky, its warming rays heralding another hot summer day, yet Grady shivered involuntarily as he searched for someone…and the source of the sound. He walked briskly, his pulse increasing with each step. He finally arrived at the main excavation area, but found it abandoned as well. Tools lay on the ground, waiting for workers to return, like everyone was on a break. But Grady knew better. Something had caused them to drop their equipment and abruptly leave the area, but what? Why would his team leave their camp in this condition and where could they have gone and how?

Grady ran his trembling hands through his hair as his mind raced through possible scenarios, none of them good.

What have I done?

He heard the sound again.

***

Posadas, Argentina
July 18, 5:43 p.m.

Grady sped along the highway, the passing countryside a blurred streak in his peripheral vision. He punched the dashboard repeatedly, thinking of how he had abandoned the search for his team. When the odd humming noise had returned, a tsunami of fear had flooded him, and he sprinted back to his Jeep and got the hell out of there. Now a new feeling overwhelmed him. Guilt. His stomach churned thinking about everyone. Especially Jennifer. What would she think about him running away like a scared kid?

3

Grady's thoughts wrestled in his mind, creating confusion, but one thing was clear: he needed to find help. Fast. Unfortunately, normal channels wouldn't work—the nature of his research guaranteed that. There was only one person he could turn to, but he had no idea what kind of reception he'd get. He'd have to worry about that later. First, he had to get back to his apartment in the town of Posadas to get his research notes. He had rented the space to be near the dig, but now he'd have to abandon it. Just like his team.

He parked his jeep outside the two-story tan and white building, badly misjudging the stall and taking up two spaces. His sweaty hands slipped off the handle as he struggled to open the door. He needed to calm himself.

Grady slowed his breathing, steadied his hand, then carefully gripped the metal lever, and popped open the driver's side door. He sprinted the short distance to his apartment complex, weaving past parked cars and hedges that lined the walkway. Climbing three concrete stairs at a time, he reached his second-floor unit and looked down to the parking lot. He had left his truck door open but couldn't worry about that now.

He opened his front door, darted inside, and locked the door behind him.

His small apartment was in shambles. Toppled bookcases and paper from his drawers lay strewn across the floor. Someone had ransacked his place undoubtedly searching for his research notes. If they had found them, his chance of finding his team had disappeared along with them. He could only pray that they hadn't discovered his hiding spot.

Grady ran to his bedroom and found his window shattered. A breeze ruffled the white curtains like a menacing ghost warning him to leave. He crouched by his bed and rolled the frame away from the corner of the wall, exposing the slatted wood floor. Jamming a key into a narrow gap, he pried up a single plank, revealing a secret compartment. He shined his cell phone light inside and sighed with relief.

His brown courier bag was still there.

He grabbed it and looked inside. Everything was there.

A slamming car door drew his attention to the lot below. He rose slightly, peering over the sill and through the smashed window.

Two men in suits moved around his car. One rifled through his glovebox while the other scanned the lot for something. Grady's heart lodged in his throat when he realized they were looking for him. One of them turned toward his bedroom window. Grady ducked.

Did he see me?

Grady slowly peered over the sill again. The men were running … toward his apartment. They'd be on him in minutes.

Grady sprinted, bag in hand, to the bathroom. He jammed the window open, then smashed the screen with his palm, partially tearing the mesh.

Pounding rose from the front door. He had to get out of there.

Grady punched the screen again, but this time the entire framed popped out. He climbed onto the toilet and out through the window. Gunshots echoed through his apartment, followed by the sound of someone kicking in the front door.

Grady scurried onto the narrow ledge that ran along the outside of the building. The wind tussled his red hair as he balanced twelve feet above the black asphalt of a neighbor's carport. If he were to drop here, he'd leave one hell of mess for his neighbor to clean up. His brown bag strap lay across his forearm as he inched along the ledge, heading toward the back of the complex.

He shuffled a few more feet, reached for the next piece of molding and gripped it. Something sharp sliced into his finger. He instinctively recoiled, titling backward, nearly dropping to the ground, his right arm flailing in the air. He lunged for the piece of trim, grabbing it lower than before. Nothing sharp this time. He

5

clamped his fingers around it and balanced himself, his heart thudding like a drum in his chest.

"Verdammt! Where the hell is he?" an angry German voice yelled from the bathroom window.

Grady turned to look.

A bald-headed man popped out. He looked to the street, then turned to Grady. An evil smile spread across his face. "Got you." He climbed onto the windowsill.

A second pursuer stuck his mustached face out of the window and glared at Grady.

The bald man slid a gun from his coat. "Auf Wiedersehen, professor." He took careful aim.

"Nein! Herrmann wants him alive! Get him and his notes!" the mustached man growled.

The bald man grunted, then put his gun back in his pocket. "It'd be easier to shoot him." He slid onto the ledge, moving fluidly, like a gymnast. He quickly closed the gap with Grady.

"I'll get down to the parking lot, and make sure he can't get away," mustache man barked.

Grady's fingers ached from holding on, but he couldn't stop. He shimmied to the corner of the building and hopped down onto a neighbor's balcony. He landed awkwardly, tumbling onto the sandpapery floor, knocking over a potted plant in the process. The ceramic container smashed into a section of stucco wall, shattering into pieces.

Grady tried the slider.

Locked.

He grabbed a chunk of the smashed pot and launched it at the glass, which shattered on impact. He ducked inside the apartment and found it empty. He ran to the front door, threw it open and sprinted into the second story hallway, nearly running over a neighbor.

"Verlo! Watch where you're going!" The man screamed.

"Sorry."

Grady hit the landing, running at full speed. He reached the ground and broke into a dead sprint, then flipped a quick look at his apartment before turning the corner. The bald man popped out the front door, spotted Grady, and sprinted for the stairs.

Grady ran along a tall row of flowering hedges, which exploded outward as the mustached man barreled into him. The two sprawled into the road, kicking and hitting then rolled to a stop, the man straddling Grady. He pressed his huge hand into Grady's throat, cutting off his air and grinning as he squeezed.

A roaring engine, followed by a car horn, blared from down the street. The man spun his head and looked over his shoulder, loosening his grip on Grady's throat. Grady used the distraction to shove him off and the man tumbled into the street, in front of the approaching silver sedan. The speeding car ran over his head, popping it on the asphalt. The driver skidded to a halt and hopped out of his car, mouth hanging open as he stared at the dead body.

Grady paused a moment, then vomited into the street, his body shaking with a mixture of adrenaline and shock. He wiped his mouth with his bloodied shirt sleeve.

Gunshots rang out from his building.

"You're dead, motherfucker!" The bald man had caught up to him.

Grady staggered to his feet and raced down the walkway toward the parking lot. He stopped in front of a gate and pulled the handle. Locked.

He hopped onto an adjacent wall, then jumped over the gate and tumbled onto the brick walkway on the other side. Popping to his feet, he resumed his mad dash. Moments later, a soft grunt arose from behind him. Grady turned to see the bald man jump over the gate, hitting the ground in stride.

You've gotta be kidding me!

Grady needed to slow his pursuer to have a chance to escape. He ran by a row of trash cans, pulling them to the ground in front of the bald assassin. The sound of cursing and banging tin behind him told him his plan worked, but had he bought enough time? Grady emerged from the walkway and sprinted for his truck. The door was still open. He dove into the vehicle, started the engine, and threw it into reverse. The truck lurched backward, speeding out of the parking space. Grady hit the brakes then threw it into drive just as the windshield shattered under a barrage of gunfire.

Grady ducked, then mashed his foot onto the accelerator. He peered over his dashboard, spotting the bald man standing in the road in front of him, taking aim. The assassin squeezed off several rounds, which buzzed over Grady's head, shattering the Jeep's rear window.

Grady aimed the truck straight ahead, nearly crushing the bald man, who dove to the side moments before impact. Grady looked at his rearview mirror. The bald man was running to his car.

Chapter 2

George Washington University, D.C.
July 20, 9:02 a.m.

Dr. Nick Randall lifted the lid of the white storage box, which sat on the end of the workbench. Inside were dozens of artifacts from a graduate anthropology project from the previous spring's fieldwork session at Point Rosee, Newfoundland. Carefully wrapped, labeled, and separated by material type, each bag contained several smaller bags filled with stone, wood, and metal artifacts. Randall ignored these, carefully pushing them aside to reach the bag he wanted.

"Not interested in those other bags?" Keisha Lewis asked, a smile forming on her lips.

Randall looked over his glasses at Keisha, and chuckled. Caught red handed, like the proverbial child with his hand in the cookie jar. Only this cookie jar was a box full of artifacts from a recent excavation and the prize wasn't a sweet desert. "Of course I'm interested in them. Just not at this particular moment."

"Uh huh," Keisha's voice dripped with sarcasm. She was Randall's favorite graduate student, funny, driven and as smart as anyone he had ever worked with.

"What?" Randall replied, putting up his hands to emphasize

9

his innocence. He continued to dig through the box and with a little additional searching, found the bag and pulled it out. Inside were several bone fragments.

The fragments were found in excavation unit 902, level B, as indicated by the designation 902B, carefully printed on the bag's label. These would be the first artifacts Randall and Keisha catalogued today. He emptied the contents of the bag onto his cataloguing mat, which had a series of measured circles used to help organize the artifacts during the sorting process. He made vertical groupings by what body part the bone fragments came from to simplify the data entry process.

He lifted an oval shaped piece and studied it more closely, then handed it to Keisha. "Tell me about this one."

Keisha accepted the fragment, turning it over in her hand, looking at it from different angles. "It's from a man's skull, which was shattered by the impact of a heavy object."

"What sort of object?" Randall asked.

"Based on the deep, v-shaped indentation, probably a sword blade."

"Is there anything odd about that?"

Keisha knitted her brow, confused, but only for a moment. She grinned widely, solving Randall's riddle. "The indigenous population didn't use swords, which raises the question of who did this?"

Randall smiled and nodded.

"I'm sure you have a theory Dr. Randall," Keisha handed him back the skull fragment.

She was right, he did have a theory. "Vikings."

Keisha raised an eyebrow. "Vikings?"

"The descendants of the Vikings left sagas explaining that Leif Erikson led an expedition to the east coast of North America. The stories described good harbors and abundant natural resources."

"But they're just stories, not hard evidence."

"That's true, there wasn't any concrete proof until 1960,

when a site at Newfoundland offered the first clues. Since then, there've been multiple excavations of the site," Randall replied.

"Is that why you took the fieldwork class to Point Rosee?" Keisha asked.

Randall nodded, Keisha had missed the trip because of a family emergency. She had nearly lost her mother to cancer and had to fly home to care for her. The fieldwork class had discovered additional evidence of a Viking presence in the frigid lands of the northernmost regions of the Canadian Island, including this piece of skull. "Sorry you had to miss the trip, but I thought you might enjoy cataloguing the artifacts."

Keisha smiled. "Thanks for thinking about me, and thanks for offering me the job this summer."

"You earned the job. You're one of the brightest students I have and you're going to have a wonderful career. Just don't forget about us little people when you make it to the top."

This earned a laugh from Keisha.

"Nick Randall?"

Randall turned to face the door and found a tall, thin, young man propped against the frame. The stranger was dressed in dirty khaki pants and a rumpled, blue short-sleeve button shirt. His face was long, and narrow and sported a neatly trimmed beard and mustache, which rested beneath a broad nose and bright green eyes. His red hair was a scraggily mess, like he had been for a long ride in a convertible. "Can I help you?"

The stranger crossed his arms, licked his lips, and rapidly tapped his foot against the floor. "You're Dr. Nick Randall?"

"That's right. And this is Keisha Lewis, one of my graduate students."

"My name's Jim Grady."

"Is there something I can do for you?"

"Do you mind if we speak in private?" Grady asked. There was something in the way he spoke, more a demand than a request.

He then fidgeted with his buttons before letting out a deep sigh. "Now, please."

Randall looked at Keisha. "Can you give us a few minutes?"

"Sure, I can enter the grades from the summer session quiz," Keisha rose to her feet. "Nice to meet you Jim."

Grady gave a curt nod then watched Keisha exit the room and slowly walk down the hall before turning in the direction of the stairs. Grady's eyes followed her closely and he mumbled under his breath until she was out of site. His eyes then fell to Randall.

"Grab a seat," Randall gestured to a black mesh back chair on the other side of the work bench.

Grady jumped into the open seat, sinking into the gray foam top. "I'm in a bit of trouble."

"What kind of trouble?"

"My team disappeared from our dig site and I don't know what to do."

Randall frowned. "I don't follow you."

"We were excavating a site in Argentina, but I was called back to the university. I was gone for a couple of days, and lost contact with my team. I tried calling and texting but couldn't reach anyone."

"You're an archeologist?"

"Yeah, and like I said, I lost contact with my team."

"When did this happen?"

"A few days ago."

"Have you gone back to the site?"

"Yes, but no one was there. I looked everywhere: the dining hall, the main excavation area, even their tents, but couldn't find a single person," Grady rocked back in forth in his chair like a metronome keeping time for a musician.

"Did you call the police?"

"Yes."

"What did they say?"

"They weren't any help. They said it might be tomb

12

robbers."

"I guess that's possible."

"It can't be. There was no ransom note, no signs of struggle, nothing," Grady gripped the arm of his chair and leaned forward. "It's like they were there one minute and gone the next."

"What are the police doing now?"

"Not a damn thing."

"That can't be."

"They didn't believe me. They acted like I was crazy and told me to call them if I heard back from anyone about a ransom."

"But they're the police, they have to do something."

"They're not."

"Can't you have the university work with them? I'm sure if you get your administration involved the authorities will have to listen."

"I tried that, and it didn't work."

Randall contemplated the situation. Jim sounded serious, but how could his entire team have vanished? "I'm really sorry to hear about this, but I'm not sure how I can help."

"I've followed your work for some time, and I know you're not a normal archeologist."

"Gee, thanks."

"I don't mean it that way. You have an open mind and consider possibilities outside of the norm."

"Where are you going with this?"

"What do you know about San Ignacio Mini?" Grady asked, his knee working up and down like a jackhammer.

"I've never heard of it before. Why?"

"It's a Jesuit mission in Argentina."

"Is that where your team disappeared?"

"No, but there's another site not far from there, hidden in the jungle. That's the site we were excavating. We were looking for an artifact called El Corazon del Diablo. Have you heard of it?"

Randall shook his head.

"According to legend, The Devil's Heart was a sacred stone that possessed great power. The Inca wanted it so badly they pillaged nearby tribes hoping to find it. There're stories about the stone being discovered, then lost again, throughout the ages."

"How did it get its name?"

"It's blood red with two lumps on top."

"And how do you know so much about it?"

"You want the long version or the short version?"

"Let's start with the short."

"I learned about it during my doctoral program, from a laborer named Humberto. He came from a very poor family and was having a tough time supporting his wife and kids, so I shared my supplies with him and even gave him a few bucks every now and then. Right before the project ended, he brought me this."

Grady opened his courier bag and removed a single piece of parchment paper and handed it to Randall, who immediately recognized the writing as Quechua, a native South American language, spoken primarily in the Andes. It took him a moment, but he eventually recalled enough of the language to understand the document. Randall lifted his eyes toward Grady, whose leg was nervously bouncing again. "Go on."

"When I got back to the university, I started researching the legend. It wasn't easy, because there's not a lot of information about it, and I didn't want to broadcast my research, but eventually I confirmed it wasn't just a legend. Then I spoke to my mentor, Dr. Vogel, and told him about the stone. I wasn't sure how he'd react, but he encouraged me to pursue it. He even found funding for my trip to Argentina."

"All of this is really fascinating, and good for you to chase your dreams, but I still don't understand what you want from me."

"I was hoping you'd help me look for my team, and the stone."

Randall furrowed his brow. "Do you want me to speak to the police for you and see if I can get them to do something?"

"No. I want you to come with me to Argentina."

"Jim, I'd like to help you, but I'm a scientist, not a private eye. I think you need to work with the authorities to find them. I'm sure there's a simple explanation behind this. Besides, I don't know the first thing about looking for missing people."

Grady's eyes darted around the room, finally coming back to rest on Randall. "There's more to the story about The Devil's Heart."

Now Randall leaned toward Grady. "If you have something to tell me, just say it."

"The origin of the stone is… mysterious."

"How?"

"Most of my information is from indigenous tribes in the area. The stories they told me were passed down through generations."

"And?"

"The Devils Heart isn't from Earth."

Here we go.

"I went back to ask Humberto how he got the parchment. He didn't want to tell me, but before I left, he shared one additional thing. He gave me a cardboard matchbox and inside was a small piece of red stone."

"What makes you think it's not from Earth?"

"I had a buddy of mine—a chemist at the college—run tests on it. He found trace elements he couldn't identify. He researched it more and discovered these elements were very dense and had the same qualities as elements in the actinide series."

"You mean, like uranium?"

"Uranium and plutonium."

"Did you have your friend run any other tests?"

"He was going to, but the stone disappeared. He swears he had it locked up and didn't tell anyone about it, but when he came to work the next day, it was gone. Now my team's missing too, and

I don't have anywhere else to go."

Grady pressed his palms into his red eyes. His stubble-covered face and ragged appearance gave all the outward signs of a man at the end of his rope. In his many years of teaching, Randall had always had a soft spot for anyone in trouble, rarely turning down a request for help, remembering the kindness others had shown him when he was nearly forced out of teaching. But Grady's story set off numerous red flags.

"Will you help me?" Grady asked.

Randall squirmed in his chair. "I can see you're worried about your team, but the help you need is beyond anything I can do."

Grady's shoulders slumped.

"Maybe I can call some friends to see if they have any ideas."

Grady angled his eyes to Randall. There was a sadness in them. "You don't remember me, do you?"

A look of confusion washed over Randall's face.

"I can't say I blame you. It's been twenty-two years, and I was just a kid, but I sure remember you. My dad always talked about how you were his favorite student. I could tell, he loved you like a son."

Randall's eyes went wide. "You're Ben Grady's son?"

Grady nodded.

Dr. Ben Grady was the reason Randall loved archeology. He had taken Randall under his wing and taught him everything he knew about the field. When Randall had explained that he needed to leave graduate school because he could no longer afford it, Dr. Grady arranged for a paid internship. But even more than this, Ben Grady had invited Randall into his life, introducing him to his family, and welcoming him into his home. Ben had been like a second father to Randall, who had lost his own father when he was just teenager. It had been a crushing blow when Randall learned of his passing. Sitting across from Jim now, he realized the two of them shared a similar story. Jim was only seventeen when his father had passed, same as Randall.

"Will you help me?"

Randall owed everything to Ben Grady. How could he refuse his son? "I'll help you Jim."

Grady smiled. "Thank you." He wiped his eyes with a ragged sleeve and cleared his throat. "What do we do first?"

"There's someone who might be able to help us, but first I'd like to meet Dr. Vogel."

"I can take you to see him, he only lives a couple of hours from here."

"Give me some time to wrap things up here and then we can go."

"Perfect, I'll be back around one."

Chapter 3

Rhodes, Greece
July 20, 9:23 pm

Father Enrico Bianchi's cassock waved in the breeze as he walked from the rectory to his church, *Sancta Maria*. An unseasonably cool summer wind carried off the Mediterranean, washing away any stray clouds that lingered in the sky. He walked past the white plastered walls and looked up to the small niche above the door, which contained a beautiful statue of the Virgin Mary. Opening the door, he entered the narthex of the church. Built in 1743, it was the main Catholic Church on the island of Rhodes. He dipped his fingers into the baptismal font, then made the sign of the cross on his forehead.

He made his way through the nave of the old church, walking past frescoes depicting the Stations of the Cross. The beautiful artwork recounted Jesus's final walk through the streets of Jerusalem to his crucifixion. He paused for a moment, leaned on one of the wooden pews, then contemplated a life of service. He opened the door to the Blessed Sacrament Chapel and went inside. No one was there. He sighed, saddened that venerated practices such as this were no longer popular with parishioners.

The old priest took a knee near one of the back rows and began to silently pray. Finishing the Rosary, he heard a soft creak from the pew behind him.

"It's nice to see that for some, the old ways still hold sway," a gruff voice said from behind, in an accent that Bianchi couldn't place.

Fr. Bianchi finished his prayer, raised his head slowly, and addressed the man without turning. He spoke slowly, his gravelly voice belying his age. "Sì. The practice of the Faith knows no fads and doesn't give in to the whims of popular culture. Is there something I can do for you, my son?"

"You can tell me the location of your society's most sacred artifact," the man said. His words were heavily accented, perhaps German.

"The most sacred item in this room— in fact, this entire church, is up there," Bianchi said, motioning to the tabernacle, where the Eucharist was stored.

The stranger grunted. "That's not what I meant." Bianchi felt the cold steel barrel of a gun pressing into the back of his neck.

"How dare you bring a weapon into the house of God!" Father Bianchi chided; his hands balled into fists. He tried to stand but was met with a strong hand, pushing down on his shoulder, forcing him to remain kneeling.

"Your faith is strong, old man. Perhaps I'll put it to the test if you don't provide the information I seek." The stranger cocked the gun's hammer.

Bianchi closed his eyes, unworried about the prospect of dying. "I have lived a long and fulfilling life serving my Lord. If it is my time to be called back to His side, I will go willingly. My soul is prepared to meet Him. Can you say the same?"

The stranger laughed. "You may feel that way now, old man, but I know something that might convince you otherwise. Get up, you're coming with me."

"And if I refuse?"

"You have two lovely nephews and a brother in Italy. It

19

would be a tragedy if something were to happen to them."

"What sort of a man makes threats against the lives of the innocent? I will go with you out of love of my brother and nephews, but woe to you for harboring such evil thoughts. It is better that you had never been born than to threaten to kill children."

Chapter 4

Potomac, Maryland
July 20, 2:37 p.m.

Concrete skyscrapers fell away to green suburbs as Randall and Grady sped along U.S. 29, to Dr. Vogel's home in Potomac Maryland. The highway wound along the edge of the Potomac River, skirting the Virginia and Maryland border. They traveled Northwest from D.C., past C.I.A. Headquarters and Langley Virginia, which lay directly West. As they crossed The Beltway, most signs of civilization faded to open countryside.

Thirty minutes prior, Grady had returned to Randall's office eager to get going. Randall had used the two-hours to finish his work and call some colleagues to learn more about Grady. A teacher friend had confirmed that Grady worked at the university but didn't know about his current fieldwork. Grady's reputation was a hard-driven researcher who wasn't afraid to question established archeological norms. As Randall's friend had put it, "He likes to push the envelope when it comes to conducting research. Kind of like you."

During the ride, Randall learned more about Grady, asking him what had happened after his father passed. Grady explained that he and his mother had moved back to Waco, Texas, to be near her family. After graduating from high school with honors, Grady applied for and was accepted to the University of Texas at Austin, where his formal archeology education began. After graduating, Grady began teaching at the school.

"Are you working there now?" Randall asked.

"No. I left a few years ago."

"Why?"

Grady turned and looked out the passenger-side window.

Not wanting to press, Randall switched gears. "Do you remember Francisco Andrade?"

"How could I forget him? He's the largest human being I've ever seen. He towered over me when I was a kid."

"I called him and he's going to arrange for someone to take us to your site."

"How much did you tell him about what happened?"

"Enough to make him worry. He insisted we take security guards with us, and to tell you the truth, I don't think it's a bad idea."

"When can we go?" Grady asked.

"He'll call me when everything's arranged," Randall steered the truck onto the offramp that led into the town of Potomac.

"He's going to have to hurry. I booked us a flight leaving tonight," Grady said.

Randall turned to Grady. "Don't you think you should have checked with me first?"

"My team's missing. I didn't think you'd mind."

Randall bit his tongue, not wanting to start an argument. "We'll have to cut this meeting short. I'll need time to pack and make arrangements for someone to watch my house."

"If it makes you feel better, I paid for the flights myself."

Randall took a deep breath and sighed. Grady was missing the point; it wasn't about the money. They drove on for several minutes, neither man speaking. Grady cleared his throat, then motioned to the upcoming intersection. "That's his street."

Randall turned onto Riverwood Drive, a beautiful tree lined

street on the outskirts of town. Tall sycamores blotted out the sun, creating a false sense of late afternoon on the shady street. Following Grady's directions, Randall pulled his car into the driveway of a beautiful two-story brick home, with a burgundy Buick Riviera parked in the driveway.

The lot was an oval shaped clearing of grass, surrounded by the same tall sycamore trees that lined the road. The nearest home was half a mile away and invisible from the driveway. Secluded was the word that came to mind.

"Looks like he's home," Grady exited the truck.

Randall followed him to the tall, arched front door.

Grady knocked, and they waited. No one answered.

Randall scratched his head. "Try the doorbell."

Grady pressed the button and the two men waited again. Several more minutes passed, but still nothing.

Grady tried the doorknob. It was locked.

"I guess he's not here," Randall said.

"That's his car," Grady pointed to the Buick. "Let's try the rear door. His office is around back."

The two men shuffled to the rear of the house. As they approached, Randall noticed the back door cracked open. A sliver of darkness announced that there were no lights on inside.

Grady frowned. "That's weird." He pushed the door open slightly. "Dr. Vogel!"

There was no response.

"Why don't you try again?" Randall said.

"Dr. Vogel, its Jim." Grady knocked as he spoke.

Randall stepped past Grady and pushed the door open. Daylight washed into the home, revealing an empty room.

"Dr. Vogel, are you home?" Grady asked, his voice rising.

Randall scanned the room. Neatly arranged, checker patterned furniture by the fireplace created a warm welcoming environment. "I thought you talked to him before you came to my

23

office."

"I did. He said he'd be here."

The two men walked past the stairs and down the hallway into the den. It was empty, like the rest of the house.

"Something's not right," Randall said.

"I'm going to check his office," Grady slid past Randall and entered the door on his right. "Nick, he's over here!"

Randall hustled into the adjoining room and found Grady kneeling by the professor, who was seated in a large, upholstered recliner, his wrists and legs bound by rope.

"Are you okay?" Grady asked, trying to loosen the cord binding his hands.

"I am now. I don't know what I would have done if you hadn't come," Vogel said.

"What happened?" Randall asked.

"I was working in my office and heard something behind me. I turned and found two men with guns. I was shocked and asked what they were doing. One of them hit me in the head and told me to sit down," Vogel turned to face Randall, revealing a large, oval shaped red and purple lump on his forehead.

Grady left the room.

"What did they want?" Randall asked.

Vogel shrugged. "They went through my things, but before they left, they tied me up and warned me not to call the police, so I've just been sitting here."

"Did you get a look at their faces?" Randall asked.

Vogel shook his head. "They wore masks."

Grady returned with a bag of ice and a kitchen knife. He cut Vogel's hands free then gave him the ice. "Put this on your head." He handed the ice to Vogel who gingerly placed the bag on his lump, then winced in pain.

Grady knelt by the chair, then cut the rope around Vogel's legs. "We need to get you to a doctor."

"It's just a small bump Jim. I'll be fine."

"What were they looking for?" Randall asked.

24

"I have no idea. I was preparing my class materials for the fall term when they came," Vogel replied.

"Have you been working on something special?"

Vogel shook his head, lifted the bag of ice, and ran his hand over the lump.

"You have no idea why they were here then?" Randall persisted.

"None. They came, looked and left."

"You need medical attention," Grady said. "And we need to call the police."

Vogel grimaced. "I'm sorry about this. I know you wanted to talk about what happened to your team."

Randall shifted on his feet. "I think that'll have to wait. Jim's right, we need to call the police, then get you to the hospital."

Vogel nodded. "I suppose you're right."

"We should take him to the doctor first," Grady said.

"When we call the police, they'll send the paramedics." Randall turned away from Grady, pulled his phone from his pocket and dialed 911, then explained what had happened. He clicked off. "They're on the way."

A short time later, emergency units arrived. Having provided as much information as possible to the police, Randall joined Grady as the paramedics lifted the sides of Vogel's gurney, preparing to take him to the hospital.

"I'm sorry I can't go with you to the hospital. We're flying out later tonight and I need to go back to D.C. to pack.," Grady said.

Vogel smiled. "No need to worry my boy, I'll be fine."

"Do you have anyone to stay with when you get out?" Randall asked. "The police don't think it's a good idea for you to come back here until they've had a chance to investigate."

"I have a friend I can stay with," Vogel replied.

Grady patted Vogel on the shoulder. "I'll call and check in

once we get to Argentina."

The paramedics loaded Vogel into the ambulance and pulled away, leaving Randall and Grady standing in the driveway.

"Things just aren't adding up," Randall frowned. "Is there anything you haven't told me?"

Grady held up his hands and shrugged.

"I guess we better get back to D.C." Randall walked to his truck and hopped in. Jim entered on the passenger side.

Randall fired up the engine and headed back onto the road.

Chapter 5

Arlington, Virginia
July 20, 4:46 p.m.

The ride back to town was quiet, both men frayed from the events at Vogel's home. Randall pulled his truck to the curb near his house.

"Why are we here?" Grady asked.

"This is my house, and I need to pack for the trip. You're welcome to help yourself to anything in the fridge. I'm sure you're hungry."

Randall opened the front door, walked in, and set his keys on the end table.

"It's about time," a female voice called from the couch.

Randall flinched at the unexpected sound, then turned in the direction of the voice. "Sam. What are you doing here?"

"We were supposed to have lunch today, remember?" Sam rose from the couch to give her father a peck on the cheek.

Grady stood in the doorway and cleared his throat.

Sam brushed a stray strand of brown hair from her eyes. "I didn't know you had company."

"Jim, this is my daughter Samantha."

"Nice to meet you," Sam said. "How do you know my father?"

Randall dropped onto the couch. "Why don't you sit

27

down."

He explained the situation to Sam, starting with Jim's background and ending with what had happened to Jim's team and their visit to Vogel.

"My dad's said so many wonderful things about your father throughout the years. I can't think of anyone who's had a bigger impact on his life."

"Thanks Sam, that's nice of you to say."

"I'm also sorry to hear about your team. Is there anything I can do to help?"

Grady's glance pivoted to Randall, his eyes seeking guidance on how to answer.

"We're flying down to Argentina tonight to look for them," Randall said, noting Sam's raised eyebrow. "It's the least I can do for Jim."

Sam slowly nodded. "Jim, would you excuse us for a minute?" Sam rose from the couch, looked at her father and nodded her head toward the kitchen. Randall picked up the cue and the two walked around the corner and out Jim's view. "Do you think that's a good idea, given your recent history."

Randall looked into his daughter's eyes. She was worried and for good reason. His last two projects had nearly turned deadly, through no fault of his own. "Francisco arranged for private security to escort us to the site. We'll be fine." He smiled.

Sam folded her arms, clearly not buying it. "You're going because this is Dr. Grady's son and you feel an obligation to him. I get that, but I'm worried Dad."

"I know, but I promise I'll be careful. We're just going to visit the site, poke around a little bit and see what we can find. I'll be back home in a couple of days."

Sam unfolded an arm and brought her hand to her chin. It was a move Randall had seen many times before and it meant she was contemplating something. And Randall knew exactly what she was contemplating. Her eyes flicked to her father, she smiled, then walked back toward Jim.

"Sam?" Randall called out after his daughter, following her back out of the kitchen.

"Jim, what time's your flight and what airline are you flying?" Sam pulled out her cell phone.

"Avianca, flight 247, leaving at 7:12," Grady said.

Randall shot Sam a look. "I don't think that's a good idea."

"Based on your history, I disagree. Besides, the Fall term is still a few weeks off, so I'm not busy. A trip to Argentina sounds right up my alley."

"You're a professor too?" Grady asked.

"Uh-huh."

"Where do you teach?"

"Jim's team is missing. This could be dangerous, and I don't want to have to worry about your safety," Randall interrupted.

"You said we'd have security," Grady blurted.

Randall glared at Grady, who withered under his stare.

Sam placed her hand on her father's forearm. "You always taught us that family takes care of each other and you told me on many occasions that Dr. Grady was like a second father to you. If Jim needs our help, then I'm going."

Randall frowned, pinching his eyebrows. "The last time you came on a trip with me, you were nearly killed."

"Last time, you were kidnapped by that psycho Francis Dumond, and I went looking for you. This time we'll have security with us. Besides, Dumond's gone, remember? We're just going to the site to look for clues for a few hours. It's not the same."

Frances Dumond. Randall shuddered at the name. The crazed industrialist had sent a team of mercenaries to kidnap him and steal his discovery. In the process he also captured Sam and threatened to kill her. He damn near succeeded, killing one of Randall's graduate students in the process. Luckily, they stopped him. Now he was dead, and that chapter of his life was closed.

29

"Found the flight and bought the ticket with PayPal," Sam said. "Now all I need to do is pack. I'll book an Uber to pick you boys up first, then have it swing by my house to get me. Does that work you?"

"Can I reimburse you for the flight?" Grady asked.

Sam wrinkled her nose. "I wouldn't feel right if I took your money."

Randall shook his head. "I don't like this, but it sounds like I don't have much of a choice."

"You don't," Sam said, walking to the door. "See you both in a couple of hours."

Chapter 6

Posadas, Argentina
July 21, 6:08 a.m.

Randall, Sam, and Grady sat in the economy section of the 777 bound for Posadas, Argentina, after a short layover in Buenos Aires. The early morning flight wasn't full, so Sam found an empty seat across the aisle from her dad. Having gotten several hours of sleep during the flight, they were now wide awake with anticipation of what they'd find. During their Miami layover, Grady had contacted a groggy Dr. Vogel, who was at his friend's home. He had been released from the hospital with a clean bill of health, and despite the late hour, was chipper as ever. He asked Grady to keep him updated on their progress and had taken a special interest in learning more about Randall. As usual, speaking to his mentor had calmed Grady's nerves.

"How are we are going to find our ride to the site?" Grady asked.

Randall looked out the window of the plane as it began its descent into Libertador General José de San Martín Airport. "Francisco said his contact would meet us at the terminal."

"What's his name?" Grady asked.

"Dr. Enrique Hernandez," Randall turned from the window.

Grady yawned. "Have you ever met him?"

Randall shook his head.

31

"How will we find him?" Sam said from across the aisle.

"Francisco gave him my picture, so he'll be looking for us."

Grady nodded and sank back into his seat as the plane taxied to the jetway. A short time later, the three made their way up the ramp and into the busy main terminal. Among the throng of international business travelers and people on vacation, Randall spotted a tall, thin man with jet-black hair and a craggy tan face holding a sign with his name. Randall tapped Sam's shoulder and motioned to the man.

"Is that Enrique?" Sam asked.

Randall scratched the stubble on his chin. "Must be. Let's go meet him."

The three walked to Hernandez, Randall reaching him first. "Dr. Hernandez?"

"Si. Please call me Enrique. I'm assuming you're Nick Randall?" Hernandez asked through a thick Spanish accent.

Randall nodded. "This is my daughter Samantha, and that's Dr. Jim Grady."

Hernandez smiled and nodded to them. "You must be tired and hungry. Would you like to get some breakfast before we make the drive to the site?"

"I'd like to go now. My team's been missing for two days and we can't wait any longer," Grady said.

"Fernando spoke about a security team to escort us, have arrangements been made? Randall asked.

"Si. They're just waiting to be notified."

"Great, please let them know we'd like to go as soon as possible. Enrique, we'll follow you," Randall said.

Chapter 7

Southwest of Parque Nacional Iguaçu, State of Paraná Argentina
July 21, 10:12 a.m.

The team had been on the road for hours, leaving behind the concrete skyscrapers and city streets of Posadas. They now drove through lush, green, rolling hills and dense jungle, intermittently broken by small towns interspersed along the way. Randall sat quietly next to Sam as the four academics rode in the lead jeep, headed for the ill-fated archaeological site, their security detail following closely behind. Grady explained that the dig was Northeast of them, lying in a section of rainforest between San Ignacio and Iguaçu National Park, near the Argentina-Uruguay border. After the brief geography lesson, Grady went silent. He stared out the window, his mind clearly elsewhere.

Randall had sensed the tension rising in Grady as they approached their destination, his knuckles turning white from his grip on the edge of his seat.

The thought of losing an entire team to some unknown fate weighed heavily on Randall's mind. Filled with concern for Jim, as well as for Sam's safety, he made multiple attempts to convince her not to go, but she had refused.

Despite the feeling of frustration, Randall respected his
daughter's wishes. In fact, her stubborn, independent streak was
one of the things he loved most about her. He just wished now that
he had also packed a weapon in case they ran into trouble. It wasn't
that he didn't have faith in their security detail, he simply felt
responsible for Sam's safety. When he had hunted with his father
as a teen, his father had always explained that its best to be
prepared for any situation and not to rely on others for your safety.
Randall's time in the military had solidified this thought process
and he wished now he had heeded his words.

They had passed San Ignacio Mini nearly two hours ago,
the road becoming nothing more than a narrow band of dirt, parting
the dense jungle, which towered overhead on both sides of them.
Their driver pulled the Jeep off the road and through a small
opening in the rainforest, revealing the camp. A semi-circular patch
of land framed by a ring of trees; the area was slightly larger than
the infield of a baseball diamond. Several small tents were neatly
arranged on one side of the area, with a larger one sitting near its
center. Beyond the larger tent were several vehicles and a trail that
cut through another opening in the brush. They drove through the
camp, then stopped near the trail head. The second jeep carrying
their two security guards pulled alongside them. The main
excavation area lay beyond the opening.

The site was just as Grady had described earlier. Equipment
and tools lay scattered about, as if the team were just taking a short
break from work. An eerie quiet enveloped the camp, only the
sounds of birds and small animals rustling through the brush
occasionally breaking the silence.

Randall exited the vehicle first. The fluttering tent flaps
were the only movement coming from the once busy
archaeological dig.

Sam appeared by her father's side. "Kind of spooky."

Randall nodded in agreement, his mind trying to take in
what had happened. Grady had vividly described the abandoned
site but seeing it in person was a chilling experience. Randall's

mind raced with possible scenarios of what might have happened to the team. They all ended with one unsettling realization: they probably hadn't survived.

"I'm surprised there's no police tape or any sign of an investigation," Sam said.

Grady walked to the trail's edge. "It's too remote. Once the authorities finished, they packed up and left."

"We better get started. Jim, can you show us the layout of the camp? If we walk through it, we may get some ideas of what happened," Randall said.

Mateo Diego, the first security guard walked up to Randall. "Con permiso. Dr. Randall, please give us a moment to get ready." He grabbed his pack from the jeep with a muscular, tattooed arm. He checked his weapon, sliding it into its holster, then clipped a radio onto his belt. His partner Tomas followed suit. He nodded for Randall to continue.

Grady led the team on a tour of the site, the two security guards taking the rear. First, he took them through each tent, hoping to find clues. There were none. He nodded to the large tent in the center of the camp. "That's the mess hall, we'll head there next."

Randall nodded, then heard a sound rising from the center of the camp. It was a humming noise whose pitch was slowly increasing. He turned to Grady, noting the color had drained from his face.

Mateo whispered to Tomas who drew his weapon. He whistled, and waved for Sam, Hernandez, and Grady to move behind him.

Mateo pulled even with Randall, drawing his gun as well. The two men crept toward the main tent.

The pitch of the hum climbed higher with each step they took. The air seemed charged with energy, the particles vibrating in rhythm to the sound.

Randall and Mateo stopped by the entrance to the tent. Mateo pointed at Randall, then the tent flap. Randall nodded. He was to open the flap when Mateo gave him the signal. Mateo readied himself, pointing his gun at the tent. He nodded. Randall drew back the flap.

Chapter 8

Mateo swept the tent entrance in small arcs. He glanced at Randall, then looked back to tent. He walked in, disappearing from Randall's view.

Randall waited. And waited. It was taking too long. Something must be wrong. The sound suddenly stopped.

"Senior!" Mateo called from inside.

Randall hustled in.

The stench of rotting food was overwhelming. Randall covered his nose, searching for Mateo. He was standing by the far corner, a bandana tied around his face, his gun in the holster. He looked over his shoulder, motioning for Randall to join him.

Randall jogged to his side.

Mateo's hand was clamped around a piece of tent canvas. He let go and the humming returned. A heavy strap, used to secure the tent to the ground, flapped on the outside of the tent. It had slowly ripped a hole in the fabric, allowing the wind to whistle through.

Mateo pulled down the bandana, a broad smile on his face. "Aquí está tu fantasma! Here's your ghost!" He punched Randall in the arm and laughed.

Randall closed his eyes, shook his head and chuckled. The two men exited the tent.

"What happened?" Sam asked.

"It's a tear in the fabric. The wind was whistling through it."

"That's great, but my team's still missing," Grady said.

Randall nodded. "You're right. Take us to the main excavation."

The area was a large, precise rectangle, measuring sixty by forty feet. Randall noted the neatly excavated test pits, carefully cut into the dark brown soil to varying depths. Small flags marked items of interest as picks, shovels, and dirt sifting baskets lay where the workers had left them. Tucked away in the southwest corner of the site was the main pit, which sank deep into the ground, accessible by a dozen steps cut into the earth. Opposite the steps was a large opening, which led directly into an underground chamber.

Randall descended the steps, sinking below ground level, which was now two feet above him. He approached the opening, which resembled a doorway carved from the dirt and framed by decaying logs. Grady arrived by his side a moment later, flanked by the others.

"Is this the opening Jennifer was going to explore?" Randall asked, his eyes fixed on the doorway.

"Yes, we found it some time ago. We had excavated enough space to expose the door covering, but I was called away before we opened it. When we found this, we realized it was the underground tomb where, according to legend, the stone was hidden."

Randall peered into the opening. The sun sat directly perpendicular to it, so no light illuminated the interior. It was a pitch-black rectangle set into the earth. Randall's heart beat faster, his palms growing cold and clammy.

He removed a flashlight from his pack, then Shot Sam a glance. "I guess there's nothing I could say to make you stay outside."

"Not a chance," Sam responded, her face set in stone.

"Professor, I will go in with you and Tomas will stay outside to guard the entrance," Mateo announced.

Randall nodded. "I'll go first." Randall clicked his light on. The beam sliced the darkness, revealing an open space just beyond the entrance. He ducked under the rotting log serving as the doorway's header, then walked into the inky underground world.

Once inside, Randall paused, giving his eyes time to adjust. He shone his beam in slow arcing motions, studying the interior. The passageway was roughly hewn into to the earth, forming a rectangular tunnel with a ceiling that arched deep underground. He breathed the musty air in slow gulps, acclimating to his new surroundings. His eyes adjusted to the darkness and he began his slow march down the corridor.

After twenty feet, he discovered stone steps that led him deeper into the earth. Before proceeding, he turned to see if everyone else had followed. Noting all the members of the team inside, Randall descended the staircase. The ceiling was appreciably lower here and he crouched to avoid hitting his head. Reaching the bottom of the steps, he shined his light toward the end of the path, then froze in stunned silence.

The short tunnel opened into a large, circular room with multiple entrances leading in different directions. The room was approximately thirty feet in diameter and resembled a train station hub. He panned his light, examining the area. Beautiful, fading frescos adorned the walls between the openings.

"What did you find?" Sam called out from behind.

"This is amazing," Randall approached the nearest fresco. The image depicted a medieval landscape with knights battling enemies, protecting the contents of a small, ornate container they carried. Randall shifted his light to another image. This one showed a holy man in Christian garb, blessing the knights who delivered the package to him.

"Nick, you have to see this!" Grady's voice called from another part of the chamber. Randall turned away from the painting, shining his light around the room.

"Where are you?"

"I'm to the left of the frescos you were studying."

Randall pivoted to his left, seeing a beam of light pointing at the wall. He also noted two other lights in the room. The halo they cast outlined Sam and Enrique, but he couldn't find Mateo. It appeared that everyone was studying different sections of the chamber.

Randall walked toward Grady's voice, arriving by his side. "What did you find?"

"Take a look at this painting," Grady said, motioning to the wall in front of him, his features eerily outlined by the glow of his flashlight.

Randall examined the wall. The fresco was painted in several panels. The first portrayed a single ship bearing a white cross on its black mainsail. The other panels detailed the journey of the ship from a small island south of Sicily, across the Atlantic Ocean, to the coast of Brazil. The cargo was transferred to a smaller vessel, which made its way up a network of rivers to an inland location.

"Does this mean what I think it does?" Grady asked from behind.

"I think so. Let's check with Sam and Enrique," Randall turned to search for the others. He saw only one additional light aside from Grady's and his own. "Sam?" No answer. "Enrique, are you there?"

"I'm over here," Enrique replied, wiggling his light. He was standing next to the wall near the third opening. Randall walked to his side, then shined his light on the section of wall in front of them.

The frescos showed a mission under construction in one panel and then an indoor scene in the next. A religious man, seated in a tall chair, wore a red cope, a circular, ankle length cape, commonly used by bishops and priests, with a purple stole draped around his neck.

"He must have been a bishop," Randall commented.

"Why?" Enrique asked.

"He's wearing a mitre," Randall pointed to the hat in the fresco. "Only bishops and abbots are permitted to wear these and, based on the rest of his outfit, he's not an abbot."

Seated on either side of the bishop, in lower chairs, were men dressed in black robes, bearing the same white cross from the ship. A knight bowed before the religious man, holding up a familiar ornate box in homage.

Randall strode to the fourth and final opening, the one that Sam had been near earlier.

"Sam, where are you?"

"I'm inside," Sam replied, her voice floating down the short corridor.

Before searching for her, Randall studied the final frescos. These depicted the knights fighting men wearing black uniforms with yellow chest plates on horseback. The knights were taking the worst of it. Several had broken away from their comrades, carrying the wooden box into the jungle. The final image showed the knights entering an underground passage and placing the box into an alcove, cut into the wall. Nestled inside was a red heart. Jim was right. The legend was true.

"Dad?"

"Coming."

Randall walked through the six-foot tunnel, which emptied into a small, square chamber. Through the beam of his light he saw Sam kneeling next to an open stone sarcophagus, its lid propped against its side. Carved into the cover was a shield with the now familiar cross emblazoned in its center. The rest of the room was empty except for a smashed stone jar.

41

Sam peered into the coffin, studying the contents. "I think it's a knight, but most of the organic material has decayed. It's mostly skeletal remains."

Randall walked to her side, shining his light into the sarcophagus. Just as Sam had described, a skeleton lay inside, its arms folded across its chest, clutching the hilt of a sword. Moving his light up the wall, Randall noted a small alcove carved into the stone above the knight. It was about the size of a shoe box but was empty.

"Looks like we're late to the party," Randall commented.

"Uh huh. Whatever happened to Jim's team must have had something to do with this knight."

"We should check with the others to see what they've found," Randall turned away from the coffin and shone his light toward the main chamber. "Jim, have you found anything?"

No reply.

Sam joined him near the exit of the chamber.

"Jim, Enrique, did you search the other chambers?" Randall called out as he walked back through the tunnel.

Again, only silence.

"Mateo? Are you there?" Randall and Sam entered the main chamber. There were no lights, beside their own.

"What's happening Dad?" Sam asked.

No sooner had the words left her mouth when multiple lights switched on, flooding the tomb with brightness. Randall recoiled, temporarily blinded by the sudden glare.

"Drop to the ground now!"

Chapter 9

Randall shielded his eyes, disoriented by the bright lights and loud voice. He failed to get down fast enough, and was met with the force of a boot, striking the back of his knee. His leg buckled, and he tumbled to the ground.

"Pick him up!" the disembodied voice growled through the throng of lights.

Thick, gloved hands grabbed under his arms and hauled him to his feet. Still temporarily blinded, he struggled to see how many people were there.

"Who are you? What do you want?" Randall asked, still shielding his eyes. There was no response. Instead, a kick to his behind informed him that he was expected to walk back out of the main tunnel.

"Sam, are you okay?" Randall asked.

"I'm alright," Sam responded.

A metal, circular object jabbed into Randall's back. "Shut the hell up!"

Randall turned his head slightly to one side. "Jim, Enrique … are you there?" There was no response.

"What did you do with our friends?" Randall demanded.

43

The answer was a blow to the back of his head. Randall winced in pain, grasping the growing lump on the back of his skull. As he slowed down, another boot to his backside told him to speed up.

They made their way back up the steps into the main tunnel. Randall saw three black-clad men with weapons leading the way, followed by Sam and another man tasked with watching her. Randall resisted the urge turn around, sensing he'd earn another blow to the back of his head. After several minutes, the group exited the mouth of the underground network and into the light of day.

Mateo and Tomas lay on the ground, their hands and feet zip tied together. A small contingent of armed men stood guarding Grady and Enrique. The soldiers wore black military fatigues, and masks, which obscured their faces.

"Get over there with the others," growled a voice from behind Randall, who complied, joining the rest of the group. As he did, he turned to see how many men had been following him out of the tomb. He was surprised to see only one.

Randall counted ten heavily armed mercenaries, their bulky shapes cutting an imposing figure against the dark earthen background.

"Who are you and what are you doing at this site?" one of the mercenaries growled.

"We're from a local university and we're looking for our friends who disappeared a few days ago. I'm assuming you had something to do with it," Randall answered.

The mercenary didn't respond. Instead, he turned to another soldier who held a radio pack. "Contact the colonel and let him know we have additional prisoners inbound." He turned to face Randall. "I'll ask you again. Who are you and what are you doing at this site?" the mercenary moved to within inches of Randall's face.

Randall could feel the warmth of the man's breath. "Like I said before, we're looking for the archaeologists who were here a few days ago. We're worried about them and want to know if they're safe."

He was rewarded with a sharp blow to the stomach. Randall doubled over in pain.

"Leave my father alone!" Sam yelled before another mercenary pushed her back.

The man in charge motioned for Randall to be lifted back to his feet. Two other men obliged, hauling him back up. The lead man removed his black mask.

"How sweet, you brought your daughter, and what an attractive young lady she is," the mercenary said, smiling grotesquely.

"If you lay a finger on her, I'll…"

"You'll what? Call me bad names? You don't seem to get it. You're in no position to make demands."

A soft thudding sound appeared from the west as two black helicopters closed in on the site. They circled nearby and touched down softly, behind of row a trees directly north of the camp.

"Get them onto the chopper, we'll interrogate them back at the base."

Chapter 10

Enemy Base, Location Unknown
July 21, 5:34 p.m.

Father Bianchi rested on his side in the cell, remaining as still as possible, the slightest movement sending a torrent of pain ripping through his chest. Although not a doctor, the priest assumed he had multiple bruised, if not broken ribs, the result of twice-daily beatings by his captors. He lay quietly on the filthy mattress, a small puddle of blood forming under the gash below his right eye.

Despite the intense pain, Bianchi hadn't divulged the information his captors so desperately craved. His act had been so convincing that he sensed they were beginning to doubt if he knew the location of the stone. He prayed for the strength to continue resisting his abductors, knowing that once they found the relic, they'd be unstoppable.

The sound of the cell block opening down the corridor caused Bianchi to stir. He had just completed his most recent session only an hour ago; it was far too soon to be interrogated again. He lifted his head to peer through the metal bars of his cell, causing pain to radiate through his chest. Through the fog of discomfort, he could see his captors escorting four additional prisoners into an adjacent lockup. There were three men and one woman.

Bianchi rested his head on the pillow again, a wave of relief washing over him as he realized that he would have a brief respite from additional beatings. Relaxing his body, he allowed himself to fall into a dream-like state.

His mind raced back to when he had entered the Order many years ago, a fiery, young seminarian bent on social justice. A native of the town of Asolo in Northern Italy, he had been sent to live with his aunt in America prior to joining the seminary. His enthusiasm, while admirable, had rubbed many of the older priests the wrong way. As a young candidate, he'd questioned everything. Highly intelligent, he had difficulty taking instructions from his superiors. Especially those he felt were intellectually inferior. He smiled at the memory, realizing that he had suffered from the sin of pride.

The situation had become so severe that the young candidate was called before the bishop. Bianchi recalled the terror he had felt prior to meeting the leader of his seminary, not sleeping at all the night before. As he waited in the hallway outside of the bishop's office, all he could do was pray for guidance. When the bishop's secretary announced he was ready to see the young seminarian, the final walk into the office had seemed like the march of a death row inmate.

Bianchi was surprised at the humble office of his religious Order's leader. Bishop Meckler had a simple wooden desk, with pictures of his mother and brother prominently displayed on top. On the wall directly behind him was a large, simple wooden cross, and a picture of a strapping young man wearing a baseball uniform. The photograph was ancient, a black and white picture taken on a dirt infield. Bianchi studied the young ball player's face, then looked down at the man sitting behind the desk. The bishop was grinning from ear to ear. Bianchi immediately recognized the similarities between the old priest's face and that of the young man in the picture.

"I primarily played center field at St. Mary's academy and batted first in the lineup. I had quite the left-handed swing at the time. I could hit for average and power, and my coach, Brother Scalisa said I was the toughest out in the league," the Bishop reported proudly. "Of course, I don't think I could catch up with a fastball today," the priest smiled, his kind old eyes brimming with mischief.

It had been a seminal moment for Bianchi, who immediately felt at ease in the Bishop's presence. Far from wanting to kick him out of the Order, the old priest had other ideas in mind for the young candidate. He would study under the tutelage of a different, smaller Order.

"I hear you have an interest in pugilism."

Embarrassed, Bianchi nodded. While at the seminary, he had nearly come to blows with other candidates and even a priest or two.

"Very good! We have to be ready to fight for what we believe in!" Meckler had said, tapping the young priest on the arm.

After the meeting, Bianchi's personal belongings were moved from the seminary to his new home, where his education on the faith and his special Order began in earnest. At first, he wasn't sure of his new calling, but with time, he came to accept and even cherish belonging to the Order of Hospitallers. The ancient, medieval group, charged with protecting Christian travelers so long ago, had morphed over the years, but their calling was still the same: to serve the faith, and Father Bianchi had sworn an oath to do so. Now that oath was being put to the test by his captors. Although their plans were a mystery to Bianchi, he was sure of one thing. Their goal was evil on a scale unknown. Years of studying and training had led him to this point in his life and he wasn't about to fail.

The priest was called back to the present by loud voices down the hall from the other cells. He could hear the four new prisoners talking about being taken from a place called San Ignacio Mini. His heart raced at the news as pieces of the puzzle continued to fall into place. His captors clearly knew the history of the red stone, but did they know how close they were to discovering it? Bianchi shivered at the thought. He reaffirmed his commitment to protecting the secret of his Order. Even at the cost of his life. It was a small price to pay to maintain the safety of western civilization.

Chapter 11

Randall paced the concrete floor of their musty prison cell, assembling his thoughts and trying to devise a way out. The glow of the overhead neon lights caused him to squint as he walked, causing further distraction. Sam studied the steel barred door and heavy lock, while Ernesto and Grady sat quietly on the bunk. Their captors had likely played a role in the disappearance of Grady's team, but the missing archaeologists were not in the cellblock. Neither were Mateo or Tomas, who Randall hadn't seen since the jungle. When they had been ushered into their cage, Randall had noted another prisoner in a nearby cell. Randall watched him closely now, but the man remained motionless. It was entirely possible he was dead, but there was no way to be sure.

"I don't think we'll be getting out of here anytime soon. The bars and lock are solid," Sam commented from across the space. She discontinued her examination and walked over to a cot, plopping down on a threadbare mattress. Randall joined her.

"What do we do now?" Sam asked.

Randall thought for a moment. "I don't think there's much we can do but wait and try to figure out why these guys want the stone."

"Maybe's there's something else in that tomb that they want," Sam replied.

"They want the stone," Grady chimed in. "I don't know how, but they must know about the legend."

Sam wrinkled her nose. "What would they do with the stone if they had it?"

"I'm not sure," Grady said, his voice trailing off. "But I'm sorry I involved you two."

"We're adults and agreed to help, so no need to apologize," Sam replied.

While appreciating his daughter's fortitude, Randall couldn't help but worry for her safety. If their captors had taken and possibly disposed of an entire archaeological team, they wouldn't think twice about killing them. Randall shuttered at the thought. He couldn't allow his mind to go down that rabbit hole.

"No, you don't understand." Grady looked up at Randall and Sam. "I wasn't completely honest with you."

Randall's eyes narrowed. "What do you mean?"

Grady let out a long sigh. "I never contacted the authorities. I was worried that if I did, word would get out about my discovery."

Randall shot Grady a look. "What else haven't you told us?"

"Before I came to see you, I was assaulted and nearly captured at my apartment building. It was probably the same guys who brought us here. I'm sorry I didn't tell you earlier," Grady hung his head.

Randall set his jaw. Grady lying to him and risking his own safety was bad enough but putting Sam in danger really angered him. If something happened to her, he would never forgive Grady, or himself. His eyes bored through Grady and his muscles tensed. He had to relax. Anger wasn't going to help them. He breathed deeply, rubbing the back of his neck. "No more lies, Jim. From this point forward, you need to come clean about everything. And for your sake, nothing better happen to Sam."

The door to the cellblock opened and four soldiers entered. Three of the men stood outside the cell, their weapons trained on their captives. The fourth operated a control panel, inset into the wall. With a loud clank, the cell door opened.

"Out of the lockup, hands behind your heads! Schnell!" the lead soldier barked.

Randall and his group exited the cell, the soldiers taking positions to their side, rear, and front. They marched to the pace of the lead guard who led them into a small, warmly appointed room before ordering them to sit on a large sofa.

The room was about twelve feet long and maybe a couple of feet wider, the walls painted a soothing sandy brown color. The floor was a simple repeating striped navy pattern of carpeted squares, not unlike those found in office buildings. But this was no ordinary office. As Randall surveyed the room, he immediately noticed the priceless artifacts occupying tabletops and wall cubbies throughout. Ornately decorated gold crucifixes and marble statues of Mary the mother of Jesus and other saints were carefully displayed throughout the space.

Grady studied the artifacts as well, his gaze transfixed on items concealed in a thick case of Lucite. Protected within were a band of thorns, a dark metal sword with a sheet of gold foil around its center, and a goblet. The young professor was in trancelike state, staring at the items, his gaze unwavering.

The door to the room opened again and a man dressed in a crisp, black suit entered. His six-foot tall, athletic frame moved gracefully as his piercing azure eyes scanned the room. His chiseled face, framed by perfectly combed blond hair wore a broad smile that exposed perfectly aligned teeth, so white they reflected the light from the fixtures.

His gaze fell to Randall first, then to Sam, and finally came to rest on Grady, who was still staring at the three relics.

"I see you're enjoying my collection, Dr. Grady. I assure you that those were not easy items to obtain," the stranger commented in English tinged with an accent that Randall couldn't place.

Upon hearing his voice, Grady lifted his eyes and looked directly at the stranger.

"The Arma Christi … are they real?" Grady asked, his voice belying his awe.

"I'm impressed, you know your Judeo-Christian history quite well. The crown and spear are quite real. Sadly, the goblet is just a replica," the stranger replied, his smile growing larger.

"What's the Arma Christi?" Sam asked.

"They're the instruments of Christ's Passion: The Crown of Thorns, the Holy Grail, and the Spear of Destiny," Grady said, turning back to the artifacts. He turned to face the stranger again, "How did you get them?"

The stranger walked over to the desk, taking a seat in the high-back executive chair. He opened a drawer, removed an ashtray, a pack of cigarettes, and a silver lighter. Extracting a single cigarette from the pack, he placed it between his lips and lit it with the flame from the lighter. He clicked the silver lid closed, setting it down on the desk in front of him. Taking a long puff, he exhaled slowly, savoring the moment. "Let's just say I'm well connected and leave it at that."

"There were two other men with us, Mateo and Tomas. What have you done with them?" Randall asked.

"They were of no use to us, so we disposed of them," the stranger replied.

"Bastards!" Jim spat.

"Who are you and what do you want with us?" Randall asked, keeping calm.

The stranger turned to Randall, studying him carefully. "Dietrich Herrmann. As you can see, I'm a collector of rare items and, based on my research, Dr. Grady may have information that could lead me to another artifact I seek. Isn't that right, Professor?"

"If you're looking for the Devil's Heart, you know

everything I know. My research led me to that site outside of San Ignacio Mini, but the tomb was empty. Someone else must have already found it."

Herrmann's eyes narrowed, the smile evaporating from his face. "Do you think I'm a fool? I've been watching you for some time. You're the first person to find the clues that led to the secret chamber, and I believe you know more."

"I swear to you. Every clue I have pointed to that tomb."

Herrmann crushed his cigarette into the ashtray. "You'll help me find the stone or your friends will pay with their lives."

Grady shook his head. "I don't have any more information. Please let my friends go. They don't know anything about this legend."

"Perhaps you need a bit more convincing," Herrmann said, nodding to a guard, who grabbed Sam by the arm and dragged her to Herrmann's side.

"Wait. We'll help you," Randall said.

Herrmann cocked his head in Randall's direction "And you are?"

"Nick Randall. I'm an archeologist at George Washington University. Jim came to me for my help because I specialize in finding and retrieving rare items. I can help you find the stone, but I need some time."

Herrmann stared at Randall, a look of confusion in his eyes. A moment later, the smile reappeared. "And what's your interest in this young lady?"

"She's my daughter. If you take us back to my office, I have Jim's notes there, along with additional research about the stone," Randall lied.

"I have a better idea. My men will search your office and bring me anything they find," Herrmann hissed. "Take them back to their cell."

"Wait." Randall threw up his hands. "Even if you find my notes, you might not be able to decipher them. Take us with you and I'll answer any questions you have."

Herrmann's face went blank, his eyes moved side to side, clearly contemplating Randall's proposal. He looked at Sam, then at Randall, his eyes narrowing. "Nein! You will stay here while my men retrieve your notes and you will answer my questions when they return. But I warn you, if you are lying, your daughter will pay with her life."

Chapter 12

The guards marched the group back to the lockup. On the way, Randall noticed that the other prisoner was gone. Grady dropped onto the cot, holding his drooping head between his hands. It was clear to Randall that if they were going to find a way out, it would be up to him. If Herrmann had only bought his lie, they would have gotten out of this place, greatly increasing their chances of escaping. Now, he had put Sam's life in grave danger.

"Senior Randall, what are we going to do?" Ernesto asked.

Randall looked at Ernesto, then Sam. "I'm not sure, but I've bought us a few hours. Once they search my office and can't find anything, we'll have to convince them that they need us alive. Jim, we need another possible location for the stone."

"I told you, there aren't any."

"It doesn't matter if it's real. We just need something to convince Herrmann. We need to give Francisco more time to figure out we're missing."

Sam's eyes went wide. "A ruse! Dad, that's a great idea!"

"Right. If we can think of a plausible location, we might be able to convince them to take us out of here. Once we're on the outside, we'll try to escape. Jim, we need—"

An enormous explosion interrupted Randall, shaking the walls and causing bits of the ceiling to fall to the ground.

"Qué pasa?" Ernesto asked.

Another blast, this one closer than the first. Larger chunks of concrete rained to the floor.

"Get under the cots!" Randall yelled, pushing Sam toward cover. Sam scrambled under a bed.

"You too, Jim!" Randall grabbed the young professor and shoved him under a second cot. Ernesto, followed suit, diving under another bed, leaving only Randall exposed. With no other shelter, Randall ran to a corner, knelt, and covered his neck and head with his arms.

The clatter of small arms fire echoed in the distance as the sound of confusion and men barking orders joined the fray.

"Everyone stay down!" Randall yelled.

Another explosion shook the chamber, dropping more fragments on them. Stone chunks smashed to the ground, one striking the top of the bunk protecting Sam. The blasts were getting closer. They were trapped.

"What are we going to do?" Grady asked.

The door to the cellblock exploded inward, raining sparks of fire and metal everywhere. Soldiers toting assault weapons burst through the door, fanning out into the area.

Randall counted five men total. Their uniforms were different from their captors, but their weapons and demeanor carried the same threat of death.

"Flip the cots down for protection!" Randall yelled.

His words caught the attention of one of the soldiers, who headed straight for Randall's cell. He scanned the area as if looking for someone or something.

"Where's Father Bianchi?" the soldier asked.

Caught off guard, Randall could only blink. He realized the solider might be referring to the prisoner in the other cell. "I don't know. He was here earlier but was gone after we were interrogated."

57

The soldier studied Randall's face before turning to his team. "Open the cell and take them with us."

Another soldier nodded, moving for the cell door. "Back up and get behind a cot." He placed a small piece of gray clay on the metal lock.

Randall didn't need an explanation; they were blasting the door open. He dashed behind one of the cots and a moment later, a small explosion announced their freedom.

"Come with us!" the lead soldier ordered.

The group complied, joining the soldiers who had opened their cell. They exited and made their way down a corridor. As they moved, Randall noted additional men dressed in the same uniform as their rescuers … or new captors.

The sounds of battle raged all around as the two forces collided. Gunfire intermingled with small explosions as parts of the building turned to rubble. The stench of smoke mixed with burning flesh was overwhelming.

Another explosion rocked the facility, shattering an external wall. Light from the setting sun flooded the hallway. The force of the blast knocked Randall to the ground. He smacked his head against the tile floor hard enough to split his lip. The coppery taste of blood filled his mouth as he struggled back to his feet. His ears ringing, he looked desperately for Sam. He spotted her lying on the ground several feet away. She wasn't moving.

Randall sprinted to her, kneeling by her side. He gently lifted the hair from her face, exposing a large gash on her forehead. Sam's eyes fluttered open and she coughed violently.

"Are you alright?"

"I think so. Where are Jim and Ernesto?"

Randall searched the area, his view obscured by smoke. The sound of voices echoed down the corridor. "I think they're down the hall," Randall helped Sam to her feet.

The two raced toward the voices and, turning the corner, found Grady and Ernesto with a small group of soldiers. Instinctively, the soldiers raised their weapons toward Randall and

Sam.

"They're with me!" Grady yelled.

The soldiers lowered their guns but kept a watchful eye on Randall and Sam as they approached. The lead soldier stood next to the empty cell where Randall had seen the other prisoner earlier. As he approached, Randall noted captain's bars on his lapel.

A corporal pushed past Randall. "Captain Tassone, we've been unable to locate Father Bianchi."

Tassone frowned. "Search the rest of the area, round up any survivors, and bring them here for interrogation."

The corporal nodded, signaling for the other soldiers to join him. The squad sprinted away, leaving the group.

For the first time, Randall noticed a small insignia embroidered on the soldier's uniform. The mark was familiar, but it took Randall a moment to recall where he had seen it. His mouth fell open as his mind made the connection. It was the same symbol he had seen on the painting of the knights in the tomb: a black background with a white cross emblazoned in the center.

Chapter 13

Randall stood next to the hulking form of Captain Tassone. He studied the insignia on his lapel. "It can't be. You're one of them?"

"It's okay Nick, I explained everything to the Captain. He says they can help us get home," Grady said.

"What are you both talking about?" Sam asked.

"My Order is an old one," Captain Tassone replied, "largely forgotten by modern man. We prefer it that way because the work we do is meant to be known only by a select few."

"Your corporal mentioned you were looking for a priest, why?" Randall asked.

"He's a member our Order and we were sent to rescue him."

"But your Order were knights, not priests," Randall said.

"There were multiple sects within the Order. There were knights who defended travelers and fought the wars, medical personnel who ministered to the sick, and religious members," Grady stated, joining the discussion as the captain nodded in agreement.

Randall turned to look at Grady, feeling like the odd man out. "You know about this Order?"

"The Knights Hospitaller, also known as The Order of the

Knights of St. John. They were formed during the Middle Ages by Gerard Tum, their Founder and first Grand Master. Their job was to protect pilgrims making their way through the Holy Land. The pilgrimage was dangerous, and the travelers faced poor weather, bandits, and unsafe roads. It was common for pilgrims to arrive in the Holy Land sick and needing help," Grady explained.

"But what does that have to do with the Devil's Heart?" Randall asked.

"Over time, the Order became one of the most formidable military groups in the Holy Land. Tum acquired territory and money for the Knights throughout Jerusalem and beyond. They also obtained many religious artifacts, some of which the Order still has today. I guess they either found the stone or were ordered to protect it from marauding forces," Grady replied.

"Our Order did possess the stone, but we lost it. It's our responsibility to find it and keep it from falling into the hands of those who wish to wield its power for dark purposes. The men who captured our priest, Father Bianchi, believe he knows its location. My men and I were dispatched to save Father Bianchi and prevent this group from finding The Devil's Heart."

Randall listened, amazed at the story unfolding before him. "Who are these men and why do they want The Devil's Heart?"

The captain stared at Randall and then at Grady, clearly sizing them up. "They're a group that escaped from Germany immediately before Berlin fell to the allies in World War II. Some of them smuggled out weapons and technology developed by the Wehrmacht during the war. We believe they've been secretly developing these weapons at this base."

"Where exactly are we?" Sam asked.

"Isla de los Estados. We fear they're seeking The Devil's Heart to power a Wunderwaffe," Tassone explained.

"Wunderwaffe?" Randall asked.

"Wonder-weapon," Grady answered.

Randall's eyes widened at the explanation. "What sort of wonder-weapon are we talking about?"

"We're not certain, but based on our intelligence, it's an offensive weapon meant to deliver a large payload over long distance," Tassone replied.

The group stood in silence, the captain's last words hanging in the air like a thick blanket of smoke, choking all remaining hope from them.

Finally, Randall spoke. "Captain, what's your next move? Do you have any idea where the Nazis might take Father Bianchi?"

Tassone shook his head. "This was the only confirmed location my sources had for the Germans. We believe they also have a station in Germany but haven't been able to verify it."

"Sounds like we're back to square one," Sam said.

"I might know someone who can help us," Randall replied.

"Who?" Sam asked.

"Uncle Peter," Randall replied, referring to another close family friend that his children treated as an adopted relative. Dr. Peter Moloney was a Professor and Chair of Catholic Studies and Theology at St. Thomas University in Minnesota.

Sam raised an eyebrow. "How can he help?"

"He's an expert in middle age theology and his doctoral studies focused on the hierarchy of the Catholic Church and its affiliations. He's read more medieval manuscripts and books than anyone in the field and knows more about the Church than anyone west of the Holy See. He might be able to give us some insight into the history of the Knights that could help explain where the Nazis might look for the Devil's Heart."

"Do you really think he'll know more about the Knights than Captain Tassone?" Grady asked.

"Captain Tassone is a military man and I'm sure his knowledge of the Knights is extensive, but Peter is a researcher and has devoted most of his adult life to learning arcane facts about the church. He's also assembled one of the best historical reference libraries at his University. If we can ask him some questions about his research, he may be able to tell us about some obscure stories that might point us in the right direction. Trust me when I tell you, he knows all the conspiracy theories and tall tales. Captain, what do you say?"

Tassone shook his head. "I must report back to my commander and, with all due respect, as civilians you would only slow my team. We will evacuate you before German reinforcements arrive and will then part ways."

"Captain, I understand your hesitation, but if what you're saying is true, we don't have a lot of time. My friend Peter might be able to help us find the Nazis and your missing priest, and every minute we delay, the less likely we'll be able to pick up their trail."

"I'm sorry, but no."

"I owe you for saving my daughter's life and I promised Jim I would help him find his people. I'm simply saying if you don't have any additional leads, why not try?" Randall persisted.

Tassone shifted on his feet.

"Please, Captain, if my father says Uncle Peter can help, maybe he can. You have to trust us," Sam said.

"I don't really see a downside to our offer. If we get out of line, you can kick us to the curb. The worse you'll do is have three strangers tagging along for a ride," Randall said.

"I will take you to safety and consider your offer but must speak with my superiors. We have studied this group for many years, and I can't imagine your friend will have useful information for us," Tassone said.

"Fair enough," Randall nodded. "Can you arrange for travel to Minnesota? That's where Peter lives."

"Yes, but first we need to leave this island," Tassone answered.

As if to emphasize the point, the sound of intensifying gunfire erupted in the distance.

"Captain, we've neutralized their surveillance system, but

63

Nazi reinforcements are on the way."

"We cannot risk being captured. Fall back to the choppers," Tassone ordered.

Tassone led the group to a waiting chopper in the adjacent courtyard. As it ascended into the sky, the arriving German forces fired skyward, landing little more than glancing blows. The dark chopper raced into the sky until the Nazi forces and their compound were little more than a speck on a distant island.

Chapter 14

Georgetown, Washington D.C.
July 22, 5:42 p.m.

Dr. Vogel waited patiently, having chosen an outdoor table
at the Rye Bar in Georgetown for this meeting. Dressed in navy
cotton pants and a long sleeve blue striped button shirt, he blended
in with the rest of crowd seated at the restaurant. The fading sun
filtered through the overhanging trees, reflecting off the C&O
Canal, capturing the reflection of the vine covered brick façade of
the building across the way.

The outdoor seating afforded Vogel a secluded
environment, away from the prying eyes of diners seated in the
main part of the restaurant. From his table, he could also see the
entrance of the restaurant. He would know when his direct report
arrived with the information about the recent escape from the
island compound. Dr. Konrad Vogel led a double life, a fact known
only to a select few. In fact, his last name was nothing more than
another deception to hide his true German heritage.

His professorship provided him with valuable information
for his true passion, re-establishing the Reich to the position of
power it so greatly deserved. His chosen profession also provided
him with ample time and freedom to lead his subordinates in their
quest. To his associates at the university, he was a sweet,

grandfatherly figure. Fools! It was in his role as General Vogel that his true brilliance shown. His men would follow his word to their deaths if he so ordered it. And he had done so in the past and wouldn't hesitate to do so again if the situation required it. Vogel folded his hands across his chest and leaned back in his chair.

Patience is a virtue.

It had been a motto he lived by his entire life. A necessity given the incredible discipline and self-sacrifice needed to carry out his mission. A mission inherited from his father; a man haunted by the demons of his own failure.

His family had lived in a small compound, carved from the Argentinian jungle. As a boy, Vogel was homeschooled, rarely interacting with other children his own age. As such, he craved the attention of others, especially his father. Unfortunately, he rarely received it. Instead, his father obsessed over an object he referred to as his greatest creation. Night after night, his father would come home late, his nose buried in schematic drawings or other material related to the device. It was almost as if his son didn't exist. The worst part was that the boy knew very little about his father's research. He only knew that his father worked nearly around the clock to finish it, neglecting his family in the process.

When Vogel turned thirteen, he made a decision that would alter the course of his life. He would see, firsthand, the object of his father's obsession. But discovering the nature of his father's work was risky. His father was secretive about the device, only saying it would change the world, and was his duty complete. If his father found out about the plan, Vogel would face a beating. Though rare, when he had earned his father's ire, he had paid for it with many strikes of a riding crop across his backside. On some occasions, the beating had been so severe, he had been unable to sit for days. As such, he had to wait for his father to be away before implementing his plan.

Vogel tracked his father's routine, carefully watching when he came and went. Once he knew his father's schedule, he devised a plan to secretly follow him on his bicycle. School and other commitments forced his attempts to weekends and breaks, but he persisted. The task proved more difficult than he had anticipated. He had to learn the route in parts, following along as far as he could go and then the next time, starting from the last endpoint.

After months of failed attempts, he finally discovered the location of his father's lab. He now had to watch his father's movements even more closely, searching for a pattern, which might lead him to a day when his father's lab would be unattended. The opportunity came on a balmy fall day. Listening in on a loud telephone conversation between his father and one of his associates, he learned that his father would attend a meeting elsewhere.

Seizing the opportunity, the boy rode out to his father's laboratory, intent on finding the truth. Alas, he hadn't planned properly and found the grounds monitored by security guards. Undeterred, he waited until the guards were gone and used his bicycle as a step stool to climb over the wall, scraping his leg badly. Dropping down on the inside of the compound he was shocked to see multiple buildings. How would he determine which contained his father's project? He skulked about the grounds, walking up to the window of one of the buildings. He peered inside. Was this his father's lab?

A heavy hand fell on his shoulder. Frozen by fear, he stood rigid.

"Was machst du gerade? What are you doing here?" A male voice called out from behind.

The boy thrust his elbow into the guard's stomach, then sprinted around the corner of the building, searching for a way in. He ran straight into several men wearing lab coats, knocking himself and one of the men to the ground in a violent collision. The guard caught up with Vogel, towering over him. The guard grabbed him by his arm and hauled him to his feet, marching him into an adjacent building, where an older man, also dressed in a guard's uniform asked him a series of questions. Upon discovering who his father was, the older guard ordered his underling to take him home.

When he got there, his mother was waiting outside the front door, arms crossed. The guard opened the rear door to the sedan where Vogel was seated, but he refused to exit the vehicle. His mother grabbed him by his arm, dragged him out of the sedan and marched him into his father's study where he would wait for over two hours until his father finally arrived. His heart skipped a beat upon hearing the clicking sound of the doorknob turning. His father walked in, set his hat on the desk of his study, and pulled up a chair next to him. Vogel straightened his back, ready for his punishment.

His father cleared his throat. "I heard you visited my facility today."

The boy nodded.

"And what did you learn?"

"That I should have planned better before trying to break in," the boy replied, flinching in anticipation of a strike to the face. Instead, his father did something unexpected. Something he had rarely done over the course of the boy's life.

"Look at me," his father said. The boy complied, turning to look his father in the eye, feigning bravery. "What do you know about my research?"

"Nothing."

His father told him the story of his work for the Third Reich, the weapons his teams had created, and how they had struck terror in the heart of their enemies. He spoke of the V-2 bombs, which streaked across the English Channel, ripping apart the illusion of England's safety. The powerful Panzer tanks, which annihilated the inferior versions operated by the allies. As he spoke, his eyes flashed with passion as he relived his glory days. It was the first time his father had ever shown such emotion and the young boy longed to be a part of it.

"All of these creations, as incredible as they were, paled in comparison to the greatest device we ever created. Die Glocke."

"What's that?" The mesmerized young boy, asked.

His father wrinkled his nose, showing frustration at his son's inability to understand the name of his life's work. "You would call it the Bell," he said, translating the device's name to its English equivalent.

"What does it do?"

"It was a device unlike anything the world has ever known. It could travel anywhere at any time, slipping past the enemy's most advanced detection systems. It was to be my crowning achievement. The Fuhrer himself charged me with its completion. I will never forget the day he visited my laboratory in Poland. He grasped my shoulder and told me this would be the pinnacle of the Reich itself, a beacon proclaiming the superiority of our people," his father said, eyes alight with pride.

"What happened? Did you finish it?"

His father's face morphed, his eyes closed, and his shoulders drooped. "Nein. Before we could complete our task, the Russians invaded, taking back the part of Poland containing my lab. We were forced to flee for our lives, taking our plans with us. We had to destroy the near working prototype we had completed."

"You had to destroy the Bell?"

"Ja. We wouldn't allow the communist scum to take our work. We moved all we could take in our vehicles, then set fire to the facility, detonating explosive charges placed in key locations to ensure they would find little more than charred and twisted metal," his father replied, eyes narrowing.

His father went on to explain how, with the assistance of wealthy benefactors loyal to the Reich, a small cadre of scientists had been secretly spirited from Germany to Argentina. The same benefactors had graciously funded the building of the compound and living spaces for the scientists and their families. The boy listened closely, hanging on his father's every word. As he listened, he basked in the attention lavished by his father, never having

69

experienced it before. The day had marked a watershed moment in his existence. Although his father would never again spend such time with him, it was enough to spark a drive in the boy, a drive to follow in his father's footsteps.

Previously a mediocre student in math and science, the boy threw himself into his studies, sure that if he became a scientist, he would finally win his father's affection. He rose to the top of his class, demonstrating his father's incredible analytical skills. But his intelligence wasn't the only family resemblance. On every occasion possible, the boy reminded everyone of his family's social ranking. Rivals, who sought to dethrone him, met various nasty fates, suffering a broken arm or leg in a dubious accident.

His iron grip only tightened as he grew older, taking his place by his father's side when he had completed his studies. Still, his father held him at arm's length, causing the younger man to lash out at others around him. Vogel became a tyrant, those crossing him being incarcerated or worse, deposited into the middle of the jungle without supplies, the equivalent of a death sentence.

Eventually, he bestowed the title of General on himself, making him the unquestioned leader of his small tribe of renegade Nazi castoffs, operating under the militaristic structure of their predecessors. Descendants of a group of graduates of the Reichsführer school of the Nazi Party, the group called themselves Der Orden des Tyr, a reference to the bravest and boldest of the Norse gods. Appropriated by the Nazis in their zeal to realize an idealized Aryan heritage, all members of Vogel's society were forced to wear the rune mark of Tyr, a small arrow. At the age of eighteen, each member of the Order had the mark tattooed on the inside of their wrist as a sign of loyalty to Vogel.

Despite Vogel's growing power, his father remained aloof, withholding information about their work. It wasn't until his father was on his deathbed, their creation close to reality, that he finally disclosed the secret behind the device. The General sat by his father's side, when an amazing secret was shared between father and son.

The technology for the craft was not of terrestrial origin. The concept was presented to them by creatures, claiming to be visitors from another world. While sharing information with the scientists of the Third Reich, they had not provided them with full details of the device. Instead, they wanted the German scientists to learn how the craft would work so that they could create it from materials found on Earth, and design it in such a way as to allow humans to operate it. Components were provided to allow for reverse engineering, but the Nazis lacked the technology to truly understand all aspects of the design. As such, progress had been painstakingly slow. However, the process had allowed the German war machine to create advanced technology, which was then applied to other disciplines, such as rocket building.

The key, according to his father, was finding a rare stone, whose properties would allow it to serve as fuel for the craft. "Find the stone and finish die Glocke" was the admonition from father to son. He died a short time later, and Vogel swore upon his father's grave that he would complete his work at any cost.

"Will your guest be joining you soon?" the server asked, calling Vogel back to the present.

He looked up at the uninvited intrusion, sneered and nodded his head. "Ja."

"Excuse me?"

Vogel, realizing where he was, changed his expression, donning the false character he had developed over many years. "My apologies. Yes, my friend should be along shortly."

"Very well, I'll give you a few additional minutes," the server left Vogel to his thoughts. A short time later, the soldier entered the restaurant, spotted his commander, and walked directly to his table. The man's suit was badly wrinkled and his eyes bloodshot, but this was to be expected as Vogel had ordered him to take the first available non-stop flight from Argentina.

"General," the man said, nodding and taking a seat next to him.

"Pick up a menu like you're ordering, we're in a restaurant," Vogel said. "Were you able to obtain the location of the stone?"

The man's eyes flicked up from the menu to his commander. "Negative sir."

Vogel's eyes went wide, his nostrils flaring. He wanted to slam his fist on the table but couldn't risk the scene in public. "What information was Herrmann able to attain from the priest and the others?"

"Very little. The priest insists he doesn't know the whereabouts of the stone. He claims it's only a legend."

"And the other prisoners?"

"They escaped with the help of the armed soldiers who stormed our compound."

"Incompetence!" Vogel growled. "I've planned this operation for decades, patiently waiting for this moment. I won't have it stopped because a simpleton priest cannot be coerced to reveal the stone's location."

"Sir, Herrmann believes he can break the man. He feels he only needs more time."

"Tell Herrmann that I will arrive at the base tomorrow afternoon. If he's not able to obtain the information, then I will do it myself." Vogel looked up from the menu. "Go!"

The man dropped his menu and headed out of the restaurant. The server, seeing him go, tried to flag him down, but the man slipped out the door before the server could reach him. The server made his way to the Vogel's table. "Is everything okay?"

Vogel smiled. "Sadly, my friend won't be able to join me, but I'm ready to order."

Chapter 15

Isla de los Estados, Argentina
July 22, 6:54 p.m.

The helicopter touched down on the helipad of the Knight's ship, docked in a harbor on the opposite side of the island. On the surface, the vessel looked like a luxury yacht, her sleek white and blue hull and cabin shimmering in the setting sunlight. But a closer look revealed an impressive array of military firepower. After disembarking from the helicopter, Randall noted several cylindrical tubes protruding above the superstructure of the yacht. Upon inquiring about them, one of the Knights had offered a two-word response: launch tubes. As they walked through the main cabin, Randall had been surprised to find several Knights cleaning and stowing racks of semi-automatic rifles and crates of explosives. The conclusion Randall had reached was that any pirates unlucky to stumble upon this luxury cruiser were in for a rude surprise.

After a brief meeting with Tassone, the group was granted permission to roam a limited section of the deck. Though a biting cold wind swept over them, Randall and the group were happy to be out of the confines of their former cell. The ship lifted her anchor and departed from the island, but to Randall's surprise, instead of heading to the mainland, the ship headed east. Sam and Randall shared a look as their vessel drew closer to a different island chain off the coast of Argentina. Swinging to the south of the first island, they approached the southeast side of the last island in the group. Lights framed a harbor, as small and large crafts entered and exited the breakwater.

Tassone exited the superstructure and approached them.

"Captain, is there a reason we're going to the Falkland Islands instead of the mainland?" Randall asked.

"We have an agreement with the British government that allows us to utilize their military facilities."

Randall nodded. "Have you considered my offer?"

"Against my wishes, my superiors have ordered me to escort you to your friend to see if he can help us," Tassone said, his eyes narrowing. "But you'll be on a very short leash and will never be left unattended."

"Understood," Randall replied.

Tassone nodded and left.

The ship made landfall a short time later and the team was met by members of the British Royal Air Force, who arranged for Ernesto to return to his university. The rest of the team boarded a British military chopper which took them directly to Mount Pleasant airbase where they were loaded into a small, private jet that awaited them on the tarmac. Once in the air, Captain Tassone excused himself from the group. He returned wearing civilian clothes.

"I'm assuming the pilot is also a member of your Order?" Randall asked.

"Correct," Tassone replied. "Tell me about this friend of yours."

"His name is Peter Moloney and he's one of my oldest and dearest friends. He and his wife Jean were like second parents to my kids. Our families used to vacation together, and when my wife died, Peter helped us through the worst of it. He's like a brother to me."

Tassone nodded.

"He's also the head of the Catholic Studies Department at the University of St. Thomas. Peter's Catholic, which I think you would consider a plus," Randall added, smiling.

"As with every group, I have experienced bad Catholics. That doesn't mean anything to me," Tassone responded, letting Randall know that this wasn't to be a friendly conversation.

Taking the hint, Randall moved to the back of the plane, called his friend in privacy, and arranged to meet with him. He returned to his original seat, opposite Tassone.

"Were you able to reach him?" Tassone asked.

"It's all set. He'll be waiting."

"You didn't disclose the purpose of the meeting." Tassone said, more a directive than a question.

Randall glared back. "No, I didn't." He paused for a moment. "As far as Peter knows, this is just a friendly visit with Sam and me."

Tassone closed his eyes and sank into his seat. The exchange was over.

Randall walked to the seat next to Sam who was already asleep. They'd be in the air for several hours and Randall suddenly felt overwhelmed by fatigue. He dropped into the seat and closed his eyes to get some rest. He was asleep within minutes.

Chapter 16

Minneapolis, Minnesota
July 23, 1:04 p.m.

Randall was awakened by a repetitive poking of his arm. He rolled his head to the side to find a frowning Tassone hovering over him. "We'll be landing shortly."

Randall wiped the sleep from his eyes and nudged Sam awake.

A short time later, the plane touched down at Minneapolis-Saint Paul International Airport, then taxied to a private hangar. The group deplaned, entered a black town car, and fifteen minutes later arrived at Peter Moloney's house.

The walkway from the street took them past a beautifully manicured front lawn and up a short flight of brick steps to the black front door, flanked by white painted sidelights. Black wooden shutters framed white painted windows on the two-story brick home, completing the colonial revival look.

Randall knocked on the front door and a moment later his friend greeted him.

"Nick, how are you?" Moloney asked, shaking his friend's hand.

"Good, Pete, thanks for seeing us on short notice."

It was then that Moloney noticed the rest of the group. He

shot Randall an inquisitive look. "Friends of yours?"

"Sorry, I couldn't go into details on the phone."

"No problem. Please, come in everyone."

The small entourage entered the foyer of the colonial-style home.

"Where's Jean?" Randall asked.

"She's at work, I don't expect her home for a few more hours. Hi Sam," Moloney said, hugging her as the group walked to the living room. He motioned for everyone to sit down. "Grab a seat."

Randall and Sam sat on a small sofa near a leather recliner while Tassone and Grady occupied the adjoining parts of a sectional unit. Moloney was the last to sit, choosing the recliner near his friend. He turned to face Randall. "I thought something was up when you called."

Randall frowned. "What do you mean?"

"You had that sound in your voice, the one when you have big news about a discovery or some such thing," Moloney replied, grinning.

"Guess he can't fool you either, Uncle Peter," Sam winked at her adoptive uncle.

Moloney winked back, then turned again to her father. "What can I do for you and your friends?"

"Remember your doctoral thesis about the hierarchy of the Catholic Church?"

"I hope I do. I had to defend that thesis and, let me tell you, it wasn't easy."

"I was wondering what research you might have done on a group called the Knights Hospitaller?"

Moloney cocked his head and raised an eyebrow. "The Knights Hospitaller, also known as the Order of St. John. Along with the Knights Templar, they were the most formidable military order in the Holy Land but far less famous. At one time, their territory was expansive, but by the mid-1500s they were in decline. Their last great battle was defending the Island of Malta from the Ottomans under Sultan Suleiman the Magnificent. Did I pass the test?"

"Okay, sounds like you're an expert," Randall said.

"I hope so old buddy, those classes in medieval studies weren't cheap."

"Pete, are there any odd stories about the Knights?"

Moloney frowned. "What do you mean?"

Randall glanced at a stone faced Tassone. He could read his expression. Don't tell your friend what's going on.

"Were there any stories about odd occurrences that couldn't be readily explained."

"Are we talking about one of your out-there theories?"

"Maybe."

"Nick, we've known each other a long time. What's going on here?"

Randall looked at Tassone who shook his head.

Tough.

Randall explained what had transpired, beginning with Grady's visit to the school and culminating with their rescue from Isla de los Estados. He didn't disclose Tassone's identity, and Moloney was too shocked to ask.

"Jesus Nick, you could have all been killed," Moloney said.

"I know, but can you help? Are there any stories that might provide some clues?" Randall asked.

"The Malta story might help. In 1530, Charles I of Spain gave Malta and Tripoli to the Knights in exchange for an annual fee of a single Maltese falcon, which they were to send on All Souls' Day to the King's representative, the Viceroy of Sicily."

Sam smiled. "Is that what the movie's based on?"

"You got it, kiddo. The Hospitallers used the island as their base of operations against the Muslims and the Barbary pirates. That didn't sit well with the Ottomans, so in 1565, Suleiman sent an invasion force of about 40,000 men to besiege about 700 knights and 8,000 soldiers stationed in Malta."

"What happened to them?" Sam asked.

"At first it didn't go well for the Knights. They were losing men rapidly, but then a series of events turned the tide in their favor."

"Such as?" Randall asked.

"First, the Ottomans didn't have sufficient space to house that many soldiers. They were forced to live in such cramped quarters that disease spread rapidly through their ranks, wiping out a portion of their army. That demoralized their troops and kept them from finishing the job. The Knights, who knew that they were fighting for their lives, were able to rebuild their defenses and repel the attacks. Even injured knights and soldiers assisted in the battle. Pretty soon, they started to believe they could win."

"Sounds like the tide of the battle turned against the Turks," Randall said.

"Precisely. Then the Admiral of the Ottoman fleet, Turgut Reis, died and the remaining naval commanders failed use the navy to their advantage. That demoralized the Turks even more. Eventually, the Viceroy of Sicily sent reinforcements to support the Knights, and the Ottomans abandoned the siege. By the time the 15,000 Turkish troops retreated, the Knights only had around 600 fighting men left. It was a blow to the Ottoman Empire and a huge victory for the Knights."

"You're saying the Ottomans attacked the Knights at Malta because the Knights used it as a base to launch their military operations against them?" Grady asked.

"That's the standard explanation," Moloney replied.

"What do you mean standard explanation?" Sam asked.

"Your dad asked for odd stories and there are two theories behind what motivated the Turks and one of them is pretty strange," Moloney said.

79

"I don't understand," Grady furrowed his brow.

"The mainstream theory states that the Ottomans wanted a new base to launch another assault on Europe, and Malta fit the bill."

"What's the other theory?" Sam asked.

"It's been widely decried as a fairy tale and I wouldn't have even mentioned it if your dad hadn't explained what happened. It involves an ancient relic that was believed to contain great power. As the story goes, this mysterious relic would grant anyone who possessed it the power to defeat their enemies," Peter said.

"But what does that have to do with Malta?" Grady asked.

"According to conspiracy theorists, the Knights stationed in Malta possessed this relic and it's what helped them defeat the overwhelming Ottoman force. Apparently, Sultan Suleiman discovered that the Knights were hiding this relic and sent his army to capture it. If he had, it would have changed the history of Europe as we know it."

"Excuse me, Professor, but what exactly was this relic?" Tassone asked, speaking for the first time.

"I'm not sure. Some say it was a religious artifact, possibly something to do with The Last Supper or…"

"Or what?" Tassone asked.

Moloney sighed and drew his mouth tight. His eyes scanned the room. "Others say the relic was of unknown origins, possibly extraterrestrial."

Tassone sat upright. "Where was the artifact hidden?"

"That's unclear, but some believers of this conspiracy say it passed through Fort Saint Angelo."

"Based on your research, which theory do you believe?" Randall asked.

"I think the Ottomans wanted a base to attack Europe, but their leaders got sloppy with their tactics because they had such an overwhelming advantage. That theory's supported by documents written by the Turks themselves, dating back to before the siege.

There was a long, tense history between the Muslims and the Christians battling for control of the Holy Land."

"It makes sense that Suleiman would have wanted an island base off the coast of Italy," Sam agreed.

"Exactly. With his naval advantage, the Christians would have had little chance of reclaiming the island. He could have then taken Sicily and used it to gain a foothold on the mainland. From there he could have marched his troops right into his enemy's home base in Rome. By having Malta, his supply line for an attack of the mainland would have been much shorter and less vulnerable to attack."

Randall could tell that his friend's demeanor had changed. He had undoubtedly noticed the way Tassone responded to the alternate theory about the relic. As if to confirm this, Moloney turned to Tassone. "By the way, I don't believe I've caught your name."

"Scusa, my name is Gabriele Tassone," the captain said, extending his hand.

"I see you're Italian. Nick, I feel like there's more to this story. Care to enlighten me?"

Randall shot Tassone a side glance. The Captain nodded back.

"How much time do you have before Jean comes home?"

"Plenty."

Randall provided the remaining details to his friend, disclosing that Tassone was a Knight. Moloney shook his head in disbelief.

"You mean you're a member of the Order?" Moloney asked.

"Sí. My men and I were sent to rescue Father Bianchi, who was held captive by a group of devotees of the former Third Reich. These people fancy themselves the new generation of Nazis, bent on re-establishing the reign of terror wrought by Hitler and his henchmen."

"How in the world did these people end up in South America?" Moloney asked.

"At the end of the Second World War, Nazi sympathizers smuggled scientists and other members of the Reich out of the country. These men brought plans for their weapons with them and established a small, secretive community. They re-established ties with wealthy Germans who helped fund their research and recruited new members to their ranks.

Moloney looked at Randall. "I can't believe that crazy theory about Malta might be true. What are you going to do now?"

"We need to go to Fort Saint Angelo and see if we can pick up the trail to the stone before the Nazis figure things out," Randall replied.

"I agree. If you will excuse me, I will make arrangements." Tassone stood and left the room.

"Jim, I'm sorry to hear about your team, but if anyone can find them, it's this guy," Moloney said, casting a thumb in Randall's direction.

"From what I've seen so far, I would have to agree with you," Grady replied.

Randall shook his head. "I can't make any guarantees, but I'll do my best and I promise I won't quit if you don't."

Tassone returned to the group. "We are ready to go but need to hurry."

Randall stood. "Pete, I can't thank you enough for your help."

"Do you want me to go with you?"

"I don't want to risk your safety. Keep an eye on your phone though, I might call for help once we get to the church."

"Will do. God speed."

The group left Moloney's home, racing back to the airport, where the jet was waiting. As soon as they boarded, it departed for Malta.

Chapter 17

St. Anne's Chapel, Malta
July 24, 6:13 a.m.

Randall was exhausted, his body clock disturbed by the frequent air travel and multiple crossings of time zones. Though his watch told him it was 6:13 a.m., his body said something else, his circadian rhythm a thorough mess. He had slept fitfully at times but had struggled to maintain a deep sleep. During the latter part of the flight, Tassone had explained that a small contingency of men would be waiting for them when they arrived. Wanting to maintain secrecy, his soldiers would be dressed in civilian clothes. They would be accompanied by two fire teams, consisting of five men each. One team would enter the church with them, while the other kept watch outside. Now they just needed to get there.

The plane crossed the coast of Africa, exiting the continent and making its way above the Mediterranean. It soon began its descent into the sea of lights marking the Malta International Airport. Once on the ground, the jet taxied to a private hanger where ten impeccably dressed men waited for them to disembark. Tassone was the first to exit the plane as a light mist dusted the group while they descended the stairs.

"Captain, per your orders, preparations have been made.

Archive records have been retrieved and are awaiting your arrival."

"Very good, Lieutenant."

The group entered three waiting Peugeot sedans and sped toward the town of Birgu, where the Fort was located.

"Captain, how long before we get there?" Randall asked.

"The fort is 9.4 kilometers from the airport. If we don't encounter traffic, we should arrive in approximately 18 minutes."

"What'll we do first?" Sam asked.

Grady stretched his long arms. "We should check their files to see if there are any odd entries that might be related to the stone. From my recollection, the Knights were fastidious record keepers."

"Agreed. I have instructed my men to have the documents ready for us. We will review them first, then begin our search," Tassone glanced down at his watch.

"And what do we do if we find The Devil's Heart? The Nazis still have Grady's team, and if they can't get the stone, what will happen to them?" Sam asked.

Sam's question seemed to suck the air from the car, causing everyone to stare off into space. After a painful silence, Tassone responded. "We cannot, under any circumstances, give The Devil's Heart to the Nazis. Doing so will place hundreds of thousands of lives in danger. I'm sorry, Dr. Grady."

Randall winced. The Captain was right, but it didn't make the situation easier to accept. Whatever plans the Nazis had for the stone were sinister, and to trade it for the lives of Grady's team members would be morally wrong. By the same token, leaving his team's fate in the hands of their German captors was equally wrong. There had to be a way to achieve both goals.

The three Peugeots made their way into the city of Cospicua, past the loading docks used to transport goods to the island nation. Bolts of lightning streaked through the sky, illuminating the Grand Harbour in fits as the cars plied their way to Birgu. Tassone explained that the city resembled a crooked finger pointing out into the harbor, with the Fort at its tip. They would reach their destination in a few minutes.

Randall glanced out the side window through the streaks of water, the rain growing heavier as they approached their destination. The road they followed ran perpendicular to the ocean, providing views of the many beautiful boats lining the docks. The lead car turned right from Xatt ll-Forn Road into a narrow passage that fed into a parking lot adjacent to the complex. Tassone's men exited their vehicles, forming a protective perimeter around their guests. Randall, Sam, Grady, and Tassone exited their car and strode toward the Fort, pelted by an unrelenting assault of rain.

"As we discussed, we will begin by reviewing the files from the archives. They are awaiting us in St. Anne's Chapel. Please follow me," Tassone raised his voice to be heard above the storm, then picked up the pace, jogging at a slow trot.

Even in the foul weather, the view was breathtaking in the mercury vapor lights that illuminated the site. The fort was a stone-walled fortification that towered over the harbor. The first level was a combination of stone walls, sheer rock face, and archways, which created the base upon which the rest of the structure had been built. Multiple buildings and courtyards were contained within the multilevel citadel, forming a mazelike structure through which the group zigzagged toward the chapel.

Unlike the whitewashed stones on the exterior of the fort, the walls on the interior were constructed of neatly stacked, rust-colored bricks. The group moved along cobblestone paths, past cannons that spoke to the facility's distant past as a coastal defense from marauding forces. They made their way higher along the facility, moving toward the far northern tip of the fort as The Grand Harbour fell away beneath them. Slashes of lightning briefly illuminated the many small boats that dotted the waters of the harbor.

The group crested a hill and walked onto a flat courtyard of interconnected white and brown stones, slick with rain. They crossed the opening and approached a single building at the far end. An arched doorway containing a heavy wooden door, framed by beautiful natural stones, formed the entrance to the structure. High above the door was a single bell, above which was an ornately carved cross. They had arrived at St. Anne's Church.

Tassone ushered the group into the Narthex of the tiny chapel. The interior of the church was simple, yet beautiful. White-washed stone walls featured artwork depicting the life of Christ, his mother Mary, and the early Saints of the Church. Additional paintings hung in the many niches of the chapel which were framed by high arching entryways resting on stone columns. Candles burned near the altar and several rows of chairs lined the floor in the Nave. The strong scent of incense filled the air as they traversed the floor toward a small wooden desk to the right of the Nave. A lone man, wearing a dark suit and matching somber expression, waited by the desk.

"Captain, here are the documents you requested," the man said as Tassone approached. He gave the captain a key ring.

"Thank you, Lieutenant. Take a defensive position with the other men outside."

The lieutenant exited the building, leaving the captain and three academics to review the archival documents. The papers were encased in several well-worn, black trunks, stacked neatly by the desk. The containers resembled steamer trunks like those used by travelers during the heyday of oceanic voyages. A single heavy lock on each chest ensured the safety of the documents within.

Tassone hefted the first trunk onto the table. Thumbing through the keys on the ring, he found the one he needed. He opened the chest, revealing neatly bound, hardcover booklets, carefully arranged within.

Randall frowned upon seeing the binders. "What's this?"

"The original documents are priceless artifacts, many of which are fragile and damaged by the ravages of time. To prevent further harm, we scanned them, organizing the images by date and source. What you see in these trunks are the copies of the original manuscripts and papers."

"You said they're organized by date and source?" Grady asked.

"That's correct," Tassone answered.

"Do you have an index system for the copies?"

"In fact, we do," Tassone lifted the first binder from the trunk and flipped it open. "As you see, this folder outlines all of the documents within this chest and cross references the document to the corresponding number of the binder."

As Tassone explained the system, he removed a second binder, showing the group the raised number on the spine.

"Quite a system you have," Sam commented.

"Given the number of documents within our possession, an orderly filing system was a necessity."

"Where do we start?" Grady asked.

"I suggest we each take a trunk, review the source list, and see if we find any entries that refer to artifacts matching the description of the stone." Randall suggested.

Tassone opened a trunk for each team member, and the research began. Hours passed as each person reviewed the contents of their trunk. Several false starts raised hopes that were soon dashed. After reviewing nearly every trunk, hopes of finding a clue dwindled.

Sam stretched her arms over her head and yawned. "Sounds like the rain stopped."

Sam was right, the incessant ticking of water droplets striking stone had ceased.

"There's only one trunk left," Jim said.

"Might as well get to it," Randall craned his back while Tassone opened the lock.

Randall removed the binder, flipping it open on the desk in front of him. Before long he hit upon an entry, he motioned for the others to join him. "Take a look at this."

"What is it?" Sam asked.

"Hopefully not another false start," Jim said.

"It's an entry with the source listed as Gerard Tum," Randall replied.

Tassone nodded. "Yes, there are several documents attributed to him in our records."

"Look at the entry date," Randall said, his index finger resting near the number.

Tassone frowned, shaking his head. "That's impossible."

"What do you mean?" Sam asked.

"Gerard Tum passed away in 1120, but this entry is dated 1792," Grady answered. "This must have been their way of hiding a clue that this was an important transaction. Only members of the Order or people familiar with them would have noticed this discrepancy."

Tassone nodded in agreement. "We must look at this more closely."

"It's in Volume 92, let's grab it," Randall pointed to the trunk.

Grady hefted the binder in question and brought it over to the table. Flipping through the pages, he finally arrived at the entry. "It's from the personal journal of a priest named Fr. Demarco Dicce. It's written in Latin."

Captain Tassone moved to Grady's side. "Would you mind?" he said, reaching for the entry. Grady passed it over to him. As Tassone read, his stony appearance changed. His frown slowly straightened, eventually becoming a smirk. His eyes softened, a raised eyebrow and slight nodding of his head communicating a sense of surprise.

"What does it say?" Randall asked.

"Fr. Dicce explains that a relic was brought to the church by a Knight who did not give his name. The artifact was kept at the church, which was common at the time, as many relics discovered by the Knights were brought to the Chapel. According to Dicce, the artifact was retrieved from a site near San Ignacio Mini in South America at the behest of Pope Pius VI. It was then hidden in the monument of Grand Master Nicolas Cottoner at the Chapel of Aragon."

"When did Pope Pius VI reign?" Randall asked.

Tassone's grin blossomed into a full-blown smile. "February 1775 to his death in 1799."

"Then this must be the Devil's Heart, but where is this monument?" Sam asked.

"There's only one church that fits the description," Grady said. "The Co-Cathedral of St. John."

Tassone closed his eyes and nodded his head.

"How far away is it?" Sam asked.

"Here, in Valleta," Grady answered.

Sam turned to Tassone. "How long will it take us to get there?"

"It's just across the harbor. We can be there in twenty minutes."

Chapter 18

Co-Cathedral of St. John, Valletta Malta
July 24, 11:11 a.m.

The rain had subsided, the clouds reluctantly giving way to the first rays of sunshine when the Peugeots pulled to a stop on the Triq il Merkanti in front of the cathedral. Tassone barreled out of the car, instructing his men to form a perimeter around the church, his speech fast and high pitched. He strode toward the front door while the rest of the group followed, trying to keep up with him. Randall grinned as he listened to the Captain, seeing him animated in a way he hadn't seen before.

As the group neared the cathedral, one of Tassone's men approached him, speaking as he walked so as not to slow his commander. "We've established a perimeter and all occupants have been removed from the church."

"Well done Sergeant, return to your post and keep your radio ready. We may need assistance moving the relic."

The sergeant saluted his captain, sprinting back to his position. Tassone pushed open the cathedral door and walked in without breaking stride. The others trailed close behind.

Upon entering, Randall took two steps, then stopped in his tracks. His gaze swept over the interior of the church, his mind overwhelmed by the beauty and grandeur that met his eyes. Unlike the simplicity of the Chapel of St. Anne, this cathedral was built on a grand scale, during the height of the Baroque period, utilizing highly detailed and lifelike artwork and statues to produce dramatic grandeur. Humans reached toward the heavens and cherubs trumpeted horns in the many paintings that adorned the interior, all framed by tall, carefully sculptured columns that stretched to the arched ceiling.

"This is incredible," Sam commented.

Tassone nodded. "The interior was decorated by Mattia Preti, a Calabrian artist and Knight. Preti designed the intricately carved stone walls and painted the vaulted ceiling and side altars with scenes from the life of St. John."

"The artwork is beautiful. The detail work of the three-dimensional statues at each column are extraordinary," Randall commented.

Tassone smirked. "They're actually two-dimensional paintings. Preti created the illusion of three-dimensionality by his use of shadows and placement."

As the group walked by the first column, Randall noted that the captain was correct. Feeling a bit sheepish, he chose to not comment further on the artwork.

"Don't be concerned with your error, you aren't the first to fall victim to Preti's incredible skills," Tassone said. "The carvings you see were all undertaken in-place—in-situ—rather than being carved independently and then attached to the walls. The Cathedral was built from Maltese limestone, which allowed for such intricate carving."

"What about the marble floors?" Sam asked.

"A series of tombs, housing 375 knights and officers of the Order. There's also a crypt containing the tombs of several Grandmasters," Tassone announced proudly, stopping next to an ornately carved section of wall that jutted out from the side. The sculpture depicted cherubim victoriously trumpeting in the sky, hovering above statuettes holding a ledge, which housed a bronze plaque commemorating the individual for which the artwork had been created.

"The monument of Grandmaster Nicolas Cottoner," Tassone said.

"Incredible," Sam said.

"The stone's inside this artwork?" Grady asked.

"According to Father Dicce's journal, yes. It was common at the time for artists such as Preti to conceal valuable relics in works of art. In fact, being a master craftsman, Preti would have been able to create a secret compartment that blended seamlessly into the artwork itself," Tassone explained.

"How do we open it?" Randall asked. "We certainly don't want to damage it."

"Agreed," Grady said.

As the group pondered the situation, Randall noticed an irregular ticking sound coming from the wall facing the exterior of the building. The noise, at first infrequent, grew in intensity. Randall looked around the empty cathedral as the rest of the group watched the captain intently. No one else seemed to hear the sound. Had the rain returned? This sounded different. Randall walked toward the nearest exterior wall, trying to determine the source of the sound.

He returned to Sam's side. "Do you hear that?"

Sam frowned. "Hear what?"

"That clicking sound. It's getting louder and more frequent."

The front door of the Cathedral burst open and a Knight rushed inside, sprinting straight for the group as bullets ricocheted off the entryway.

"We're under attack! We've lost contact with most of our men but have reports of sniper fire and a company of enemy soldiers closing on our position."

Tassone straightened. "Get on the radio and call for immediate reinforcements, we must protect this church."

"We've tried contacting our base, but something's interfering with our transmission," the soldier responded.

Randall grabbed Tassone's arm. "What's going on?"

"The Nazis must have followed us. We led them straight to the stone! Corporal contact all remaining troops and pull them back into the main part of the cathedral!"

"We need to find the stone now!" Randall pushed his way to the monument and sent Sam a worried look. "Captain, I'll help until the end, but please, you need to protect my daughter. Is there somewhere inside the church she can hide?"

The door to the cathedral opened again as two more of Tassone's men joined the group inside. As the heavy doors swung closed, the sound of gunfire rang through the exterior courtyard. The Nazis were closing in.

Tassone grabbed the corporal. "Take Ms. Randall to the crypts and guard her."

"Dad, I'm not leaving you."

"Please Sam, this isn't the time to argue with me. You weren't supposed to be here in the first place."

"But..."

"No buts. Corporal, take her."

"Ms. Randall, please come with me."

Sam looked at her dad, but his worried expression conveyed everything she needed to know. To her credit, she didn't argue, for which Randall was grateful. Sam and the corporal disappeared from the chapel.

"There has to be a lever here somewhere to open this. Any thoughts?" Randall asked.

"Try the carvings and look for a single stone to depress. Anything that might act as a lever," Grady answered, joining Randall.

The gunfire grew louder.

The doors to the church burst open again as one of

93

Tassone's men dragged another soldier inside. The blood from his chest wound left a streak of crimson across the marble floor.

"Captain, the enemy is approaching from all sides. They have RPGs and are preparing to use them."

"I need a head count," Tassone said.

"We're it."

The door to the Cathedral shattered into a million fragments as an explosion ripped through the nave of the church, sending shards of wood and metal careening inward. The shockwave caused the entire team to drop to the ground for cover as smoke billowed through the opening.

"Cover fire toward the door!" Tassone ordered as his remaining men took defensive positions, their weapons trained on the entrance of the church.

They waited. Nothing happened.

"Inside the church!" an amplified voice called out from the courtyard. "We have you surrounded, lay down your weapons and come out."

"We need to find the damn switch to open this thing!" Randall growled, searching frantically for a way to open the monument's secret compartment.

Tassone glared defiantly toward the shattered doorway. "Steady, men."

"You're outnumbered and overpowered. Come out now and you'll be spared."

"Professor?" Tassone asked.

"Nothing yet," Randall replied, his heart beating like a ticking metronome.

"Someone must have heard the gunfire, the police have to be on their way," Grady said.

"They won't arrive before we're all dead," one of the soldiers observed grimly.

"This is your final warning," the voice called out.

Randall discovered a small depression in an otherwise smooth piece of marble. "I think I found it!"

As he spoke, several canisters shot through the front of the church. Gas poured out, obscuring their view of the damaged opening.

Randall looked back to see multiple uniformed men storming inside, flames spewing from the barrels of their weapons. Bullets hissed by his head, bouncing off the statue and walls, creating sparks that danced like fireflies through the smoky church. He was forced to dive to the ground to avoid the deadly hail of lead.

"Concentrate fire on the doorway!" Tassone ordered.

His men complied, firing in unison at the intruders.

Bodies fell as the invaders were temporarily repelled. The victory was short lived as more soldiers poured into the church.

Bullets and bits of limestone and wood rained down on Randall and Grady as they lay on the ground, covering their heads and necks as best as possible. The acrid smell of smoke filled the church as the Nazis moved toward them. Tassone and his men took the worst of it, the enemy homing in on the flashes emanating from their muzzles. One by one his men were picked off.

"Professors, run!" Tassone shouted, coming to his feet, and rushing the intruders, gun blazing.

"Come on!" Randall grabbed Grady and sprinted in the direction the corporal had taken Sam.

The two men wove through the various niches and nave of the church, finally arriving at the sanctuary. Randall turned to look back at Tassone. The captain lay on the floor, his gun by the side of his mortally wounded body. He had bought them just enough time to escape and paid with his life.

Randall spotted a staircase to his left. He dragged Grady toward it, then headed down the steps to the crypt area beneath the sanctuary. They sprinted downward, taking several stairs at a time, finally arriving on the lower level. A short hallway fed into an arched entryway, marking the entrance to the crypts.

"Stop or I'll shoot!" The corporal popped out from a niche in the wall.

"It's us, we're all that's left. The Nazis killed the rest of your team!" Randall yelled. "Where's Sam?"

"I'm right here, Dad," Sam stepped out of the shadows of another recess.

"We've got to get out of here. Corporal, is there another way out besides those stairs?" Randall asked.

The soldier stared blankly at Randall. The sounds of shouting from above let him know the enemy would soon be there. "There may be another way through the crypts. Follow me."

The four wove their way through the catacombs, past stone crypts containing the remnants of venerated Knights. The dank, musty air was smothering, making it difficult to breathe.

"Legends speak of a path that leads from the crypts to a panel in the chapel. It should be this way," the corporal said. The sound of boots hitting the bottom of the stairs echoed through the tombs. The Nazis had arrived.

"Fan out and find them!" a Nazi ordered.

"Stay close to the walls," the corporal whispered.

The group threaded their way through the tombs, arriving at a niche containing a stone coffin.

"It should be here," the corporal searched for a secret panel.

Randall craned his neck, peeking around the corner toward the staircase. "They're getting closer," he whispered to the group, pulling back into the niche.

Failing to see Grady next to him, he bumped him, knocking him toward the wall. Grady staggered backward, hitting an urn sitting in a small alcove cut into the stone. The urn wobbled on its base, tumbling toward the ground. Grady dove for it, trying to catch it before it hit the floor. He failed. The urn smashed onto the stone, made a loud cracking sound on impact, then rolled into the main floor of the crypt.

"Shit!" Grady whispered.

"This way!" a Nazi soldier called out from the end of the

crypt.

"Hurry!" Grady shouted.

Randall moved to the corporal's side, pushing, and pulling on sections of wall, outcrops, and anything else he could get reach.

Boot steps thundered through the crypt, growing louder each second.

"Dad?"

"Working on it…"

"Schnell!"

Randall's mind raced, he had to find the panel. He pressed on an inlaid sculpture of the Knights' crest with one hand, while groping along the ledge above with the other. A section of wall buckled in front of him. He tumbled in.

"Einfrieren!" a German voice called out behind him as the section of wall closed behind him, sealing him inside the passage.

Randall scrambled to his feet, running back to the section of wall that had just closed. The rest of the group was still on the other side … with the Nazis.

"Move and we'll kill you!" a voice shouted from the other side of the wall.

"There was another man, where is he?" a separate voice barked.

"He went in there!" the first voice answered.

Randall heard pounding on the wall. They knew where he was.

"Run, Dad!" Sam yelled.

"Halt den Mund!"

"Sam!"

There was no response.

Randall pulled his cell phone from his pocket. Flicking on the light, he shined it down the passageway, then looked back at the wall. "If you son of a bitches hurt her, I'll kill every last one of you!"

"He's on the other side. We have to get through the wall!" a German voice responded.

"Hurry Dad!" Sam yelled.

"I can't leave you!"

"Go!" Sam screamed.

Randall flinched. He moved toward the wall, then turned to run and froze again.

"I…"

"Dad!"

"Shut her up!"

Randall blinked and balled his fists.

What do I do?

"Get the explosives!" a German voice ordered.

Randall cursed, then sprinted down the path. He made it several feet, then looked back. The sound of activity on the other side of the wall grew louder.

I'll save you Sam … I promise.

Randall sprinted down the darkened path into the unknown.

Chapter 19

Randall raced ahead, the upward slant of the tunnel draining him of energy. He paused a moment, leaning has back against the cold stone wall, hands on knees to catch his breath. Sweat rolled down his back and his head pounded with pain. He had to keep going, the Nazis were only minutes behind him. He reached the end of the passage and, using his phone light, he examined it. Carved into the rock was a shield, baring the symbol of the Knights, the outline a carved groove forming its perimeter. He pressed the center of the shield and, hearing a click, he pushed harder. A section of wall pivoted open.

Randall stuck his head through the opening and looked around. He was back in the sanctuary of the church. He exited the passageway and pushed the stone panel closed. To his surprise, the section of wall hiding the passage was a beautifully sculptured work of art, its high arching top blending seamlessly into the background.

For the moment, he was hidden in a small alcove. Randall peered out, looking into the nave of the church. Lying amidst the chunks of wood and stone were Tassone's body and the bodies of several dead Nazis the captain and his men had killed. The

99

Germans were all dressed in nearly identical suits.

The smell of gunfire and dust filled the nave. Randall crept over to the bodies, darting in and out of the niches for cover. Upon reaching the first dead Nazi, Randall stopped to examine him. He was facing down and appeared to be approximately Randall's height and build. Randall rolled him over. The top of the man's skull was missing, the result of a bullet tearing through his head. Randall nearly vomited.

The sound of German voices from the staircase leading down to the crypts was growing louder. They were coming back up.

Randall dragged the Nazi into an adjacent alcove, quickly removing the man's pants and jacket. Changing into the dead soldier's clothing, he jogged from the niche directly toward a gun lying near another dead German. He picked it up and made his way to the entrance of the church.

In the distance, he heard someone yelling orders in a mixture of German and English. Accompanying the angry voice were thunderous footsteps growing louder by the moment. Randall sprinted toward the charred remains of the front doors. Daylight spilled through the opening. As he closed within a few yards, a man with a gun walked inside. He was wearing the same suit as Randall and the dead Nazis.

"Where is the colonel?" the man asked in English.

Randall stopped and raised his gun slightly. He stared into the man's face.

The soldier glared back. "The colonel?"

"Back there," Randall said, jerking his thumb toward the sanctuary. "They were looking for the professor down in the crypts."

The man's eyes narrowed as he examined Randall. "And what are you doing?"

"The professor may have exited through the courtyard. I'm trying to find him before he escapes," Randall said. "Colonel's orders."

The Nazi's eyes relaxed and he moved aside for Randall, who wasted no time sprinting out of the church. Lying in the street, next to their squad car, were two dead police officers, the word PULIZIJA stenciled in blue across the back of their black jackets. Randall scanned the area. Several civilians peered from behind walls and out of windows, trying to make sense of the carnage.

Randall jogged to the side street where Tassone's men had parked their cars. He was relieved to find the vehicles still there. The driver who had taken him to the church was crouched behind a car, his gun drawn. Seeing Randall, the driver waved him over, obviously recognizing who he was despite his disguise.

Randall ran to him. "We have to go, they've captured my daughter and Dr. Grady," he said, then opened the passenger door. The soldier stood motionless as Randall entered the car.

"Where's the captain and why are you wearing that suit?" the soldier said, staring blankly at Randall through the car window.

"Captain Tassone is dead and so are the rest of your men," Randall replied. "The suit's a disguise. Without it, the Nazis would have recognized me."

The man just stood there, eyes wide, his hand glued to the door.

"I'm sorry about your captain and your fellow Knights, but if we don't leave now, they'll capture us as well."

Still no movement.

Shouts rose in the distance. Before long, the Germans would realize he'd escaped. The droning of sirens in the distance joined the chaos. More pulizija were on the way. It was a toss-up who would find them first, the Nazis or the authorities. Tassone's soldier stood rooted in place.

"Soldier, your captain died to keep the enemy from obtaining the Devil's Heart and to protect my daughter, Dr. Grady, and I. He's gone. Are you going to complete your mission or allow the Nazis to win?" Randall barked.

The Knight snapped out of his trance, pulled the driver's door open and hopped inside. He turned the key and the engine roared to life. The two men sped back in the direction they had come earlier.

"Where are we going?" Randall asked.

"Somewhere safe. I need to report back to my superiors to let them know what happened. They'll know what we should do next."

Randall pressed back into his seat and pounded his fist on the armrest. His anger slowly subsided, replaced with concern. He couldn't stand leaving Sam and Grady with the Nazis, but he had no choice. If they had caught him, no one would have known what had happened. At least now he could try to save them.

The car raced along the streets of Malta as the sun burned brightly above, the rain all but a distant memory. All Randall could do was wait and hope that the Knights might have an idea to help them.

Chapter 20

Sam stared down the nave of the church through what had once been the front door of the cathedral. She and Grady were surrounded by Nazis, each brandishing a weapon.

Upon seeing Captain Tassone's body, Sam fought back tears. He had bravely sacrificed his life to defend them and his sacrifice had allowed her father to escape. Sam set her jaw and defiantly glared at her captors.

"You look angry, Dr. Randall," a voice said from behind.

Sam turned to see who had spoken and immediately recognized the man. "You're the one from the base in Argentina," she said, her head cocked to one side. She quickly resumed her death stare, finding a new target for her hatred.

"I'm flattered you remember me."

"Don't be too flattered, I've already forgotten your name."

"My name is Dietrich Herrmann."

"Why do you want the Devil's Heart?"

Herrmann chuckled. "I'm impressed. Most people in your situation would be more concerned with their well-being."

"You didn't answer my question."

A flicker of anger flashed in Herrmann's eyes. "While I appreciate your curiosity, I don't believe you're in a position to demand information."

Herrmann turned to face Grady. "Dr. Grady, you came here because you believed the stone was hidden somewhere inside.

103

Where?"

"I don't know."

"I see," Herrmann walked up to Sam. He extended an open hand, into which one of his men placed a serrated knife. He held it below Sam's chin. "Does this help jog your memory?"

Sam's eyes went wide. "Don't tell him anything."

"Frau Randall, it would be wise for you to keep your mouth shut," Herrmann said, pressing the tip slightly harder into her skin. A drop of blood trickled down the blade and Sam winced.

"Stop, I'll tell you!" Grady yelled.

"I'm waiting."

"It's in the Chapel of Aragon," Grady said, motioning for Herrmann to lower the blade.

Herrmann grabbed Sam's arm, still holding the blade against her throat.

"Escort the good professor to the chapel," Herrmann said to his men, nodding in that direction.

The group moved as a single unit, Grady leading with two Nazis following behind, one with his gun pressed into Grady's back. Herrmann followed holding Sam, knife still to her throat.

"It's in there," Grady pointed to the monument of Grand Master Nicola Cottoner. "We couldn't figure out how to open it, but apparently there's a secret compartment hidden inside."

"Open it," Herrmann demanded.

A look of bewilderment crossed Grady's face. "We don't know how?"

A Nazi pushed past Grady, carrying a small satchel to the monument. He opened it, revealing a small cube of putty with wires and a small digital clock attached to it.

Grady's eyes went wide. "You can't do that. That's a priceless artifact!"

A soldier smashed the butt of his rifle into Grady's back, knocking him to the floor.

"Stop!" Sam yelled.

Grady rolled on the ground in pain as the soldier finished

placing the charge. Sam broke free of Herrmann's grip, kneeling by Grady's side.

"Are you okay? Let me help you up," she gently grasped Grady's arm.

Herrmann stood over them, smiling. "Set the timer."

The soldier complied, then walked away as the timer began beeping, the digital numbers counting down.

Herrmann nodded at Sam and Grady. Soldiers grabbed them by their arms, then prodded them with guns to their ribs. The group shuffled away from the monument, taking shelter in the adjoining chapel. A small explosion, followed by a puff of smoke, announced the detonation.

The Nazis forced Sam and Grady back into the Chapel and Sam watched in anger as Herrmann approached the now destroyed priceless work of art. She coughed, the smell of gunpowder filling her lungs. She waived her hand in front of her face to dissipate the smoke. "There's a special place in hell for people like you."

Herrmann turned, his eyes tight and his lips curled into an angry frown. He nodded once at Sam and Grady, jabbing a finger at the ground next to him. Sam felt a gun press into her back as she was prodded to walk to Herrmann's side. Another Nazi did the same to Grady and when they reached the monument, Herrmann placed his face inches from Grady's.

"Where is it?" he hissed.

Grady blinked. "What do you mean?"

Herrmann jabbed a single finger into the broken monument. Grady looked inside. The Devil's Heart was gone.

Chapter 21

Knights Base, Gozo Malta
July 24, 12:17 p.m.

The Peugeot sedan sped along the rugged coastline of the island of Gozo, weaving along the winding road. Randall stared out the window, lost in thought. Having taken the Channel Lines ferry from Malta, it had been slightly more than an hour since they left the cathedral. Known for its tranquility, Malta's sister island was greener, more rural, and smaller than its larger neighbor to the south. Baroque churches and old stone farmhouses dotted the countryside, as the car wound its way around the island.

Randall and his driver had barely spoken since fleeing the Germans. Instead, Randall focused on the situation … and worried about what could be happening to Sam and Grady.

"You never told me where we're going," Randall said.

"I'm taking us to a safe house used by my people. It's a small headquarter away from the main part of the city. I need to speak with my superiors to make sure they know what happened."

"How much longer until we get there?"

"Maybe ten minutes."

Randall nodded, sinking back into the rear seat of the car. All he could do was wait. The car crested a small hill and Randall spotted yet another white stone compound on the ocean side of the road. As they approached, the driver slowed, taking a gravel path to the far side of the structure, away from the main thoroughfare. Randall glanced out his window. Seeing the beautiful white stone structure with multiple buildings, he thought the compound resembled a quaint ocean-side retreat.

Randall exited the car and followed the driver up to the gate, where he pushed a button on a black intercom box.

"ID?" a voice called out through the speaker.

The driver held his identification near his face and looked directly into the camera. A buzzing sound announced that the gate was unlocked. Walking into the compound, Randall noted the pool and lounge area, complete with umbrellas and chairs for sunbathing. The driver moved briskly through the courtyard, heading directly for a set of stairs at the far left-hand corner of the facility.

The men went down a flight of stone steps and arrived at two doors. One was made of glass, revealing a kitchen and small dining area and the other was a non-descript wooden door with the word "Maintenance" written in the center and a small card reader at shoulder level. The driver ran his ID through the card reader and the door opened.

Randall was shocked by the sight that befell his eyes. State-of-the-art computer stations and big screens occupied most of the space. Manned by at least a dozen staff, the room was a high-tech command center. A short man with a thick black mustache looked up from his desk, peering over a pair of brown-rimmed glasses. He shot to his feet, trotting toward the driver and Randall.

The driver offered the man a salute and the man nodded in return.

"Where are the rest of your men?" the mustached man asked.

"We were ambushed, Captain Moretti. Only Dr. Randall

and I escaped," the driver said, motioning to Randall.

Moretti raised a brow in Randall's direction, clearly sizing him up. He turned back to the driver. "And the artifact?"

The driver shook his head, then looked at Randall.

"It wasn't there. I was able to open the monument where it was supposedly hidden, but the stone was gone," Randall replied.

Moretti sighed and shook his head. "All of those men died for no reason."

Randall shifted on his feet. "I'm truly sorry for the loss of Captain Tassone and his men. He gave his life to protect us, and his men fought bravely, but the job isn't done. My daughter and friend were captured by the Nazis, and we need to rescue them. I can't do it on my own."

Moretti studied Randall closely, running his fingers over his mustache. He narrowed his eyes.

"We're also your best chance of finding the stone," Randall said. "My colleague, Dr. Brady, is an expert on the subject, and his team disappeared searching for the Devil's Heart in South America. I'm pretty sure the Nazis kidnapped them too, so there are many people relying on us to find them."

"Dr. Randall, you have an impressive academic record, and an interesting extracurricular background as well," Moretti stated, revealing that he had conducted research on Randall.

Randall shook his head. "I didn't realize I was on someone else's radar."

"Despite this, I cannot allow you to become involved any further."

"My daughter is being held by mercenaries; I have to do something."

"While I appreciate your situation, the seriousness of this matter stretches far beyond your daughter."

"Captain Tassone trusted us. In fact, we could have walked away from this whole thing, but we chose to help. Now my daughter may pay with her life. That doesn't seem like a fair reward."

Moretti scratched his chin with an extended index finger.

"Doesn't our faith call upon us to assist others in need? The situation with my daughter, Dr. Brady and his team certainly seems to fit the bill. Besides, you need my help. I've been inside of the Nazi compound and met them."

Moretti softened. "Perhaps we can use your use assistance. You can share your knowledge of the base and monitor the situation from our operations center."

Randall shook his head. "I need to be in the field. If you have a file on me, you know I'm not going to just sit around and watch."

Moretti stared straight ahead, clearly weighing the situation and whether to directly involve Randall in the field. If he didn't, Randall would need to take another tact. Sitting in a control center while Sam was in danger was unacceptable.

"Very well, you can join my men, but understand that we cannot guarantee your safety. If you become a distraction, I won't hesitate to remove you."

"Fair enough. What do we do next?"

"We were focused on finding the stone at the cathedral, we'll need to put people in the field to find a new lead."

"That could take weeks or months."

Moretti gave a curt nod.

"People will die if we wait and the Nazis could find the stone. I think I know where we need to go next," Randall said.

"Where?"

"Back Isla de los Estados."

Moretti again raised a brow. "   The Nazis will be on high alert. I need more of a reason than your daughter and friend to risk my men."

"There was an older gentleman there. A priest. Captain Tassone and his men were looking for him."

"You saw Father Bianchi? Captain Tassone reported that

they were unable to find him."

Randall nodded. "When the Nazis marched us into a cell, I noticed him in a separate area. He wasn't moving."

Moretti sighed. "They may have killed him."

"Possibly. But he may still be alive. The compound is fairly large, and they may have just moved him to a different part."

"If Father Bianchi is still alive, he's our best hope of finding the stone," Moretti said.

"So we agree we're going back," Randall said, hoping to convince Moretti.

"We'll leave shortly."

Chapter 22

Isla de los Estados
July 25, 6:28 a.m.

After leaving the cathedral, the Nazis transported Sam and Grady on multiple flights, consisting of over a day's worth of travel. Fearful of what awaited them and not wanting to let their guard down, Sam and Grady rotated sleeping, each person dozing for a couple of hours while the other kept watch. The last leg of their journey brought them back to the same Nazi base they had been rescued from earlier. This cell block, however, was different from their earlier enclosure, prompting Sam to wonder about the size of the facility. She paced the floor of the cell trying to think of a way for them to escape, while Grady sat on the bunk, staring at the ground.

The only items in the cell were two metal bunks bolted to the floor, a threadbare mattress on each, and a bucket in the corner. The outside of the lockup was an empty, six-foot-deep room that led to a heavy metal door, which was locked. Making matters worse, their captors watched their every move courtesy of a video camera mounted in the corner.

111

"There has to be a way out," Sam said, checking the lock on the cell door again.

"Even if we got outside the cell, there's no way we're getting through that thing," Grady pointed to the thick metal door that lead out of the room. "Besides, they'll see us trying to escape and send armed guards to stop us."

"We can't just sit here."

"We don't have a choice."

The words had no sooner left Grady's mouth when the tumbler on the door lock clicked. Sam looked in the direction of the sound. Two guards entered, followed by Herrmann, who was wearing a dress uniform, resplendent with medals and ribbons. He walked up to the cell door, stopping two feet short of the bars.

"Enjoying your stay?" Herrmann said, clicking his heels together as he grinned.

Sam wanted nothing more than to punch him in the mouth, removing that goddamn smile. She could feel the muscles in her neck tighten as rage filled her. She tried to relax, realizing that she had to maintain her composure if they hoped to survive.

"I've been in nicer places ... but I've been in worse as well," she replied, managing her own fake smile.

Herrmann frowned. "You're brave now, fräulein, but I wonder if you would be so courageous under more dangerous circumstances." He nodded for the guards to open the door. One soldier marched to the cell, key in hand, to open the lock, while the other pointed his gun directly at Sam.

"Back away from the door!" the solider with the key snarled. Sam complied, moving deeper into the cell.

Grady looked at her, then pushed off the cot, coming to his feet.

Sam signaled for him to remain seated. This was no time for heroics.

When the door was open, the guard lifted his gun and pointed it at Grady's chest. He walked into the cell and Herrmann followed closely behind.

"Professor Randall?" Herrmann motioned for Sam to exit the cell.

She looked over at Grady, then to Herrmann. As she exited, her attention turned to the guard outside. He was now pointing his weapon directly at her head.

"Halt!" the guard ordered. "Hands up!"

Sam complied as Herrmann brushed past her. The guard covering Grady slowly backed out of the cell, locking the door again.

"Where are you taking her?" Grady asked, walking up to the bars.

"Don't worry, Herr Brady, we'll take good care of your friend," Herrmann said in a lilting tone.

Sam marched down the hallway, led by Herrmann and a third guard who had been waiting outside the main door. Flanked on both sides by Nazis, Sam knew that escape was impossible. The group passed several doors, stopping by one with a small glass window set two-thirds of the distance from the floor. Sam was too far away to see what was inside the room, but as the lead guard opened the door, a wretched odor spilled out.

"After you, fräulein," Herrmann extended his arm toward the open door and Sam felt a push from behind. Having no other options, she entered the room.

She was immediately overwhelmed with the stench of animal feces and sweat. Examining the room, she noted that the area was broken into two sections separated by a steel gate with metal bars spanning from floor to ceiling. On one side of the gate was an enormous jungle cat, pacing the floor. On the other, Sam saw an elderly man seated on a stool in the center of the concrete floor, his clothes rumpled, his eyes red and his thinning gray hair a mess. She gasped at the site. The elderly man slowly turned to face her. He rose to his feet, flattening the wrinkles from his pants and shirt.

"You pigs! What have you done to him!" Sam ran to the man, bracing him around his shoulders to steady him. "Are you okay?"

The elderly man nodded and smiled weakly.

Sam turned to face Herrmann. "I don't know how, but I'm going to make you pay for the things you've done." She turned back to face the elderly man. "What's your name?"

"I'm Konrad Vogel, and you are?"

"Samantha Randall. Don't worry, Mr. Vogel, I'll find a way to get you out of here."

Vogel's eyes lit up and he grasped Sam's arm. "You wouldn't happen to be related to Nick Randall?"

"As a matter of fact, I'm his daughter. How do you know him?"

"Enough of this," Herrmann said, pushing past his guard and stepping next to Sam. "Take him out of here," he said, waving his hand at the guard to take Vogel from the room.

"Until we meet again," Vogel released Sam's arm, and followed his escorts out of the room.

Sam turned to face Herrmann. She brushed a strand of hair away from her face as she locked eyes with the Nazi. Herrmann simply smiled, taking a seat on the stool vacated by Vogel while his two remaining guards trained their weapons on Sam.

"Are you familiar with the large feline specimens in South America?" Herrmann asked.

Sam shook her head no. Herrmann had just confirmed she was back on the South American island compound.

"This beautiful creature is known as a *Panthera onca*, more commonly referred to as a jaguar. It's the third-largest feline in the world, after the tiger and the lion, and it's the largest in the Americas. This fearsome creature is largely a solitary, stalk-and-ambush predator at the top of the food chain. Are you familiar with how it kills its prey?"

"No," Sam replied curtly, bracing herself for what was likely to come.

"The jaguar has an exceptionally powerful bite, even relative to the other big cats. This allows it to pierce the shells of armored reptiles, employing an unusual killing method." Herrmann pointed to his head. "It bites directly through the skull of its prey between the ears to deliver a fatal bite to the brain. A truly horrible way to die."

Sam looked over at the large cat, loping around its small cell, its eyes locked on them.

"The specimen you see normally consumes five pounds of meat each day, but alas, this poor thing hasn't eaten for several days," Herrmann said, contorting his face into a fake frown. "While these animals frequently attack much larger species, they don't typically feed on humans unless provoked ... or starving."

Herrmann nodded to one of his guards, who retrieved a long pole with a serrated tip from its cradle on the wall. Placing the device through the bars, the guard proceeded to poke and prod the big cat, which hissed, revealing massive incisors. The jaguar roared at the pole, swatting it with huge paws.

"The barrier you see is a cleverly designed gate, held in place by a lock and a counterbalance attached to a pulley system," Herrmann pointed to several cables attached to the ceiling of the jaguar's cage. "When the lock is released, only the weight of the counterbalance holds the gate in place, but there's a special feature to this counterbalance. A plug holds the sand weighing it down. Once the plug is removed, the sand slowly trickles out, making the counterbalance lighter and lighter until..." Herrmann slammed his boot to the ground, creating a loud snapping sound. "The gate springs open, allowing the creature to enter this side," he pointed to the ground near Sam. He drew back his outstretched arm, tenting his hands and grinning broadly. "Where is the Devil's Heart Professor?"

"I don't know."

Herrmann nodded to the guard, who pulled a lever on the

wall. A rushing noise rose from the jaguar's side of the cage. Glancing over, Sam saw the source of the sound. The plug from the counterbalance, suspended several feet above the floor, had been removed and sand now flowed out freely, slowly piling on the ground.

"I'm waiting, fräulein…" Herrmann tilted his head as he stared at Sam.

"I have no idea where the stone is. We thought it would be in the cathedral, but it was gone."

Herrmann closed his eyes and shook his head. "Professor, Professor, Professor. Do you take me for a fool?"

Sam shrugged. "I don't know what you want me to do. I have no idea where the stone is."

"I will give you one last chance. Tell me what you know about the location of the stone. Surely you and your colleagues have some theories?"

"We don't. We had just gotten to the church when your team arrived," Sam said.

Herrmann kicked the stool, which fell over and skidded across the room. Sam flinched at the sound of the metal chair slamming against the wall.

"You're a foolish woman and your silence will cost you dearly. I wonder if you'll be so brave when there's nothing between you and this exquisite creature?" Herrmann asked. "We'll find out in the next two hours. If you come to your senses and decide to save yourself, we'll be watching. Auf wiedersehen, fräulein." Herrmann straightened his jacket and walked to the door.

"Kommen!" he barked at the guard, who slowly backed out of the room, gun still pointing at Sam. He took the serrated pole with him.

The gate between Sam and the prowling cat creaked upward. The jaguar moved closer to the gate, swiping a huge paw at the bottom bar. It growled softly as it probed the opening, waiting for an opportunity to join Sam.

Chapter 23

Off the coast of Isla de los Estados
July 25, 6:39 a.m.

Randall peered through the binoculars that Moretti had provided. Given the nature of the mission, the Knights had expedited the strike team's travel to South America to search for Father Bianchi. They were about to land their Zodiac boats on the Northern side of the craggy shoreline of Isla de los Estados for this mission. Moretti had explained to Randall that the first assault on the Nazi stronghold, led by Captain Tassone, had been an overt show of force. The Knights had launched an amphibious assault from the Southwest side of the island, sailing from the Southernmost tip of Argentina, and concentrating their firepower in one spot, thereby overwhelming the Nazi defenses. In contrast, Moretti had decided the second incursion called for a stealth attack.

Though the Germans would undoubtedly be on high alert, the Knights were banking on them not expecting another assault so quickly. As such, Moretti had told Randall that their team was landing on a small section of beach away from the main fortifications. The beach offered a high cliff, obscuring the ocean

117

from direct view of the Nazi compound. The team would have to traverse a steep incline, thereby exposing them to attack from above, but it was a chance they would have to take.

Randall tapped his leg impatiently, worrying that with each tick of the clock Sam's life might be in greater danger. Worse, he had no idea if she and Grady had been brought back to the facility. If not, their best chance was to find Father Bianchi and hope that he might know where they were being held. The wait was excruciating. As a father, he would have preferred the quickest route to the Nazi stronghold, but he had been voted down. In fact, the other Knights had questioned even allowing him to join the assault, despite Moretti's agreement to allow it. But Randall had convinced them that, since he was the only member of the team who had been on the inside of the complex, his knowledge of the layout would be an asset to the mission. He hoped now that he hadn't overplayed his hand.

As self-doubt crept into his mind, Randall simply had to remind himself that his only daughter was in danger. That was reason enough to go. For the second time in his life, he worried that his decision to take on a dangerous assignment had put Sam in jeopardy. The first time had been in Peru, trying to find a lost city. Fortunately, things had worked out then, and he could only hope that their luck would hold.

Someone tapped his shoulder. He turned to face Moretti, who signaled that the first boat had made landfall and they were next.

The driver of the boat, a baby-faced Corporal named Antonio Esposito, cut the engine as they drew within yards of the shore. Pivoting the boat motor out of the ocean on its hinge, he hopped into the waist-deep water. Esposito hit the sand running, pulling the Zodiac out of the surf with the assistance of his other team members, Sergeant Greco and Lieutenant Bruno. The group worked like a well-oiled machine, duly impressing Randall with their synchronicity.

The Knights dragged the inflatable craft onto the sand,

pulling it alongside the shoreline bushes that dotted the beach. Cutting branches from the plants, they camouflaged their craft from prying eyes.

Their Zodiacs hidden, the teams worked their way along a ravine, which snaked its way up the hillside toward the main structure on the island. In near silence, the Knights worked in units, the first group moving forward while the second provided cover fire in case they were discovered. Utilizing this back and forth strategy, the team made its way to the top of the first ridge. Following closely behind the leaders, Randall jogged in a crouched position, finally arriving by Moretti's side.

In the distance, they spotted a low-lying structure. Taking a pair of binoculars from Esposito, Randall examined it. Through the lens, he could see the detail of the masonry wall, stretching from the side of the hill to the outer edge of the ridge. The wall wrapped around the structure at a ninety-degree angle, almost directly away from them, forming the outer part of the Nazi compound.

Randall dropped the binoculars, and looked toward Moretti, who was also studying the facility. After several minutes, he too lowered his binoculars, motioning for Randall to come closer.

"There's a ravine twenty yards to our left that terminates at the section of wall near the hillside. It should offer us cover from any sentries or surveillance cameras. We'll follow it until we come to the wall and find a place to breach the compound," Moretti said, motioning for Lieutenant Bruno to lead his men in the direction of the ravine.

After twenty minutes, the team arrived near the end of the gulley. Moretti, Bruno, and Randall conferred about their next steps.

"Take three men and circle around to the top of the ridge. I want intel about guards and the layout of the courtyard," Moretti told his lieutenant, who separated from the group to carry out his orders.

"What do we do in the meantime?" Randall asked.

"We wait," Moretti replied.

Randall sipped water from a canteen, drumming his fingers on the outside of the container. After what seemed an eternity, a call came over the radio.

"We're in position. There are two guards inside the wall of the compound directly in front of your location. They're following the inner perimeter of the wall, moving at a right angle away from you, toward the corner near the cliff," Bruno reported.

"What about security cameras?" Moretti asked.

"There's a single camera on the exterior of the building, facing your direction."

"Watch the guards on the ground and let me know when they're out of range, and prepare to disable the camera," Moretti released the radio button.

"Roger that. Setting up laser and scope."

"Disable on my mark," Moretti turned to Greco. "Get ready." The soldier motioned for four of his men to move into position. Two stood at the base of the wall, while two stood several feet back in a crouched position.

"The guards turned the corner, you're clear," Bruno reported.

"Disable the camera."

A moment passed. "Affirmative. Camera disabled."

"Over the wall," Moretti ordered his team, he then turned to Randall. "Watch them to see how they do this."

The two soldiers at the base of the barrier, pressed their backs to the wall, then crouched, cupping their hands, creating a foothold for a third soldier to shimmy up and grab the lip of the wall. The climbing soldier then pulled himself to the top and offered an outstretched arm to a fourth man who was now being pushed up by the soldiers at the base of the wall.

As Randall eagerly studied the technique, two men slipped over the wall, taking positions on the inside, watching for the Nazi guards who might return at any time. Two at a time, additional

120

team members followed them over until the entire team, including Randall, had entered the compound. The last man over, Sergeant Bruno, sprinted to the others at a nearby doorway.

Moretti motioned for Esposito to join him. Esposito hurried to his side and produced a long, snakelike device attached to a handheld monitor, known as a borescope. Feeding the tube under a gap in the door, he peered at the monitor, examining what lay inside the building. He rotated the device for a full look inside. "All clear. No guards or cameras in this area."

A second soldier joined him, carrying a small gun-like device and placed its wire-like tip into the door lock. After a few seconds, he twisted the knob and opened the door.

Esposito and Greco sprinted into the building guns raised as Randall and Moretti followed them in. They moved down the hallway and arrived at a doorway. Esposito took a position facing the door, while Greco opened it. Esposito moved in, followed by the others. A single Nazi looked up from a desk. He reached for a gun, but Esposito knocked it away. Facing multiple armed soldiers, the Nazi lifted his arms in surrender.

"You're holding a priest and two others hostage here. Where are they?" Moretti asked.

"Ich spreche kein Englisch," the guard replied.

Moretti pointed a finger at the Nazi's nose. "Don't pull that with me. Wo sind die Gefangenen? Where are the prisoners?"

The guard blinked. "I don't know what you're talking about. I haven't seen any prisoners."

Moretti backhanded the man. He removed a pistol from his holster, placing the gun to the man's temple. "Where?"

The man sat motionless, only his eyes moved, blinking several times.

Moretti cocked the gun. "Last chance."

"They're being held nearby, but the woman may not be alive."

Randall pushed past Moretti. Gripping the Nazi by his collar, he pulled the man within inches of his face. "What do you mean? Talk now or so help me I'll kill you!"

"Colonel Herrmann has her in the interrogation area," the Nazi said.

"Where?" Randall shook the man violently.

The Nazi pointed out the window to another section of the building, which veered to the right of their current location. It appeared to be a single room, jutting out from the main part of the structure.

"Take us! Now!" Randall slammed the man back into his chair, still gripping the front of his shirt.

Moretti holstered his weapon, placing his hand on Randall's arm. "We'll find your daughter," he said, "but we need to be careful. If we run out there and get killed, we'll be of no help to her."

Randall released his grip on the Nazi and backed away. As he did, Moretti grabbed the man's face, turning his head until their eyes meet.

"How many guards between us and the girl?"

"Two guards stationed outside the door."

"Any additional security?"

"No."

"Moretti squeezed the man's face, his fingernails digging into his cheeks, drawing blood.

"There's a security camera in the hallway!"

Moretti released the Nazi's face. "Undress."

The Nazi's eyes went wide. He turned to look at Randall.

"You heard the man," Randall said.

The Nazi complied, removing his shirt and pants. Moretti motioned to one of his soldiers. "Private Conti, bring the serum."

Conti brought a small zippered pouch, the size of a man's toiletry bag, to his captain. Moretti motioned to the Nazi and pointed to the chair. "Sit."

The Nazi looked at Moretti, then dropped into the seat.

122

Greco dressed himself in the Nazi uniform while Conti opened the bag. He removed a vial and needle. Seeing it, the Nazi tried to stand, but Moretti and Randall pinned him to the chair. Randall held his arm while Conti inserted the needle. In less than a minute, the Nazi was out.

"He'll be unconscious for several hours."

Randall's body shook from the adrenaline coursing through his system. "We need to find Sam."

The team made its way toward the interrogation room, stopping at the first corner. Greco used the borescope to peer around the turn. At the top of the wall, half-way down the corridor, Greco spotted the dome-shaped security camera. He turned and nodded for Conti who joined him, dropped his gear bag, and retrieved a gun scope, with a cylinder mounted beneath it.

Randall turned to Moretti who must have read his expression of confusion.

"A laser attached to a rifle scope to disable the camera. The laser damages the camera sensor, blinding it," Moretti explained.

Conti, prone on the ground, slowly peered around the corner, laser in hand. A few seconds passed. "It's disabled, go."

Greco led the way, the rest of the team following him. They stopped short of the end of the hallway, the interrogation room just around the corner. Greco screwed a silencer onto his pistol, then slid the silenced weapon under his coat and into the small of his back. If the Nazi had been honest, two additional guards were waiting outside the door. Greco nodded to Moretti, then turned the corner while the rest of the group waited. Two muffled blasts were followed by a whistle, alerting them that the coast was clear.

Randall broke for the hallway, but Moretti held him back, one arm across Randall's midsection, the other clutching his pistol. He tapped the side of the barrel to his pursed lips. At first, Randall didn't understand. Moretti whistled in response to Greco's signal and a double whistle came back, letting him know it wasn't a trap.

Moretti led his team to the interrogation room, stopping at the door, but Randall would have no further delays. He pushed past Moretti, opened the lock, and forced the door open, his nose registering a foul odor.

"Dad?"

Randall spotted his daughter and raced to her side. "Sam!" He hugged her as soon as he reached her. "I thought you were—"

He was cut off by a loud roar and spun around. To his horror, he saw the jaguar ... and the nearly open gate.

"We have to get out of here!" Sam yelled, tugging at Randall, who was frozen in place.

The gate had lifted nearly two feet from the floor and the jaguar had wedged its head and one shoulder into the opening. A few inches higher, and it would have enough room to squeeze under.

"Come on, Dad!" Sam dragged Randall toward the door, but before she could reach the handle, the door flew open and both Moretti and Conti entered the room, guns at the ready.

Randall frantically motioned toward the exit. "Go, go, go!"

More sand flowed from the counterweight and the gate creaked up as the jaguar roared in anticipation of the kill.

Moretti and Conti froze in surprise, mouths agape.

"Get the hell out!" Randall yelled, sprinting past Conti before nearly hitting Esposito, who had just dragged one of the dead Nazi guards into the room. Randall hit Moretti square in the chest with an outstretched arm, shoving him back toward the hallway.

They reached the door and Sam yanked it open just as Conti, who was nearest the jaguar, screamed, firing his gun wildly. The cat was through the gate.

Randall pushed Sam and Moretti into the hallway, then grabbed Esposito as well. The four tumbled through the door, landing on the floor outside the room, Randall's heel lodged between the door and frame. The door opened again as Conti struggled to escape from the huge cat. He managed to get one arm and leg through the opening before the Jaguar began dragging him back inside.

Randall scrambled to his feet, and grabbed Conti's arm, pulling with all his strength. The private grabbed Randall's shirt with his free hand, his eyes wide with terror. The two were no match for the sheer brute force of the beast. The screaming soldier was yanked back toward the cell, pulling Randall with him.

Chapter 24

Randall was nearly through the door when he felt a tug on his collar. He turned to see Sam and Moretti trying to pull him back into the hallway. His forward motion into the room slowed, but he continued to inch forward, caught in a tug of war between man and beast.

Conti cried in agony as he was eaten alive, still gripping Randall's shirt. A piece tore off and Randall tumbled backward into the hallway onto Sam and Moretti and the door slammed shut. The three lay on the ground panting and sweating and Randall checked his body. Aside from a torn shirt, everything was still there. The shrieking from inside the cell ended abruptly as Conti met a gruesome fate.

Closing his eyes, Randall lay on the floor of the hallway, a split lip filling his mouth with the coppery taste of blood. He remained motionless, momentarily unable to move as he gasped for breath.

Sam stood over him, her face ashen. "Are you alright?" She was shaking uncontrollably.

Randall nodded, still unable to speak. Moretti grabbed him under his arms and lifted him to his feet.

"That poor man," Sam covered her mouth, closed her eyes, and shook her head.

Randall searched the face of his daughter, who was clearly shaken by the narrow escape and Conti's death. There was nothing he could say to soothe her as he struggled to grasp the situation as well. He glanced at Moretti, who said a silent prayer and made the sign of the cross for his fallen comrade.

"We must move," Moretti said, taking a pistol from Esposito.

Randall turned to Sam and hugged her again. "I thought I'd lost you."

Sam managed a weak smile. "I'm fine, Dad, but I'm sorry that man lost his life trying save me."

Randall nodded. "So am I." He looked at the door, then back to Sam. "I know this is difficult, but we still need to find Grady. Do you know where he is?"

"We were being held in the same cell before the Nazis brought me here. I can show you where." Sam said. "They're holding another prisoner, too. His name is Mr. Vogel."

Randall furrowed his brow. "Dr. Vogel is here?"

Sam nodded. "He said he knew you. How?"

"He's Jim's mentor. Jim and I visited him back in Maryland. Someone ransacked his house looking for something."

"What were they looking for?"

Randall shrugged.

"Well, he's here. I'm not sure where, but I saw him a little while ago."

"Signorina, time is short. Did you see another man here? A priest?" Moretti inserted himself into the conversation.

"I'm sorry, but no."

"Then you must lead us to Professor Grady," Moretti said.

"He's this way," Sam replied, turning away from her former holding cell. She led the group down the hallway, explaining the layout of the area surrounding the cell and where the guards were posted. Moretti once again assigned Sergeant Greco to infiltrate and subdue the guards.

Sam pointed with an outstretched finger. "The cell is around this corner, second door on the left."

Moretti nodded to Greco, who left the group and rounded the corner. After a few moments, they heard the unmistakable sound of the silenced gun firing twice. Moretti whistled, and his sergeant responded, letting him know it was safe. Gun drawn, Moretti turned the corner first with Sam and Randall following closely behind. Greco stood over two dead Nazi guards; his weapon raised as he watched the door to the cell. Moretti searched the dead guards and, finding a gun, handed it to Randall who tucked it into the small of his back as Greco had done earlier.

Moretti continued his search, finding the cell keys. He gave the keys to Greco and backed away from the door. Providing cover for his sergeant, Moretti nodded for his man to enter the cell. The soldier burst through the door with Moretti trailing him. From the hallway, Randall heard additional muffled bursts from the silenced gun. A moment later, Moretti popped out the door, waving Randall and Sam into the room.

Upon entering, Randall saw Grady pressed against the bars of the cell, eager to get out. Standing next to him was Dr. Vogel who, though disheveled, appeared to be in good health. Sprawled on the floor was an additional German guard, his face contorted in a look of surprise.

"Sam, I'm glad to see you're okay!" Grady said, as Greco opened the lock.

Grady stepped out of the cell and turned to Randall. "Thank you for coming for us! I didn't think we'd ever get out."

"Dr. Vogel, I'm surprised to see you here," Randall said.

Grady stirred, clearly pumped from the excitement. "These bastards caught Dr. Vogel and brought him to my cell after they took Sam."

A tugging sensation at Randall's elbow drew his attention. It was Moretti.

"We need to move quickly, my friends. They know for

certain we're here now. This way." Moretti led the group out of the door and back into the hallway where Esposito stood watch. Greco and Esposito alternated lead and cover positions, offering protection as the group moved back in the direction they had originally come.

"We're almost there," Moretti said as they approached the last hallway. The team made it halfway down the corridor when the exit door burst inward and four armed Nazis stormed in. Firing a quick volley, they killed Greco, then paused momentarily, as if confused.

"Take cover!" Moretti yelled, dropping to a crouch and opening fire on the approaching Germans. He dropped one with his first shot.

Randall dove for the floor, striking his head against the wall as he fell. "Dammit!" He held his head, writhing in pain as bullets whizzed by. As he rolled on the floor, he noticed the door they had just passed.

"Sam, go for the door!" Randall yelled.

Sam grabbed Vogel, who stood defiantly staring down the Nazis, and pulled him into the room with her.

Randall scrambled to a crouch behind Moretti, who dropped another German soldier. Randall glanced to the other side of the hall. Esposito lay sprawled on the ground, his eyes staring vacantly into space. Gunfire ripped at the wall directly above Randall's head. Plaster chips rained down and the smell of gunpowder and dust choked the air.

"There's a room right behind us!" he yelled into Moretti's ear.

"You go!" Moretti replied, firing his last round.

Randall ran in a crouch for the door just as the remaining Nazis unleashed a torrent of automatic gunfire. He threw the door open, looking back at Moretti who barely avoided the hail of metal slugs, diving for his fallen comrade's weapon. Having seen

Randall open the door, the Nazis now fired at him and Randall burst into the room as bullets crashed against the door.

He tumbled to the ground, rolled, and popped up on his feet. His eyes darted around the room. Seeing everyone huddled to one side, he joined them only to discover another older gentleman in the room. The elderly man's physical condition was poor, his eyes sunken into his head and his face littered with bruises and cuts.

"What's going on in here?" Randall asked.

"This is Father Bianchi. The Nazis took him hostage because they think he knows where to find the Devil's Heart," Sam answered, kneeling by his side.

The group ducked almost in unison as gunshots rang out from the hallway.

Randall turned to Bianchi. "Are you okay?"

"Si, Signore, but I won't be for long, unless you can remove these," Bianchi said, lifting his arm, which was handcuffed to a metal rail on the wall.

Randall studied the area until he found what he needed. A wall of wooden cabinets behind Bianchi would easily absorb a bullet.

"Stand back," Randall motioned for everyone to move away from the priest. "Extend your hand as far as you can then turn your head, Father." Randall removed the gun from the small of his back and, taking careful aim at the handcuffs, fired. The bullet split the chain between the cuffs then lodged in the cabinets as planned.

Bianchi grinned. "Thank you, it worked!"

"This is all great, but what about the Germans outside?" Grady said.

"You're right. Find a place to hide and something you can use as a weapon," Randall said.

The shooting outside the door stopped. Randall crouched near the wall facing the door, while the others scrambled for cover. If the Nazis came through, it was up to him to defend the group.

Randall's heart pounded as he pressed against the wall. He

130

focused on the situation at hand, relying on his experience from his Reserve Officers' Training Corps to steady his nerves. He raised his gun, his breathing slow and steady. There were no sounds coming from the hallway.

They waited.

Minutes ticked by. Nothing happened.

Randall remained in position, ready to engage if needed.

A soft shuffling sound arose from the hallway outside. Slowly, the door opened inward, creaking on its hinges.

Randall closed one eye, taking aim.

The door inched open. The dark barrel of a gun poked through, paused, then disappeared back out.

A moment later, the door burst open and a man entered the room, rolling on the floor, then popping up into a low squat. He took aim at Randall, who adjusted his sights onto his target and slowly depressed the trigger.

"Professor?"

"Moretti, thank God it's you". Randall heard a loud sigh of relief as the Knight lowered his weapon.

"Thank God indeed and I'm glad you're okay," Moretti smiled as he holstered his gun.

"Moretti?" Bianchi said from the corner.

Moretti spun to face him. "Father Bianchi! You're alive!"

Moretti strode over to Bianchi and the two men embraced. Moretti examined the priest. "We thought you were dead."

"You two know each other?" Sam asked.

"Si. Padre and I have worked together for years," Moretti said.

"Of course, you're both Knights," Grady said.

Randall motioned toward the door. "I'm glad for the happy reunion, but we still need to get out of here."

Moretti nodded. "Follow me."

Moretti checked the hallway and, not seeing any additional

Nazis, signaled for the others to follow. They made their way to the exterior door and Moretti looked through the small window. He slowly opened the door, pointing his gun to the right. Moving outside, he turned to check the other direction. Still no signs of the enemy.

"This way," Moretti said. "My men are over here."

The group snaked their way through the courtyard toward Moretti's soldiers. As they approached, one of the guards motioned for the group to stay back. The group quickly backtracked around the corner of the nearest building, Randall taking the rear to make sure everyone else was safely hidden.

Randall peered around the corner, his head pressed to the wall, minimizing his exposed profile. At first, he only saw one of Moretti's men prone on the ground, his weapon trained in front of him. Then he spotted two Nazi guards, one on his radio, the other clutching an assault rifle. Based on their body language, the two were on alert, searching for them. Randall flinched when a hand touched his arm. Spinning, he saw Moretti, who motioned for him to settle. The two peered around the corner just in time to see the Nazis sprint in the direction of the building where Grady, Vogel, and Bianchi had been held prisoner.

The area clear, the group rounded the corner, arriving by Moretti's guard, who was now on his feet. "Captain, the Nazi patrols have increased."

"How frequently do they pass by?"

"Every fifteen minutes, but our lookouts report additional activity in the compound. More Nazis are on the way. We don't have much time."

As they spoke, Moretti's second guard joined the group. The men hustled into position, settling near the wall as they had done earlier. The first soldier climbed to the top.

"You next," the soldier said to Sam, who shimmied up and over the wall. Randall watched Sam disappear to relative safety.

Grady went next, followed by Vogel, who was assisted by one of Moretti's men.

Randall turned to Bianchi. "You're up."

The old priest nodded. He took a running start, planted a foot in the hands of the soldiers at the base of the wall and stretched up, demonstrating surprising spryness as the soldier on top hauled him over.

Randall prepared to go next, but Moretti grabbed his shoulder. He gave a quick slashing motion over his throat and before Randall could even respond, one of the soldiers led him around a corner and dragged him to cover. Moretti and his other men took defensive positions around him.

"Don't make a sound," Moretti whispered.

Randall cast a glance in the direction of the wall. Several Nazi soldiers approached the spot where Bianchi had climbed only minutes earlier. They looked up and down the wall, one of them kneeling in the spot where the soldiers had helped the others over. The kneeling soldier rose to his feet, scanned the inside of the compound, and gripped his weapon tightly. A second Nazi looked down the wall away from Randall and the others, then flipped his gun and looked in their directions.

Randall withdrew, unsure if they had been seen.

The four men squatted motionless against the wall, trapped, the Nazis only ten yards from them. After what felt like an eternity, Randall chanced a glance around the corner. The Nazis were slowly marching along the perimeter of the facility, away from Randall and the Knights. Their guns raised; they carefully scanned the surrounding area as they made their way along the wall. After several excruciating minutes, the Nazis disappeared around a bend.

Randall received a hard tap on the back, followed by Moretti's men coming to their feet. In quick, fluid motions, Moretti's men were in position near the wall again. One of them shimmied to the top, demonstrating incredible athleticism.

Moretti motioned for Randall to go next. He sprinted, hopped up and hoisted himself up the wall. He was nearly at the top when he heard shouting. He turned to look in the direction of the commotion and immediately regretted looking. The two Nazis were back. Their earlier action of leaving had likely been a ruse to flush the Knights out and their plan had worked. A hundred yards to his right, one Nazi yelled into his radio while the other took careful aim. The cracking sound of bullets filled the air, followed instantly by shards of concrete ripping free of the wall.

"Get over, now!" Moretti shouted.

Snapping out of his trance, Randall reached for the outstretched hand of the soldier at the top of the wall and shimmied the rest of the way up. He scrambled over the top and dropped to the ground on the other side as the shooting intensified. From the inside, Moretti shouted to his team to keep going, while more German voices joined the fray.

The Knight at the top of the wall, extended his hand to help the next soldier but his head jerked back as a bullet ripped through his skull, sending his body tumbling off the wall.

"Let's move, we have to get out of here!" A Knight on the outside of the wall grabbed Randall's arm and pulled him towards the ravine.

"Your captain's still in there! We can't leave!" Randall protested.

"Captain Moretti gave explicit orders. We need to get all of you to safety!"

Bianchi placed his hand on the Knight's shoulder. "My son, we cannot leave him."

Before the Knight could protest, Randall pulled free of his grip and sprinted to the base of the wall and tried to climb up. He failed and turned to face the Knight. "Help me up!"

The Knight glared at Randall.

Bianchi ran to Randall's side and gave him a boost. He pushed him partially up the wall but struggled to get him high enough.

"Get over here and help!" Randall yelled at the Knight.

The Knight shook his head, then sprinted to the wall and

boosted Randall the rest of the way up. Randall peered over and saw Moretti engaging the enemy. He fired his final shots, tossing the spent weapon aside.

"Up here!" Randall yelled.

Moretti jerked his head in Randall's direction. He froze for a moment, his eyes narrowing as if questioning Randall's judgement for climbing back up.

"There's no time to argue!" Randall yelled, extending his arm to Moretti.

Moretti ran to the wall, jumped, planted the toe of his boot in a gap and grasped Randall's outstretched arm. Bullets ricocheted around him as he pulled himself up. He was two feet short when his left arm jerked toward the wall, a splatter of red appearing beneath it. He cursed in pain.

"Come on, just a little further!" Randall grunted as Moretti's full weight pulled him down.

Moretti struggled to pull himself up with his one good arm. Bullets whizzed by, striking the wall around him. Randall watched in horror as another grazed his leg. Moretti's face contorted in pain.

Randall reached his entire upper body over the wall. He grasped Moretti's right arm and pulled with all his strength. He lifted the captain so that his arms and shoulders cleared the top of the wall. Struggling with the added weight, he lost his balance, tumbled back off the wall and landed hard on his side, the wind knocked from him.

Moretti flopped on the top of the wall, his head and torso on the outside, his legs and feet on the inside of the compound. Another Knight scaled the wall and pulled his injured captain the rest of the way over.

Sam raced to her father, who rolled on the ground in pain.

"Get up, Dad! We have to go!"

Pulling him to his feet, she threw his arm over her shoulder, carrying him down the canyon. Randall glanced back to see Moretti's soldier supporting him on one side as they followed the rest of the group out. Several Knights stayed behind, providing cover fire so the remainder of the team could escape.

The group struggled over the uneven terrain, making their way back to the ocean. As they followed the contour of the river, occasional bursts of gunfire announced that the Nazis were still in pursuit. When they finally arrived at the beach, they quickly uncovered their hidden boats.

Randall turned to Moretti as he arrived with the aid of one of his soldiers. "What about the rest of your men?"

"They're not far behind. We must hurry to ensure your safety."

Dragging several of the inflatable boats into the water, the group made their way back to the relative safety of the ocean, leaving the Nazi stronghold behind.

Chapter 25

Falkland Islands
July 26, 10:31 a.m.

A distant, craggy shoreline loomed in the distance, growing as the Knight's ship approached the now familiar outline of the Falkland Islands. Waiting on the Mare Harbor dock were several military vehicles lacking the traditional British military insignias. Dutifully standing aside them were several serious looking men, watching the Knights' ship as it docked. They tied the ship to the dock and assisted the group as they disembarked, leading them to the awaiting vehicles, which whisked them Mount Pleasant airbase.

When they arrived, Moretti's men tried to assist him, but he declined, saying his leg injury was simply a flesh wound as was his arm. Before leaving, he turned to thank Randall for pulling him up the wall. The two shook hands and Moretti headed inside. After a short wait, a private charter flight picked them up and they departed for the island of Rhodes to take Bianchi back to his church.

On the ride, the remaining members of the party broke into groups, with Grady and Vogel catching up with each other, while

Randall and Sam conversed with Bianchi. The old priest had many stories, and Randall sat quietly, listening in amusement as Sam fired a barrage of questions at the cleric. But when the subject of The Devil's Heart was broached, the tone became serious.

"What do you know about the history of the stone and its possible whereabouts? Who do you think has it now?" Sam asked.

"These are very good questions. Are you familiar with the reason the Nazis want it?" Bianchi asked.

"From what we understand, they want to use it to power a super weapon, but we don't really know any details about it. I'm still amazed that there are living, breathing Nazis with ties to the Third Reich running around South America and other parts of the world," Sam said.

"This evil group has been plotting for decades, patiently waiting to acquire the stone and put their plan into action," Bianchi replied.

"What exactly is their plan?" Sam asked.

Bianchi shifted in his seat, looking out the window of the plane, then casting a glance at Vogel and Grady, who sat several rows back. He finally brought his eyes back to rest on Sam and Randall. He sighed, his body sinking into the seat. His face looked haggard and he suddenly appeared much older. "Hitler had an affinity for the occult. He sought many things that held supernatural powers, hoping they would bring him an advantage against his adversaries. Some were religious artifacts dating back to the times of Christ."

"We saw several of them back at the Nazi base," Sam said.

Bianchi grunted. "His henchmen were very effective at collecting relics on his behalf, but it wasn't until they stumbled upon the ruins at San Ignacio that their current plans began. They advised Hitler of an artifact of great power—greater than the Christian relics he sought and possessed—entombed at the mission."

"The Devil's Heart," Sam said.

"Hitler was told that the stone held incredible power.

Enough to allow him to fuel his ever-growing arsenal of super weapons. In fact, Hitler believed that if he possessed it, it would give him the ability to destroy any weapon the Allies could build. He became obsessed with obtaining it."

"But the Nazis never acquired the stone," Sam said.

Bianchi shook his head. "Hitler dispatched Hermann Göring, his second-in-command, to lead an expeditionary force into the jungles to find it. They searched the ruins of San Ignacio, torturing many Jesuits in the process. But the stone wasn't in the mission or even in the underground tombs. By this time, the tide of the war had turned against the Reich, and Hitler had no choice but to recall Göring to focus on the relics he already possessed."

"Did your people remove the stone from the mission and bury it in the underground tomb Jim's team found?" Sam asked.

"The stone hadn't been in South America for over a hundred years. Even if Göring had found the area your friend discovered, he wouldn't have acquired The Devil's Heart. Several Knights had retrieved the stone from the mission over a century ago, bringing it where they could guard more closely."

"Where did they take it?" Sam asked.

"They took the stone back to Europe. Originally, it was in Malta, but the Knights decided it wasn't safe there either, so they moved it again."

"Do you know where it is?"

Bianchi closed his eyes and nodded.

"Are you sure it's safe?" Sam asked, her eyes growing wide.

"It's well hidden."

"Father Bianchi, you said that Hitler was told about the stone's existence. Who told him?" This time Randall asked.

Bianchi snorted a short laugh. "You wouldn't believe me if I told you."

"You'd be surprised at the strange things we've heard in the

139

past few years. Not much shocks us anymore," Sam replied.

The old priest looked daughter, then father in the eye. "During the Blitzkrieg, the Nazis seemed unstoppable. Their advanced weaponry and military superiority didn't go unnoticed. Several men paid the Fuhrer a visit at his headquarters."

"The S.S. allowed strangers to visit Hitler? That seems unlikely. He was notoriously paranoid about who met him," Randall said.

"Si, but for all his power Hitler couldn't prevent these men from visiting him."

"Who were they?" Sam asked.

"According to stories relayed by high-ranking German soldiers captured after the war..." Bianchi stopped in mid-sentence, his lips pursed tightly and his eyes staring at the ground.

"Please, Father," Sam said.

"They weren't men. After their initial meeting with Hitler, they revealed their true identity."

"Which was?" Sam persisted.

Bianchi lifted his head, his eyes meeting Sam's. "They claimed that they, and the stone, were not from this world which is why it possessed such incredible power. They convinced Hitler that they could help him win the war by providing him with the designs for a weapon far more advanced than anything the Allies possessed."

"What was in it for them?" Randall asked.

"An agreement was struck that the two groups would share governance of the new world order. On the surface, the Nazis would be the official rulers of all conquered nations, but these creatures would be granted power over various parts of the world that they sought. In addition, Hitler agreed to provide them with human subjects for experimentation."

"And if these creatures could change their appearance and look like humans...?"

"Then everyone else would assume that they were operatives of the Third Reich," Bianchi said, finishing Sam's thought.

The three sat in silence, Randall contemplating the terrifying ramifications of a Nazi victory in World War II.

"But what about the Devil's Heart? What kind of weapon do the Nazis want to use it for and why?" Randall asked.

Bianchi leaned in. "What do you know of the so-called superweapons the Nazi scientists were developing during the war?"

"Jim's more of an expert than I am, but apparently they were working on numerous Wunderwaffe," Randall answered.

"Have you heard of die Glocke?"

"I'm not sure what that is."

"You may know it from its English translation the Bell. It was the result of an experiment carried out by Third Reich scientists working for the S.S. in a German facility known as Der Riese near the Wenceslaus mine in Poland. The device was made of hardened metal, measuring approximately nine feet wide and fifteen feet high and was shaped like a large bell, hence its name. It had two counter-rotating cylinders filled with a metallic liquid and emitted radiation when active," Bianchi said.

"What was it designed to do?" Sam asked.

"It's a craft designed to travel anywhere by distorting space and time. It can move from one place to another instantaneously, drop its payload and leave," Bianchi answered.

"You mean theoretically? You said it was an experiment," Randall said.

"The device exists, probably built with the assistance of the creatures that visited Hitler. The only thing needed to make it work is The Devil's Heart. If the Nazis find the stone, they can attack anywhere in world, without being detected." Bianchi replied.

"How do you know this?" Randall asked.

"My group attained the transcripts from an interrogation of former Nazi SS officer, Jakob Sporrenberg, who confirmed that the device was under construction near the end of the war."

"That was over 70 years ago. There's no way of knowing if they ever completed it. Besides, it could have been destroyed or he could have been lying," Randall replied.

Bianchi sighed again and closed his eyes. "You raise a good point, but while I was being held captive, I heard conversations among the guards about its existence. When the Nazis questioned me, their only interest was the location of The Devil's Heart. They want the stone to activate the device."

"But what do they plan to do with it?" Sam asked.

"They could transport a chemical or biological weapon and unleash it in the middle of a crowd. They could also deliver a bomb to a heavily populated area or invade a military installation. The only thing I can say for sure is that whatever the purpose, the desired outcome is evil on a scale the world has never known."

Chapter 26

Randall and Sam sat quietly contemplating the information Bianchi had shared as Grady walked up and took a seat by the priest who fingered a metal cross hung around his neck.

"Professor Vogel was telling me about his time with the Nazis. Sounds frightening!" Grady said, studying everyone in the group. "What gives, you look live you've seen a ghost."

"Father Bianchi was telling us what he knows about the Nazi's plans, and it's not good," Sam said, not looking up.

Vogel joined the group, taking a seat opposite Randall. "My friends, I cannot thank you enough for rescuing me. Jim shared your harrowing ordeal and I must say, you're not at all like other academics I've known."

Sam smiled. "After some of my dad's recent adventures, I'd have to agree with you." Sam elbowed her father, eliciting a laugh.

"What do we do next?" Grady asked.

"I must return to my Order to ensure that the stone is still safe. Once we arrive in Malta, my associates can take you anywhere you want to go. I cannot ask you to put yourselves in further danger. As you've seen, the Nazis will do anything to possess the stone," Bianchi rubbed his reddened eyes.

143

"There's no way we're going to let you carry the load by yourself. My dad and I are here to help as long as you need us," Sam replied.

Caught off guard, Randall's expression suddenly became serious again. "Sam, I never meant for you to be a part of this. I really don't want…"

"Forget it, Dad, I'm not leaving," Sam interrupted, holding her hand up. "Where you go, I go."

"Count me in, too. I still need to find out what happened to my team. I just hope they're okay," Grady said.

"Then it's settled, we'll all help you," Vogel added his voice to the chorus.

"Such true friendship rekindles my faith in mankind. Perhaps there is still a chance for us." Bianchi's eyes sparkled as he spoke.

The remainder of the flight went by quickly and the plane touched down at Rhodes International Airport. Upon landing, the plane taxied to a hanger tucked away at the far eastern end of the facility. As they disembarked, Randall noticed men in suits holding the doors open to several cars. The group quickly entered them and sped away from the airport, hugging the coastline as they traveled to their destination.

"Father, what's the name of your church?" Sam asked, seated between Randall and Bianchi.

"The Church of Our Lady of Victory, or Sancta Maria," Bianchi smiled as he spoke.

"You've missed her, haven't you?" Randall asked.

"Si. She is not the biggest or most beautiful, but she is my home. I've been honored to serve this parish for many, many years."

"How long will it take us to get there?" Sam asked.

"No long. Twenty or thirty minutes at most."

Randall looked back at the car directly behind him. Through the front windshield, he could make out the shapes of Grady and Dr. Vogel in the backseat. He turned back to face

Bianchi. "Once we retrieve the stone, what's next?"

"My Order has kept it safe for over a thousand years. I will turn it over to my superiors and they will protect it."

"They won't tell you its new location?" Randall asked.

Bianchi folded his hands across his lap, then shook his head. "Although we are all members of the same Order, secrecy between groups is maintained to prevent the entire organization from being compromised. Once the stone is moved, only a few will know its whereabouts. This is the way the secret has been kept all this time and how it will be long after I'm gone."

"Does that bother you?" Sam asked.

Bianchi closed his eyes and sighed. "I'm an old man. I have seen much and have served my Lord well. There will be great relief in having this burden removed from me."

"Will your Order help Jim find his group and secure their release?" Sam asked.

"My people will do everything in their power to rescue his friends. As you have seen from Captain Tassone's actions, we are a dedicated group willing to sacrifice our lives for the innocent."

Bianchi was right. Randall remembered the way Tassone had paid the ultimate price to protect them, never worrying for a moment about his own wellbeing. The strategy the priest spoke of made sense. By compartmentalizing the Order, it was easier to protect important secrets. If the Nazis recaptured Bianchi after the stone was moved, there was no way the old priest could divulge its location … no matter what they did to him.

The thought made Randall shudder, but he pushed it aside. There was no sense worrying about something that wouldn't happen. The stone would soon be in a safe new place, the Knights would rescue Grady's friends, and Father Bianchi would get some well-deserved rest.

Chapter 27

Sancta Maria Church, Rhodes Greece
July 27, 6:02 a.m.

As the group drew closer to Sancta Maria, Bianchi grew
more reticent, speaking less and closing his eyes for short periods
of time. Was he saying a prayer or just tired? The first of the two
Fiats pulled alongside an open gate, which lead into the courtyard
of the church. A tall bell tower loomed over the parking lot, its
cream-colored walls and dome framed by a beautiful cobalt sky
punctuated by an occasional white cloud. A sense of serenity fell
over Randall as he stepped out of the car and breathed in the clean
air. Sam exited after him, walking over to his side as Bianchi
followed behind.

"She is beautiful, no?" Bianchi asked.

"She is," Randall answered, turning to look at Sam, who
smiled broadly back at her father.

The doors to the second Fiat opened and Grady and Vogel
rejoined their friends.

"What a lovely old church," Vogel commented. "When was
it built?"

"Sancta Maria was built in 1743 by the prefecture of the
Franciscans of Constantinople who opened it to re-establish their
mission in Rhodes. It's the main Catholic church here."

"Father, is this where the stone is hidden?" Grady asked.

The smile faded from Bianchi's face.

"I'm sorry, father, I'm just worried about my team. They've been missing for some time now and finding the stone is the only way we can help them," Grady cast his eyes downward.

Bianchi walked over to him. "It isn't you who should feel badly for asking, it is I who should feel badly for not thinking about your friends. Yes, the stone is here, and I will take you to it. Come, let's go inside."

Bianchi led the group into a small chapel inside the church. Simple wooden pews lined the sides of the short hall, which held a central walkway that led to the front of the building. A black, wrought-iron fence framed the altar over which hung a portrait of St. Joseph holding the infant Christ. A Catholic from birth, Randall was moved by the chapel's simplicity, which added to the air of mysticism.

"This way," Bianchi said, moving toward a small opening to the left of the altar. Arriving by his side, Randall looked around, wondering what came next.

"Help me move this," Bianchi said, lifting a small wooden podium with Randall's help. Setting it aside, Bianchi focused on the space where the podium had been. A small cylindrical nub of metal rose about an inch above the tile floor. Taking a closer look, Randall noticed that it had tiny holes interspersed throughout.

"Is that a microphone connector?" Sam asked.

Bianchi cocked his head to one side. "Yes and no." Taking the metal cross from a chain hanging around his neck, he twisted it in the center, removing the bottom cover to reveal a series of staggered, metal rods.

"A key," Sam said.

Bianchi placed the key into the metal cylinder, sliding the rods into the openings. When it was fully inserted, Randall heard a sharp click. Bianchi twisted the key, then stepped back as a section of tile slowly sank beneath the rest of the floor. After a few minutes, a thin staircase filled the spot where the podium had once stood.

"This way," Bianchi headed down the steps.

Randall watched the priest disappear beneath the floor, then followed him down the stairs beneath the church. It was a tight fit, barely enough room for an adult to squeeze through. Randall pressed his hand against the stony wall to guide himself through the dimly lit opening, which grew cooler as he moved down. As Bianchi exited the circular staircase, wall-mounted light fixtures blinked to life, fully illuminating the lower level.

Randall followed him into the underground structure finding himself on flat ground again, facing a short hallway with arched niches cut into the wall on both sides. The stale air that filled the chamber tickled his nose. Bianchi stood ten feet down the passage in the middle of the narrow opening. He clasped his hands behind his back as he waited. Randall pivoted, turning back towards the staircase. Sam reached the bottom of the stairs, followed by Grady and Vogel.

"Professora, could you please stand next to the second niche on your left?" Bianchi said to Sam, pointing to an alcove several feet from the staircase. Sam obliged, walking over to the niche, while her father, Grady and Vogel walked over to Bianchi. Sam peered into the arched opening, which came to a peak approximately six feet from the floor.

"Do you have a flashlight?" Bianchi asked.

Sam searched her pocket for her cell phone, pulled it out and hit the light app. "Got it."

"Very good. Please shine your light towards the peak of the arc."

Bianchi watched as Sam, who was five feet away from him, shined her light inside the alcove as instructed. When she was ready, he knelt on the ground by a round seal approximately two feet in diameter, set into the floor of the hallway. At the center of the seal was the symbol of the Knights, with St. Peter's keys emblazoned in the center of the cross. A large circle encompassed

the cross, with a second larger circle forming the edge of the seal.
Within the concentric circles were symbols unlike anything
Randall had ever seen. He and Grady stood entranced by the beauty
of the artwork while Bianchi pressed the symbols on the floor, in a
sequence dictated by some ancient source that only the old priest
understood.

Bianchi paused. "Are you ready?"

"Ready," Sam said.

Bianchi pressed one last symbol. As he did, Sam giggled.

"What's happening?" Randall asked.

Sam poked her head out and looked in father's direction.
"There was a hidden pocket in the wall that opened when Father
Bianchi pressed those buttons."

"If you would be so kind, please walk into the opening and
shine your light near the top in the back. Sam disappeared for a
moment, then reappeared holding a small, wrapped item. Sam
walked over to the group, object in hand, wrapped in cloth and tied
with string. Randall had to step aside for his daughter to pass by in
the narrow space.

"I almost didn't get it out before the panel closed again,"
Sam said giving the item to Bianchi.

"Grazie!" Bianchi took the item, cradled it in his hand, then
tugged the string. Unfurling the cloth, he revealed a beautifully
carved metal key, the type people associate with hidden treasure
chests.

"I feel like a pirate," Sam said.

"This is a treasure unlike anything the wealthiest kings have
ever seen," Bianchi strode deeper into the passageway. He stopped
by the last alcove on the right, his empty hand disappearing
beneath a small ledge near the bottom of the niche. A moment later
his other hand, the one holding the key, disappeared under the
ledge as well. A loud clicking sound was followed by the sound of
stone rubbing against stone as the wall of the alcove retracted

several feet.

"Per favore, can you bring your light?"

The group walked over to Bianchi, Sam illuminating the way. As they approached, Randall noted a small ledge protruding from the recess with an opening on top.

Sam shined her light into the hole as Bianchi reached in, plucking out a smooth object with rounded edges. He brought it into the beam of light.

"The Devil's Heart," Bianchi whispered.

He cradled the crimson-colored stone, which possessed two uneven, rounded humps on its top and light grey striations throughout. It was easy to see how it had gotten its nickname.

"It's incredible to think that it may not be from this world," Grady said, joining Sam, Randall, and Bianchi as the priest gave the stone to Sam.

"Thank you for retrieving it for us," a voice called out from the distance.

Randall's head snapped up just in time to see several armed men file into the hallway from the staircase above. He immediately recognized the familiar suits.

"How in the hell...?"

"The stone, please," one of the armed men said, walking ahead of his team. He carried a pistol in one hand, the other outstretched to Sam.

"You can't have it," Sam clutched the stone to her chest.

The lead Nazi pointed his gun at Sam's sternum. "By the count of three. Ein. Zwei."

"No!" Bianchi stepped between the Nazi and Sam.

A single shot rang out in through catacombs, striking Bianchi in the chest. He fell to the floor, blood spilling through the fingers covering his wound.

Sam knelt next to Bianchi as he writhed on the floor.

Randall rushed over to the fallen priest, grasping his hand. "Father..."

"Do not lose hope my son. There is always another way,"

150

Bianchi closed his eyes and drew his final breath. Randall held him a moment then gently set him on the floor.

"You son of a bitch!" Randall rose to his feet, taking a step toward the lead Nazi.

"Stop!" The German's eyes went wide with anger. He raised his gun at Randall, taking careful aim.

"Das ist genug! Lower your weapon!" Vogel yelled, pointing a finger at the Nazi.

"Ja mein Herr General," The Nazi lowered his gun and put it back into his holster. He clicked his boots and saluted Vogel.

"The stone, Fräulein," Vogel said softly to Sam. She gave it to him without a sound.

He cradled it in his hands, gently stroking the stone as if it were a long-lost pet. He lifted it to his eyes and examined it closely as he slowly walked toward the Germans.

"I don't understand. Why did he call you General?" Grady asked.

"I'm sorry, Jim, but I haven't been entirely honest with you. Although you've been an excellent student, my interest in you hasn't been academic," Vogel commented, not breaking eye contact with the stone.

"What do you mean?" Grady asked.

"He's one of them," Randall said. "The tattoo on his wrist. That Nazi has it as well," Randall gestured at the soldier who shot Bianchi.

Grady stared at his mentor's wrist, then at the Nazi's. "My God. How could I have missed it?"

"It's just a tattoo. Anyone could have missed it," Randall said.

Grady shook his head. "No, it's not.

Randall turned to look at Grady, who stared directly at his mentor.

"It's the ancient rune symbol for Tyr," Grady said. "It was a loyalty badge for graduates of the Reichsführer schools and was featured on Nazi literature during the Third Reich."

"I've been waiting for this moment for years—since I was a young boy, in fact. I can still remember my father speaking of the glorious Wunderwaffe of the Third Reich and how the Fatherland would crush all who opposed it. The weapons were incredible, but one stood above the rest. Die Glocke!"

"Your father was a Nazi scientist?" Randall asked.

"Nein! To call my father a scientist is an insult to his memory!" Vogel said, shooting Randall a hard glare. The veins in his neck protruded as he clenched his teeth. Slowly he relaxed his jaw, his eyes softening. "My father was a visionary who oversaw the construction of many of the Reich's most incredible facilities. He didn't get nearly the credit he deserved for his magnificent accomplishments." Vogel turned back to the stone, squeezing it in his fist.

"Who was he?" Grady asked.

Vogel snorted. "His name was Hans Kammler and his greatest desire was to acquire this stone and use it to power die Glocke, but he never had the chance. His work was interrupted by the Allied invasion, and he was forced into hiding, trying to complete his work in secret. Now I will lead my glorious Orden des Tyr and finally finish what he started.

"That can't be. Hans Kammler died near the end of the war. His driver attested to seeing his body buried," Randall said.

"His body was never found. There were reports that he had escaped to South America, and by the looks of things, I would say those reports were accurate," Grady turned to look at Vogel.

"As I said before, you were always an excellent student," Vogel said.

"Except your father wasn't a visionary. He was a cold-blooded killer and a coward. So are you and your so called Order of Tyr," Grady took several steps toward Vogel, whose eyes filled with rage.

"You would be wise to hold your tongue!" Vogel growled.

"Hans Kammler built concentration camps and weapons facilities. The blood of millions of innocent people is on his hands!" Grady moved within several feet of Vogel as the other soldiers raised their weapons at him.

"Silence! My relationship with you will only afford you so much mercy! Another word and you will die!" Spit flew from Vogel's mouth as he raged at Grady, his empty fist shaking in anger, his other clutching the Devil's Heart.

Sam walked next to Grady and placed her hand onto his shoulder. "You have to let it go for now. We'll find a way to escape," she whispered in his ear.

Vogel took several deep breaths and straightened his hair with his free hand. He steadied his voice. "I have business to attend to. Captain, escort Dr. Grady and Fräulein Randall back to the base. Dr. Grady could still serve a useful purpose and our associates will want to examine her," Vogel said to the lead Nazi soldier, who gave him a quizzical look.

"Mein General, what about Herr Randall?" The captain asked.

"We have no use for him. Put him in there and let Dr. Grady close it. He watched the priest operate it," Vogel nodded to the opening where Sam had retrieved the stone, his words little more than an afterthought.

"You can't leave my father there. He'll die!"

"That's not my concern," Vogel said curtly. He turned and walked up the staircase.

"You, into the space. Now!" the captain barked, motioning with his gun for Randall to move.

Sam looked at her father, tears welling in her eyes.

Randall squeezed Sam, feigning courage for her behalf, while his mind raced at the thought of being sealed into the alcove. "I'll be okay."

"I'll never see you again," Sam sobbed.

"We'll see each other again. I don't know how, but I promise you we will."

"Move!" The Nazi yelled.

"If you lay a finger on my daughter, I'll hunt you down and kill you," Randall set his jaw, his eyes afire.

The Nazi cocked his gun and pointed it at Sam's head.

Randall relented and walked to the opening. The alcove was three feet deep and made of solid stone. He stepped inside, then turned to look out. A second Nazi prodded Grady with the barrel of his gun, forcing him to kneel by the seal on the floor.

Grady looked at Randall forlornly, "I'm sorry."

"Close it now!" The Nazi pressed the barrel of his gun into Grady's neck. He turned his eyes from Randall and pressed the symbols on the floor. The sound of stone grinding against stone announced the closing of the alcove wall. Randall's final sight was Sam holding her cupped hand over her mouth, tears streaming down her face.

Chapter 28

Randall heard the muffled, yet unmistakable sound of boots clicking against stone growing fainter as the Nazis undoubtedly led Sam and Jim out of the lower level and up the stone staircase. Soon, they were gone, and he was alone with his thoughts.

The air was dank and musty, and it was all he could do not to curl up into a ball and await asphyxiation. Randall walked deeper into the niche his arm extended forward to keep from running into the back wall in the inky darkness. He took no more than a couple of steps before touching stone. He ran his hand against the wall, feeling the coldness of the blocks that now imprisoned him. Feeling a groove, his finger traced it until it ran into the side wall. He continued to grope through the darkness, trying to find another way out. After failing to find anything, he slumped to the floor, sitting with his back against the cold wall.

He had never imagined this would be his final fate, sealed into a stony tomb. A wave of sadness washed over him as he realized he would never see Sam or his son John again. Sadness morphed into anger at the thought of what the Nazis would do to Sam. What did Vogel mean when he said their associates would be interested in Sam?

Randall pounded his fist on the floor and cursed. He rested

his palm against the floor, his wrist and forearm running up the cool rocky surface. He shivered against the cold, which permeated his back, legs, and arms, but his wrists were coldest of all. Almost like there was a breeze blowing against them, but how was that possible? Randall scrambled for his phone, shining the light against the corner where wall met floor. The fit was tight, but he could clearly see a seam. He checked the side wall and floor and found no seam. He then crawled back to the entrance which led back into the hallway where they had been earlier. It looked the same as the back wall.

Hope flooded through Randall, there may be a way out. He shined his light on each wall, searching for a lever or some way to open the back passage—if there was one. He carefully studied each side of the small enclosure but found nothing. Disappointed, he sat back on the ground again, steadying himself by pressing his hand against the floor. He felt a stone seam with his palm and slid his hand along the floor. A circular arc was cut into the stone. Flipping his phone light back on, he scooted to the side and swept the ground with the beam. The same seal Bianchi had used to open the niche was carved into the floor beneath him.

Randall scrambled to his knees and studied the strange symbols he had seen earlier. He carefully recalled the order Bianchi had tapped earlier when Sam had retrieved the stone. He pressed the symbols in the same sequence and was rewarded with the sight of the back wall sliding open. Fresh air flooded the chamber and Randall breathed in deeply, the sensation of being freed from his tiny tomb making the air seem particularly sweet.

Not wanting to chance the wall closing again, he hurried through the opening and into a stony passageway. Scrambling forward, he noticed a dim glow ahead. The sight inspired him to sprint onward, wanting nothing more than to escape the underground tomb. Randall drew within several feet and recognized the sight—a rectangular grate set into the top of the wall with daylight streaming through.

He peered through and realized the grate was at street level and that if he could open it, he would be on the sidewalk outside of the church. Randall studied the latch, which looked ancient. He grabbed the handle and pressed with his remaining strength, but the latch didn't budge. Randall leaned on the lever, throwing his weight onto it, growling as he strained to open the grate. With a sudden jerk, the latch released, sending Randall to the ground. He smashed his knuckles on the floor then popped back up to his feet, cursing and shaking his hands, which throbbed with pain.

He propped the hatch open then climbed onto the curb and into daylight. Shielding his eyes from the blinding sun, he gained his feet and scurried ahead, turned a corner, and made his way down an alley which emptied onto a major thoroughfare.

Stores lined both sides of the street. Randall jogged to the end of the block and turned into an open-air market, threading his way through the carts and merchants. Brightly colored clothing hung from racks set up by vendors in the town market, but most booths featured fruits and vegetables neatly displayed for visitors to peruse and purchase. Randall hurried past them, sprinting through the streets, zigzagging down one road, then turning to run down another.

Randall needed help but didn't know where to turn. The Nazis had clearly eliminated the Knights stationed at the church and might still have eyes on the police as they conducted their investigation. Tiring, he slowed to walk, a strategy forming in his mind. He turned east and headed toward the coast.

Arranged in a rectangular grid pattern, the streets alternated between tall buildings and small shops. Randall finally arrived near the water, spotting the area where the fabled Colossus of Rhodes once stood on a spit of land jutting into the harbor. He stopped to assess the situation. The coordinated nature of the Nazi attack and the slow response from law enforcement might mean that the Nazis were working with local government officials. If that were the case, Randall would have to find help somewhere else.

But where?

It suddenly occurred to him that on a past trip to Crete, he and his wife Ann had seen an American naval base in nearby Souda Bay. If he tried to call the base, whoever answered the phone would likely think the call a prank and hang up on him. Worse, if the Nazis were monitoring him, it would tip them off that he had escaped. He'd have to travel there and try to speak to someone in person. Although he wasn't sure how his story would be received, he decided it was worth the risk.

The next question was how to get there. Buying a plane ticket meant using his credit card, which, again meant possibly tipping off the Nazis. The same was true of renting a car. His one advantage was that the Nazis thought he was sealed in the tomb and he couldn't afford being discovered. He had only one option. Checking his cell phone, Randall found a ferry that could take him to Crete. It would be a long trip, 10-14 hours depending on conditions, but it would be the safest way to travel without alerting the Nazis. He would pay for his ticket in cash and blend in with the tourists.

Randall took a deep breath, looking back in the direction he had come. The only thing he could think of was Sam. Was she okay? What would the Nazis do with her? He agonized over the decision to leave, but eventually decided this was his best chance to help her. He headed to the dock.

***

After nearly half a day on the ferries, Randall finally arrived at the United States Naval Base at Souda Bay. His only focus was to get help for Sam and Grady. Unfortunately, he wasn't sure how. While pacing the decks and weighing his options, he had decided to try and contact someone from his recent past who might have the authority to get someone at the base to listen to him. General James Flores was a man with deep connections as demonstrated by the many pictures he had with past presidents in his office. The problem was that Randall had no idea how his call would be received. Although he had tried to help the General retrieve another artifact, he had failed and though Randall had risked his life, the General had been clearly disappointed. Randall got his answer when his multiple messages had gone unreturned.

Now he had no choice but to try and reason with the base commander without Flores assistance. He replayed various scenarios in his mind, trying to determine the best way to state his situation. Unfortunately, there was no way to know how the military would respond when he revealed that Nazis were developing a super weapon powered by an alien rock. There was a distinct possibility that he would simply garner blank stares and be asked to leave the base, wasting nearly an entire day in the process. He'd just have to chance it. The clock was running, and he had no idea what the Germans had done with Sam and Grady and he couldn't wait for a better opportunity to present itself.

The taxi pulled up to the base's main gate. Randall paid the driver, exited the cab, and walked directly to the guard station. When he was twenty feet from the entrance, two armed military police exited the guard house. Sporting assault weapons, they strode directly at Randall, the look on their faces serious but inquisitive.

"Can we help you, sir?" one of the MP's asked, his body language informing Randall not to move any closer to the base entrance.

"I'd like to speak with your commanding officer," Randall replied.

The MPs shared a look.

"What's the purpose of your requested meeting?"

"I'm an American citizen and my daughter and friend have been taken hostage by a paramilitary group on the island of Rhodes and I need help."

The taller MP shifted on his feet, his eyes belying his confusion. "Sir, if you require assistance for your daughter and friend in a foreign country, you'd be best served to visit the

159

American consulate."

"I understand what you're saying, but I can't wait for political back channels to try and rescue them. The group that's holding them attacked and killed multiple priests at a church in Rhodes. I need immediate, armed assistance to get them back."

"I'm sorry, sir, but there's nothing we can do. You can contact the consulate or the local authorities for help."

"The people that are holding them are extremely powerful and well connected! I can't trust the local authorities. For all I know, they could be working with them."

"Sir, I'm going to have to ask you to turn around and leave the base."

"I don't think you understand, I'm not leaving until I speak with someone."

As Randall addressed the taller MP, the second spoke quietly into his shoulder mounted microphone, never breaking eye contact with Randall. A moment later, the sound of sirens rose from the distance.

"Place your hands behind your head and remain completely still," the lead MP said, gripping his weapon more tightly.

Randall raised his hands as ordered, placing them behind his head. "I understand this sounds crazy, but you have to believe me. I'm an Archaeology professor from the United States and a colleague approached me asking for help. We stumbled upon a secret plot, and my daughter and friend were taken hostage. You can confirm what I'm saying by checking the news. I'm sure the police on Rhodes have found the bodies and damage at the church by now."

"Search him for I.D.," the lead MP growled. The other complied, pulling Randall's wallet from his front pocket.

"He's telling the truth about his name. Nick Randall, from D.C."

"Please, my daughter and friend are in serious trouble. I just need to talk to your commander."

"Be quiet and turn around," the lead MP ordered.

Randall turned. "Look, if you just give me a chance to explain I'll…"

"I'm placing you under arrest," the MP said.

Randall felt the cold metal handcuffs biting into his wrist as his left arm was twisted behind his back, followed by the right. Next came the sensation of being pushed toward the guard shack as two Humvees pulled up, sirens blaring and lights flashing. Several more military police exited the vehicles, guns at the ready. Randall was pushed into the back seat, joined by an armed officer who handcuffed him to a bar on the seatback.

A few minutes later, they arrived at the base jail, where Randall was escorted down the gray hallway to a cell. His pleading fell on deaf ears and the guards locked him up and left. Randall called after them to no avail. Alone, he trudged over to the cot and dropped down, hands on his head, struggling to figure out what to do next.

Chapter 29

Souda Naval Base, Greece
July 27, 2:18 p.m.

Several hours passed. Randall had heard footsteps down the hall several times, raising his hopes of someone arriving with good news. Each time before those hopes had been dashed as no one ever came to his cell. He sighed, sitting on the edge of his cot, arms draped across his knees. Once more boot steps approached, but this time they stopped outside his cell. He looked up to see a uniformed officer looking back at him.

"Are you Dr. Randall?"

"Who are you?"

A broad smile spread across the man's face, and Randall noted for the first time that his uniform didn't match the others.

"So, you're Nick Randall. You look just like my dad described," the officer said, his eyes scanning Randall from head to toe.

"Sorry, I didn't catch your name," Randall rose to his feet and walked to the cell door.

"I didn't tell you my name," the officer grinned.

Randall had to fight back the rising anger. "Look, son, I don't have time to play games. Someone I care about is in danger and I came here looking for help. If you can help me, great. Otherwise, I'd appreciate you finding someone who can."

The officer laughed. "Sorry, Professor, it's not often I meet someone who bested my dad. He's a bright guy and his list of professional accomplishments is long. My name is Michael Flores."

Randall puzzled for a moment. Then it struck him. General Flores had spoken of a son in the Air Force, stationed in Europe. Had his messages gotten through? "You're James Flores' son?"

"I'm flattered you remembered my dad!"

"He said you were stationed at Ramstein."

"I am, but we regularly run joint command exercises with the Navy. I spend almost as much time here as I do at Ramstein. When I heard your name, I had to come and see if you were the Nick Randall my dad had talked about. Everyone at the base is worked up over your talk about a paramilitary group on Rhodes taking your daughter hostage. They're not sure if you're a deranged lunatic or if something strange is going on over there. They were getting ready to send you in for a psych evaluation when I told them I'd like to meet with you first."

"I can't say I blame them for thinking I'm nuts, but I sure am glad you're here," Randall said, rubbing the back of his head. "Do you think you can get me out of this cell and arrange a meeting with the base commander?"

"Give me a little time and I'll see what I can do."

"Thanks, Michael. By the way, not that I don't appreciate your help, but I'm worried about my daughter. Do you think you can make this happen quickly?"

Michael laughed out loud and shook his head. "Boy, my dad was right about you! Yes sir, I'll get right on it."

Michael turned to go, leaving Randall with a glimmer of hope.

Chapter 30

Nazi Base, Germany
July 27, 1:21 p.m.

Sam paced the floor of her cell, walking past Grady, who sat on his cot, staring into space. Although she wasn't sure where the Nazis had taken them, she considered the possibilities. They had been in the air for about three hours, after which, they had been transferred to a car for the remainder of the trip. Although blindfolded most of the time, her captors had removed the cover shortly after they were transferred from the plane to the car. They had then traveled along a lonely stretch of highway, through a heavily wooded area.

She recalled her memory of European and African geography and mentally drew a circle, with its center on Rhodes. A flight south would have placed them somewhere in Africa or the Middle East. Since they had driven through a forest, she eliminated this possibility. That meant they were either in Russia, Eastern Europe, or Western Europe. Given current geo-political alliances, she felt Russia was a stretch, leaving them in either Eastern or Western Europe.

Many of the Eastern European countries had suffered during the Nazi and Soviet occupations during the World War II, leaving them less likely to ally themselves with her captors. That left Western Europe as the primary possibility and, since her captors were German, and since they were in the middle of a forest, Sam surmised they were somewhere in Germany, perhaps even Bavaria. She turned to look at Grady, who now sat with his head in his hands, staring at the concrete floor.

"I'm so sorry that I dragged you and your dad into this mess," Grady said. "If I had known what I was getting you into, I never would have asked for help."

"There's no way you could have known that the Nazis were responsible for your team's disappearance. Aside from a few conspiracy theorists, no one would believe there was a powerful group of Nazis running around trying to take over the world again.

"I guess maybe the conspiracy believers aren't so nuts," Grady said, eliciting a laugh from Sam.

"Good point," she sat next to him.

Grady looked up. "I have to say, you're taking this pretty well. I don't know how you're keeping it together with these lunatics holding us hostage. This is the scariest thing I've ever dealt with."

"It's not the first time this has happened to me." Sam replied.

"What are talking about?"

"My dad and I were held captive by a crazed industrialist in Peru a couple of years ago."

"You're kidding!"

Sam shook her head. "And if it makes you feel any better, I'm still scared as hell!"

"You don't look it."

The tumbler to the cell block clicked. Sam turned to face the door and saw a familiar face enter the room.

"Professor Randall, how wonderful to see you again," Dietrich Herrmann's snakelike smile was an unwelcomed site for

165

Sam. "Although I'm surprised you managed to escape, I must say, I believe your luck has finally run out." Two armed guards joined him.

"To be honest, the feeling's not mutual," Sam folded her arms across her chest.

Herrmann shrugged. "What do the French say? C'est la vie."

"What do you want from us?" Sam asked.

"Ah, an excellent question! We had some help developing die Glocke, and our benefactors requested a small payment in return," Herrmann replied.

A chill ran down Sam's spine. "What does that have to do with us?"

"You'll see shortly," Herrmann approached their cell, stopping just outside with his guards.

A moment later, the door behind Herrmann opened again and two additional men entered, carrying a small case no larger than a man's toiletry bag. Goosebumps rose on Sam's skin as they approached. Something simply wasn't right about them, but Sam couldn't put her finger on it. Then it struck her. Their heads and faces were cleanly shaven, void of even the faintest hint of stubble anywhere. They walked slowly, blank expressions on their faces. They stopped outside the cell. One of them opened the bag, revealing a syringe and four vials.

"If you think I'm going to let you draw blood from me, you're crazy!" Sam backed away from the cell door as Grady rose to his feet.

"All in the name of science," Herrmann said, nodding to one of the guards, who opened the lock.

The two bald men walked into the cell, their heavy gazes on Sam.

"You're not going anywhere near her!" Grady stepped directly in front of the two men. They momentarily shared a glance, then one turned to face Grady, locking eyes with him. Grady slowed then stopped in place, frozen.

Sam watched in horror as the second man slid past Jim and approach her. She backed away from him, stepping deeper into the cell until she felt the hard metal bars pressing into her back. Unable to move any further, she stared into the eyes of the second bald man, breathing in shallow gulps.

The man removed the syringe from the bag and lifted the needle to his mouth, never breaking eye contact with Sam. Removing the cover of the syringe with his teeth, he moved toward her, dead eyes staring through her. Sam wanted to scream. Wanted to swat at the man and run, but she was paralyzed. All movement except her shallow breathing stopped.

The bald man grasped her arm, straightening it as he pressed a bony finger into her skin searching for a vein. Clearly satisfied he had found what he needed; he swabbed the spot with an alcohol wipe. A thought occurred to Sam. Although the man had five fingers, she could only feel three gripping her arm.

Struggling is useless. The more you fight, the longer it will take for you to regain control over your body.

Sam realized the man drawing blood was communicating with her. She rolled her eyes up to carefully study his face. To her horror, the man's appearance transformed into a hideous creature with black elongated eyes. She looked down at her arm and saw the creature's gray, mottled fingers grasping her arm as it drew her blood. Sam cast her eyes at the other man standing next to Grady. It now looked just like the creature stealing her blood.

It released her arm, having filled the four vials. Backing away, its appearance transformed back into a bald man. The second creature joined the first and they left the cell, then exited through the door they had entered earlier.

Slowly, Sam regained control over her head and neck. She looked up to see Herrmann's evil sneer as he nodded to the guard to close the cell door again.

"Auf Wiedersehen," Herrmann said. One of his guards held

the door to the cell block open as the two bald men and Herrmann exited. A moment later, they were gone, leaving Sam and Grady to contemplate what had just happened.

Chapter 31

Souda Naval Base, Greece
July 27, 2:48 p.m.

Randall paced the floor of the Souda Bay cell. He had stridden it so many times he knew the dimensions well enough to walk it with his eyes closed. As much as he tried to put his concern for Sam out of his mind, being trapped in the cell and not knowing what was happening to her was overwhelming.

I've gotta get out of here!

He heard boot steps and looked up to see Michael approaching with military police from the base. Good to his word, Michael had returned with a guard who opened the cell for Randall.

"Thanks, Michael. Are we going to see the base commander?"

"I've arranged for you to meet with him, but I can't guarantee how you'll be received. If you don't mind, I'm going to tag along."

"I don't mind at all. I'll take any help I can get."

Two burly armed guards escorted Randall and Michael

169

through the facility. Their intense demeanor while escorting an unarmed fifty-year-old college professor seeming a bit excessive.

The trip to the base commander's office only took a few minutes and upon arrival, one of the guards held the door open as Michael stood at the doorway. "After you, Dr. Randall."

"Thanks," Randall said before entering the office and taking a seat. Michael entered next, followed closely by the two MP's. One stationed himself in the corner opposite Randall, his angry glare locked on the professor's face. The second stood by the doorway, obviously prepared to keep Randall from making a break from the office. Despite the circumstances, Randall couldn't suppress a grin. He stared down at the floor and shook his head, the irony of the situation not lost on him.

"What's so funny?" Michael asked.

"I traveled for nearly a day, hell bent on finding this place and now these guys are worried that I want to leave," Randall replied.

"He's just doing his job. It's a military thing," Michael replied.

The base commander arrived at the office door a moment later. Michael rose to his feet, standing straight as a flagpole as the commanding officer entered his office, walking around to the front of his desk.

"At ease," he said, dropping his hat onto the desk before lowering himself into his desk chair.

The commanding officer wasn't what Randall expected. Judging him to be little more than five and half feet tall, Randall found himself curious how a man of his stature commanded so much respect in an environment known for excessive masculinity. Studying him more closely, Randall noted the graying patch of short hair circling his nearly bald head. His thick, short neck fed into his stocky frame and his arms and legs were broad and short. Randall suddenly understood where the term 'resembling a fireplug' came from.

The officer studied a file on his desk, making Randall wait

for several minutes. He finally looked up; his dark brown eyes boring into Randall. "To what do we owe the pleasure, Dr. Randall?"

"I appear to be at a disadvantage here. You know who I am, but I don't know who you are," Randall replied.

"Commander Doug Zakarian," he said, his hand shooting out toward Randall and squeezing like a vice. Randall clamped his hand around the commander's, trying his best to return the solid handshake. Neither man broke eye contact.

"My daughter and friend were taken hostage by a group of German paramilitaries in Rhodes. I was lucky enough to escape, and I came here searching for help to rescue them."

Zakarian released his death grip and swiveled back in his chair. Randall noticed for the first time that the folder he had been reading was labeled: *Randall, Nicholas—Operation Ice Hammer,* a reference to the assignment he had received from General Flores.

"A little light reading before our meeting?" Randall said, nodding at the file.

"First rule of war; know your opponent," Zakarian replied, continuing to study Randall carefully.

"I'm your opponent?"

"You walk onto a secure military base, demanding to meet with the base commander, spouting a crazy story about paramilitary forces taking your daughter hostage, so until proven otherwise that's how I view you."

"You're aware of my history with General Flores?" Randall asked wanting to change the tone of the meeting.

"Affirmative. When the captain here mentioned that his father knew you, we pulled up the record. Sounds like you were a thorough pain in the general's backside."

"Is that what the file says?" Randall asked, raising a brow.

Zakarian picked up the file. "That and more. It also says you played an instrumental role in something called 'Operation Ice

171

Hammer.' Most of the file is redacted—apparently someone at the Pentagon doesn't trust an old sailor like me with information like this," Zakarian tossed the file on the desk, causing it to skid toward Randall.

"Maybe it has something to do with your attitude," Randall prodded. It was clear Zakarian didn't like him so why place nice.

Zakarian glared at Randall.

"Commander, with all due respect, Dr. Randall has nothing to do with that file being classified. All I know is that my father spoke respectfully about the professor and his interactions with him. Of course, he couldn't share specifics with me, so I guess the military doesn't trust us flyboys, either," Michael said, trying to break the tension.

Zakarian shifted his gaze to Michael and then back to Randall before exhaling loudly. "How do you know they're German?" Zakarian leaned forward, dropping his clasped hands on his desk.

"They told us. They have an operating base off the coast of Argentina and probably another one somewhere nearby. Commander, I'm not here to cause you any trouble, I just need some help."

"Why come to my base? Why not go to the consulate or the local authorities?"

"These men who've taken my daughter are well financed and powerful. To be honest, I didn't know if I could trust the local authorities. It's entirely possible they've been bought off. As for the consulate, I can't afford to wait around for back-channel negotiations. My daughter is in danger and, to put it bluntly, if I have to rescue her alone, then that's what I'll damn well do."

Zakarian raised an eyebrow. He opened his desk drawer and retrieved a stubby cigar. Placing it into his mouth, he reached back into the drawer, retrieving a silver-plated lighter with what appeared to be a special forces insignia engraved in its side. His elbows now on the desk, he lit the cigar, taking a puff before addressing his guest. "How in the hell do I know you're not blowing smoke up my ass?"

"You don't, but I'm guessing you already know that based on whatever is in that file. Are you going to help me?"

Zakarian leaned back in his chair, chewing on his cigar. "What were you and your daughter doing in Rhodes when these Germans took her hostage?"

"Research."

"Bullshit! If you want my help, you better be straight with me. I'm not about to risk the lives of my men to go on some wild goose chase for someone who's lying. I don't give a goddamn what Captain Flores, or his daddy have to say about you. I don't know you from Adam!" Zakarian spoke through teeth clenched around his cigar. His face turning red.

"Fair enough, but I don't think you'll believe me if I tell you."

"Why don't we find out?"

Randall squirmed in his chair uncomfortably. He glanced over at Michael, who held his chin in his hand. Turning back to face Zakarian, Randall pursed his lips, not sure if he wanted to divulge the full story. He studied the commander who was clearly not someone to be taken lightly. He had no other choice, but to tell him the truth. "A colleague, Dr. Jim Grady, discovered previously unknown ruins in the South American jungle. He was searching for a rare, priceless artifact, but this group of Germans found out about his research and wanted the artifact for themselves. They kidnapped Grady's archaeological team and tried to force him to turn over the relic, but it wasn't at the site."

The commander nodded for him to continue.

"My daughter and I tried to help Jim find his team, and the artifact, but were captured in the process. Now the Germans are holding my daughter and everyone else as prisoners."

Zakarian slowly removed the cigar from his teeth. "What's the artifact and why do the Germans want it?"

Randall swallowed hard. "It's a stone, one that shares characteristics with uranium. The German's are a remnant of the Nazi party from World War II and they've developed a super weapon and need the stone to power it."

"Nazis, you say?"

"Yes."

"And the weapon is…?"

"A device called the Bell that can travel anywhere at any time, moving from one spot on the globe to another almost instantaneously and undetected."

"And you don't want to go to the local authorities because you're afraid they might be working in cahoots with the Nazis?"

"Yes. I didn't know who I could trust, so I thought you were my best chance."

Zakarian leaned back into his seat, stroking his chin while puffing on his cigar. He sat upright, moving to the edge of his seat, his eyes locked on Randall's. Removing the cigar from his mouth, he frowned. "That's the biggest load of crap I've ever heard in my life. I warned you Randall."

"I'm telling you the truth!"

"Take him back to his cell," Zakarian motioned for the guards to gather Randall, then pointed at Michael. "You're staying here. We're going to have a little talk."

The two MP's took positions on either side of Randall's chair. Looking up at each of them, Randall stood and, giving Michael a last look, shuffled toward the door of Zakarian's office, his escorts in tow.

Chapter 32

Nazi Base, Germany

July 27, 3:02 p.m.

Sam sat on the edge of her cot, staring through the bars of her cell. Her feet nervously bounced as she tried to wrap her head around the fact that she had just had her blood taken by creatures, unlike anything she had ever seen before. "What just happened?"

Grady, also in shock, sat on the floor shaking his head and muttering to himself. "I have no idea."

Sam replayed the situation in her mind, each time arriving at the same frightening conclusion. She had just encountered extraterrestrial beings who were working with the Nazis. The tumbler for the lock on the cell block door clicked loudly again, causing Sam to nearly jump from the bed. Her eyes followed the door as it swung inward, and two armed Nazis enter the room.

175

"Back up!" one guard growled, pointing his Heckler & Koch handgun through the bars while the other unlocked the cell door.

"What do you want now?" Sam asked, still sitting.

"You're moving to a different area. Up!" the Nazi leaned forward slightly, moving his gun closer to Sam's head.

Sam complied; the fight drained from her. The guard removed a set of handcuffs from his belt and placed them on Sam. She looked over at Grady, who faced the same fate. The two guards led them out of the cell block and into the hallway. A short time later, they were standing outside another locked metal door.

"Halt!"

Sam and Grady stood staring at each other while the guard opened the door.

"In," the guard said, removing their cuffs.

The room was a holding area with multiple cells filled with nearly 30 people.

"Jenn!" Grady said, pushing past Sam and running to one of the cells. A woman inside extended her arms through the metal bars, reaching out to embrace Grady.

"Jim, it's you!" Jenn said, trying her best to hug him through the metal barrier.

A Nazi guard strode to Grady and struck him hard in the back of his head, knocking him to the concrete floor.

"Stop, you're hurting him!" Jenn cried.

Sam ran to Grady, pushing by the Nazi and kneeling at his

side to examine him. Blood flowed freely from the wound on the back of his head, a large lump forming where the guard had struck him. She rolled him over, but he was unconscious. She put her ears to his mouth, watching his chest, slowly rise and fall.

"He was just happy to see her! Why the hell did you have to hit him?" Sam glared at the guard, who sneered back at her. He raised his gun, ready to strike Sam.

"Enough! Back to your post!" a voice boomed from across the room, causing the guard to recoil in fear.

Grady stirred, rolling from side to side as his eyes slowly opened. "My head…" He moaned, gingerly touching the expanding lump on the back of his skull.

The man who had called out from across the room walked to the cell, stopping in front the guard whose expression now resembled that of a teenager caught sneaking into his room at two in the morning.

"You fool! Your job is to guard the prisoners and prevent their escape, and nothing more! Your insubordination is unacceptable!" he slapped the guard with the palm of his hand, then turned to face Sam. "My apologies, fräulein, this brute will not hurt your friend again. My name is Dr. Brauer, I'm the lead scientist at this facility."

Sam nodded, helping Grady to his feet.

"Do you require medical assistance, Herr Doctor?" Brauer said to Grady.

"No, I'm fine."

"Why are you holding these people?" Sam asked.

177

"We need them for research we're conducting with our …
associates," Brauer replied.

"You mean you're using them as lab rats for your
experiments," Sam said.

Brauer shrugged. "All in the name of science. Sometimes
certain sacrifices must be made for the greater good."

Sam folded her arms across her chest. "That's easy to say
when you're not the one making the sacrifice."

Brauer motioned for the guards to open the cell door. They
pushed Sam and Grady inside before locking it once again.

"Auf Wiedersehen," Brauer left the room.

"Are you hurt, Jim?" Jenn asked.

"I'm fine," Grady embraced her. He then turned to Sam.
"Samantha Randall, meet Jennifer Artemis. Jennifer was the lead
scientist on the archeological site by San Ignacio." As Grady
spoke, Jennifer's gaze never broke contact with him. She grasped
his hand and gave a gentle squeeze while he spoke.

Jennifer turned to look at Sam. "I wish we could have met
under better circumstances."

"I can't tell you how happy I am that everyone's okay.
How've they been treating you?" Grady asked.

"They take turns roughing up the men, interrogating them,
and they've drawn blood from all of the women," Jennifer
answered.

"They drew blood from me, too," Sam said. "Do you know
why?"

"I overheard Dr. Brauer and another scientist saying they're searching for some sort of genetic markers. As best as I can tell, they're testing for some sort of compatibility," Jennifer answered.

"Compatibility for what?" Sam asked.

"I'm not sure, but they came back and took one of our researchers, Margaret, and we haven't seen her since."

A banging sound came from the door to the main facility. Sam turned and saw Brauer, two guards, and another man marching toward the cell. The man next to Brauer was holding a clipboard, carefully reviewing a sheet of paper. Brauer's gaze fell on Sam. He scrutinized her like a teenager studying a frog before a high school science experiment.

"Open the door," Brauer instructed one guard, while his partner pointed his gun into the cell.

"Step back!" the guard said. The prisoners complied.

Brauer's gaze was locked on Sam. "You're coming with us."

Chapter 33

Randall once again paced his cell, wringing his hands and shaking his head. His only plan had been a bust, and now his intended helpers had become his captors. In the distance, he once again heard the unmistakable sound of boots clicking on the concrete floor, but this time they were moving much more quickly.

"Guess that didn't go as planned," Michael said, arriving at Randall's cell. "Come on, we've got to go." He produced a large key and opened the mortise lock, then pulled the door open.

"Why are they letting me out?"

"They're not, that's why we have to hurry." Michael glanced over his shoulder and grabbed Randall's arm, dragging him from the cell.

The two men ran down the hall, hugging the wall as they went. Coming to a corner, Michael stopped, put his arm in front of Randall, and pushed him against the wall. He glanced around the corner.

"Are you telling me you broke me out?" Randall asked.

"That's about it. We need to get out of this building without being seen. The guards inside all know who you are. Once we get outside, we'll be okay. Come on!" Michael said, once again grabbing Randall's arm and resuming their dash. They raced down the hallway, heading for the exit. A door to their left opened inward, releasing the sound of men talking from inside. The sound of their voices grew louder. They were about to walk into the hallway.

Randall spotted a door on his right. He jerked Michael's arm, pulling him with one hand as he pushed the door open with the other. They dashed inside before realizing it was a janitor's closet. Randall pulled to a quick stop, but Michael, not having time to react, ran into Randall's back, catapulting him into the wall. Randall's forehead struck the cinderblock, causing him to yelp.

"Shit!" Randall rubbed his head.

"Sorry. That was close!" Michael said.

Randall steadied his nerves, his heart thumping like a jackhammer.

"Listen to the door to make sure no one saw us," he whispered to Michael, who did as instructed.

After a couple of minutes, he shook his head. "I think we're okay." Michael cracked the door open and peered into the hallway. "All clear!"

The two resumed their race, stopping just short of the exit and pressing their bodies against the side wall. The door possessed a small window with a view outside. Michael peered through the glass.

"We're good to go," Michael pressed the panic bar, opening the door and the two men stepped outside. They walked briskly, putting distance between themselves and the cell block.

"As long as they haven't discovered you're missing, we should be able to get to the airstrip without a problem," Michael said.

"Why are we going to the airstrip?"

"We have to get to my plane. Here, put this on," Michael handed Randall an ID badge.

Randall checked the picture. "I don't look anything like this guy." He clipped the badge on his pocket.

"It'll work from a distance. I don't plan on stopping long enough to let someone have a close look," Michael replied.

The two men moved quickly along the outside of the jail structure, hugging the wall as they went. The warm Mediterranean sun was a welcome reprieve from the fluorescent light of the military jail.

They turned the corner of the building and Randall spotted the airfield about half a mile away. They picked up their pace. Lining their path to the airfield were multiple rows of equally spaced semi-circular buildings separated by narrow walkways.

"Base barracks," Michael said.

Randall nodded in reply, recalling his own days of service. They quickly covered the remaining ground separating them from the airfield. They approached the second to last barrack when two sailors rounded the corner from the pathway between the two buildings. Engaged in a lively conversation, they seemed unaware of Randall and Michael as they approached.

Randall's eyes went wide as the sailors drew closer. One was the guard at the gate that had arrested him. The man stared at Randall his head tilted to the side as if trying to recall who he was.

They closed to within several feet, still walking toward each other. The sailor's eyes went wide with recognition. "You're that nut who said his daughter had been captured! What the hell are you doing out here?"

Randall lunged at the sailor, grabbing him by his arm and spinning him into the wall. The man tumbled to the ground unconscious, his forehead scraped and bleeding. Randall tripped as well, falling onto the grass strip. He looked up to see Michael and the other sailor staring, mouths agape. After a moment, the other sailor stormed at Randall, towering over him.

"What in the fuck are you doing?" the sailor said, fists clenched, his eyes filled with rage. After a moment, the look changed to one of bewilderment.

"Hang on, fella," Michael pressed a gun into the man's ribs.

"You're committing professional suicide buddy. They'll

send your ass to Leavenworth for treason!" the sailor seethed.

"Then I better not get caught. Back away from the man on the ground," Michael said in a stern voice. The sailor complied. "You okay, Dr. Randall?" Michael asked.

"I'm fine, thanks," Randall stood and dusted himself off. He inspected the area to see if anyone else had noticed the altercation. Everything appeared to be normal.

Michael nodded. "Good, we better get going."

"Going where? I'm not going anywhere with you two!" the sailor said.

"You'll do exactly what I say," Michael ordered. "We're going toward that plane over there," Michael nodded toward the airstrip.

Randall glanced over and saw a fighter jet sitting on the apron, its canopy open. "Does that have two seats?"

"Yes, it's the F/A-18F Super Hornet. We use it for carrier-based operations. Let's get going," Michael poked the gun into the sailor's side to get him to move.

The three made their way toward the jet as aviation personnel moved about in the distance, servicing other planes. Randall eyed them warily. They were cutting this very close. They walked within several feet of the Super Hornet.

"Pull the chalks from the wheels," Michael said to Randall.

"You'll never get away with this," the sailor mumbled.

Randall returned to Michael's side. "What do we do with him?"

Just as the words left his mouth, the sailor spun, knocking the gun from Michael's hand. He sprinted toward the staff working near one of the hangers. "Call the tower, they're stealing a plane!"

"Crap! Come on!" Michael moved toward the ladder on the side of his plane.

He scrambled up first, plopping himself into the pilot seat as Randall shimmied up after him. He awkwardly tumbled into the rear seat of the jet as its engines roared to life and it started rolling. He righted himself as the cockpit closed then looked out the glass and saw armed sailors sprinting toward them.

The plane accelerated, picking up speed as it taxied to the airstrip.

"Tower to pilot of F-18, you're stealing government property. Shut down immediately!" a voice cackled from the speaker.

"Tower, this is Captain Flores, sorry about the confusion, but I need to take Dr. Randall to Ramstein."

"Flores goddamn it, I thought that was you. Do you realize what you're doing? You'll be court-martialed for this! Turn that plane around right now!" This time it was Zakarian's voice.

"With all due respect I can't do that commander," Michael responded.

The plane sped down the airstrip, heading directly toward several armed sailors, their guns raised and pointed at the cockpit.

"Then you leave me no choice," Zakarian replied giving the order to open fire. Small bursts of flame followed by puffs of smoke emanated from the sailor's weapons as bullets bounced off the fighter's cockpit.

The jet raced down the airstrip, lifting into the air as Michael pulled back on the yoke. Randall was pressed into the backseat by the g-forces created by the take-off. A short time later, they were at cruising altitude, heading for Ramstein Air Base and a meeting with Michael's father.

Chapter 34

Randall settled into the seat of the fighter, his body finally recovering from the g-forces applied by their quick escape. Peering out the window, a sense of calm came over him as he stared out at the bright blue sky.

"You still didn't explain why you busted me out of my cell," Randall said, utilizing the built-in microphone system in his helmet, which Michael had shown him.

"I wasn't completely honest with you. We train a lot at Souda but that's not why I was there. My father got your message and told me to go and keep an eye on you and Captain Zakarian caught wind of it. Base Commanders don't appreciate other officers interfering with their operations, and he took it out on you. While he was reading you the riot act, I texted my dad to let him know what was happening and he ordered me to get you back to Ramstein. By any means."

"You're kidding. He didn't order you."

Michael turned his head around as far as possible. "Believe it or not, even though he's my father, he also outranks me ... and Commander Zakarian."

"Then why not just tell Zakarian to transfer me to Ramstein?"

"Even though he outranks the commander, there's still a lot of red tape to transfer a prisoner, and sometimes the branches don't exactly play nicely together. Commander Zakarian would have thrown up roadblocks to keep you at the base for a while and based on the nature of your story, my dad thought the situation was time sensitive."

"To be honest with you … after the way we left things, I didn't think I was your dad's favorite person."

"What do you mean?"

Randall frowned under his face mask, unsure of how much he wanted to divulge to Michael about his experience in the Antarctic and his father's role.

"Is this thing working?" Michael asked through his mic.

"How much did your dad tell you about what happened?"

"Not much. He just said you and your son were trying to help him find a relic he was looking for. Sounds like you almost found it, but not quite."

"Anything else?"

"Yeah, he said you were one of the most reliable men he had ever met, putting everyone else's safety above your own. Trust me when I say this, that's high praise from my dad."

Randall cocked his head to one side, truly surprised by the news.

"He also said he couldn't tell if you were exceptionally brave or extremely stupid for putting your ass on the line so many times," Michael chuckled.

Randall smiled at the revelation, shaking his head from side to side. "Well I guess that makes two of us. Aren't you worried about stealing this jet though? Won't there be consequences? You not only stole government property; you broke a prisoner out of jail and threatened to shoot an American serviceman. I'm no expert, but doesn't the military frown at that type of behavior?"

Randall could see Michael's head bobbing up and down. He assumed Michael was laughing. The young man clearly had a better sense of humor than his father.

"Like I said, I was simply following orders and my dad has highly placed connections in both the military and the government. He's personally met with every president in the past two decades and enjoys a close relationship with the Joint Chiefs. I'll get slapped on the wrist but not much else. My dad on the other hand is going to have to call in some favors and deal with a lot of flak, but whatever you've gotten yourself into must be important enough for my father to risk it," Michael answered, scanning the skies around them. "So, back to your adventure with my dad."

"Okay, you win, but you probably won't believe me," Randall said.

"Try me."

"Your dad was running a top-secret program with the help of a guy named Shaw."

"Colonel Shaw?"

"That's the one. They were trying to develop an antidote to a mind-control substance and were secretly funding my son's work. My son John is a bioengineer. He and his research partner had developed a compound to help erase targeted memories in people who had suffered traumatic experiences their life. The idea was to help patients move past their tragedy."

"Sounds like a noble pursuit, but what does that have to do with mind control?"

"The compound worked but had an unintended side effect. It temporarily left the subject open to suggestion. The military wanted it for their own use and to derive a compound to stop the mind-control effects. They wanted it so badly that Shaw tried to kidnap my son. We stopped him and inadvertently found out about your dad's facility in Dulce."

"Dulce? My dad never told me he was stationed in Dulce."

There was a twinge of surprise and disappointment in Michael's voice. Randall cringed. He had never intended to cause trouble for Flores. He stopped talking.

"It's okay, Dr. Randall. Please go on."

Taking a deep breath, Randall continued. "The government was aware of another mind-control substance and was trying to secure it before anyone else did. Unfortunately, a faction of the Chinese military found out about it and wanted to get to it first. We battled with them in the Antarctic and beat them to it."

"But my dad said you weren't able to get what you were looking for. I'm assuming he's referring to the substance you found."

"On our way back to the U.S. base at McMurdo, we had a run-in with another group, and I traded the substance for a friend's life."

"I see."

"Your dad was upset by the thought of a rogue group possessing a mind-control substance, but the government still had my son's compound, so I guess it was a wash."

Randall sat back into his seat, waiting for Michael to reply. He didn't. An awkward silence filled the cockpit of the fighter jet as the two men sat isolated in their own little worlds.

The silence was short lived. The F/A - 18 missile warning system buzzed to life.

"What's that?" Randall asked.

"It's our warning system, a missile locked onto us."

Michael pulled back on the yoke, taking the plane into a steep climb as the warning system continued to wail.

Michael scanned the skies around them. "Look for a contrail!"

Randall turned to look as far behind the plane as possible.

The plane banked hard right, making a tight turn that shoved Randall deeply into his seat.

A missile detonated in the air no more than thirty feet behind them.

"Captain Flores, this is Captain Marcus, I'm ordering you to return to Souda Base."

"Looks like we have company. I count four bogies,"

Michael said as Randall recovered from the g-forces. "Captain Marcus, I'm operating under the orders of General Flores. I repeat, I have been ordered to bring the prisoner to Ramstein."

Randall looked out the canopy, spotting one aircraft slightly above and to their right and another slightly above and to their left.

"Negative, captain, you are to return to Souda base with the prisoner immediately," Marcus said.

"And if I don't?"

"We have orders to shoot you down."

"I thought this might happen. They're flying F-22 Raptors, we're outmatched in a dogfight," Michael said.

"Michael, I appreciate what you're trying to do for me, but you've already taken too many risks. If you want to turn back, I understand and I'm ready to accept whatever punishment they have for me. Just talk with your dad to help my daughter," Randall said.

"Surrender? I don't think so. I love a good challenge. Don't worry, Professor, we're not going back to Souda," Michael throttled the engine and pulled back on the yoke. The plane surged forward into a steep climb, leaving the other jets behind as if standing still.

The pressure on Randall's body was unlike anything he had ever experienced. It felt like someone had thrown enormous sacks of sand over every square inch of his body. He struggled to move his arm but couldn't.

The warning system buzzed to life again, the red flashing indicator glowing brightly as Michael pitched the plane into a turn.

"Hang on!"

Randall heard the mechanical sound of chaff and flares launching as countermeasures. An explosion emanated from somewhere behind them.

Michael angled the supersonic jet into another steep climb, fighting to keep his pursuers at bay. The warning indicator wailed loudly, letting them know they were still in danger.

The jet banked hard to the right as a missile slid by them, curling back to find its target.

More countermeasures.

Randall nearly blacked out as Michael pushed the jet to its limits. The plane leveled out for a moment, allowing Randall to recover from his lightheadedness. He felt nauseous.

"Flores bring the plane down. Don't make us do this!" Marcus shouted through the helmet-mounted speakers.

Michael ignored his warning, putting the plane into a sharp dive. The staccato sound of gunfire emanated from behind as tracer rounds punctured the air around them, some finding their mark on the Belly of the plane.

Michael buzzed the treetops, pulling up at the last moment. The German landscape buzzed by at a frightening speed.

The threat indicator screeched on, announcing another impending threat. Michael pulled the jet up slightly, taking it into a tight, curling arc.

The threat warning hit a high pitch. Their pursuers had missile lock on them.

"Flores turn back now. This is your final warning!" Marcus announced as additional tracers struck their plane. Another warning system screamed to life and the jet lurched downward.

"We have mechanical failure!" Michael yelled into his helmet mic.

"Jester One, you have clearance to launch in three, two…"

"Delay that order," a new voice announced from the communications system. "Souda Base flight team, this is Admiral Stigler, disengage now."

The missile warning system remained active.

"Flight control, request verification of message sender," Marcus said.

"Souda Base flight team, verification code Delta, Delta, Sigma, Zero, Four, Niner."

"Verification identified, breaking off pursuit," Marcus said. Randall watched the jets bank away.

"Captain Flores, what's your status?" Stigler asked.

"I have multiple system failures," Michael replied.

"You're cleared for landing on runway two. Can you reach the base?" Stigler asked.

"Affirmative sir, I'll do my best."

Michael nursed the wounded fighter plane along as Ramstein Airbase came into view.

"Are we going to make it?" Randall asked.

"I'm working on it," Michael grunted as he fought the controls.

The airfield grew larger; even from their current altitude, Randall could see emergency vehicles scrambling in anticipation of a crash.

"Shit!" Michael said as the plane lurched down again. "I'm losing her!"

Randall sensed them dropping quickly.

"Mayday, mayday, Ramstein, prepare for crash landing!"

The ground rose with frightening speed as the damaged jet closed on the runway. At the last possible moment, Michael pulled up the stick with all his strength. The plane hit the runway with a jarring thud, momentarily bouncing back into the air.

The wheels touched down again a moment later. Michael lowered the flaps, raised the air brakes, and engaged the wheel braking system. Utilizing every component on the craft, Michael attempted to slow their forward motion, the end of the runway looming a short distance ahead.

The braking action of the plane pulled Randall forward, causing the restraint system to dig into the front of his body.

"Come on baby, hold together," Michael said as the plane jerked from side to side, still moving far too quickly to stop safely.

The sound of straining metal came from the landing gear, then the plane suddenly dropped on the right side. It skidded down the runway, sparks flying from the right wing as it lurched to the right.

Michael struggled to keep the damaged jet from veering off the runway. The right wing sheared off and flames erupted from the Belly of the plane.

"Hang on!" Michael yelled.

The Hornet skidded from the runway and into the weed-strewn field to the side. Sirens wailed in the distance as emergency crews converged on the injured jet.

They finally stopped.

"Let's get out of here!" Michael popped the canopy open.

Randall pressed the release lever on his safety harness. The latch wouldn't budge.

"It's stuck!" Randall yelled. Michael removed his helmet, stood on his seat, and looked backward.

"Hit it again!" Michael instructed.

Flames licked the outside of the craft, growing higher as Randall struggled to free himself.

"It's not working!" Randall shouted. The smell of burning jet fuel and rubber filled the air as the heat intensified, the flames now reaching the cockpit.

Randall cursed, struggling to free himself. Michael leaned over him, knife in hand. In one fluid motion, he cut the strap and yanked Randall out of his seat. The two men tumbled over the side of the plane, hurtling to the ground.

They landed on the hard dirt, Michael's body absorbing most of the blow as Randall fell on top of him. Michael yelped in pain. They rolled through the flames, their clothes catching fire. Safety crews arrived, dumping flame retardant on and around them.

The two men rolled to a stop and Randall tumbled to the side. He looked at Michael, whose right arm was still burning. A firefighter finally doused the flame, but Michael rolled in the dirt in obvious pain.

Though injured, they had reached Ramstein.

Chapter 35

Ramstein Airbase, Germany
July 27, 6:50 p.m.

The emergency crew helped Michael and Randall into an ambulance, then took them to the base hospital where they found a familiar face waiting.

"Son, I'm glad you're all right," General Flores grasped his son's shoulder while the doctor examined his injured hand. He turned his head to Randall. "Professor, I wish I could say I'm surprised to see you again, but I had a feeling it'd only be a matter of time."

"I wouldn't be here without Michael. He put his career and his life on the line to break me out of the brig at Souda Bay. I'm in his debt," Randall said, nodding to Michael, who smiled back.

"Michael told me about your daughter and friend. I think we can help. In fact, we may know where they are," Flores commented.

Randall furrowed his brow. "How's that possible? You just found out about this a few hours ago."

"You of all people should know that we have our

resources," Flores replied.

Randall shook his head. "I suppose you're right."

"Once our doctors finish looking you over, my men will escort you to the meeting room," Flores said.

"I'd prefer we meet right now."

"No. You've been through a serious incident; I want to make sure that you're one-hundred percent. I'll see you soon." Flores gripped Michael's shoulder again, then exited the examining room.

The doctors made quick work of treating Randall and Michael; whose injuries were minor. Save for Michael's burned forearm which wasn't serious enough to warrant much more than bandages, the two had suffered little more than bumps and scrapes. Soon, they joined the elder Flores and another soldier in the meeting room. The area was small, accommodating a dozen people at most. An oval shaped wooden table sat in the center of the room with high-back rolling chairs neatly arranged at evenly spaced intervals around its perimeter.

Flores motioned for Randall and Michael to take a seat.

"How's the arm?" Flores asked.

"It's fine, general, just a minor injury. I'm ready for duty," Michael replied, earning a nod of approval from his father.

"Will Admiral Stigler be joining us?" Randall asked.

Flores shook his head. "The Admiral was conferenced in using a secure sat line to speak with the pilots from Souda Base. He's at an undisclosed location at the moment. Dr. Randall, when Captain Flores contacted me about your presence at Souda Naval Station, I have to say, I was a bit surprised. To put it bluntly, it takes guts to walk onto a United States military installation and make a request the way you did," Flores said.

Randall shrugged. "I didn't have many options."

"Your timing was fortuitous, and after the captain contacted me, I had my team do some research," Flores said.

The soldier placed folders in front of Randall, Michael, and the General.

"What's this?" Randall asked.

"The results of our research. Dr. Randall, the information you are about to review is classified and cannot be shared with anyone outside of this room. I don't believe I need to explain the legal ramifications of violating this order. Do you understand?"

Randall nodded.

"Good. We believe we've found where the Nazis are holding your daughter and friend."

"How did you find them so quickly?" Randall asked.

"Once Captain Flores contacted us, we began tracking flights and ships bound from Rhodes to Germany. We identified a flight from a private airfield, which flew directly to a small airport in Bavaria. We then traced a small caravan of vehicles leaving the airport, which headed into the countryside."

"What makes you think those were the Nazis?"

"Their destination was a remote area of the Black Forest. There's nothing nearby except an old farm. No hotels, no shops, nothing of interest in the area … except for what we discovered when our reconnaissance satellite passed overhead."

"Which is?"

"Inside your folder, you'll find infrared and ground penetrating radar scans, which led to the discovery of a large underground facility. Based on this, we hit the area with a full sensor suite and found concentrated radiation levels that were abnormally high in one part of the structure. The nature of the readings suggested some sort of testing facility utilizing an unknown, radioactive substance. It didn't take much to connect the dots from there," Flores explained.

Randall studied the contents of their folders, dumbstruck by what he read. The size of the hidden facility was massive. The large underground structure extended several stories beneath the forest floor. The size of several aircraft hangers, it was completely hidden from view, save for a dilapidated farmhouse, which sat directly above the compound. As he studied the files, he was immediately drawn to a circular structure set at the end of the facility.

"What's this?" Randall asked.

"That's where they're testing the device," Flores answered. "The shape of the ringed structure matches photographs of the area known as "The Henge" in the vicinity of the Wenceslas mine. Except this one is larger."

"That can't be…" Michael mumbled.

"I don't get it. What do you mean?" Randall asked.

"The Wenceslas mine area is where the Nazis supposedly tested a device called die Glocke or the Bell, but there was never any verification of the project other than reports by some prisoners of war. It was just considered part of the lore of the Third Reich and Hitler's infatuation with the paranormal," Flores answered.

"What does Michael know about your command?" Randall asked Flores.

Flores's gaze shifted between Randall and his son; his mouth drawn up into a tight bow. "Lieutenant, can you please excuse us?" Flores asked his direct report, who immediately rose to his feet and walked out of the room, leaving only Flores, Michael, and Randall.

Michael sat back into his seat; his arms crossed over his chest.

"My son isn't aware of the extent of my command or the true nature of my position," Flores stated, taking a deep breath. "It began nearly twelve years ago, when I was approached by the Secretary of Defense on behalf of then President Mercer. The President wanted me to head a task force to coordinate research and rapid response into 'uncommon' phenomenon."

"What sort of uncommon phenomenon?" Michael asked.

"There were a number of items we were tasked to investigate: unidentified aerial phenomenon, unexplained oceanic events, the discovery of structures and objects that didn't fit typically accepted archaeological theory and historical narrative."

"Like the unexplained disappearance of American citizens," Randall interjected, his eyes narrowing on the general.

"That's correct," Flores answered, closing his eyes.

"What does this all mean, Dad?"

"It means your father has been keeping a lot of information from you and your family," Randall replied.

Flores dipped his head and nodded. He raised his head and looked into his son's eyes.

"Dad, is this true? Exactly what's been going on?"

"When I was asked to head this task force, I had a lot of questions. The things I saw were beyond conventional explanation. At first, I didn't believe some of the things I heard and read, but eventually, I saw them with my own eyes. Once I was a part of the group, there was no leaving it."

Michael cocked his head to one side. "You were forced to stay?"

"Yes and no. I don't think they would have let me out, but once I knew what was happening, I felt I owed it to our family and our country to help. This became my responsibility. I couldn't just walk away."

The pain in Flores eyes was palpable. A pang of guilt struck Randall. "In fairness to your dad, I can relate to him. I kept secrets from my family for years. I thought I was doing the right thing and it cost me my wife and nearly destroyed my relationship with my daughter," Randall said, his voice trailing off.

An awkward silence fell over the room. Michael sat blinking and shaking his head.

"I'm sorry, son."

Michael looked at Randall, then at his father. A smile crept over his face. "I never thought I'd see the day when my own father would ask for my forgiveness. Okay, Dad, apology accepted, but I want to know everything. No more secrets."

The general nodded. "I'll tell you everything I'm allowed to share."

Randall cleared his throat. "Back to the Nazi base. What happens next? I'm sure you have heavy fire power stationed close by that can overwhelm the Nazis."

"Germany is a sovereign nation so ending a large contingent of American troops and equipment uninvited, isn't possible," Flores responded.

"Have you reached out to the German government and told them what's happening? I'm sure they wouldn't be happy about Nazis operating on their soil again," Randall said.

"This is a very delicate situation, one that our government doesn't necessarily want to disclose to other parties," Flores replied.

"You're not going tell the government of one of our closest allies what's going on in their backyard?" Randall asked.

"No. Aside from not wanting to disclose the situation, there's also no way of knowing if the Nazis have assets placed within the German government," Flores answered.

"What do we do?" Michael asked.

"We're prepared to send a covert extraction team to the facility, free the hostages, and destroy the weapon." Flores turned to Randall. "I don't suppose I could convince you not to join the exercise?"

"Not a chance. These maniacs have my daughter and there's no way I'm going to sit by and let someone else try to save her," Randall said, rising to his feet.

"I could simply deny you access to the mission."

"And I can go public with all I know about this and other operations within the government."

Flores held up his hands. "We've been down this road before. You'll go with the team."

"I'm going, too," Michael said.

Flores turned to look at his son. Upon seeing the expression on his face, he simply nodded. "You'll leave in an hour."

Chapter 36

Nazi Base, Germany
July 27, 6:59 p.m.

Sam once again found herself behind bars, having been escorted to a different part of the facility by Dr. Brauer and a Nazi guard. Although she was no longer with Grady, she had company. Sam found herself sharing a cell with three other women she had never met. Being the newest member of the group, she listened intently as each relayed their story. Each of the women had been abducted by the Nazis and brought to this facility. The Germans had never explained why they had been targeted, but in turn, each had been separated from the others and taken to another area of the facility for a short time.

"None of you remembers what happened after being taken to the waiting area?" Sam asked.

"That's right. They take you there, force you to sit alone in the room, then you lose consciousness. When you wake up, you're on a gurney in a recovery room, then you're escorted back here by two guards. Each time I've returned to the cell, the girls tell me I've been gone for a little over than 24 hours," Eileen Loughlan said. At 52 years old, she was the senior member of the group. Her short black hair sported streaks of silver, and she spoke with authority. "My guess is they pump some sort of sleeping gas into the room to subdue you, right before conducting experiments on you."

"The strange thing is, we never have scars when we come out," Julie Wolf, the second woman in the group, added.

"Julie's right, the only sign that something has happened is soreness in our abdomens," Eileen added.

"Margaret, have you experienced the same thing?" Sam asked the member of Grady's team.

Margaret nodded her agreement.

"Well, I don't know what they're doing, but I'm sure as hell not going to stick around to find out," Sam said, rising to her feet.

"What do you suggest we do?" Eileen asked.

Sam surveyed the room. "See that up there?" she motioned with her head toward a corner-mounted surveillance camera. "We're going to use that to get out of here."

"What do you mean?" Margaret asked, her eyes wide.

"You've each been taken multiple times, and come back in pain, right?" Sam asked.

Eileen nodded.

"If one of you is really hurting, do the guards come and check on you?" Sam asked.

"Sometimes they'll bring us a pain reliever, but that's about it," Eileen replied.

"It's almost like they're afraid to enter the cell. I don't know if it's because we're women or if they're worried about the types of test being conducted," Margaret added.

"Good, we'll use that. How many guards normally come?" Sam asked.

"Two. Always two," Eileen replied.

Sam turned to Julie. "You were the most recent one back there, right?"

Julie was on her bunk, rubbing her stomach. She nodded. "I

just got back an hour ago."

"You mentioned abdominal pain after the episodes. How bad does it hurt?" Sam asked.

"It depends. Mostly not too much, but there've been times I've just curled up in ball to ride it out," Julie replied.

"How do you feel right now?" Sam asked.

"It hurts, I won't lie, but not as bad as some of the times."

"What do you have in mind?" Eileen asked, drawing her hair back and securing it with a rubber band.

"They're watching us at all times, and we're going to use that to draw them out," Sam replied.

"How?" Eileen asked.

"Julie, we'll need you to pretend like you're in excruciating pain. The rest of us will act like we're really worried about you. We'll lure the guards in to check on you, then we'll jump them!"

Margaret rubbed her hands together. "Are you sure that's a good idea?"

"It's a bloody brilliant idea and we need to do it now!" Eileen shot Margaret a hard glare. Margaret turned away, looking down at her feet.

"Can they hear what we're saying?" Sam asked.

"No. There's been no indication they can hear us. They just have the video feed," Eileen answered.

"Julie, I want you to really sell the pain. Roll around and grab your stomach. Once we have the guards inside the cell, I want you to moan even more. Make them think there's something really wrong with you," Sam said.

"And while one of them checks on you, we'll jump the other guard and take him down. Then we'll take out the man checking on you," Eileen said, her hazel eyes wide with anticipation.

"Right! The key is going to be distracting them. Julie, you're going to have to really fool them. The minute the second guard is distracted, Eileen and I will take him out," Sam said.

"What about the guard checking Julie?" Margaret asked, clearly nervous.

"You're going after him. Just keep him from getting to his gun," Sam said.

"I don't know if I can," Margaret whispered.

"Yes, you can. I know you're afraid, but so am I. If we don't do this, those creeps will control our fates and I won't allow that," Sam said, lifting Margaret's chin so she could make eye contact. "You have to trust me."

"Okay."

"Let's do this. Julie, once I sit down, wait a minute then start," Sam said, taking a seat on the edge of a cot.

Julie rolled away from the camera, her back to the group. A moment later, she started softly moaning and rocking from side to side. The intensity of her movements slowly increased until she rolled into a fetal position, drawing her knees up toward her chin.

Eileen shot up from her bed and moved to Julie's side, stroking her head, a look of concern on her face.

"Sam, come over here," she said, speaking slowly, her eyes wide with fear for the sake of those monitoring the camera.

Sam darted up, quickly arriving by Eileen's side, while Margaret sat clutching her knees to her chest on the adjacent bed. Sam checked Julie, pressing her palm to her forehead. Sharing a scared look with Eileen, she moved to the edge of the cell, as close to the camera as possible.

"Hey, over here! We need help!" she yelled, waving dramatically at the camera. "She's sick. Help!" Sam motioned toward Julie. She waved again, then sprinted to Julie, who was now writhing as if in serious pain.

A few moments later, the door to the cell block burst open. "What's going on in here?"

"Something's wrong with our friend. It started a while ago, and it's getting worse! What did you animals do to her?" Sam yelled, turning to face the two guards. As she did, Julie let out a loud, painful yelp.

"It hurts, God it hurts! Make it stop!" Julie said, clutching her stomach.

The plan was working, the first guard grabbed his keys and unlocked the cell, entering the space while the other stood in the doorway.

"You two, move!" the first guard ordered. Sam and Eileen dutifully responded, moving away from Julie, near the entrance to the cell and closer to the second guard, who stared at Julie, hands clutching his assault rifle tightly.

The first guard moved next to Julie. He looked over her midsection, then tried to see her face. He placed his hand on her shoulder. Julie flinched, grabbing her midsection, and crying.

"What are you doing? You're hurting her!" Eileen wailed from the doorway.

"I'm just trying to help!" the first guard said, recoiling and running his fingers through his thinning hair.

Sam watched the second guard out of the corner of her eye. Younger than the first, his face was ashen, his grip on the gun loosening.

"Don't just sit there, do something!" Eileen cried out.

It took all Sam had to keep from smiling—Eileen's performance was Oscar worthy.

"Where's the pain?" the first guard asked.

"My stomach … it hurts so bad," Julie cried, sobbing loudly.

Come on Julie, one more time…

"Oh God! Make it stop!" Julie blurted, drawing the first guard closer to her. The second guard's grip had loosened to the point of nearly dropping his weapon.

"Now!" Sam yelled, throwing a vicious elbow into the younger guard's face, knocking his head backward into the metal bars. He dropped to the ground unconscious as Eileen scooped up his weapon.

The older guard froze, his eyes wide with surprise. He turned to face Sam and Eileen, his hand going to his holster. Julie jumped up from the bed, hopping onto his back, digging her nails into his face.

"Margaret!" Eileen yelled, causing her to pop up and lunge at the stunned guard, hitting him from the side. The guard and Julie tumbled to the ground. They hit the concrete floor, the guard's gun jarring loose and sliding toward the cell door.

Sam bent over and picked up the weapon. She cocked the hammer, walked over to the guard, and stood over him.

"Don't move, I know how to use this and won't think twice about putting a bullet in your head!" Sam said, towering over the injured guard. Streaks of blood trickled down his face, which was contorted with a mixture of anger and bewilderment.

"You bitches will pay for this!" he growled.

"Julie, get his keys and his cuffs," Sam said.

Julie obliged, bringing them to Sam. "Roll over!" Sam ordered.

The guard sneered but did as instructed.

"Hands behind your back. Do it!" Sam yelled. "Julie, cuff him."

"Let's get out of here," Sam said. The four women exited the cell, locking the door behind themselves. "We have to hurry they probably saw everything on the camera!"

Chapter 37

En Route to Nazi Base, Germany
July 27, 7:09 p.m.

Riding in the heavily upgraded, stealth-optimized MH-60 Blackhawk helicopter, Randall leaned forward in his seat to listen to their team leader, Captain Bill Eckert, provide last minute instructions. The chopper was a modified version of the radar-evading craft used in the Osama bin Laden raid and had been chosen for the operation to ensure that their journey through German airspace went unnoticed. The plan was simple: Randall, Michael and two Special Forces Operational Detachments, totaling 24 men, would be inserted into the Bavarian Forrest, near the suspected base. Two additional Blackhawks would wait nearby to provide additional cover fire and a quick evacuation if needed.

"Alpha team, you'll lead the assault into the farmhouse while Delta sets up a perimeter. Burke, DeGray, Fernandez, your job is to protect Randall and Flores when we land," Eckert pointed at the leaders of Alpha team, then pivoted back to Delta team. "Identify anyone who leaves the compound to determine if they're friendly or hostile. No one leaves without our knowing. Randall and Flores, you'll accompany the second wave of Alpha team, after

Franklin, Chung, and O'Brien sweep the building. Stay by Staff Sergeant Donaldson and he'll take care of you. Any questions?" Eckert asked, patting the mountain-sized Donaldson on the shoulder as he spoke. Eckert checked his watch. "ETA to LZ is three minutes."

The choppers buzzed the tree-tops, staying as low as possible to avoid detection. The whisper-quiet chopper blades cut through the air as the dense evergreen forest parted and their landing area came into view. The first Blackhawk softly touched down and the first wave of Delta team disembarked, fanning out to create a defensive perimeter around the clearing. Randall's chopper was next.

Randall jumped from the helicopter and landed with a soft thud onto the forest floor. The moment the last man jumped from the chopper, the pilot lifted off again, banking back and to the left, and disappearing. The raid had begun.

The smell of pine was thick and the cold morning air bit into the exposed flesh of Randall's face. He looked around and saw Michael standing next to Captain Eckert, who was waving him over to them. Randall jogged to the two men. They then fell into line, following the lead members of Alpha team, who moved silently through the dense forest, heading in the direction of the farmhouse.

Sunlight filtered through the foliage, creating a checkered pattern on the shapes of the men ahead of Randall. After a short time, Franklin signaled for the group to stop and drop. Crouching behind a tree trunk, Randall peered around the stump and noticed a road ahead in the distance. He immediately realized that it was the single road from the aerial photograph. They were close to the farmhouse.

The group moved in single file, parallel to the road, but far enough from it to be hidden from any vehicles traveling the highway. Before long, the edge of the tree line appeared and through a hazy view of staggered pines, Randall could make out the shape of a large structure. They had arrived.

Chung unpacked a suitcase-sized object, flipping the top open to reveal a complex piece of electronic equipment. He studied the computer screen, which showed multiple lines of data with a small green square on the side. Punching a sequence of keys, the color of the square turned to red.

"Electronic signals jammed, sir," Chung reported to Eckert, who nodded.

"Delta team, I want scopes and infrared on the farmhouse," Eckert whispered into his throat-mounted microphone, squatting down just inside the tree line. He waited a few minutes before getting a reply.

"Four hostiles spotted and neutralized on the perimeter. No thermal footprints inside the structure," Burke reported back.

"Roger, maintain perimeter. Alpha strike team, recon the structure," Eckert ordered. "Randall, once we secure the interior of the building, you'll join the second wave as they go in. Get ready."

Randall and Michael squatted next to Eckert waiting for the signal. Moments later, they received an update.

"Structure secured," O'Brien reported into Eckert's earpiece. He nodded.

"Alpha second wave, go!" Eckert ordered.

Randall and Michael followed Donaldson and his men into the farmhouse. Upon entering, Randall was surprised by what he found. The interior of the building was as different from the exterior as winter is from summer. The inside of the farmhouse was sleek and modern with painted concrete floors and stainless-steel storage cabinets. Banks of florescent lights lined the ceiling. Most were off, but the active units provided ample light to illuminate the large room. Four corner-mounted security cameras would normally provide a 360-degree view of the interior of the farmhouse, but Eckert's men had jammed the signal, allowing them to enter undetected. The only thing that wasn't immediately apparent was how the lower part of the facility was accessible.

Randall assessed the room, turning to take in the whole view. The wall perpendicular to the entrance of the farmhouse contained two large roll-up doors on tracks that fed into the ceiling. They were solid metal doors, made to look like wood slats laid end on end to match the rest of the exterior walls.

Michael pointed to O'Brien, who was examining the ground while Franklin searched the rest of the building. The concrete floor was separated into four large grids, one of which was directly in front of the roll-up doors. That segment was fifty feet wide by a hundred feet long with faint tire tracks spanning its length.

Franklin motioned for O'Brien to join him. O'Brien obliged jogging to his side. Franklin had found the control panel.

"It's an elevator pad for vehicles to access the lower level," Michael whispered into Randall's ear. A moment later, he heard a quiet whirring sound as the pad slowly sank into the ground. As it dropped down, a hidden recessed ladder came into view.

Franklin, O'Brien, and four additional Alpha team members climbed aboard the pad, fanning out to the perimeter, and dropping to the ground, weapons pointed outward. A hand patted Randall's shoulder. He looked up and saw Donaldson motioning for him to join the men on the pad.

Randall and Michael stepped onto the pad, joining the rest of Alpha team. They were soon joined by Chung, who sprinted into the facility and jumped on board as the platform descended. As they moved to the center of the slab, Donaldson pushed down on Randall's shoulder, forcing him into a squatting position. He then took a position directly next to Randall, serving as his personal bodyguard.

"Alpha team accessing lower levels," Donaldson whispered into his microphone.

"Aren't we a little exposed?" Randall asked the squad leader.

As he spoke, two soldiers dropped a large black bag by his side, unzipped it and extracted a tripod mounted machine gun.

With Swiss watch-like efficiency, they fed the chain mounted ammunition into the weapon and were ready.

"Never mind," Randall said.

The pad slowly dropped, ground level now several feet above their heads. A few minutes later, the concrete shaft gave way to open space as the pad reached the second level. O'Brien and Franklin, lying prone on the floor, scoped rifles aimed toward the opening, fired several rounds from their weapons. The pad continued to drop as wisps of smoke rose from the silencers of the discharged rifles.

The pad came to a stop, now on the second level. Three men lay dead on the ground, blood trickling from the bullet wounds in their heads and chests. Alpha team moved off the pad and onto the lower level, guns drawn.

They entered a long hallway that fed deep into the underground complex. The opening was a drab, grey rectangle, which slowly arced to the right. The floor of the tunnel resembled an asphalt street with a slashed line painted down the middle and two huge lanes on either side. The facility was clearly designed to handle large motorized vehicles.

Randall and Michael followed Donaldson and his team onto the second level. The soldiers moved in leapfrog fashion, the lead members moving forward then stopping and offering cover while the second group then took the lead. Randall marveled at their efficiency. He looked over at Michael, who now wore a serious look as he clutched his assault rifle.

Donaldson motioned for the team to stop and nodded to Chung, who looked through a scope at the open space in front of them. The soldier scanned the area, whispered into his sergeant's ear, and slowly moved forward with two other men. Donaldson then relayed the information to the remaining members of Alpha squad. "All clear."

A bank of ceiling-mounted lights lit their way as they

moved through the tunnel, hugging the wall that formed the inside part of the arc. Chung led the way, now ten yards ahead of the rest of the group. He stopped and stared at the wall, then spoke into his mic.

Once again, Randall felt a familiar tap on his shoulder. Looking up, he saw Donaldson motion for him to join Chung. Puzzled, Randall slowly made his way to the soldier's side. Once he arrived, he understood.

The soldier looked confused, staring at a sign posted on the wall of the tunnel. The writing was clearly unlike anything the man had ever seen before, but Randall recognized it from his previous operation with General Flores at a secret facility in Antarctica. His pulse quickened.

Randall removed his reading glasses from his pocket and studied the sign. It took him a few minutes, but he deciphered the cryptic message. He nodded to Chung and pointed at Donaldson. Chung nodded back.

Randall jogged to the sergeant whose head was cocked to one side.

"What does it say?" Donaldson asked.

"Low levels of radiation present. No safety gear required," Randall responded.

"How were you able to read it?"

"I've seen the language before."

Donaldson shot Randall an inquisitive look, to which Randall shrugged, his outer demeanor hiding the concern rising inside of him.

"Move forward," Donaldson ordered quietly.

The team moved deeper into the complex. A metal door, inset into the left-hand side of the wall, came into view. Chung and Franklin took crouching positions facing the door, while Donaldson stood directly in front of it. Donaldson counted down from three using his fingers. When he hit two, the door swung inward and a younger Nazi rushed out through the door, angrily rubbing the back of his head. He stopped suddenly upon seeing

Alpha team, then his eyes went wide.

Franklin popped to his feet, covered the Nazi's mouth, and slammed him against the wall. "Where are you holding the hostages?"

The Nazi's eyes darted around the hallway, a look of despair growing as he spied the members of Alpha team.

"I asked you where you're holding the hostages. I'm going to remove my hand from your mouth and you're going to quietly answer me, otherwise I'll add some ventilation just below your chin," Franklin removed his serrated combat knife from its sheath and placed it on the Nazi's throat. Sweat ran from the Nazi's brow. "Do I make myself clear?"

The Nazi nodded his head quickly. "The female prisoners escaped. We don't know where they are," the Nazi gasped.

"What about the others?"

"Others?" the Nazi asked.

"Don't fuck with me!" Franklin snarled, pressing his blade against the Nazi's throat.

The Nazi blinked. "They're a level down in our main holding area. This is a secondary containment unit we use to hold our experimental subjects…" The Nazi's voice trailed off.

Franklin's eyes narrowed. "What do you mean, experimental subjects?"

The Nazi hesitated.

"Spit it out!" Franklin said, now pressing his forearm into the Nazi's chest, compressing his body against the wall.

"Several of the women. We need them for experiments," the Nazi stammered.

Randall pushed by Franklin, bringing his face within inches of the Nazi's. "One of the women you're holding is an archaeologist, five-foot five inches, dark brown hair. Where is she?" He squeezed the Nazi's face between his thumb and forefinger.

The Nazi blinked repeatedly, the sweat now coming in sheets down his face.

"Where is she!?!" Randall yelled, shaking the Nazi's face.

"She's one of the women who escaped," the Nazi answered.

Donaldson pushed past Randall and pointed a finger at the Nazi. "You're coming with us. Franklin, get the layout of the facility from him and location of guards and surveillance cameras. Then you and O'Brien, make sure that room's clear. Randall, I need to speak with you,"

Donaldson grabbed Randall's shoulder and steered him away from the Nazi. "I know you're worried about your daughter, but we'll find her. Right now, we need to interrogate him and get as much information as possible. That's our best chance of rescuing everyone and finding that stone."

Randall's body shook, the adrenaline coursing through his veins. He struggled to contain his anger and fear. The thought of Sam suffering at the hands of the group that produced the likes of Dr. Mengele, and his horrific human experimentation, was almost too much to bear.

"Professor, are you with me?" Donaldson asked.

The haze slowly parted from Randall and he turned to look at the sergeant. "You're right, let's see what information we can get."

Randall and Donaldson made their way to the soldiers interrogating the Nazi. A moment later, Franklin and O'Brien returned with another Nazi in handcuffs.

"We found him cuffed in the cell. Apparently these two were sent to check on four female prisoners in the block, one of whom appeared to be suffering abdominal pains," O'Brien reported, nodding toward the first Nazi the group had found.

"What else did you find out?" Donaldson asked.

"This is a tri-level facility, topside is the entry, this second level is where genetics and biological research is conducted, and the third level is a testing platform for die Glocke. The main cell block is also located on level 3. That's where Dr. Grady and the other team members are being held. We also know all access points for the three levels," Franklin replied.

"Do we know what kind of biological testing is being conducted?" Donaldson asked.

"Negative, sir. This man is just a grunt. He knows basic information about the facility and prisoners, but little more," Franklin answered.

The older Nazi appeared totally defeated, his arms zip-tied behind his back.

O'Brien pointed his assault rifle at the Nazis. "What do you want to do with these two, Sergeant?"

"Take them topside. Captain wants us to extract them to Ramstein for a full debrief. The rest of the team will continue down to level 3. Remember, our primary mission is the safe recovery of the prisoners and securing the stone," Donaldson said.

Two members of Alpha team escorted the prisoners to ground level, and the rest of the group, made their way to level 3. Utilizing the information provided by the Nazis, the team split into two units. The first took the stairwell at the end of level 2, while the second took the maintenance access near the vehicle pad.

Donaldson had expressed surprise at the lack of resistance they had encountered thus far, but their prisoners provided the reason. The Nazis were in the final testing phase of the Bell and were enjoying the fruits of their labor at a celebration near the testing area.

Randall's group hustled down the stairwell by the vehicle pad they had taken from the surface. If their prisoners were correct, this would put them close to the main cell block. Their job was to rescue the research team being held captive and get them back to the surface. Randall hoped beyond hope that he would find Sam there since they had not seen any of the four women who had escaped from level 2.

213

The team approached the final landing that lead to the door onto level 3. O'Brien and Franklin took crouching positions covering the opening, and Chung checked the door and found it unlocked. Randall stood several steps up from the landing, waiting for the area to be cleared.

Chung nodded, then peeled the door back and the two crouching men sprung through the opening, guns first. Short bursts of gunfire erupted and then ended. The rest of the team followed through with Randall bringing up the rear. As they emerged, they found the bodies of three Nazis lying on the floor.

"Sir, two hostiles escaped. They headed down the corridor toward the testing area," Chung reported to Donaldson.

"They'll form up with their team soon, we can expect heavy resistance." Donaldson motioned to his communications specialist. "Let the other squad know we've been discovered." He turned to the rest of his team. "Set up the SAWs ten yards ahead of the cell entrance. We'll need cover fire to free the prisoners. The rest of you, follow me."

Two members of Alpha team sprinted down the hallway with their machine guns while the remainder of the team made their way to a metal door inset into the wall. If their Nazi prisoners had been truthful, this would be the cell block where the others were being held. Unfortunately, the element of surprise was gone.

O'Brien and Franklin took their positions outside the cell door, while Chung removed a tactical battering ram from his gear bag.

"Breach the door on my mark," Donaldson said. Everyone took their positions. Donaldson nodded, then Chung reared back and drove the ram into the door which popped open. O'Brien and Franklin immediately entered the breach, disappearing from the view.

A torrent of gunfire erupted from the other side of the door. Donaldson ordered two additional team members to enter. The shooting subsided, turning into an occasional burst, before stopping entirely.

"Area's secure," Chung reported.

The rest of the group entered the cell.

Randall stared around the space, shocked by the size of the block. Near the door, Franklin tended to an injured comrade. Farther in, O'Brien's lifeless body lay on the ground near two dead Nazis. Locked in two separate cells were over a dozen people … but he didn't see Sam.

"Nick! Over here!" A voice called out, drawing Randall's attention. It was Grady.

Chung was already at the cell door, opening the lock. Randall walked over to Grady, noticing for the first time that two people in the jail cell were injured, apparently struck by stray bullets. One was holding her arm, the other, his thigh. Franklin, having finished assisting his injured team member, was now tending to them.

"Thank God you came. I'm not sure what would have happened if you hadn't," Grady said, extending his hand.

Randall shook it but didn't smile. "Do you know where Sam is?"

The expression on the younger professor's face changed, providing his answer before he spoke. "I'm sorry."

Donaldson jogged to Randall, having determined that the injuries to the freed prisoners weren't serious. "Dr. Randall, we need to get these folks out of here ASAP. The Nazis know we're here, so every second counts."

Almost as if on cue, the staccato sound of machine gun fire erupted down the hall of the complex. It was immediately followed by the sound of multiple weapons returning fire. The Nazis were on their way.

"Chung, Franklin take point. The rest of you, follow my men out of the cell. Stay close to the wall and get ready to drop on my order," Donaldson barked to the group. "Let's move!"

Chung and Franklin led the group through the door and

back into the passageway. Bullets ricocheted through the tunnel, spraying sparks, and bits of concrete into the air. The two soldiers sprinted back toward the stairwell while the others followed, their progress slowed by their injured comrades and carrying Obrien's body.

Randall and Grady were next to last to exit the cellblock as Donaldson covered their retreat.

As he exited the door, instead of following the others, Randall turned in the direction of the firefight raging deeper inside the facility. Grady stayed by his side.

"What the hell are you doing?" Donaldson yelled.

Randall stopped. "I'm not leaving without my daughter! I know you have your job to do, but so do I!"

"You're going to get yourself killed!" Donaldson bellowed.

"Sir, we're at the exit point topside," Chung radioed.

"Exit the facility now!" Donaldson growled into his microphone.

"Sir, what about the rest of the team?" Chung replied.

"I gave you an order. Move out!"

"Affirmative," Chung replied.

"Here, take these," Donaldson said to Randall and Grady, giving each man a sidearm. "Had any training?"

"ROTC and hunting with my dad," Randall said, taking the gun.

"Good, because I can't guarantee your safety and you have to be ready to use them."

Randall turned to Grady. "I appreciate what you're doing, but you don't have to come. In fact, I'd feel better if you left with the others."

"Nothing doing. I dragged you and Sam into this mess, and I'll be damned if I'm going to abandon you now," Grady replied.

"I'd suggest less talking and more paying attention to the situation before you both get your asses shot off and mine chewed out. Follow me!" Donaldson barked as he made his way down to the members of Alpha team manning the machine guns. They weren't far, having set their position around a bend in the tunnel.

As the group turned the corner, the grim situation became apparent. One of the two members of Alpha team lay on the ground with his back propped against the wall, firing his service weapon while the other manned his SAW. Both sported wounds and were pinned down, doing everything possible to repel the enemy.

Randall counted five Nazis returning fire on Alpha team with assault rifles. A moment later, two others came into view. Alpha team was badly outnumbered. Randall heard a loud blast directly behind him and watched one of the Nazis fall to the ground, a large blood splatter on the wall behind him. A second later, another loud clap was followed by a second Nazi reeling backward into the wall, his limp body dragging to the ground, leaving a bloody streak on the concrete behind him.

Mouth agape, Randall spun in time to see Donaldson taking aim on another Nazi. This time, however, the enemy turned to face the new threat.

"Get down!" Donaldson yelled, grabbing Randall by the shirt, and dragging him to the ground next to him. Grady had already dropped to the floor.

Several rounds whizzed over Randall's head, narrowly missing him, careening into the tunnel beyond.

Another short burst of cracking sounds announced Donaldson returning fire with his assault rifle. A third Nazi fell to the ground as the Sergeant proved to be a one-man killing machine. Randall and Grady opened fire as well, adding to the mayhem taking place in the constricted passageway. The distraction proved fatal for the Nazis as the Alpha team member manning the machine gun poured a steady stream of munitions directly at them.

A fourth Nazi dropped to the ground and the remaining men retreated.

"You two wait here," Donaldson ordered.

The Sergeant made his way over to his men. Randall's ears

rang from the harsh, repeated sound of gunfire, bringing back memories of his days on the firing range. Donaldson checked his machine gunner. The soldier nodded, communicating that he could still provide cover fire. Donaldson then aided the injured man on the ground. Helping him to his feet, he wrapped the injured soldier's arm over his shoulders and helped him walk back toward Randall and Grady.

"Sorry Randall, but we can't go that way. In a few minutes, this place will be crawling with Nazis. We need to get out of here," Donaldson announced. "We still have the other team and they may have found your daughter. We'll go back up to the second level rally point and check with them. It's our best chance."

Randall glanced down the passageway where the Nazis had retreated. His heart sank in his chest, but he knew Donaldson was right. He nodded his agreement and had to hope that the other squad had found Sam.

Chapter 38

Sam, Margaret, Julie, and Eileen continued their escape plan. They snaked their way along the tunnel of the Nazi facility, heading in the same direction they had been led when they were first brought to level 2. The other women, having been held at the facility for an extended period-of-time, realized that the testing facility lay in the opposite direction. As they reached the staircase that led up to the first level and freedom, Sam stopped, letting the others move past her. As Eileen opened the door, she turned to look at Sam, who stared back at her.

"What's going on?" Eileen asked.

"I'm not going with you," Sam replied.

"What do you mean?"

"I can't let them launch this weapon. If they do, God only knows what kind of trouble they'll cause. Thousands of lives could be in danger," Sam answered.

"Sam, I know you mean well, but what can one woman do against a Nazi army? Please don't take this as a slight, because even a group of well-trained soldiers couldn't stop them. I think our best bet is to get up to the surface and contact the authorities," Eileen replied in a motherly tone.

"You're right. That's why I want the three of you to go up and do exactly that. Find a way to contact the police or the military and get help as quickly as possible."

"You can't be serious," Margaret said, joining the others.

219

Sam smiled. "I've been in tough situations before. I'll be fine."

Eileen studied Sam carefully then finally broke the silence. "If you're staying, then I'm staying."

"You two are nuts!" Margaret cried, throwing her arms in the air, and pacing around.

"I'll stay, too," Julie said, nodding and folding her arms for emphasis. "These guys deserve a little payback for what they've done to us."

Margaret's mouth hung open, her gaze shifting between the other three. After several moments, she took a deep breath, closing her eyes as she gathered herself.

"Margaret, you don't have to come with us. You can go for help. In fact, it might be a good idea if you did," Eileen said.

"Are you crazy? I'm not going by myself! I have no idea where we are or what I'll run into!"

"Then it's settled. We'll all stick together," Sam said.

"What do we do next?" Eileen asked.

"First we need to find a radio or some other way to try and call for help. Then we need to find where they're testing the weapon and see if we can get the stone back or at least find a way to slow down their progress," Sam said.

The four women headed deeper into the facility. They quickly passed the entrance to their former cell, heading into unchartered territory. The further they went, the more doors they encountered and the higher the risk of being caught.

They passed a room with a small window and Sam peeked through the corner of the glass. Several small tables sat neatly arranged on the floor and lockers lined the far wall. In the corner, she noticed a flat screen TV angled in such a way that she could tell it was on but couldn't tell what was showing.

A pounding sound came from across the hall. Sam snapped her head around just in time to see a door opening.

"In here!" she whispered, grabbing Julie and Margaret by the arms, and hauling them into the room. "Come on, Eileen!"

Eileen paused, staring at the opening door. She realized what was happening and bolted toward Sam. The four women crashed through the door, which swung shut behind them.

Sam—still holding Julie and Margaret's arms—found herself face to face with a young man standing by one of the lockers. He stared at Sam, frozen in surprise, one arm in a white lab coat, the other bent behind his body, ready to slide into the second sleeve.

Sam released her friends and removed the pistol from her waistband. She poked it into the stunned man's face. "Take off your lab coat."

Chapter 39

Alpha team returned to level 2 and found Franklin, Burke, DeGray and Fernandez waiting for them near the top of the stairs. Michael was with them, keeping a watchful eye on the corridor that led into the main part of the facility.

"Where are the others?" Donaldson asked, leaning the injured soldier against the wall.

"All of the prisoners are topside, sir. Chung escorted them up the main pad and back out about fifteen minutes ago. We were a little worried when we didn't see any of you come up after us," Franklin answered.

"Have you heard from the other squad?"

"Affirmative. They located the testing area and, just as our Nazi friends reported, the whole facility is down there celebrating."

"I'm not so sure that's the case anymore," Grady said.

"Did they see the missing women?" Randall asked.

"Negative. They conducted an initial recon of the area and sent two soldiers back to report in. The rest of the team remained in place. Sorry, Professor," Franklin answered.

Randall's heart sank at the news.

"You say they found the testing area, but did they see the weapon?" Donaldson asked.

Franklin nodded. "The weapon's there and the Nazis were

preparing to test it. An older man was giving a rah-rah speech to the troops, getting them pumped up. For all I know, they could have already tested it by now."

"We'll have to hope they haven't. If we're not able to get the stone, we'll have to resort to plan B," Donaldson announced.

"Hold on. What's plan B?" Randall asked.

Donaldson set his jaw. "In the event we're not able to retrieve the stone, we were ordered to destroy it and the weapon as well."

"You son of a bitch! When were you planning to tell us?" Grady yelled, stepping up to Donaldson and bumping him. The Sergeant stood his ground, not giving in to emotion.

"I understand how you feel, Professor, but we cannot allow the Nazis to successfully test and launch this weapon. We don't want to destroy it, but if we can't retrieve the Devil's Heart it's our only viable option.," Donaldson said in an even tone.

"This doesn't bother you?" Grady asked, turning to face Randall.

"Let's just say I've been here before with General Flores," Randall replied.

Michael winced at the reference to his father.

Randall turned to Donaldson. "You realize that the fallout from the detonation could very well bring down this facility? At the very least, the radioactive contamination will kill everyone in this place, not to mention every living thing for several square miles in any direction."

"That's why we've ordered the evacuation of all non-military personnel. Once Chung got the prisoners topside, he called in the choppers to evac them out. We have an additional one waiting to evacuate you two as well," Donaldson replied.

"Forget it! I'm not leaving without Sam," Randall said, shaking his head vigorously.

"That's what I thought you'd say. Okay, you can come with

us, but if we're not able to retrieve the stone, you know what we need to do," Donaldson locked eyes with Randall. "And I won't tolerate anyone getting in the way of our mission."

Chapter 40

Wearing lab coats found in the staff lounge, Sam and the other three women walked through the facility feeling less conspicuous. Although she didn't want to, Sam had been forced to tape the young lab assistant's mouth shut with duct tape and tie his hands behind his back before forcing him into a locker.

While searching the staff lounge, three of the four women had also found personnel badges, adding further legitimacy to their disguises. Only Julie had failed to procure one, so she walked behind the others. To finish out their costumes, each also carried clipboards or manuals acquired from the break room.

As they progressed into the facility, the long arcing tunnel opened into a much wider area. Banks of ceiling-mounted Mercury Vapor lights illuminated the cavernous room, creating the appearance of daylight. The path they followed now sloped downward into a massive, circular area with a small elevated platform spanning the outer perimeter. Staggered at regular intervals were large concrete columns that rose from the floor of the elevated platform to the top of the facility. Sam estimated that the height of the building—from the floor of the lower arc to the steel reinforced ceiling—was easily 50 feet, and its diameter at least 200 feet. The enormity of the underground complex was staggering.

Sam scanned the area, quickly understanding why the rest of the facility had been largely empty. Hundreds of people filled the platform and floor of the structure. Large, wall-mounted monitors captured the scene from a dizzying array of angles, showing videos of the construction and development of the weapon.

Despite the awe-inspiring size of the complex and the sheer number of people present, Sam's attention was immediately drawn to the center of the lowered floor. There, sitting on its own elevated platform was the device for which the structure had been built. With one look, Sam understood where it had gotten the nickname the Bell.

The craft was pear shaped, the top rounded and smooth, converging on a smaller rounded structure sitting on its top. Small, square windows formed a ring just below the upper dome. The sides of the vessel flared outward several feet above the ground, forming a skirt, which then turned ninety degrees down, creating a two-foot-wide flat band around the craft, which then curved back under, completing the bell shape.

More ominous still was the flat black matte finish of the weapon, which sported a large swastika embossed on the side facing the main floor. Sam estimated that the craft was approximately fifteen feet tall by eight feet wide.

As the women drew closer, Sam spotted two technicians standing over a control panel with a video monitor. Overhearing their conversation, Sam realized that they were monitoring the weapon systems in anticipation of the test run. Standing directly behind them and keeping close watch was the now familiar face of Dr. Vogel. Sam involuntarily clenched her fists, remembering how he had betrayed them.

A hand gripped the back of her arm and Sam felt the unmistakable sensation of a gun being pressed into the small of her back. She turned her head to see Colonel Herrman's smirking face.

"Fräulein Randall, how kind of you to join us."

Chapter 41

Randall and his group made their way down the spiral flight of stairs, finally arriving at a small landing in front of a solid metal door. Randall took a position at the rear of the group while Franklin got into position, ready to jump into the breach if the Nazis were on the other side. Donaldson tested the handle and found it locked. He signaled for Burke, who would serve as the breacher. Burke removed a handheld battering ram from his bag and took a position near the door. Donaldson trained his assault weapon on the door and signaled for Burke to go. Burke unleashed a brutal strike with the battering ram, caving in the door near the locking mechanism and causing the door to swing open. Donaldson and Franklin stepped through the opening then stopped and lowered their weapons.

Randall peered around the soldiers then understood their odd reaction. Directly in front of them was the Nazi superweapon sitting on an elevated platform. The passage had taken them to a point directly behind the Bell.

Donaldson motioned to his men, and DeGray and Fernandez moved through the door and into the staging area. As the team fed through the doorway, they were amazed at the level of commotion. An amplified voice roared over the loudspeakers about the greatness of the Third Reich and how they had reached their crowning achievement. The voice then spoke about crushing the enemies of the Fatherland, like the prisoners found in the facility today.

Randall and Michael shared a look. The Bell blocked their view of what was happening but also hid them from the Nazis. A huge ventilation shaft in the wall behind them spewed cold air into the area as they crouched behind the superweapon, peering around it to see what was transpiring.

Hundreds of people filled the facility, their attention riveted to several massive wall-mounted video screens. As he looked up at one of the monitors, Randall's blood ran cold. Four women in white lab coats were being held at gunpoint by the Nazis, standing to the side of a man speaking at a podium. He immediately recognized Dr. Vogel as the speaker. Worse still, he recognized one of the prisoners. Sam.

"These treacherous women are part of a plot to thwart our efforts to return Germany to its greatness! As they will learn, enemies of the state will feel our wrath as we once again exert our Aryan right to lead the world!" Vogel cast a disparaging glare at Sam and the others as the crowd roared in response.

Randall turned to look at Donaldson, who had ordered his men to begin searching for access into the Bell. Randall crept next to him. "What are we going to do?"

Donaldson's look provided the answer.

"I'm not going to let them kill my daughter and those other women," Randall poked his index finger at Donaldson.

"Once we get the stone, we'll find a way to rescue them," Donaldson responded.

"Not good enough," Randall lowered his finger and cocked the hammer of his Glock.

"Randall, don't!"

Randall popped up from behind the Bell. "Sam! Get down!"

The entire facility turned to face him as he fired round after round at the podium. Caught off guard, Vogel dove for cover. The Nazis guarding Sam and the others raced toward Randall, returning fire.

Randall dove back behind the Bell as a volley of gunfire ripped past him. Bullets glanced off the Nazi superweapon and the ground, striking the surrounding concrete walls. A shower of debris and sparks rained down like fireflies dancing on a foggy night.

"Goddammit! Are you crazy?" Donaldson glared at Randall. He turned to his men, "Return fire!"

Donaldson's men opened fire on the Germans, causing lab personnel to scream and duck for cover.

"Hit them with the grenade launcher! No rounds near the podium!" Donaldson ordered.

Heeding his commander's orders, Robinson fired three 40-millimeter grenades in rapid succession from his M32, semi-automatic grenade launcher. The ensuing explosions rocked the facility, sending debris and bodies cartwheeling into the air. All-out panic followed as non-military personnel streamed out of the area seeking shelter.

The Nazis, limited in their ability to fire heavy weapons for fear of damaging the Bell, continued raining rounds on Randall's group.

"We're pinned down. We need to move to higher ground to take out their position," Donaldson said.

"Sir, there's an access point there," Robinson pointed to a vertical groove cut into a section of wall that ran from the floor to the observation deck, ringing the area around them. Metal rebar steps were spaced two feet apart in the groove, creating a built-in ladder. The ladder was partially blocked from the Nazis' view by the Bell, but above it was a clear stretch spanning about eight feet to the upper level.

Donaldson tapped Enriquez shoulder. "Enriquez take Robinson with you and get up to that platform and take out their positions with the grenade launcher," Donaldson indicated the three major pockets of Nazi shooters. "We'll give you cover fire on my mark."

Donaldson informed each team member of their plan. Each man would rotate shooting to create a steady cover fire while Enriquez and Robinson climbed to the upper level.

"Now!" Donaldson reached around the Bell and fired concentrated bursts while DeGray did the same from the other side of the superweapon.

The two soldiers began their ascent, climbing as quickly as possible. Offered some protection by the superweapon and the cover fire of their squad, they climbed higher. Enriquez finally reached the open gap for the final leg to the top.

The Nazis, having to take cover from the rounds fired by Donaldson's team, couldn't get a bead on the ladder. Their shots bounced off the Bell, striking harmlessly to the side of Robinson and Enriquez. Unfortunately, as the soldiers climbed higher, they became easier targets for the Germans.

Both men were now in the open space, Enriquez four feet from the upper level. Robinson trailed about a foot below. The Nazi shooting was less frequent, but the shots were landing closer to the ladder. A step away from the upper level, Enriquez's right shoulder burst open in a bloody explosion as a high-powered rifle round dug into his upper back. His hand flew off the rung.

He grasped desperately at the rung with his shattered arm. Another shot and his left leg slammed into the concrete wall. The lead slug entered the back of his calf and exploded out the front causing Enriquez to teeter on the metal step.

Another round ripped into his left arm and he fell from the wall, unable to grip the metal rebar. His body tumbled down, over Robinson who reached out to try and save his friend. Robinson grabbed a piece of his shirt, but the force of gravity was too much. Enriquez tumbled past him; his uniform ripped from Robinson's grasp. The soldier dropped to the ground, crashing against the concrete floor.

"Shit!" Donaldson yelled.

Robinson paused on the ladder. The Nazis now had only one target left. He started back up the ladder as bullets slammed the wall all around him.

"Come on Robinson, get your ass up there!" Donaldson yelled.

Randall picked up an assault rifle and turned to Donaldson, interrupting him before he had a chance to give further commands. "I have an idea, but I need you to cover me!" Donaldson arched an eyebrow.

Randall sprinted around the corner of the Bell into full view. He fired his weapon on full auto, yelling as he ran. The gunfire around Robinson stopped as the Nazis focused their fire on the shrieking target below.

The distraction allowed Robinson to finish his climb. He scrambled over the concrete lip to the observation level, dropping onto the other side.

Randall completed his mad rush, finally arriving on the back side of the Bell, collapsing to the ground in exhaustion.

"You're one crazy son of a bitch," Donaldson helped Randall to his feet.

"Are you okay?" Michael asked, shaking his head and grinning.

"I think so. Did Robinson make it up?" Randall asked, still bent over trying to suck in as much air as possible. Sweat streamed down his face and his hands shook noticeably.

"Yea, he's up there," Donaldson pointed to the upper level. A moment later, they heard a loud explosion, followed by another near the Nazi's main position. Almost in unison, they peered around the Bell, realizing that the onslaught of gunfire had subsided.

From a prone position on the observation level, Robinson fired round after round of grenades at the Nazis, sending debris and bodies flying into the air. The assault caused the remaining German force to retreat deeper into the facility. Sensing the opportunity, Donaldson and his men pushed forward, leaving the cover of the

Bell, and taking control of the entire circular test area.

Randall searched for signs of Sam. He spotted a woman with long black hair wearing a white lab coated. She turned. It wasn't Sam. He cursed.

"I need to look for my daughter," Randall yelled into Donaldson's ear.

"You need someone to go with you, these Nazis aren't giving up the fight," Donaldson replied as return fire whizzed over their heads as if to emphasize the point.

"I'll go with him," Grady said, joining the two men squatting behind work crates.

"Cease fire!" a voice called out in a heavy German accent. The shooting from the Nazis stopped immediately.

"Hold you fire, men," Donaldson ordered, searching for the source of the order from his Nazi counterpart.

A gray-haired man, dressed in suit pants and a blue shirt with rolled up sleeves, came into view, clutching a woman's arm with one hand and holding a Glock to her head with the other. Randall immediately recognized them both. Vogel was holding Sam hostage.

"You will move away from the device or Fräulein Randall will meet a tragic end," Vogel said, a stern look on his face.

"We can't do that," Donaldson yelled back.

Vogel forced Sam down a flight of stairs, using her as a human shield. He pressed the barrel of his gun against Sam's head even harder. "Do not test me."

"Sergeant, for God's sake, he's going to kill my daughter. Let him have the damn device!" Randall said.

Donaldson's eyes narrowed as he aimed his weapon at Vogel, unable to get a clear shot. "The clock is ticking," Vogel hissed.

"Please, let him take the damn thing. It's not worth Sam's life," Randall pleaded.

Donaldson whispered to his men. "If you get a clear shot take it."

Sam and Vogel reached the bottom of the staircase and stopped. They were twenty feet from the Bell. Vogel cocked the hammer of the gun. "Move now!"

Donaldson grunted; gun still pointed at Vogel.

Vogel shoved Sam toward the Bell.

Vogel strode to the Bell, keeping Sam between himself and Donaldson's men.

"It'll be okay," Randall said to Sam as they drew near.

"I can't let him take it," Donaldson leveled his assault rifle directly at Sam.

Randall reached out. "No!"

A shot echoed from above, a bullet striking Donaldson's left shoulder, jerking him slightly to one side. He fired, narrowly missing Sam and Vogel.

Randall dashed between Donaldson's men and Sam. "Hold your fire! Hold your fire!"

Before anyone could respond, Vogel shoved Sam to the device then hit a hidden button on the black matte metal. A door hissed open, revealing the inside of the craft. He stepped into the interior, still holding Sam's arm, and keeping her between the soldiers and himself. He released Sam's arm, but kept his pistol to her head.

"Let her go," Randall said.

A sickening smile spread across Vogel's face. "Let her go? I have no intention of letting your daughter go." Vogel dragged Sam into the craft.

"Wait, no!" Randall yelled, sprinting for the door.

"Auf Wiedersehen Professor," Vogel pressed a button inside the vessel and the door slid shut.

Randall pounded on the side of the Bell yelling for Vogel to let Sam out. The overhead lights dimmed, and a loud buzzer boomed through the cavernous opening, pulsating to the beat of the strobe lights that sprang to life. Tall, tapered slots, running from the ceiling to the ground, popped open as thick metal doors crept along tracks in the floor, slowly cutting off the vessel from the rest of the complex.

The noise and lights created a dizzying din, only adding to the sense of confusion. Oblivious to the lights and sounds, Randall continued beating on the exterior of the craft, screaming for Vogel to release Sam. A red pulsating light beamed from the windows at the top of the ship, starting on one side and circling the vessel, faster and faster. The craft began to vibrate and hum, ratcheting up the anxiety in Randall. His hands ached from beating on the metal walls of the vessel. He punched, kicked, and slapped at the Bell, cursing Vogel, and calling for Sam, his voice growing hoarse.

He felt something heavy drop onto each shoulder, clamping down like metal vices, followed by the sensation of being dragged backward. Randall struggled to get free, now punching the meaty hands pulling him away from the ship … and Sam.

Despite his protests, he was forced away from the Bell. He looked backward. It was Donaldson and Burke. The world moved in slow motion. He looked from one man to the other, then to the blinking strobe lights and encroaching metal blast doors. One word came to mind. *Nightmare*. Only this wasn't a bad dream. It was reality.

Randall watched hopelessly as Donaldson and Burke dragged him out of the Bell's containment area and up the ramp while the blast doors closed around the craft. The humming reached a near deafening pitch, causing Donaldson and Burke to release Randall and cover their ears.

The hum sounded like a high-pitched dog whistle. It pierced Randall's skull, causing his teeth to clatter. Just as the humming reached its crescendo, the metal blast doors turned translucent, showing the outline of the vessel inside. A moment later, the sound was gone, and so were the Bell and Sam.

Chapter 42

Randall sat on the cold concrete floor, blinking, and staring at the metal doors.

"What the hell just happened?" Robinson asked from behind him.

"I think it worked and I think we're screwed," Michael answered.

Randall looked back to see Michael and Robinson standing side by side, looking at the blast doors, shaking their heads. The fog in his mind parted. He jumped to his feet and bolted for a small office to the side of the main floor. A shadow in the window darted away as he approached.

Randall reached for the doorknob. It was locked. He walked over to a dead Nazi lying on the floor, pried a Glock from his hand, and walked back to the office door. He fired round after round, nearly emptying the magazine into the lock, which disintegrated under the barrage. He kicked the door open and entered the room, scanning the floor from side to side. The force of his kick slammed the door shut behind him. On the far side of the room, a man cowered in the corner, shielding his eyes from Randall who walked up to him.

Lifting his chin with his left hand, Randall immediately recognized the face. It was Herrmann. Randall pointed the Glock at his forehead.

"Where did he take her?" Randall's gaze bored through the man.

"I … I don't know," Herrmann replied.

Randall cocked the hammer of the gun. "You're either going to tell me, or I'm going to put a bullet through your skull."

"I swear, I don't know where Vogel has taken her. Please, you must believe me," Herrmann said, his eyes wide and his voice quivering.

Randall grabbed the man's face, gripping it tightly between his thumb and index finger. "I'm going to give you one last chance. Where did Vogel take my daughter?" He growled.

The door burst open behind them and Robinson hustled into the room. "We have to go. The Nazis are coming and this time there's dozens of them!"

"Get up!" Randall ordered, grabbing Herrmann under the arm, and dragging him to his feet. "Move!" He shoved him toward the door, following close behind. The two brushed past Robinson who backed away, clearly sensing that Randall meant business.

"Randall, over here!" Donaldson called.

Randall shoved Herrmann in the back roughly, letting him know he needed to move in Donaldson's direction. He noticed a red splotch on the sergeant's shoulder where the bullet hit.

"You okay?" Randall asked.

Donaldson gave a curt nod. "I had my men scout ahead. There's a platoon of Nazis on the way."

Randall's mind flashed back to his time in the service. It took a moment but then he recalled that meant as many as forty men.

"We need to find a way out of here," Donaldson answered.

"We can use the staircase we came down," Randall said.

Donaldson shook his head. "Now that they know we're here they'll seal off that end. We don't have enough fire power to get through."

"Ask him if there are other exits," Randall said, motioning to Herrmann with his gun.

"Where are the exits at this end of the facility?" Donaldson asked the Nazi.

Herrmann just stared back blankly.

Donaldson's voice rose. "Did you hear me? I asked how we can get out of this facility."

"There are only two ways out, through the stairwell and that way," Herrmann replied grudgingly, pointing in the direction of the incoming Nazis. "The stairwell doors automatically lock when die Glocke is activated. They must be reset from above.

"Then it sounds like we're going to have to take our chances and go with the stairwell, but we need to open the blast shield to access it," Donaldson responded.

"How do we do that?" Randall asked.

"The shield's too thick for a breaching charge," Donaldson pointed a finger at Herrmann's nose. "How do we open the blast shield?"

Herrmann shook his head. "I don't know how."

"What do you mean you don't know how? Who the hell does?" Donaldson growled.

"What purpose do the blast doors serve?" Randall asked.

"They close when die Glocke is activated to shield us from the radiation generated by its propulsion system. Our ventilation system absorbs the radiation then pumps out the contaminated air and circulates fresh air into the chamber."

Randall shifted his stance. "How long does the system take to purge the radiation?"

"We've never used the system, but the doors stay closed until the radiation reaches a safe level."

"How long is that?" Randall asked.

"I don't know," Hermann responded.

"How much radiation is produced?" Randall continued, a solution forming in his mind.

Hermann stiffened. "I won't tell you."

Donaldson grabbed the Nazi by the throat and started to squeeze. "You'll answer the man's question, or I'll crush your windpipe," he said in a matter of fact tone that conveyed his seriousness.

Hermann's eyes went wide with fear and he struggled to free himself from the Sergeant's grip. Donaldson released some pressure but kept his hand firmly in place.

"Our scientists theorize the initial radiation level could exceed 3,000 millisieverts," Hermann managed to croak out.

Donaldson and Randall shared a look, before Donaldson released Hermann.

"It's a 50/50 chance at best that we survive the radiation at that level," Randall said grimly. "If the system can get it down to 1,000 millisieverts we should be okay."

"Agreed, but how long will that take and how will we know?" Donaldson asked.

"That's a good question," Randall looked at Hermann. "You must have a sensor in the containment area. Does the control panel show the radiation level in real time?"

Gunfire punctuated the conversation reminding everyone that time was short.

"Yes, but I'm not sure how to access the information," Hermann replied, clearly a defeated man.

"What do you mean?" Donaldson growled.

"I don't know the password," Hermann replied. "I wasn't granted access."

"Get him out of here," Donaldson ordered Robinson, who took Hermann away. "This is a waste of time," Donaldson said in disgust.

"Maybe it's not," Randall said.

Donaldson locked eyes with Randall "What are you talking about?"

"Remember how much cold air was blasting us when we were behind the Bell?"

"Yeah, so?" Donaldson said, his irritation starting to show.

"We were in front of the air duct that feeds air into the chamber and it was nearly six feet tall. There must be another duct the same size to vent the air to the surface."

"That could be our ticket out. We need to get those blast doors open."

"Can we hold out for ten more minutes?" Randall asked.

Donaldson shook his head. "Once the Nazis get here, they'll pin us down and wait us out. The only reason we were able to hold them off before was their reluctance to fire heavy rounds at their toy, but that's gone now."

"We need to figure out how to access the control system," Randall walked to the podium where Vogel had spoken minutes earlier. The unit held a computer terminal with Vogel's speech still open on the screen. Randall closed the document, revealing the home screen of the computer. It was a dashboard for operating the systems in the facility, but the words were in German.

Randall searched for the controls to the blast door on the home screen. He clicked on various icons but failed to find it.

Robinson jogged to his side and set down his assault rifle. "Try that one."

"Can you read German?" Randall asked.

"A little."

Randall clicked on the icon. A new screen popped open showing additional icons. After a moment Randall found what he was looking for, a small set of doors encompassing a bell-shaped structure.

"This has got to be it," Randall clicked on the picture. A password box appeared on the screen. "It's password protected. Any ideas?"

"Germany?"

Randall typed it in. A red error message popped up.

Donaldson joined Robinson and Randall. "What's our

status?"

"We think we found the right screen, but it's password protected," Randall replied.

"Sergeant, we have unfriendlies inbound. We're falling back to your position," Fernandez reported over Donaldson's radio.

"How many?" Donaldson asked.

"Not sure. Twenty or thirty at least," Fernandez reported back.

More gunfire, this time closer.

"We need to get those doors open," Donaldson said. "Robinson take the SAW and set it up to cover the approaching Nazis. Take Nguyen with you."

"Try Fuhrer," Robinson said, picking up the machine gun and jogging toward the incoming gunfire.

Randall tried. It didn't work.

"How about die Glocke?" Donaldson suggested.

No good.

Gunshots rang out closer as rounds ricocheted off the walls, striking the outer ring of the facility. The sound of the SAW joined the chorus of violence.

"Get Herrmann over here," Randall said, not looking up from the screen.

Donaldson sprinted over to the Nazi who was handcuffed to the railing overlooking the floor where the Bell had been earlier. Donaldson was back a moment later, dragging Herrmann along with him.

"What's the password?" Randall asked the Nazi.

Herrmann shrugged.

More bullets found their way back to their position; two rounds zipped over Donaldson's head.

Donaldson removed his Glock and pointed it at Herrmann's head. "Try again."

"I don't know the password!" Herrmann squealed, glancing

in the direction that the Nazis were coming.

"Bullshit!" Donaldson cocked the hammer of the gun.

"I swear I don't know!" Herrmann cried. "Please don't kill me! I'm not struggling against you!"

"Struggle! That's it!" Randall shouted.

"Sergeant, we can't hold them off any longer!" Robinson called out over the radio.

"Randall, we're out of time," Donaldson picked up his assault rifle and fired at the approaching Nazi army while Herrmann lay in the fetal position on the floor.

Randall typed slowly and carefully into the password box. He clicked Enter. The password box disappeared.

"What the hell did you type?"

Randall grinned. "Mein Kampf."

Donaldson dropped a Nazi with a round from his assault rifle. "Randall, we need it open now."

Randall scanned the contents of the new folder and found the sensor reading for the radiation level behind the blast doors. Even in German the reading was clear, 1,113 millisieverts. Close enough. He found an icon that could only be the blast doors and clicked on it.

Overhead lights and red strobes popped to life and the blast doors slowly slipped open.

"Fall back inside the blast doors!" Donaldson yelled into his throat mic.

Randall grabbed Herrmann, jerking him to his feet and pushing him toward the opening blast doors. Flores and Grady entered next, followed by all of Donaldson's men. The Sergeant brought up the rear, offering his team cover fire.

"Where are we going?" Grady asked.

"We need to get to the ventilation shaft," Randall replied.

The group closed on the rear wall, stopping in front of the giant metal grate that covered the air vent. The sound of encroaching gunfire grew louder.

"What do we do?' Grady asked.

"This shaft is used to vent gas from the Bell, so we think it leads to the surface. We need to get it open," Randall answered.

"An explosive charge is our best bet. We just need to create a big enough opening for us to get through," Robinson replied.

"Do it!" Randall yelled as more bullets ripped through the area, narrowly missing him.

As Robinson set the charge, Randall searched the area, seeing everyone except one team member. "Where's Donaldson?"

"He was trailing, providing cover fire for our retreat," Robinson said, affixing the charge.

Randall sprinted back toward the blast doors, searching for the Sergeant, and found DeGray and Burke laying cover fire. "Where's the Sergeant?"

"Up there," DeGray said, pointing with his weapon. A terse look on his face.

Randall spotted Donaldson lying on the ground behind a sturdy workstation, taking carefully placed shots at the approaching enemy.

"Sergeant, we have to go! They're blasting the vent open!"

Donaldson turned, searching for Randall. He grimaced when he moved, clearly in pain. It was then that Randall spotted the expanding puddle of blood by his leg. "Randall, what the hell are you doing here? Get back to the vent to evacuate."

"Cover me!" Randall yelled back at Burke and DeGray.

"Damnit Randall, Sergeant gave an order," Burke said.

Ignoring the reprimand, Randall sprinted for Donaldson. Bullets whizzed by as he zigzagged his way toward the injured soldier, huffing and puffing as he arrived by his side crouched behind the overturned desk.

"I thought I told you to go."

"I'm not very good at taking orders. Do you think you can stand if I help you?" Randall asked.

"That'll make us easy targets and I'm not putting you in

danger," Donaldson replied.

"If we stay here, they'll overrun us," Randall said.

Donaldson glared at Randall.

"I'm not leaving you and neither are they," Randall gestured toward DeGray and Burke.

"If I give my men an order, they'll follow it," Donaldson growled.

"Good thing I'm not one of your men," Randall replied.

Donaldson's glare softened. "DeGray, Burke, cover fire on my mark." He shouldered his weapon. "Help me up," Donaldson said to Randall.

Randall hoisted the Sergeant onto his shoulder, ducking to stay under the cover of the workstation. "Ready."

"Open fire!" Donaldson yelled to his men.

DeGray and Burke popped up, laying down a barrage to shield their Sargent's retreat. Randall ran as best he could with the added weight and Donaldson fired small bursts, trying to provide additional cover for them as they dashed toward the ventilation unit.

DeGray and Burke, running low on ammunition were forced to reload, offering a window for the Germans to attack. Three Nazis, seeing the easy targets, stood from their respective cover, and pursued them on foot, quickly closing the gap.

"Hurry!" Donaldson yelled into Randall's ear as he fired back, hitting one of the Germans with a volley. The man's chest exploded in red as he crumpled to the floor. The small victory did little to slow the progress of the others.

"How close are they?" Randall asked.

"You don't want to know."

Shots whizzed by the two men as they surged toward the ventilation shaft. Donaldson moaned and Randall suddenly felt the weight of the Sergeant increase. He must have been hit again.

"Hang in there, we're almost out of here!"

They passed Burke and DeGray who had reloaded and now popped out from their cover and unleashed a brutal assault on the pursuing Nazis, dropping them in mid-stride.

Randall skidded to a stop, tottering as his tired body tried to hold his own weight and that of the sergeant. Robinson came to his aid, picking up Donaldson. He jogged the short distance back to the now gaping hole where the vent had previously been.

"Let's go!" Robinson switched on his gun-mounted light and hauled Donaldson into the large air conditioning duct. Randall, Michael, and Grady followed next, with the remaining soldiers bringing up the rear.

"Where's Herrmann?" Randall asked.

"Topside," Robinson replied.

The duct, bored out of the solid mountain, sloped upward, making the trek more strenuous. The group followed Robinson who, although he was carrying the sergeant, had little trouble moving forward. Randall strained to keep up, worn from retrieving Donaldson.

"You can do it, Professor," Michael encouraged.

"I'd give anything to be ten years younger right now," Randall replied.

Robinson continued forward at a brisk pace, but then suddenly stopped. He set his sergeant down gently.

Michael arrived by Donaldson and set his gun down as well. "Why are we stopping?"

Robinson shined his light forward and the reason became apparent. A large turbine blocked the way out. He studied the large, resting blades. "We can fit through, but someone needs to go first to help me pass the Sergeant to the other side."

Michael volunteered, squeezing through the opening between the blade and housing. It was a tight fit, but he forced his way to the other side.

"You're up, Sarge," Robinson said, helping the man to his feet then guiding him through the opening. His uniform snagged on the blade as Michael pulled, causing him to groan in pain.

"Hang on," Robinson eased him back, freed his shirt and passed him through to Michael.

The gunshots from the rear were growing louder. Closer.

"We've got to get moving! Professor, you're up next."

Randall passed through the opening smoothly, followed by Grady. Robinson joined them on the other side as the soldiers bringing up the rear caught up with them.

"They're gaining on us, we've gotta pick it up!" Nguyen fired a small burst back toward the lab. He passed his gun through the blades, then climbed to the other side. Fernandez was next. He entered the opening and a loud buzzing sound rose from the machinery. The giant blades began turning just as his torso and left leg were through. A huge blade spun, pinning him in place. He yelped in pain.

"Shit, we have to get him out!" Nguyen jogged back to Fernandez's side. "What do we do?"

"Can't use an explosive charge, it'll kill him," Robinson said.

The buzzing sound grew louder. The blade pressed harder. Fernandez squealed in pain.

"Hold it back!" Nguyen pushed against the blade, trying to free his friend.

Gunshots rang out and bullets ricocheted through the duct, one striking Grady in the arm. Everyone dove for cover.

Randall jogged to Nguyen's side. He pushed, trying desperately to force back the blade. Fernandez's eyes were wide with fear. The Nazis were closing in.

More gunshots. Randall watched helplessly as multiple bullets struck Fernandez. The spark of life in the soldier's eyes flickered out and his dead body slumped against the blade.

"Dammit!" Nguyen shouted.

"Come on, we have to go!" Randall pulled Nguyen from his fallen comrade.

Nguyen grudgingly complied. The two men ran up the tunnel, eventually catching the others.

"What happened?" Randall asked, seeing Grady holding his bleeding arm.

"I took one in the arm. Damn thing hurts."

They made their way up the shaft, the tunnel ahead growing brighter. Sunlight spilled through the vents announcing they had finally reached the end of the duct. Once again, Robinson set his Sergeant down and sprinted ahead. He arrived at the vent, finding inch-thick metal bars set directly into concrete. The Nazis clearly didn't want anyone trying to sneak in through the ventilation system.

Robinson jogged back to the others, who stood waiting.

"We're going to need explosives. Nguyen, do you still have the C-4?"

"Affirmative," Nguyen fetched the putty-like substance from his bag.

Robinson nodded to Nguyen. "Set the charge. The rest of you, come with me. We need to get a safe distance away."

A blast reverberated down the shaft.

"What the hell was that!" Grady asked.

"The Nazis blew out the turbine. They'll be on us soon," Robinson replied. "Let's get moving!"

Robinson led the group back down the shaft a safe distance, taking a position facing down the duct in the direction of the lab. He fired small bursts toward the turbine trying to keep the Germans from advancing. Michael and Randall joined him and provided additional cover fire.

An out of breath Nguyen jogged up to them. "Fire in the hole!"

The men dropped to the ground, covering their heads and necks. A deafening blast reverberated through the shaft.

Randall's ears rang. He stood, peering down the ventilation shaft, catching the bouncing flashlights of the Nazis jogging toward them. He felt a heavy hand on his shoulder. Turning, he saw Michael mouthing the words *come on*, but all he could hear was the ringing in his ears. He turned and sprinted toward the daylight, finally arriving at the top of the tunnel.

The group emerged from the ventilation shaft and into a wooded area, the fading daylight filtering through the forest canopy above. Still disoriented by the blast, Randall couldn't tell where they were in relation to the barn. He spotted Robinson with a map and radio, diagramming the location of the extraction point, while Michael tended to Donaldson and Grady with the first aid kit.

Nguyen was crouched down, facing into the shaft, his grenade launcher pointed toward the opening. He fired several rounds into the blackness beyond. Distant explosions emanated from within, along with the screams of Nazis being torn apart by the explosive charges.

"That'll slow them down," Nguyen rejoined the others.

"The nearest clearing is 1.5 kilometers to the northeast. That's our landing zone. The chopper will be there waiting by the time we get there," Robinson explained.

Randall looked over at Donaldson whose face was ashen. The sergeant sucked in air in short, labored breaths. "We've got to hurry, he's fading fast."

"Nguyen. Take point. Let's move!" Robinson picked up the sergeant.

Nguyen led the group through the maze of trees. The quiet sounds of nature were a welcomed relief from the near constant gunfire inside the complex, but the quiet was short lived as a new sound formed in the distance.

"Do you hear that?" Grady asked.

"Sounds like a couple of small motors," Michael answered.

The group reached the edge of the tree line, which opened onto a small meadow. Nguyen moved beyond the cover of the trees to scout ahead of the group. The whining of the motors grew louder. Randall, his curiosity piqued, poked his head out into the clearing. He looked around, failing to see the source of the noise but saw Nguyen sprinting back in his direction, wildly waving one arm while clutching his gun with the other.

The sound of the engines grew louder, the throaty noise of something mechanical accelerating along the tree line. Randall spun to his left and spotted several motorcycles bearing down on them. Nguyen crossed the tree line, multiple rounds chewing up the earth behind him.

Randall tumbled backward to avoid being pummeled by Nguyen who dove head-first into the relative safety of the trees, landing near a squatting Robinson.

"Man, these guys just don't quit," Nguyen rose to his feet.

"Gun 21, this is Able 2, Fire Mission, over. My position in the tree line marked by IR STROBE," Robinson called into the radio, activating an infrared strobe to mark their position as he called in an airstrike to one of the awaiting choppers.

"Able 2, this is Gun 21, what's your target location? Over."

"Gun 21, target location forest clearing, Bearing 95.78°, Range 30 meters and closing. Target description, enemy motorcycles, marked by IR Pointer. Danger, close clearance, over."

"Roger Able 2, Gun 21 in transit."

"Nguyen mark them with Pointer," Robinson ordered.

"Gladly," Nguyen replied, using an infrared pointer to mark the closest approaching motorcycle.

Randall and his group headed deeper into the forest, anticipating the coming attack. They spotted the approaching Nazi motorcycles which were moving quickly across the open clearing, drawing ever closer. The unmistakable sound of a helicopter rose from the distance and closed on their position, the aircraft clearly no longer in stealth mode. The sound drew the attention of the Nazis away from the ground team. Large caliber machine gun fire came next, followed by the Germans cursing and screaming as they were ripped to shreds by the aerial assault.

The sound of the helicopter blades thumped overhead, punctuated by the occasional explosion of a gas tank from one of the now burning motorcycles.

"Able 2, you're clear to proceed to landing zone," a voice called out over the radio. It was Eckert.

"Roger."

The group picked up the pace, moving past the clearing as their escort floated overhead. A short time later, they were in the landing zone. They filed into the waiting chopper which carried them back to Ramstein.

Chapter 43

Ramstein Airbase, Germany
July 27, 9:59 p.m.

On the flight back, a medic attended to Donaldson while Eckert received a full debrief. Though the sergeant's injuries were serious, the medic was able to stabilize him until they arrived at the base hospital. Grady joined him to have his injury cleaned and bandaged, while Randall and Michael were taken by jeep to meet with General Flores. Randall could only pray that the General would have some way to track the Nazi superweapon and help him find Sam. They arrived at the administrative area and were escorted straight to Flores, who paced outside his office. Upon seeing his son, Flores jogged to his side and grabbed his son's shoulder.

"It's good to see you," Flores said.

Michael smiled and nodded.

"Do you have any news about my daughter?" Randall asked.

Flores' expression turned to a frown. "Please come into my office and sit down."

The group filed in, taking seats around a small, wooden

conference table. Flores office was neat and orderly, with pictures of the General's family hung on the walls and sitting on his desk.

Flores leaned forward in his chair. "Unfortunately, we weren't able to track the weapon."

"But you were able to find the stone when the Nazis took it from Rhodes. Why can't you find it again?" Randall asked.

"This weapon is unlike anything we've seen and the way it works makes it impossible for us to track. Without any clues of where Vogel went, it's akin to finding the proverbial needle in an Earth-sized haystack."

Randall's heart sank at the news. He felt exhausted and defeated.

"But I promise we won't give up. I have our best men working on it. I'm terribly sorry and can't imagine how you must feel," Flores added.

The three men sat in silence.

Flores cleared his throat. "You must be tired. You're more than welcome to stay on the base. We have empty officers' quarters complete with a private bath and kitchen that you're welcome to use."

Randall looked up from his lap at the general's face. He could see the sincerity in his tired eyes and appreciated the concern from one father to another.

"Thanks, but if it's all the same, I'd rather be alone for a while. Can you have one of your men take me to a hotel nearby?"

"Of course. I'll have you taken to the Hotel Merkur. It's close and has a fine bar," Flores replied.

"I guess that'll do."

"I'll take you," Michael offered. "I could use a drink myself."

Flores stood. "I'll let you know immediately if we learn anything else."

Randall stood as well. "Thank you general."

Randall and Michael left the office and walked to the motor pool. By the time they reached the hotel, the sun had set. They entered under a white and blue neon sign and headed straight to the hotel bar, forgoing check-in for the moment.

The bar was a busy sea of tables and barstools filled with locals enjoying a night out. They grabbed the first two seats they found then Michael ordered for them, speaking to the bartender in German. The server brought back two shot glasses filled with clear liquid and two steins of beer.

"What's this?" Randall pointed at the shot glass.

"Korn. It's a local liquor," Michael emptied his shot glass, then sipped on his beer.

"Never heard of it," Randall picked up the small cup and finished it in a single gulp. The clear liquid burned his throat as he swallowed. He picked up his beer and took a long pull.

"I know my dad didn't sound too hopeful about finding Sam, but if there's one thing I know about my dad, he won't stop trying."

"Thanks for the encouragement." Randall wanted to believe Michael but doubted the general would be able to locate her. "You know, when your kids are small, you worry about them getting sick, breaking an arm, or even getting hurt in a car accident, but I never could have imagined something like this happening. I just..." Randall had to fight back the tears.

Michael listened intently, nursing his beer.

Randall once again lifted his stein, taking several long drinks. He regained his composure. "Are you married?"

"Haven't met the right woman yet."

"You will. You're a good man. Your dad's right to be proud of you," it was about all the conversation Randall could muster given the situation.

"Thanks Dr. Randall."

"Call me Nick," Randall finished his beer. "Thanks for the drinks, but I'm beat. I think I'm going to check in and take a shower."

"I'll let you know as soon as I hear something," Michael rose to his feet.

"Thanks."

The two men shook hands and Michael left, leaving Randall alone at the bar. He walked to the front desk to retrieve his room key and headed to the elevator. A short ride later, he arrived on the second floor and found his room. He opened the door, walked in, and turned on the light. He stumbled backward when he spotted a man seated in a chair near the window.

Chapter 44

"Ciao, Professore," the man rose to his feet, his arm in a sling.

It took Randall's tired mind a moment, but he finally placed the face. "Captain Moretti, what are you doing here?"

"I heard about your adventure. I'm terribly sorry about your daughter, but I think we can help."

Randall blinked, trying to clear the fog from his mind. "How do you know what happened?"

A knowing look crossed the Knight's face. "Can General Flores track the device?"

Randall shook his head from side to side. "Can you?"

"No, but can I do something almost as good. I can tell when it's coming."

"How will that help?"

"Did the soldiers capture Dietrich Herrmann?"

"Why does that matter?"

"You'll soon know where the Nazis plan to strike, but without knowing when, you'll be unable to stop them."

"Then there's nothing I can do to help Sam."

"Perhaps there is."

Randall locked eyes with Moretti. "I'm too tired for games."

"There's a way to find out when the Bell is coming, but it requires something I don't have and getting it won't be easy."

"Of course not," Randall rubbed his tired eyes. "Go on."

"Prior to launching the Bell, the user must enter his desired destination. The craft then manipulates space and time around the area it wishes to go, thereby creating a nearly imperceptible signal."

"Nearly imperceptible?"

"There is an artifact that can measure the changes caused by the propulsion system. Once the destination is programmed, the launch sequence of the vehicle takes a few minutes. This will provide you with a window of time to prepare for its arrival."

"A few minutes isn't much time."

"What's the saying you Americans use? Beggars can't be choosers. A few minutes warning is better than none."

"Good point. How do we get this artifact?"

"That's the difficult part."

"Because?"

Moretti bit his lip, staring directly into Randall's eyes. "The item we seek is in the Vatican catacombs."

Randall cocked his head and stared at Moretti. "And how do you propose we get it?"

"We will have to break in."

Randall's mouth dropped open. "You want to break into the Vatican and steal a priceless, religious artifact? You're supposed to be a protector of the faith!"

"My sworn oath is to protect our faith by any means necessary. We face the greatest threat ever known, not just to Christianity, but to the entire human family. The men who possess The Devil's Heart are ruthless killers and I would remind you that they systematically killed millions of innocent men, women, and children, simply because of their ethnicity and faith. Our best chance of stopping them is to take that relic, and my conscious is quite clear on the matter."

Randall shifted uncomfortably, having just been schooled by Moretti.

"Professore, you are a good man. You have risked your life and the life of your daughter for the well-being of others. In fact, your daughter is in grave danger and I am now presenting you with the best chance of saving her. Accept my offer, and let's stop these madmen."

Randall closed his eyes and rubbed several days-worth of stubble on his chin. He breathed in deeply. It was his only chance to save Sam. "When do we leave?"

"I'll have a car waiting for you in a few hours. Rest now."

"Sam's with that madman, there's no way I can rest."

"You must try," Moretti stood.

"How's your arm?" Randall asked.

Moretti removed his arm from the sling and flexed it. "This is simply a precaution. The arm is feeling much better."

"And your leg?"

"As with the arm, simply a flesh wound. It's as if someone is watching over me," a smile crept over Moretti's face.

Randall closed his eyes and shook his head.

"Get some rest, I'll be back soon," Moretti walked out the door, leaving Randall alone with his thoughts.

Chapter 45

Rome, Italy
July 28, 3:02 a.m.

Despite his concern for Sam, Randall's exhausted body had simply given out the night before and he had fallen into a deep sleep only to be awoken by Moretti several hours later. In the air now, he used the flight time to learn how Moretti hoped to track the incoming Nazi weapon. Though tired, he was fascinated by the explanation provided by the Knight on how the detection process worked. More importantly, it offered Randall the first glimmer of hope of saving his daughter.

"What exactly are we looking for?" Randall asked.

"A model of the Church of the Holy Sepulchre carved from olive wood," Moretti replied.

Randall frowned. "What's so special about a miniature church model?"

"The model isn't special, it's what's inside that we seek."

"Which is?"

"A stone as mysterious as The Devil's Heart. Even more so."

"Why's it in the Vatican?"

"Safety. Callixtus's pontificate occurred shortly after the fall of Constantinople. He was concerned with protecting Christian

Europe against a Turk invasion, and the only place he could guarantee its safety was here."

"But how does this rock let you detect the Devil's Heart?"

"When it's near the Devil's Heart it glows."

Randall furrowed his brow. "Is it bioluminescent?"

"Bioluminescence is a chemical reaction, but we believe this stone's reaction is to the radiation produced by the Devil's Heart. In nature, there are rocks that contain a mineral known as fluorescent sodalite, which will fluoresce under longwave ultraviolet illumination. This causes the rocks to glow. Our scientists theorize that a similar process is at work with this stone but will need to examine it to confirm these properties," Moretti explained.

Satisfied, Randall nodded his head and sat back into his seat. A moment later, the pilot announced that they were beginning their descent into Ciampino airport in Rome, causing the men to fasten their seatbelts. Through the side window, Randall spotted the dome of St. Peter's Basilica, singularly illuminated in a small patch of darkness that marked the outline of surrounding St. Peter's Square. Elsewhere, lighted streets formed rectangular boxes marking the main section of the eternal city. The plane landed and moments later, the team descended the airstairs of their jet and discovered a car waiting for them just outside the terminal. The driver held the door open they entered and were whisked away to a church just north of Vatican City where they waited to put their plan into motion.

During the ride, Moretti explained his strategy to Randall, who was stunned by its audacity. The Knights had utilized their extensive knowledge of the underground catacombs to enter the Vatican from beneath the surface. They had chosen Santi Michele e Magno basilica, just outside of Vatican City to undertake their plan, having tunneled over 500 feet under Saint Peter's Square and into the grottoes beneath Saint Peter's Basilica. If their estimates were correct, less than ten feet of earth lay between the tunnel and the Vatican's necropolis.

"How long have your men been working on this?" Randall asked.

"A little over ten months," Moretti replied.

"And no one noticed what you were doing?" Randall asked incredulously.

"Though not as much as in the past, the Church still wields a great deal of influence in Rome and local officials defer to church leaders. When a sizable donation was made to renovate Santi Michele, it provided the perfect cover for our tunneling operation. With the materials brought in for the work, no one questioned the quantities of lumber and the other supplies transported here."

"But tunneling from here means the monsignor of this church had to agree to your operation. How did you manage that?"

Moretti just smiled.

The car pulled up to an arched entryway sandwiched between two larger buildings, with a long flight of stone stairs disappearing within. As if reading Randall's mind, Moretti explained that the portal marked the entrance into the church. The driver of the car hopped out and opened the rear door. Randall and Moretti exited the vehicle, crossed a small square, then walked up the stone steps and to the right. Lights illuminated a spiderweb of scaffolding enveloping the sixty-six-foot façade of the church's campanile or bell tower. Moretti arrived first, opened the door for his co-conspirator, who fled into the interior of the basilica. Moretti followed closely behind then locked the door behind them.

As the two men entered the Narthex, they were greeted by a middle-aged priest wearing a black cassock. His long, slender face was framed by short dark hair and his brown eyes showed warmth and, Randall detected, a sense of sadness. Randall stopped two feet short of the priest, but Moretti moved straight in and hugged him.

"Buona sera." Moretti said.

Randall peaked an eyebrow. "You two know each other?"

"Si. This is my cousin Bartolomeo. Cugino, this is

Professore Randall."

"It's nice to meet you. Welcome to my church."
Bartolomeo gripped Randall's hand and shook heartily, answering
the question Randall had posed to Moretti in the car just moments
ago.

"Is everything ready?" Moretti asked.

"Yes, your men are down in the tunnel and believe they are
close. They were waiting for you to arrive before breaching the
wall," Bartolomeo replied, hands folded serenely across his waist.

Moretti gripped his cousin's shoulder. "Thank you for what
you have done."

Bartolomeo bit his lip and nodded, his eyes misting over.
"You will have to excuse me I have arrangements to make." He
turned from Moretti and Randall and walked slowly down the aisle
toward the sanctuary of the church, almost as if taking in the sights
for the last time.

A dawning realization set upon Randall who turned to
Moretti, meeting his eyes. "What'll happen to him when they find
out he allowed this? This could be construed as vandalism and
breaking and entering? Will he go to jail?"

Moretti shook his head. "The Holy See will not want such a
matter made public. The magnitude of such a scandal would
further harm the Church. At worst, he will face excommunication
from the Church, which in the case of my cousin would be the
worst fate possible. Even from a young age, he knew his calling
was to serve the Lord."

"Your order must know high placed people in the Vatican.
Couldn't you have just asked permission to search for the relic?"

"The Church, like any large organization has many factions
that don't agree on all matters. While they all wish to serve the
faith, their paths are divergent."

"It just seems like such a shame. He's clearly not taking it
well."

Moretti grabbed Randall's arm. "He approached us with this plan, not the other way around. My cousin understands the evil we are facing and knows his duty to stop it."

All Randall could do was stand there and nod dumbly.

"Come, we have work to do."

The two men left Bartolomeo alone with his thoughts and walked to a small alcove, with steps leading below ground. Extension cords, plugged into sockets near the chapel, ran down the stairs and into the darkness. Randall also noticed thick tubing running down the steps into the lower level of the church. His eyes followed it up until it terminated into a large rectangular metal box.

"Forced air system to provide oxygen to the tunnel," Moretti said, handing Randall a flashlight. "You'll need this."

The Knight stepped onto the first stone stair and Randall followed closely behind. As they descended, Randall was transported to another time. Beautiful frescoes adorned the ceiling and walls of the subterranean level of the church. Randall found himself marveling at the pictures showing cherubim floating above a scene of Christ and his disciples seated at a table and other paintings depicting the early life of the Christian community. The stonework was equally intriguing, featuring incredibly detailed arches with geometrically precise keystones strategically placed for support. Sculpted stone columns framed precisely formed niches which were cut into the stone. If he hadn't known better, Randall would have assumed that the features were created using the latest construction technology.

The two men walked along the lower level of the church; work lights strung by Moretti's men providing illumination. They soon found themselves at a narrow passageway with simpler stone steps cut into the earth which led down to another level. They had arrived at the catacomb entrance.

Framing either side of the tunnel were rows of narrow ledges carved out of the volcanic rock. Far simpler than the grand stonework in the subterranean church level, these loculi were little more than roughly hewn rectangles. Randall estimated a dozen or more such openings in the walls. Small by modern adult standards, the loculi were empty, the skeletal remains removed long ago.

Randall found himself dawdling amongst the ancient catacombs, the scientist in him naturally drawn to such matters. He glanced down the tunnel and realized Moretti had already turned a corner ten feet ahead of him. He jogged the remaining distance, rounded the turn, and discovered the massive results of the Knights' ten months undertaking.

At Moretti's feet lay an opening approximately four feet high by six feet wide, framed with sturdy lumber and with matching rolling carts laying side by side on its floor. Recessed into the wall, half-way up from the ground, were the now familiar string of lights and air tubing providing illumination and fresh air respectively. Just below them was a sturdy rope, anchored to the wall at ten-foot intervals. Randall crouched and peered into the gaping opening, discovering that it ran into the distance, disappearing into an infinite point somewhere presumably under Saint Peter's Basilica.

"We'll use the carts to reach the grottoes," Moretti said, dropping to a crouch next to Randall. "Lay on your stomach, like this and use the rope to pull yourself along." Moretti shimmied onto the far-left cart, demonstrating for Randall who followed suit, lying on the adjacent trolley.

Randall struggled to keep up with Moretti, experimenting with different methods to pull himself along before landing on a system that worked best for him. Even after refining his process, Randall found his arms and shoulders aching with fatigue. He had to stop and rest. He watched as Moretti continued to shrink into the distance, outworking him, bum arm, and all. After several impatient minutes, Randall resumed his forward motion, determined to make up for lost ground. Eventually he spied Moretti stopped on his cart ahead and caught him. The Knight massaged his injured arm as Randall slid by.

After another stop and a seemingly endless series of passing light bulbs, air vents and rock face, Randall heard the unmistakable sound of hammering. The realization energized him, driving him forward. The digging sound grew louder and a bright light spilled from the passageway directly ahead. As he approached the opening, the workers came into view. Wearing head lamps and using hand tools, they were hollowing out the final corner of their most recent progress. Randall's impending arrival caused them to turn in unison at the approaching sound. He pulled up several feet short of their location and stopped.

Behind him grew the grinding sound of wheels traversing the stony floor and Moretti soon rolled to a stop by his side.

"How much longer?" Moretti asked.

The digger struck his hammer against the wall facing the Vatican. A hollow thudding sound announced they were close to breaching.

"Continue," Moretti ordered.

"Do we know what's on the other side of this wall?" Randall asked.

"If our engineer's estimate is correct, we should be near the Tomb of Emperor Otto the Second." Moretti replied. He squirmed forward off his cart, then pushed it back away from the crowded workspace.

Randall sighed. Although he didn't relish the thought of damaging priceless religious artifacts, they were out of options. Making matters worse, the sound of the digging seemed exceptionally loud. Loud enough to wake the dead. "Aren't you worried that someone on the other side will hear this and come to check?"

"At this hour, most of the staff and Swiss Guard are either asleep or guarding the main entrances. This area of the grotto will be empty."

Randall nodded, impressed by Moretti's planning. It appeared that the Knight had truly considered every detail. He hopped off his cart, staying a few feet back from Moretti and the diggers. With a final swing of a hammer, a small section of wall caved inward.

"We're through!" the worker said proudly. The man enlarged the opening just enough for an adult man to enter then moved to the side to allow Moretti access. The Knight edged closer to the new hole, shining his light through. He scooted through the hole and disappeared into the darkness beyond. A moment later, he shined his light back at Randall and the diggers.

"You've done well. Thank you for your work. Take the tools back to the church but leave the carts for us. Professore, we must hurry!"

Randall poked his head through the freshly made opening into the Vatican, then shone his light around. He spotted Moretti a few feet away, checking to make sure no one was on the other side. Randall hopped down from the hole, nearly twisting an ankle as he misjudged the height of the drop. Shining his light back, he saw that the opening on this side was nearly five feet off the ground. He was now in the Vatican.

The artistry was exquisite. The stonework rivaled the greatest statues in the finest museums in Europe, a fact not surprising given the artisans hired to create them. The sarcophagi and detailed stone columns and arches created by sculptors such as Camillo Rusconi and Paolo Romano truly captured the spiritual beauty intended for the sacred tombs.

Lost in the moment, Randall felt a tugging at his arm.

"We must find the relic," Moretti whispered.

Pulled back to reality, Randall turned to face a grinning Moretti. "Beautiful, no?"

"It's incredible." Randall exhaled deeply. He had to focus on the task at hand. He walked briskly to catch Moretti. "By the way, you never told me where the stone is hidden."

Moretti turned this head to Randall but kept walking. "We're looking for the tomb of Callixtus III. When he was pope,

265

he received the stone as a gift from Jacques de Milly, the 37th Grand Master of the Order of the Knights Hospitaller."

The two men crept through the grotto, the beams of their lights washing over the tombs of various popes. Some niches contained richly colored, gold gilded paintings as well. At auction, the artwork would fetch millions, yet the thought of these works hanging anywhere else seemed inherently wrong. They belonged here, adding to the rich tapestry of over two-thousand years of the faith. Randall marveled at the sheer amount of history so close by. He decided at that moment to revisit the grotto in the future to properly study these incredible treasures.

If they didn't get caught.

"How much further?" Randall asked.

Moretti's light went out. A strong hand gripped Randall's arm, dragging him into an adjacent alcove.

"Turn off your light," Moretti whispered.

Randall hit the switch, plunging them into darkness. His eyes struggled to adjust. He listened for the cause of Moretti's concern, but only heard his beating heart. He caught a glint of metal hovering near the specter-like outline of Moretti's face. The Knight had brought his gun. Would Moretti really shoot a Vatican employee? Worst still, could the Nazis have followed them into the grotto?

They waited.

Nothing happened.

"I think we're safe," Moretti holstered his gun and turned his light back on. "My apologies, but given the circumstances, we can't be too careful."

Randall breathed a sigh of relief then continued the journey down the passage, which spilled into the main body of the grotto. Directly ahead, as far as the beams of light carried, were two rows of pillars marking the grotto proper, flanked on both sides by niches containing various tombs and statues. To their left, a walkway carried forward approximately ten feet before terminating into a wall. Moretti went right and walked past a statue of Pius VI set into an alcove. Moving past it, they faced another wall directly ahead, but as they reached it, another path revealed itself to the right. Moretti followed it as it funneled into a narrow passage.

They had been in the Vatican for what seemed like an hour but when Randall checked his watch, he confirmed they had only been inside for fourteen minutes. How much longer would it take them to reach Callixtus' tomb? Hopefully, Moretti knew where he was going. They needed to find the stone, get back to the airbase and use it to find Sam and the Nazis.

The pathway bent to the left at a ninety-degree angle and opened into an extraordinarily long hallway, with two empty alcoves to the left and a single alcove with a stone sarcophagus on the right. If they were caught here, there was nowhere to hide and only two ways out, the way they came and whatever lay at the far end of the path they now traversed.

They arrived at the stone sarcophagus and Moretti shined his light onto it. Carved into the side of the stone coffin was the figure of a man reclining on a pillow. Randall turned to see Moretti; his head bowed in prayer. The Knight finished and made the sign of the cross. "Help me open this," he said, indicating they had found the pope they sought.

Randall grabbed a handhold built into the lid and pushed. The stone screeched in protest as the lid scraped across the sarcophagus. Randall winced at the sound. The two managed to push the lid far enough to create a triangular opening into the coffin. Randall crouched next to it and shined his light inside. All he could see were the boney remains of Callixtus. Moretti leaned into the coffin, his upper body disappearing inside. When he stood again, he was holding an object wrapped in cloth.

Randall steadied his light on the object, allowing Moretti to set it on the ground and unwrap it. He did so gingerly, careful not to damage what lay inside. He removed the cloth and revealed a small wooden model of a church, about the size of a toaster. He rotated it, carefully examining the model.

After thoroughly studying it, Moretti sighed with impatience. "There doesn't seem to be a way to open it."

"May I?" Randall asked.

Moretti passed him the model and shined his light on the crouching Randall so he could have a go at it. As with the other artwork in the grotto, the beauty of the model spoke of the devotion of the craftsman who created it. Although small, the detail work was intricate, belying the hours of loving labor the artist had spent crafting the model. Small pieces of ivory contrasted sharply with the dark hue of the natural wood, creating ornate panels within the larger pieces. It seemed a shame that the model's only purpose was to hide something more important.

Randall noticed two crosses, one at the top of the tallest tower, the other on a small dome near the front of the church. He softly pressed on each to see if they served as a lever to open the hidden compartment.

No luck.

Next, he pressed on the taller dome in the center of the model. Again, nothing happened. Unsuccessful, he stood and stretched his legs.

Moretti sighed. "I can't believe the stories weren't true. We must be missing something!"

Randall shone his light on the many facets of the model. A thought struck him. Perhaps the lever wasn't a button, but a knob. He tried turning the crosses. Still nothing. He gripped the dome in the center and turned. It cracked. He stopped immediately. "I'm so sorry, I…"

"Sorry for what? We are not here for the model. We must find the stone!"

Randall studied the damage he had caused. A crack spread from one side of the dome to the other, terminating above the courtyard of the church model. His eyes followed the crack and he noticed something he hadn't seen before. In the courtyard, there was an intricately designed ivory cross centered in the middle of a circle. The circle and cross appeared to be a separate piece inserted into the courtyard.

"Is it possible…?"

Randall placed his thumb and forefinger on the circle and twisted, causing a loud click. He winced, thinking he had damaged the ancient artifact even more.

"Professore!" Moretti yelled, causing Randall to jump, thinking he had angered the Knight.

Moretti grabbed the model from Randall and flipped it over. A section of the base hung half an inch lower than the rest of the model. He grasped at the exposed edge, prying the bottom off the model.

Inside was a cylindrical hole measuring six inches deep and two-inches wide. Filling the hole was a beautiful green stone, but it was flush with the base of the model so Moretti couldn't grab it.

Randall motioned with his hands. "Flip it back over and see if it'll slide out."

Moretti tilted the model with one hand, while keeping the other under the green stone, which began to slide out but then stopped. He grabbed it and pulled it from the model.

"It's incredible," Moretti rotated the stone, examining it from every angle.

A light popped on near the far end of the path, opposite the direction they had traveled. Both men froze. The sound of footsteps, coming from the direction of the lights, grew louder.

"We need to leave," Moretti whispered in Randall's ear.

The two sped back along the hallway they had traversed earlier, hugging the walls to minimize their profiles. The lights grew brighter, followed by the sound of additional footsteps. Whoever was coming was getting closer to Callixtus' tomb … and to discovering the broken church model.

Randall and Moretti rounded the turn heading back toward the main part of the grotto. Randall peered back around the corner,

269

straining to see how many people were coming. A tall figure popped out from the far side passage no more than fifty feet from Randall, who instinctively recoiled to avoid being seen.

He turned to look for Moretti, who was gone.

Panic set in. Randall spun left, then right, searching for Moretti. He scurried in a crouch, moving in the direction he thought they had come earlier. He heard an object drop onto the stony floor just around the corner near Callixtus' sarcophagus.

"Chi è qui e che cosa hai fatto?" a voice cried out. "Who's here and what have you done to the pope's tomb?"

Randall picked up speed, moving past another alcove. Ahead was the main portion of the grotto and to his left was another path. Was it the one that led back to the exit? He moved within a few of feet of the fork.

A figure turned the corner and came straight at him.

Randall tried to pivot and turn but fell backward onto his rear.

"Where have you been? We must go!" Moretti grabbed Randall's arm and hauled him to his feet.

Additional voices joined the first, speaking rapidly in Italian. The far end of the grotto lit up as lights sprung to life.

Next came the unmistakable sound of multiple men running, their shoes clicking with each step, masking what direction they approached from.

Moretti, dragged Randall, sprinting as best he could while crouching. They made a left and passed the statue of Pius VI, staying close to the walls. They turned left again and arrived back at the opening.

"You go through first!" Moretti leaned against wall, rubbing his injured arm.

Randall studied him. There was no way Moretti would be able to climb onto the ledge.

"No, you go first, here, I'll give you a lift," Randall kneeled, then cupped his hands.

Moretti stared at him.

"There's no time to argue. Your arm is hurt. There's no way can pull yourself up!"

The clicking grew louder.

So did the shouting.

"Hurry!" Randall urged.

Moretti relented, then reached for the ledge with his good arm and placed his right foot into Randall's hands. He bounded up, aided by a shove from Randall. He rolled through the opening, letting out a small grunt as he rolled onto his injured arm.

"This way!" a voice called out from the grotto.

They were nearly on him.

Randall reached up and grabbed the ledge. He pulled and tried to find a foothold in the rocky face of the grotto wall. His shoe caught a small ledge and he pushed his way up. Nearly high enough to climb out, but the ledge crumbled, and Randall tumbled backward onto the ground.

He hit hard and rolled on the ground. Through the haze of pain, he heard voices and spotted two men illuminated by their lights. They were no more than thirty feet away, but hadn't seen him yet, their beams sweeping the main part of the grotto.

Randall forced himself to his feet and grabbed the ledge again. He dangled by both hands, trying to pull his entire weight up only using his arms.

"This way!" A voice yelled from behind.

Randall looked back, then up. Moretti reached out from the ledge, grabbed his wrist, and yanked him up. The two climbed aboard their carts and started the long journey back.

Angry Italian voices bounced through the rocky tunnel indicating their Vatican pursuers had followed them out and were close.

Fortunately, the carts gave Moretti and Randall the advantage as their trackers had to run in a crouch. Randall trailed Moretti, ensuring the Knight didn't lag with his injured arm.

Adrenaline coursed through him fueling his rope pulling frenzy. Behind him, Italian curses lagged in the distance, indicating a growing lead on their pursuers.

The damp mustiness of the tunnel filled Randall's lungs. He paused a moment to wipe his face with the sleeve of his perspiration-soaked shirt. Somehow Moretti pulled farther ahead despite his injury. Pride drove Randall forward and a short time later he emerged from the tunnel. Moretti, who was already on his feet, gave Randall his hand and helped him up from the cart.

It was now a footrace and the two threaded their way through the catacombs. Randall and Moretti hit the steps leading to the upper levels as the sound of foot falls clicking against the stony surface behind them indicated the Vatican staff had finally cleared the tunnel.

Exiting the stony staircase, Randall landed awkwardly, twisted his ankle, and went down. His ankle burned as if on fire. He stood on his good foot, then put his weight on his injured leg. It hurt like hell, but he had to keep moving. Hobbled by the injury, his pace slowed.

Moretti's worker sprinted to his side, grabbed him under his shoulder and nearly carried him through the chapel. They approached the front door, which Moretti held open.

Their pursuers had made it up the stairs and were now at the back of the chapel. Moretti sprinted to Randall's side and grabbed him under his other shoulder. The three men burst through the front door of the church and down the steps into a waiting car, which sped away just as their pursuers exited the building.

Randall looked over at Moretti who gulped in air in large breaths. Despite the exhaustion, the Knight wore a broad smile on his face. They had successfully broken into the Vatican and made off with their prize. Randall wasn't sure whether to celebrate or find another priest to offer his confession.

Chapter 46

Randall slept soundly on the flight back to Ramstein, his body beaten and exhausted from the ordeals suffered in recent days. In his dreams, he revisited happier times when Sam and his son John were young, and his wife Ann was still alive. He vividly saw their faces. The kids were running around the backyard playing tag and laughing hysterically. Ann lovingly watched them while she set the patio table for a lazy summer dinner. Randall exhaled, deeply content to simply be in the moment and take it all in.

The moment was short lived. Someone was calling to him, warning him to watch over his family. The scene changed. He was transported to a busy freeway, slick from the falling rain. A feeling of dread washed over him as he witnessed the scene unfold from a distance. Ann was driving her car, trying to merge onto the freeway. A semi-truck barreled toward her in the slow lane.

The truck was going too fast, closing in on Ann as if she were standing still. She yanked the steering wheel, swerving to the right to avoid the truck. It was no good, the truck smashed into her car, driving it into the side wall. Her vehicle flipped repeatedly, bursting into flames.

Randall watched helplessly as flames consumed Ann's car. He heard a soft voice calling out to him. It grew louder and louder. It was Ann. "Help her Nick! Help Sam!"

Randall's eyes popped open. His heart raced and his sweat soaked shirt clung to his body. *Where the hell am I?*

His eyes darted around, then he remembered. They were

flying to Germany. He breathed deeply and steadied his nerves. There was no chance he'd fall back to sleep.

Randall sat up. His entire body ached, his mind a jumble of thoughts, all jostling for undivided attention. He closed his eyes and shook his head, unsure of what to make of this latest nightmare. Was it a manifestation of his concern for Sam? He checked his watch. They'd be landing in approximately twenty minutes.

He grabbed his phone from his bag, but still had no signal. There was no way of knowing if Sam or anyone else had tried to contact him. He tossed the phone back into his bag, sat back into his seat and rubbed his eyes. He had never wanted twenty minutes of his life to be over as much as he wanted it now. Unfortunately, all the wishing in the world wouldn't speed the clock. He'd have to wait. A hopeless situation and not a damn thing he could do about it.

Time dragged by as Randall wrestled with his thoughts which were mercifully interrupted by the pilot announcing they were on their final approach. The message over the speakers caused Moretti, seated a few rows ahead, to stir.

Randall looked out the plane's window. The runway and surrounding airport loomed larger letting him know they'd be touching down in few minutes. His phone chirped several times. He grabbed his bag, fished it out and found that he now had a cell signal. He had several missed calls. He checked the numbers and they were all from the same person, and he or she had left him messages.

Randall dialed his voicemail and listened. It was General Flores. The General was anxious to speak with him, but the details were sparse. After listening to the last one, Randall noticed for the first time that Moretti had moved and taken the seat directly across from him. The inquisitive look on his face clearly conveyed his thoughts.

"Good news?" Moretti asked.

Randall shook his head. "I don't know. The general left

several messages telling me that he needs to see me. Sounds like something important but didn't leave any details."

Moretti nodded, pushed himself back into his seat and glanced out the window of the plane. "We can take you there as soon as we land."

The Gulfstream G150 touched down at Zweibrücken Airport and taxied to a private hanger where Randall found a familiar driver waiting for them. They loaded into the Peugeot and raced off to Ramstein. Randall dialed Flores several times, but each call ended in a busy signal.

The driver pulled the car up to the front gate of the airbase and a guard immediately stepped forward to greet them. "Is one of you Dr. Randall?"

"I am."

"Please come with me," the guard opened the car door.

Randall stepped out and followed his escort but stopped and turned back upon hearing Moretti's voice. "When you discover the Nazi's plan, call me at that number. I'll have something ready to help you," Moretti's driver gave Randall a small square of paper with a number scrawled on it.

Randall nodded. "Will do."

A short walk later, he found himself seated in Flores' office, awaiting the general's arrival. He dropped into the high-back leather chair; his body cradled by the rich dark material. Randall closed his eyes and sank into a quiet moment of oblivion.

Flores burst through the door. "We've been trying to reach you. Where have you been?"

"Some friends helped me locate something that might help us find Vogel."

Flores nodded, removed his hat, and took a seat at his desk. "We have some news. Apparently, Vogel is planning an attack on the G20 summit. I'm sure you're familiar with the organization."

Once again, Moretti was right, Hermann must have

provided the information. The Group of Twenty—an international forum for the governments and central bank governors from 20 major economies—was a perfect target for the Nazis. "Where?"

"They rotate locations each year. This year it's in Hamburg, Germany."

"When does it happen?"

"Starts the day after tomorrow. Advance teams for the diplomatic corps are already in place, along with a security task force. The President is in Berlin meeting with Chancellor Müller as we speak and will arrive on Air Force One in two days."

"Then there's still time to stop the meeting and keep the President safe," Randall rubbed his tired eyes.

"The forum will take place as planned," Flores replied.

Randall's eyes went wide. "What are you talking about? Is the President aware of the situation?"

"I've spoken with the Joint Chiefs of Staff, but they don't believe me. They feel that stopping the forum for, as one of them put it, 'a fanciful story' wouldn't be appropriate for the world's most powerful nation. Besides, it would be viewed as an insult to our German allies."

"That's insane! How in the world is the Secret Service going to protect him and the other leaders?"

"With your help."

"Excuse me?" Randall furrowed his brow.

"The Secret Service will be in place, as usual, but I've been directed to assist them in preventing a possible attack. They asked how I'd gotten the intel, and I told them about you. They want you there to explain what you know and help them plan the security detail."

Randall melted into his seat then looked at the floor. It was madness. He was now responsible for keeping the President of the United States and nineteen other world leaders safe from Vogel, along with figuring out how to save Sam.

"I'll be honest, I'm not sure what kind of a reception you'll receive. The suggestion to add you to the team was met with some loud complaining from the President's security detail, but they were overruled."

Randall looked up again and cocked his head to one side. Taking a moment to digest the situation, he realized that he had no other choice but to go along with the plan. "Well, if we're responsible for protecting the President, then I need to make a call."

Flores's expression shifted to a look of surprise and mild amusement. "Who?"

"Someone who might be able to help us stop Vogel."

Chapter 47

Berlin, Germany
July 28, 7:41 a.m.

As much as Randall had tried to prepare for it on the flight to Berlin, there was no way he could have anticipated the gravity of meeting with the President's protective detail. Intimidated didn't even begin to describe how he felt meeting William H. Clancy, the Director of the Secret Service, and his staff. Based on the non-descript expression on his face, the director would have made a fantastic poker player. Tall and broad-shouldered, the director's cleanly shaven head and piercing gray eyes only added to the intimidation factor. Then he remembered that they had asked for his help, not the other way around.

"How did you hear about this plot to assassinate the president and the other dignitaries?" Roy Hallett, the Assistant Director, asked Randall.

"A scientist named Jim Grady asked me to help him find his team, which had disappeared from an archaeological site in Argentina. In the process we discovered this plot," Randall shifted his gaze between Hallett and Clancy, who remained stone faced.

"The Nazi plot to build and deploy a superweapon to threaten the lives of world leaders and raise Germany to its World War II dominance?" Hallett asked, an eyebrow raised.

"That's right. Apparently, this has been in the works for decades, but the Nazis just acquired the fuel needed to power the device."

"Do you have any tangible evidence to support your claim? Photographs or videos of the device or these secret facilities?" Hallett asked.

"Not that I'm aware of, but perhaps General Flores could weigh in on this," Randall replied.

"We had a small expeditionary force that penetrated the facility in the Bavarian forest," Flores said. "Our goal was to free the hostages being held by the Germans and recapture the fuel source to prevent them from launching the weapon. We successfully freed the hostages, except Dr. Randall's daughter, who was taken by Dr. Vogel, the leader of this project. We didn't have time to take pictures or acquire verification. My men were barely able to escape with their lives." Flores glared at Hallett, curling his upper lip tightly.

"Right." Hallett turned his attention back to Randall. "And this fuel source, what is it and where's it's from?"

"It's an element of extraterrestrial origin," Randall replied.

"I see. And why again was your daughter involved in this adventure?" Hallett was smirking now.

Randall snapped. "I already told you!" He rose from his seat, stopping just short of Hallett's nose. "I know you don't believe me, and to be frank, I don't give a damn! I didn't ask to be a part of this, I was just trying to help Jim, and in the process my only daughter was taken hostage by a psychopath who's probably going to kill her if he hasn't already! If you don't want to believe me, you can go straight to hell!"

Hallett backed away from Randall, his eyes wide.

Randall turned his glare to Clancy. "We've been at this for nearly an hour now. What are you going to do? If you're not going to try and stop them, then I am! I'm not letting these bastards kill

279

my daughter. If they want to bump off the president and every other world leader, that's your problem. I'm going to save Sam!"

Clancy's cool veneer wavered for a moment, but he quickly recovered. "That's enough, Roy," Clancy ordered. "Dr. Randall, you have to understand that the events you've relayed to us, while troubling, are difficult to believe. Our intelligence community has no actionable information on the existence of a secret Nazi base or weapons programs. The chance that they have been operating in complete secrecy since the 1940s is remote..."

"Then don't do anything!" Randall turned to leave.

"But possible," Clancy said, his voice even. "At this time, I feel we need to move forward on the assumption that what you're saying may be true. I'd like for you to assist my team and provide them with any information you have that might help them detect the threat."

Randall shot a glance at Clancy, who still wore his poker face. Next, he looked at Flores, whose frown had morphed into a tight smile. Randall took a deep breath and walked back to the seat he had occupied only moments earlier. "What do we do now?"

"You'll join our team in Hamburg and share any information you have that would be helpful in preventing the attack," Clancy replied.

Hallett shook his head. "Are you serious? He's going to join the advance team on site? What's next, a vampire hunt in Transylvania?"

"Roy, we both know that sometimes the best intel can come from a source we never anticipated. It's our job to follow up on any credible threat against the president, regardless of our personal feelings." Clancy said, still maintaining eye contact with Randall.

Hallett mumbled under his breath.

"Deputy Director Hallett will escort you to the airfield. You'll fly out on a C17 transport for Hamburg with additional men and supplies this afternoon."

Chapter 48

Sam struggled against the ropes binding her wrists. For over an hour, she had rubbed them raw trying to free herself, but the knots were tied to perfection, and her efforts had earned her little more than painful burns. Making matters worse, the heat in the holding area caused her to perspire profusely, the sweat working its way under the ropes and onto her raw skin, which burned.

Unsure of where she was being held, instead of being fearful, Sam was angry. She had spent far too much time in the past week being held against her will and, to be blunt, she was tired of it. Her anger did nothing to help her escape, but it did fuel her fight to free herself. Her struggles, however, weren't helping. She was stuck until someone untied her.

She sighed deeply, wondering if her father and the others had successfully escaped the Nazi base. Realizing that she could easily slip into melancholy, she instead turned her focus to the situation at hand. Although her attempts to escape had gone unfulfilled, her time spent with Vogel in the Bell hadn't been entirely wasted. She'd had a bird's eye view of how the craft operated, watching closely as Vogel worked the controls to get them to their current destination. The Bell's guidance system was little more than a complicated, three-dimensional GPS system, allowing a user to choose not only longitude and latitude, but altitude as well.

Making an initial stop before coming to this latest hideout had afforded Sam the opportunity to see the leaving and arriving process twice. Although she wasn't sure of the purpose of each control, the operation of the craft was straightforward, and she now had a basic understanding of how it worked. Of course, the knowledge was useless since her captors were unlikely to leave her alone with their precious weapon.

Sam heard voices approaching and stopped struggling for the moment. She closed her eyes and focused on what was being said. With a little luck, she might spot an opportunity to get away.

The voices grew in intensity and she immediately recognized the loudest. Vogel. He appeared to be reprimanding someone in German. Although she didn't speak the language, the tone and cadence of his speech were unmistakable. Vogel and a second man came into view, the latter's head held low as he quietly absorbed his superior's verbal abuse. As they drew even with her cell, Vogel spat a few final words, smashing one hand into the other for emphasis. His subordinate nodded a final time, then headed off in a different direction. Vogel, walked over to Sam, applying a phony smile that nearly made her wretch.

"Fräulein. I trust you're comfortable. Is there anything we can get you?" Vogel clasped his hands and tilted his head to the side.

"How about a one-way ticket out of here?" Sam replied.

"Sadly, that won't be possible. However, your stay here is drawing to a close. We're almost ready to go on a little trip."

"A little trip? Is that what you're calling a plan to murder thousands of innocent people?"

"Sacrifices must be made if we are to achieve our goals. I'm sure there's not a single German citizen who wouldn't willfully give their life if they knew our intentions."

"If you think some mother is willing to sacrifice her child for your psychotic dream, then you truly are delusional!"

Vogel blinked repeatedly. Sam's comment had found its mark. "Young woman, there are forces at work here that you could never understand, I—"

"How dare you belittle me! You don't know the first thing about me, you condescending bastard!"

Vogel's face turned bright red and his eyes bulged from their sockets. "You have no idea what is taking place! This isn't simply about the glory of Germany; this is about the very survival of our species! Do you think for one moment that they care about any of us?" Spit flew from Vogel's lips as he spat out the words.

"Who?"

Vogel breathed rapidly; his eyes still wide. He closed them, clearly trying to calm himself.

"You mean those creatures that took my blood back at your other base, don't you?" Sam asked.

Vogel stared at the ground for a long moment, then lifted his head, the false smile returning. But this time he was clearly straining to conceal his true emotions. "We are doing this for the glory of Germany. As someone who isn't from our pure race, you couldn't possibly understand." Vogel straightened the sleeves of his shirt. "Prepare yourself, we will be leaving shortly."

Chapter 49

Congress Center Hamburg, Germany
July 28, 2:27 p.m.

Prior to leaving on their flight, Randall had called Moretti and told him to meet in Hamburg. Upon hearing about the unplanned party joining them, Hallett lost it, lecturing Randall on the importance of secrecy and clarifying that he controlled who would be on the assignment. After unsuccessfully trying to explain why Moretti was needed, Randall decided on a more direct approach. Going through General Flores, he contacted Clancy who, to the chagrin of Hallett, approved of Moretti joining the team. As a result, the Deputy Director's disposition went from unfriendly to downright hostile. Suddenly, the monstrous hold of the C17 seemed uncomfortably small.

Randall squirmed in his seat. "Assist Director Hallett, I understand you're not happy to have me here, but Captain Moretti has explained that this device he created is our best chance of preventing—"

"I don't give a damn what he has! Both of you better stay the hell out of my way, or I'll have your asses thrown in prison for obstruction of justice!" Hallett replied.

"Do you even know what we're up against with these

Nazis?" Randall asked.

Hallett locked eyes with Randall. "Don't lecture me about this assignment or anything else. Director Clancy may have forced you on me, but this operation is under my direction. If you're as smart as you think you are, you and your friend will stay out of my way."

Realizing that it would be best to allow Hallett to cool down, Randall decided to relocate. He got up and walked to the far end of the transport plane, choosing the seat farthest from the Assistant Director. On a more positive note, he was thrilled to have Michael join him in lieu of the general. Sitting together on the long flight to Germany, Randall had time to learn more about Michael and his family.

Michael relayed stories of his childhood, growing up as an army brat. He spoke of his love for his family, and how hard it had been on his brother and him, when their father was away on assignments. Due to the nature of his work, the elder Flores could never give his children a straight answer when they asked where he had been and what he had done. Michael, the older son, had shadowed his father's every move when he was home, forming a strong bond with him, even though his work frequently took him away. Despite the stress caused by his job, Michael's father was always patient with his sons, spending as much time as possible with them, given the circumstances.

Michael was also close with his mother, and brother, Anthony, the former filling in as his baseball coach, in lieu of his father. Since they moved frequently, Michael and his brother formed a close relationship. Friends came and went for the Flores boys, but their brotherly bond was strong. The main difference between the boys was their relationship to their parents. While Michael wished to emulate his father, following him into the military, Anthony decided to pursue a career in academics, like his mother. The brothers frequently compared notes about their careers over drinks and ball games.

As he listened, Randall's fondness for Michael grew. There was a simplicity about him that made him very likeable. Clearly, Michael had a steady, loving hand guiding him while he was young. In a way that only a parent could understand, Randall's appreciation for the general grew as he spent more time with his eldest son.

"We've been cleared for final approach into Hamburg, please take your seat and strap in," the pilot's voice called out over the plane's speaker system. A short time later, the military transport touched down and taxied to its hanger. As Randall departed the plane, he caught sight of a now familiar face. Moretti was waiting, leaning against the door of a car, wearing a mischievous grin. His eyes followed Randall as he made his way over to the Secret Service detachment waiting to pick them up.

"Ciao, Professore," Moretti said, embracing Randall in a hug.

"Captain Moretti, good to see you, too. This is Michael, he'll be joining us," Randall replied.

"Randall, this isn't the time for warm reunions, we have a job to do!" Hallett growled. He strode past the others and into the front seat of a waiting Chevy Suburban. Moretti grinned and shot Randall a knowing look. Two men in suits held the rear doors open for Randall, Michael, and Moretti.

The three men entered the vehicle and Moretti's grin grew wider. After the men buckled in, the Knight leaned over to Randall, shielding his mouth from the rest of passengers. "I don't think Mr. Hallett is very happy with you. I don't think he's used to taking orders from college teachers," Moretti winked at Randall.

Randall suppressed a laugh. "Do you have your device?"

"I gave it to Mr. Hallett. I think he considers me to be almost as big a pain in the neck as you." Moretti replied. "Almost!"

All Randall could do was shake his head.

The detail sped along the Autobahn, making the short trip from the airport to the Hamburg Congress Center in eighteen minutes. Although the trip was short, the second largest city in Germany and the eighth largest in the European Union didn't disappoint. Home to over 1.7 million people, the city was a contrast of old-world European architecture juxtaposed with gleaming, sleek modern buildings made of glass and steel.

As they approached the convention center, Randall noticed an uptick in security. The detail wound its way through large concrete barricades arranged to form a single path into the sprawling complex, which was crawling with members of the Bundespolizei—the German federal police— the German military, and a contingent of suit-clad agents patrolling the area.

The Suburban pulled to a stop by the steps leading up to the center, and Randall exited the vehicle. His eyes immediately panned to the top of the Radisson Hotel to his left. Easily the tallest building in the complex, it towered above the adjacent convention center and surrounding area. Although he couldn't see them, he was certain snipers were perched atop, ready to take out anyone posing a threat by ground or by air. He then turned to take in the rest of the view. The center was a low slung, multileveled concrete and glass structure with a row of trees flanking the far side, like green sentinels standing at attention. The area was lush with vegetation, reminding him of the look and feel of the east coast.

"This way," Hallett pushed past Randall and jogged up the steps to the building, flanked by two other agents.

For the first time, Randall noticed one of the agents carrying what looked like a gym bag. Moretti trailed the man closely, as if not wanting to lose sight of the bag. They entered the first floor of the three-story convention center and were immediately greeted by additional agents. The interior of the building was a beehive of activity with members of all protective agencies prepping for the arrival of the world leaders.

Randall followed Hallett, keeping him in sight as he strode down a long corridor, trailed by the agent with the bag and Moretti.

"What's in the bag?" Michael asked, keeping pace with Randall.

"I'm not sure, but whatever it is, Captain Moretti wants to stay close by it," Randall replied.

It suddenly dawned on Randall that the bag contained the device powered by the stone they had stolen from the Vatican. A bolt of guilt struck Randall, but he quickly suppressed it. The realization that Moretti's invention was in the bag caused him to quicken his pace. Randall closed the gap, following Moretti, and Hallett into a room off the hallway.

The room, in sharp contrast to the lobby, looked like NASA's mission control in Houston. Computers, voice analyzers, and a myriad of other electronic surveillance equipment filled the room, along with a full contingent of agents and technicians to man them. At the heart of the command center were several wall-mounted monitors featuring live feeds from various cameras located around the facility. They offered nearly complete coverage of every possible location the President and other dignitaries would be.

Randall couldn't help but be impressed as he took in the view. Off to his left, Moretti motioned for him to come over as the device his group had constructed was hoisted onto the table.

Randall threaded the busy command center, making his way to his friend who conversed with a technician while Hallett parted from them to get an update from his men.

"The device acts as an amplifier for the signal produced when the craft is inbound. When the navigation system is activated, the signal will cause the stone to glow," Moretti explained to the technician, who looked on, wearing a doubtful expression.

"You're saying that rock can detect this secret weapon as it travels through space and time, heading for this location?" the tech asked, eyes blinking in disbelief.

"Simply put, yes, but it's not the Bell it senses, it's the power source within the craft that causes it to glow when it's nearby," Moretti answered. "We designed the amplifier to increase the sensitivity of the stone, so it can be detected from a greater distance. Theoretically, the amplified signal can be identified over a much broader range than the stone could normally sense."

The technician frowned. "What are we supposed to do with it?" he checked his watch.

"The amplifier needs to be constantly monitored, and at the first indication that the weapon is on its way, agents need to be dispatched to all possible landing areas. We'll have, at best, a 5 to 10-minute warning before it arrives."

"How are things here?" Randall joined the discussion.

"I was explaining to this gentleman…"

"Assistant Director Hallett, I need to speak with you," the technician left Moretti in mid-sentence.

The Knight's eyes followed the agent as he jogged over to Hallett. All he could do was shake his head.

"I guess we'll have to monitor it ourselves," Randall commented.

Moretti shifted his gaze to Randall. "I guess so."

"So how does it work?"

"The stone glows when it detects The Devil's Heart. Many years ago, it was used by a Knight to track down an individual trying to steal The Devil's Heart from the church. Of course, our situation is far different. The stone itself worked well enough to track The Devil's Heart when the it was in the same building, as was the case in the past, but given the nature of the Bell, we needed a way to amplify its ability to detect the stone over a much longer distance."

"How close does the device need to be to pick up the signal?"

"Our scientists discovered a way to read the temporal disturbance created by the Bell's approach once the destination is programmed into the guidance system and the launch sequence is activated. First the device will vibrate, then it will then glow brightly when The Devil's Heart is detected."

"How long is the launch sequence?"

"Several minutes."

"Then once the stone begins to glow, we'll know the Nazis are a few minutes away."

"Yes, that's what we believe."

"Believe?"

"There was no way to actually test it, but our scientists are confident it will work."

"How confident?"

Moretti shrugged. "Pretty confident, I'd say."

Now it was Randall's turn to shake his head.

Chapter 50

6:40 p.m.

Randall and Moretti studied the site plans for the convention center, searching for potential areas where the Bell might land. In the back of his mind, Randall prayed that Vogel would bring Sam as insurance against being caught, using her as a potential bargaining chip. It was all Randall could do to push his concern for Sam out of his mind, so he could best prepare for the encounter.

While the two elder members of the group hunted for potential landing spots, Michael had been tasked with gathering information about the security detail from the agent assigned to their group. Hallett, possibly out of spite, had assigned a young field agent straight from the Federal Law Enforcement Training Center (FLETC) in Glynco, Georgia to be their liaison. Agent Benjamin Dalton was as green as the clover that dotted the countryside of his beloved childhood home in England. His family had moved to the states when he was only five, and from a young age, he had dreamed of being an agent. Whatever Dalton lacked in experience he made up for with sheer enthusiasm for his first field assignment.

"We've finished our walkthrough of the security detail around the perimeter," Dalton announced, as he and Michael returned from their assignment.

"Any idea where our friends might land?" Michael asked, drawing Randall's attention from the site plans.

"Based on what we've seen, we think there are two likely places Vogel might arrive," Moretti replied.

"And?" Daulton asked.

"Come take a look," Moretti motioned for Michael and Daulton to join him. "The physical dimensions and mass of the Bell are the first limiting factors of potential landing spots, ruling out most internal areas within the conference center. The craft will also need open space or an internal area with a ventilation system to draw away radioactive gasses generated by its propulsion system."

"That means it could land anywhere outside and adjacent to the center," Michael said.

"Yes, but with so many agents here and in the surrounding areas, I believe most external landing spots can be ruled out. Vogel will need time for the gasses to dissipate before exiting the vehicle and, if he's out in the open, he's inviting a deadly use of force the moment he opens the door," Moretti replied.

"Sounds like we can rule out any open areas within a quarter-mile radius," Ben stated.

"Correct," Moretti said.

"You can probably double that radius and maybe more, given the air support provided for this conference," Michael commented.

"I agree, and when you consider the numerous physical structures surrounding the center, I don't believe Vogel will try to land very far away. He'll want the world to know he can slip past any defense and plant a weapon to force their leaders into negotiations," Moretti said.

"Where do you think he'll land then?" Dalton asked.

"We've identified two, high probability landing spots," Moretti answered. "The first is on the top of the hotel. There's a landing pad for a helicopter that would support the mass of the Bell. The second is an underground loading dock, located here."

Moretti pointed to a spot on the opposite side of the convention center. "According to these plans, there's a large ventilation register adjacent to the dock, which would allow Vogel to vent the air before exiting."

"Maybe we can station agents there to patrol the area. Once they see him arrive, they can radio for help and surround the craft," Michael said.

Moretti's face grew grim. "We have to be careful. If we station anyone too close, the radiation from the craft will kill them, then Vogel will have time to vent the radiation, plant his weapon, and leave. The same would happen on the roof, but we might be able to head him off with air support."

"If Vogel knows this, then it sounds like the loading dock is the most likely target," Michael said. A single nod announced Moretti's agreement.

"What do we do next?" Michael asked.

"Ben, do you think you can convince your boss about the imminent threat to the loading dock and helipad, and get surveillance equipment set up in those areas?" Moretti asked.

Dalton shook his head slowly. "I don't know what happened between them, but A.D. Hallett really dislikes Dr. Randall. He made it clear at the briefing that he doesn't want any of you here and views you as a distraction to the assignment. If I tell him we need to move a detail or use equipment based on your warning, he'll refuse."

His response garnered a snort from Michael. "I've heard that about the good professor before," he winked at Randall. "Eventually, your boss will come around."

"What should we do in the meantime?" Dalton asked.

"We'll need to split up and take turns keeping an eye on the helipad and the loading dock," Randall replied. "There's four of us total, so we can rotate. One near the roof, one near the loading dock area, and one here in the command center, coordinating the show. The person in the command center can monitor Moretti's detector and let the others know when it's inbound so they can stay clear of the radiation."

Dalton cocked his head to the side. "What about the fourth person?"

Randall turned to face him. "The fourth person should stand down, get rest, and be ready to assist anyone who needs help."

"Sounds like a plan, who goes where?" Michael asked.

"Michael, you take the roof and keep an eye on the helipad. Ben, you focus on the loading area. Both of you need to keep your radios with you so we can let you know if Vogel's coming," Randall pointed to Moretti's device. "You'll need to get clear of the area to avoid contamination but stay close enough to tell us if it's arrived in your location."

Chapter 51

July 29, 5:49 a.m.

As night passed into morning, Randall walked through the double glass doors of the convention center, greeting a rising sun, burning angrily on the horizon. He shielded his eyes from the harsh glare as he adjusted from the glowing fluorescent light offered indoors to the bright sunshine awaiting him on the outside. He ran his hand over his stubble-covered chin and walked over to a coffee cart to retrieve a dose of liquid energy. Having volunteered to be the last one to take a sleep break, he knew he would need a boost.

They had been monitoring the situation for over twelve hours, but there had been no indication of Vogel arriving. The President, on the other hand, had touched down at the local airport and been whisked to his secure room at the attached hotel some time during the night. Hallett, true to form, had been tight lipped about the chief executive's arrival, but Dalton, proving to be quite resourceful, had confirmed the President's arrival at the complex. Accordingly, the team was ready for action.

After finishing a shift at the loading docks, Randall was slated to give Moretti a break next. The Knight had shown him how to monitor the tracking device and awaited his return. With another four hours of duty, Randall knew he'd need lots of coffee to stay awake, so he purchased two cups, one for now and one to nurse over his next shift. Paying the attendant and getting his drinks, he paused for a moment, closed his eyes, and deeply inhaled the rich aroma. He entered the command center, both drinks in hand, and found Moretti seated at the desk, struggling to keep his eyes open.

"Professore I'm happy you're back. Do you remember how to monitor the device?"

"Yep, I'm good to go. Any news from the boys?"

Moretti shook his head and rubbed his tired face at the same time. The Knight had a sizable set of bags resting beneath his eyes.

If he looks that bad, how the hell do I look? "I'll take it from here, go get some shuteye."

Moretti required no additional prodding. He crawled onto a couch they had moved into the command center to serve as their makeshift bed. Randall sat with his coffee and looked at Moretti who fell asleep instantly. He envied the man, wishing he could nod off himself.

Four more hours and you'll have your chance.

Two hours and a cup of coffee and a half into his shift, Randall had just checked in with both Michael and Ben. Neither had seen anything suspicious. He glanced at his watch, 7:48 a.m., the time most people were beginning their workday. Randall, however, had been awake for nearly 24 hours now. Much like gamblers in a casino, he had lost all track of time outside of the command center, his body clock fooled by the excessive exposure to fluorescent light.

His mind began to wander as he sat at the desk, resting his head on a propped fist. For some reason, he remembered a camping trip the family had taken many years back, when Sam was eight. He fondly remembered her catching her first rainbow trout, excitedly trying to reel it in.

"Daddy look what I caught! Help me grab him, he's

wiggling too much and he's slippery!" Sam exclaimed, trying to grasp the catch of the day.

"Hey, your machine's making noise," a voice called out to Randall as he extricated the small fish from Sam's hook.

Who's talking to me when I'm helping Sam with her fish?

"Mister weren't you supposed to be watching for that light to turn green?" the voice persisted.

Randall was suddenly overwhelmed by a falling sensation and awoke just in time to keep his head from slamming into the table.

What the hell!

"The light's green!" the voice called out again, causing Randall to look to his right. He was met by the familiar face of an FBI technician, headphones cradling his neck. The man was pointing in Randall's direction. "Look down!"

Shaking free of the cobwebs, Randall looked at the table in front of him. Moretti's tracking device was vibrating, the indicator stone glowing a bright green.

"Shit! Moretti, wake up!" Randall yelled, grabbing his radio. "Michael, Ben, the Bell is inbound. I repeat, Vogel is coming!"

"Roger, Nick," Michael responded. There was no word from. Dalton.

"Ben, the machine is coming, you need to evacuate the area. Do you hear me?"

Only static.

"Ben, come in, over!"

"Sorry Dr. Randall, I got your message. I'm pulling back to a safer distance."

"Thank God, I thought something had happened! Let me know if they come."

Moretti ambled over to Randall, rubbing his eyes. "How long has the light been on?"

Randall set down the radio. "I don't know, I dozed off."
Moretti glared at him.

"About 30 seconds, no more. I could see him starting to
nod off," the FBI technician said, pulling up behind Randall's
chair. "So, this thing really works?"

"Sì. They should be here in a few minutes. Then we just
need to find where they landed." Moretti replied, taking a seat next
to Randall. Two radios sat on the desk, one labeled Loading Dock,
the other, Rooftop. It was now a waiting game.

"What's your name?" Randall asked the technician.

"Caesar Duran. And yours?"

"Nick Randall, nice to meet you. Where's Assistant
Director Hallett? We need to let him know this is happening."

"The Assistant Director's with The President and his
detail."

"Can you reach him?"

Duran pulled back, eyes blinking, head shaking. "No sir, I
can't."

"Who can then?"

"A.D. Hallett made it clear that he doesn't want you here.
I'd like to help, but I can't. If I do, it'll be my ass and I need this
job."

Randall took a deep breath. "I appreciate that you're caught
in the middle and don't want to endanger your job but consider that
the most powerful people in the world are all in this complex to
decide the fate of the world's economy. Now imagine what would
happen if they all died, and you could have prevented it. You don't
want that on your head."

Randall could see the wheels turning in Duran's mind. The
man clearly wanted to do the right thing but needed a little push.
Glancing down at the man's left hand, he spotted his wedding ring.

"How long have you been married?"

Duran looked directly at him. "Seventeen of the best years
of my life."

"Do you have children?"

"Yes, a son and two daughters."

"Don't you owe it to them to make it home from this assignment? If we don't stop this attack, it will likely mean that we're all dead, not to mention anyone within several miles of this convention center."

Duran looked down at the ground and scratched his head. After a long sigh, he nodded, turned around, and walked out the door. Randall turned to look at Moretti. "What do you think?"

Moretti grabbed the radio. "Ben, Michael, do you see anything?"

"No."

"Negative."

"Keep us updated," Moretti slammed the radio on the table. "Something's not right, it's been too long. The Bell should already be here." Moretti studied the amplifier and fiddled with the settings.

"Is it possible this is a false alarm?" Randall asked.

Moretti shook his head vigorously. "If the device were malfunctioning the stone wouldn't have turned green. The Bell is here somewhere."

"Did we miss a landing site?" Randall asked, looking around the command center. The banks of computer screens showed live feeds from the multitude of cameras surrounding the complex. There was no sign of Vogel.

The door to the center burst open and Hallett stormed into the room with Duran trailing behind, his head hung down like a puppy, chastised for stealing his owner's bacon.

"What in the hell is the meaning of this? I gave specific orders not to be disturbed and now I find out it's because of you two! Goddam it, I'll have both of your asses thrown in jail for interfering with my security detail," Hallett yelled.

"The plans for this facility, do we have everything?" Randall asked, ignoring the temper tantrum.

Hallett recoiled, a look of disgust on his face. "Yes!"

"Can't be. There must be something about this center that's not included on this set of plans," Randall replied.

Hallett strode to Randall and Moretti, hovering over the desk with the architectural renderings splayed out. He scanned the pages, flipping back and forth over each. "These are all of the architectural and engineering drawings for this convention center. You're not missing anything. Your idiotic machine is clearly broken!"

"We must have missed something," Randall said, frantically flipping through pages.

"This little stunt of yours is going to cost you, I've removing both of you from this detail. Agent Gunderson escort these men to the holding area," Hallett said to another agent in the room.

"Sir, you need to see this," Duran said sheepishly.

"Not now!" Hallett growled.

Randall left Hallett's side, coming to a stop by Duran's computer screen. "What have you found?"

"Prior to any assignment, we require all plan files to be turned over for our review. I heard you and Mr. Moretti talking earlier about finding areas that could structurally support a heavy device and found that Hall H is used for auto shows," Duran announced.

Randall studied the drawings. "You're right. How did we miss this? Is there a camera nearby?"

"Mr. Duran stop what you're doing, or you'll be joining them," Hallett fumed, storming his way across the room.

Duran furiously typed on his keyboard. "I'm bringing up the feed now."

Moretti joined Randall and Duran. The technician's screen flashed to a live video feed of Hall H of the center. Though grainy and unstable, the surveillance camera provided a bird's eye view of the room from one of its corners. Sitting to one side was the unmistakable silhouette of the Bell.

"Good job, Mr. Duran," Moretti patted the man's shoulder The technician smiled.

Hallett marched over to Randall, Moretti, and Duran, teeth clenched in anger, but upon seeing the monitor, the look on his face morphed from irritation to bewilderment. "What in God's name is that?"

"Looks like Mr. Duran might have just saved the President," Moretti said.

Hallett snapped out of his trance. "I need a team on the northeast side of the facility, I repeat, full squad to the northeast side of the facility!" Hallett barked into his radio. A buzzing noise came back.

"The arrival of the Bell is interfering with the radio transmission," Moretti said, studying the screen.

"How long until it clears," Hallett asked, his voice belying his concern.

"I don't know," Moretti replied.

Randall scooped a radio from its cradle. "Hallett keep trying to contact your men. Moretti, stay by the radio and try to reach Michael and Ben." Before anyone could respond, he dashed out the door.

"Good luck, my friend," Moretti said.

Chapter 52

Randall sprinted down the hallway, shoving his way past agents and other security members, who shot menacing glances back at him. He didn't care. His only thoughts were saving Sam and stopping Vogel. He reached the end of the corridor and smashed down the handle of a wooden door with a small rectangular window, causing it to fly open. It led to a stairwell that would take him to the lower level.

He sprinted down the stairs, jumping down two or three at a time. He hit the landing, his momentum carrying his body into the wall as he slammed his back into the concrete. He ignored the pain. Slowing down could cost Sam her life. He bound down the remaining steps, reaching the door to the next level and shoved it open.

Was Sam still alive and had Vogel brought her? Panic gripped him, propelling him down the corridor like a heat-seeking missile, searching for its target. If his recollection of the plans was correct, he was getting closer.

Randall had no idea what awaited him when he confronted the Nazis, but he had to try. He fumbled for his radio, nearly dropping it as he sprinted down the dimly lit hall. He neared the spot where the pathway turned right and keyed the microphone.

"Moretti, can you hear me?"

Nothing.

He tried again. "Moretti, it's Randall, do you copy?"

Faint static with low garbled tones replied.

"I couldn't hear you, please repeat!"

"Professore! I can hear you. Are you okay?" The reply came, thick Italian accent and all. The interference from the Bell was subsiding.

"I'm fine. Have you been able to reach Michael or Ben?"

"No, you're the first one I've been able to contact."

"Call them and get them down here! Tell Hallett to do the same!"

Only silence.

"Did you hear me?" Randall rounded the corner, radio pressed to his ear. His labored breathing made it difficult to hear Moretti's reply,

"She's there."

"Who's here?"

"Sam."

"You saw her?"

Once again silence.

"Moretti, did you see my daughter on the security camera!" Randall yelled into the radio, sheets of sweat rolling down his face and back.

"Si, I saw her," Moretti replied in a low, slow tone.

"Is she alright?" Randall asked, fear causing his voice to tremble.

"They pushed her out of the Bell and closed the door behind her."

Randall stopped, focusing on Moretti's voice. "Is she moving?"

The Knight didn't answer.

A heaviness descended upon Randall like sacks of sand

tossed upon his shoulders. He struggled to stay upright and braced himself against the crème colored wall. "Moretti."

"She's lying on the ground outside of the Bell."

"Is she alive?"

No reply.

He crushed the transmit button with his thumb. "Dammit, is she alive!"

"I don't know."

Randall's heart sank in his chest. He couldn't breathe. Tears welled in his eyes and he dropped to his knees.

Please God, please no.

"Moretti, I…"

"She's moving!"

Randall's head jerked up.

"She's pushing herself up from the floor and standing! She's alive!" Moretti yelled.

Thank God!

"I'm on my way! Tell everyone, I need help!" Randall sprinted to the last flight of stairs.

The world floated by in slow motion as Randall passed multiple doors and tear-drop shaped wall sconces. The only noise was the jackhammering sound of his heartbeat.

He flew down the steps and out into the hallway then came to a stop. The dimly lit passage opened into a long space to his left, with three separate doors. A placard on the wall announced that the doors granted access to Hall H, a large meeting room on the opposite end of the complex from the G-20 forum.

Randall's radio crackled to life. He winced at the sound and turned the volume as low as possible. He crouched low, his hands nearly touching the burgundy colored carpet. He listened for any sounds coming from the adjacent room.

Nothing.

He slowly approached the first door, cracked it open and looked inside. Columns of tables and chairs were stacked against the wall directly to his left, but he couldn't see all the way into the room. He stepped in further, his right shoulder pressed against the door keeping it open. At the far end he spotted three Nazis clad in black combat fatigues, carrying a cylindrical device from the Bell. To their right was an additional man guarding his daughter with a gun.

"Sam!"

Sam turned to look at him, eyes wide. "Run!".

The guard spun, leveling his weapon at Randall, who dove out the door and into the hallway, hugging the ground. Automatic gunfire rose from the room, pulverizing the wall and door behind him. Sparks and bits of wood and drywall rained down on him as he covered his head and neck.

Randall heard a faint murmur and realized it was his radio. He dialed the volume up.

"Nick you have to hide, they're armed with fully automatic weapons!"

Thanks for the heads up.

"Get help down here," Randall said, then clicked the radio off.

He realized the gunfire had stopped meaning the Nazis would be on him in moments. He looked for any way to defend himself and spotted a wall-mounted fire extinguisher. It wasn't much but it would have to do. He quietly slipped it from its cradle, pulled the pin, and backed toward the stairwell behind him.

A door slowly opened outward, the barrel of an assault weapon poking out. A Nazi strode out into the hallway, scanning for Randall who stood off to the side, back against the wall no more than ten feet away. Their eyes met and the German raised his weapon, but Randall fired a stream of fire retardant directly at his face, causing him to jerk his gun upward, spraying the ceiling with bullets. The man cursed and stopped shooting, then wiped the foam from his eyes.

Randall's victory was short lived. The fire extinguisher was empty, leaving him defenseless. The Nazi righted himself, gritted his teeth and lifted his gun. The stairwell door burst open, and Dalton entered, distracting the Nazi who turned to face the new threat, getting off a small volley that went wide. Dalton was ready, getting off three rounds that struck his would-be killer in the chest and neck. The man's black-clad body slumped to the ground.

"Thanks," Randall rose to his feet.

"You're welcome, glad I came along when I did," Dalton holstered his weapon, then helped Randall to his feet.

The door to the banquet room burst outward again as another Nazi entered the hallway. He spotted Randall and Dalton and brought his assault rifle up in an arc. Dalton shoved Randall to the side, jerked his gun from his holster and fired at the same time as the Nazi. Both men found their mark, the German spraying multiple shots into Ben's leg and thigh, but not before Ben fired two rounds into his neck and head. The mercenary stumbled backward a step then dropped to the floor, joining his comrade. Two down.

A wobbly Dalton grabbed his injured leg as blood flowed from his wounds. Randall caught him from behind and slowly lowered him to the floor.

"Son of a bitch hurts!" Dalton said, his hands and gun covered with blood.

"We've got to stop the bleeding. Take off your jacket," Randall said. He helped the wounded agent remove his coat, then used a sleeve as a tourniquet to stem the blood flow. He turned the radio back on.

"Moretti, can you hear me? Ben's hit. Send a medic!" Randall yelled into the radio.

"Help's on the way!" Moretti replied.

"Here, take this and watch the door," Dalton said through gritted teeth. He passed his gun to Randall. "It's up to you now, you have to stop them!"

As Randall accepted the pistol, the stairwell door burst outward again, catching both men off guard. A lone man emerged, assault rifle in hand.

Randall instinctively shielded Dalton but breathed a sigh of relief when he recognized the man's face. "Michael."

"What's the situation," Michael stepped toward the injured FBI agent.

"Ben's hurt. I'm trying to slow the bleeding until help arrives."

"Dammit, we don't have time for this! Those guys are hauling something into the building while you're out here babying me!" Ben growled.

Randall's eyes flicked between the two men. "Ben's right, we need to stop Vogel. Did you see anyone else coming behind you?"

Michael shook his head.

"We go through separate doors. I'll go first and draw their fire. You come through right after and drop anyone you see, but don't shoot whatever they took out of the Bell!"

Michael smiled at the admonition. "You sounded just like my dad."

Randall grinned then looked at Dalton. "Release the tourniquet every few minutes."

"I will. Go!" Dalton motioned with one arm while holding his injured leg with the other.

Randall and Michael slunk to the doors farthest apart, then crouched beside each. Randall checked to see that a round was in the chamber, then glanced up and nodded to Michael. He held up three fingers, then counted down. Three, two, one!

Randall shoved the door open, rolled into the banquet room, then hurried behind an upended table. His plan worked. Two mercenaries spun and opened fire on him. Bits of wood splintered into the air.

Peeking around the edge of the table, Randall spotted Vogel hiding behind the weapon's casing. He covered Sam with a gun in one hand, while he fiddled with the device with the other. As he finished, it started to beep loudly. Randall surmised he had activated a timer on the likely bomb. Vogel then barked orders to his two remaining men, who again opened fire on Randall.

As the Nazis unleashed an assault on Randall, Michael kicked in the second door, catching the Germans off guard. He fired a quick burst from his assault rifle, leveling one of the mercenaries before the man knew what had hit him. He turned to the second soldier who cursed at the realization that Randall had been a decoy.

The Nazi fired back at Michael, who ducked behind another overturned table. Randall used the distraction to move closer to the mercenary … and the bomb. The Nazi realized what was happening and turned his attention back to Randall, firing another burst of rounds at him, halting his forward progress.

Michael popped up again and fired at the German, causing him to retreat for cover. Randall and Michael took turns moving forward and shooting at the Nazi, closing to within ten feet.

Randall popped up again, exposed for a moment. The Nazi spun and trained his gun on him. At the same moment, Michael squeezed off a burst of rounds, one striking the Nazi in the head, sending him reeling backward. His body thumped against the wall before slumping to the ground.

Randall nodded at Michael, then looked around the room. "Where's Vogel?"

"I'm right here, Herr Professor," he slipped from behind the Bell, pressing the barrel of his gun into Sam's temple. Her eyes were wide. "Tell your friend to lay down his weapon and come out where I can see him."

Michael didn't have to be told again. "I'm placing it on the ground, don't shoot her." He stood from behind the table, arms in the air.

Vogel turned to face Randall. "And now you, Professor."

Randall hesitated, looking at Michael and then to Vogel who cocked the hammer of his Glock. "Your weapon on the ground or I'll shoot your daughter."

Out of options, Randall set his gun on a nearby table.

"Hands in the air, if you please."

Randall complied his eyes locked on Sam.

An evil smile crept across Vogel's face. "I'm glad to see you came to your senses. Sadly though, I have to kill you now." He moved his gun in a sweeping arc, from Sam's head, to Randall.

Michael dropped to the ground and grabbed his assault rifle, bringing it to his shoulder. But Vogel was too fast. He spun to face Michael, using Sam as a shield. He fired two rounds, striking Michael in the chest, propelling him backward and over a chair.

"No!" Randall screamed, snatching his gun from the table. He fired at Vogel, who was now exposed from pivoting to Michael. The shot grazed Vogel's leg. The Nazi cursed, then spun to face Randall, firing two rounds, into his thigh and arm. Randall tumbled to the ground and dropped his gun.

Randall looked up at Vogel and tried to stand, but his injured leg failed him, and he fell back to the floor. He lay there staring at the Nazi, helpless to save his daughter.

"I had considered sparing your daughter, but not anymore," Vogel said.

"No!" Randall yelled.

Vogel swung the gun toward Sam, who punched his arm, knocking the gun off course as it discharged into the wall. Sam pulled her other arm free of his grasp and unleased a brutal elbow strike across Vogel's face. He recoiled in shock, the gun spilling from his hand and clattering on the floor.

Vogel recovered and slapped Sam hard across the face. He then backhanded her and knocked her backward. He scrambled for his lost gun, found it, and picked it up, but Sam had already hoisted a chair above her head and smashed it down on his head. Vogel staggered to the floor, a large gash on his head. He looked wide-eyed at Sam, the Glock still in his hand. He lifted the barrel, but

Sam was too fast, dealing another blow with the chair, this time landing a shot directly to his temple. He slumped to the ground, blood trickling from both ears.

Chapter 53

Randall lay on the floor, his leg and arm throbbing. He ignored the pain, more concerned about Sam, who he couldn't see due to an overturned table that blocked his sight. "Sam! Are you okay? Are you there?"

"I think Vogel's dead."

"Thank God you're okay! Where are you?"

Randall heard footsteps, then saw Sam who was walking over to him. She was shaking. "I killed him."

"You did what you needed to do."

Sam nodded, taking a deep breath, her hands on her knees. Sam reached out a trembling hand to help her father up, but Randall declined.

"Check on Michael, I think he's hurt."

Sam straightened and looked around the room, then sprinted from view.

"He's hit," Sam shouted to her father.

Randall could hear the worry in her voice. "What's happening."

"He's not responding."

Randall struggled to stand, but his injured leg was useless. He tumbled back onto the floor, cursing. "There's a radio by the door, call for help."

"Michael, please!" Sam called out.

Randall heard groaning, followed by the sound of rustling. Footsteps approached and he looked up to see Sam steadying Michael who had a hole in the front of his shirt.

"Are you okay?" Randall asked.

Michael looked down at his chest and placed his pinky finger into the bullet hole. "I'm fine," he unbuttoned his shirt and revealed a Kevlar vest.

"I'm glad you're okay," Randall said, once again trying to struggle to his feet.

"Easy, Dr. Randall," Michael motioned for Randall to stay put.

The doors to the room burst inward and secret service agents streamed in. Men and women in suits dispersed throughout the space and surrounded Randall and the others.

"Keep your hands where I can see them!" an agent yelled, gun drawn, eyes locked on the group now huddled in place.

"We're the good guys. We stopped them," Randall said, nodding in the direction of the fallen Nazis.

The agent cocked the hammer of his SIG Sauer and pointed the barrel directly at Randall. "Don't move and keep your mouth shut!"

All Randall could do was blink and wince in pain as his leg throbbed with each heartbeat. A small commotion arose near one of the doors, and Randall turned to look. A familiar face strode into the room, flanked by other agents. Hallett scanned the area, then saw the group and made a beeline for them.

"Lower your weapons, they're with us," Hallett said, coming to a stop and crouching over Randall. "You can all put your hands down, you're safe."

"Assistant Director Hallett, we need you over here," a voice called out from the other side of the room, near Vogel's body.

Hallett's eyes shot over to the agent who signaled him. "I'll be right back."

"Take your time," Michael said, helping Randall from the

floor. He and Sam set Randall down gingerly on a padded chair, which Michael had flipped upright.

Randall grimaced in pain. The bullet wound searing like someone was jabbing a hot poker into his thigh. A combination of the pain, blood loss, and fatigue overwhelmed him, and he became light-headed.

"Are you okay?" Sam asked, steadying her father. "How are your leg and arm?"

Randall checked his arm first. The bullet had just grazed it, but his leg was another matter. "I just need a moment," he took a deep breath. "Has anyone checked on Ben?"

"Agent Dalton has been tended to," one of the agents responded.

"Dr. Randall, can you come over here?" Hallett yelled. He stood next to the Bell but focused on something lower to the ground. Despite his obstructed line of site, Randall immediately knew that he was by the weapon the Nazis had unloaded. The sound of his voice betrayed his concern.

"He can't really walk, he has a bullet in his leg," Sam replied for her father.

Hallett sprinted toward them.

"What do you know about that weapon they unloaded?" Hallett asked, his demeanor entirely transformed from earlier.

"Nothing. We hadn't been able to check it out," Randall answered.

"It's a thermonuclear warhead, and by the design, it appears to be Russian," Hallett said.

"You mean the Russians are helping the Nazis?" Sam asked.

Hallett shook his head. "When the Soviet Union collapsed, we were worried about their nuclear stockpile falling into the wrong hands. They've accounted for most of them," Hallett replied.

313

"But not all," Sam said.

"Right. This must be one of the warheads that went missing," Hallett said.

"Can your people disarm it?" Michael asked.

"We're bringing in an ordnance expert."

Randall glanced back and forth from Michael then to Hallett. "Then what's the problem?"

Hallett took a deep breath. "It's set on a timer. We have less than thirty-two minutes to detonation."

"How far away is your expert?" Sam asked.

"ETA is four to six minutes."

"That's cutting it awfully close," Sam said

Michael shook his head. "If they're not able to disarm it, there's no way we can get everyone away from here in time."

Hallett nodded in agreement. "We've notified The President and the other leaders. Marine One is on the way, but it's a few minutes out. Once it gets here, we'll load as many people as we can take and try to get them as far away as possible. As for the rest of you…"

"I want you to get Sam and Michael as far away from here as you can. You owe me that!" Randall grabbed Hallett's arm.

"Wait a minute, I'm not leaving you!" Sam gripped her father's hand so tightly that he momentarily forgot about the pain in his leg.

"I'm with Sam. I'm staying here with the rest of you," Michael said.

Randall shifted uneasily. "There's no reason to endanger the two of you. There's nothing you can do to help."

Sam grasped her father's chin. "I could say the same about you. They'll disarm the bomb and we'll all be fine."

Several agents sprinted toward the entrance of the ball room. Something was up. Hallett's hand went to his ear. "It's okay, send him in."

Moretti walked three feet in, then stopped. Upon seeing his friends, he jogged to their side. "Professore, you're injured."

"I'll be fine. Is there any news?"

"Si, the explosives specialist has pulled up. She's coming now."

A tall, dark haired woman, wearing a protective vest and carrying a small bag, entered the room.

"Excuse me for a moment," Hallett walked over to the woman, then guided her to the bomb.

"I want to see how she disarms it. Michael, help me up," Randall reached for Michael's arm and Moretti jumped in as well, helping Randall to his feet and delicately moving him toward the nuke. Sam followed behind, ready to steady her father should he stumble.

As they arrived, they caught the tail end of the conversation between Hallett and the explosives specialist. "Is there anything else?"

"You now know everything we know Agent Kwan," Hallett answered.

"And who are they?" Kwan nodded toward the others as she set up her equipment.

Hallett turned to face Randall. "This is Dr. Nick Randall and his team. They're the ones who informed us of the plan to assassinate the world leaders. Without their help, we never would have stopped them."

Kwan remained emotionless, her focus laser-like as she went about the task of disarming the weapon. Not even the sight of the Bell seemed to phase her. "You can be here, just stay out of my way," she said, never breaking eye contact with the bomb. The timer continued its relentless countdown. 26 minutes and 3 seconds to detonation.

Kwan ducked under the device, scanning its surface with her eyes, and running her hand along the metallic skin. She found what she was looking for, retrieved a small, handheld tool from her bag and started removing several hex head screws from the device.

After several minutes, she set her tool down and removed an inset panel from the side of the bomb.

Seated in a chair near the demolition expert, Randall watched in fascination. His heart beat a little faster as he glanced at the timer. The glowing numbers tumbled under 19 minutes. He looked at Kwan, her hair pulled back in a ponytail, not a drop of sweat on her smooth white skin.

"I was worried about this," Kwan said.

"What is it?" Hallett asked.

Kwan reached into her tool bag. "There's a secondary detonation device that's rigged to blow the bomb early if someone tampers with it."

Randall felt a hard squeeze on his shoulder. He turned to see Sam, fear shining in her eyes.

Hallett craned his neck to look at the exposed innards of the weapon. "Can you disable it?"

Kwan nudged him aside, going back to work inside the open panel. "Yes, but it's going to take longer than I had originally thought."

"How much longer?" Michael asked.

"The more questions I have to answer, the longer it'll take," Kwan snapped back.

The timer continued its slow, impassionate descent to zero. Its glowing green numbers menacingly announced that time was short. 14 minutes and 55 seconds remained.

A young agent pushed his way past the others, making for Hallett's side, then whispering into his ear. Hallett nodded.

"More good news?" Michael asked.

"The President and the other leaders decided to stay. They felt it wasn't right to save their own lives when tens of thousands of innocent citizens wouldn't survive," Hallett said.

Kwan set her tools down. "One down."

She picked up her wire cutters with her right hand. Showing the first signs of stress, several droplets of sweat had formed on her brow. She raised her left hand to wipe it, causing the cuff of her long sleeve shirt to pull back, exposing her wrist.

Randall's eyes went wide. "Stop her! She's going to detonate the bomb!" Randall launched from his seat, using his good leg. He nearly buckled in pain as the bullet wound roared to life. He ignored the searing sensation, grabbing Kwan's arm as she reached to cut the wire. The two tumbled to the ground, Randall coming to rest with Kwan perched above him. He fought with all his strength as she struggled to free herself.

"Randall, what the hell are you doing!" Hallett yelled eyes bulging.

Michael wasted little time, backhanding Kwan on the side of her head, sending her tumbling off his friend.

"Stop him!" Hallett screamed to his men, motioning for them to grab Michael.

Randall sat upright, pointing at Kwan. "She's with them! She's helping the Nazis!"

Moretti sprinted to the demolition expert, securing her arms behind her back.

Hallett watched in utter confusion as his agents drew their weapons, pointing them at Randall and Michael. "What are you talking about?"

Randall pointed at her wrist. "She has the same tattoo as Vogel! It's the tattoo worn by their group! Check for yourself."

Hallett walked over to Vogel's body, checking his wrist. He noted the unmistakable tattoo. Then he and two agents, strode to where Moretti detained Kwan, who struggled to free herself from the Knight's grasp. "He's crazy! What the hell are you doing!"

Hallett pointed to her arm. "Let me see your wrist."

"Which one, Professor?" Moretti asked.

"The left one."

Moretti freed Kwan's left arm. She tried unsuccessfully to shield it from Hallett, who grabbed her hand, pulling back the sleeve. There on the inside of her left wrist was the same arrow tattoo as he had found on Vogel.

Hallett's eyes narrowed, moving from her wrist to her face. "You'll face the death penalty for treason."

"Who gives a damn, we'll all be dead soon anyway," Kwan hissed.

Hallett motioned to his agents. "Get her the hell out of here."

Moretti and Michael lifted Randall from the floor, helping him into a seat, his wounded leg hurting like hell.

"Looks like you were right again," Hallett said, shaking his head. "I can't understand how they could have gotten someone so close to us."

"She must have been Vogel's failsafe. They've had a lot of time and resources to invest in this. Besides, their supporters are fanatics," Randall replied.

"Signore, we still have that to contend with this," Moretti said, pointing to the nuclear warhead.

Hallett headed toward the device. "Shit!"

"How much time?" Randall asked.

"10 minutes and 22 seconds. There's no way I can get someone else here to disarm it in time."

Randall immediately shot a worried glance to Sam, who walked calmly to his side. Tears formed in his eyes as she hugged him. "I'm sorry, Sam."

"It's okay, Dad. At least we're together."

A somber pall fell over the group as everyone came to terms with what would soon transpire. The blast would result in the fiery death of tens of thousands of innocent people instantaneously as the heat and shockwave of the thermonuclear explosion moved out in a uniform circular motion, away from ground zero. Tens of thousands more would succumb to a horrific fate as the radiation from the blast spread further and further, killing many more in the coming days, weeks, and months ahead.

Michael shuffled toward one of the doors out of the room. "If you'll excuse me, I need to call my mom and dad."

Moretti reached out and grabbed him by the arm. "Scusa signor, but I might need your help."

Michael turned to face the Knight his brow furrowed. "What do you mean?"

"We can still stop this catastrophe from happening, but we must hurry. Signora, you traveled with Vogel, no?"

Sam looked at Moretti, confusion filling her eyes. "Yes."

"Bene. Did you watch him when he operated the Bell?"

Sam nodded, a broad smile forming on her lips. "Dad, I think I can operate it!"

Randall shook his head. "No way! There's no way I'm going to let you jump into that thing, take the bomb, and die!"

"We don't have time to argue. We have to do it!" Sam shot back.

"Show me, and I'll go!" Randall replied.

Moretti stepped between father and daughter. "Per favore, neither of you will go. I will be the one."

Randall and Sam turned in unison to face the Knight.

"But you'll die," Sam said quietly.

A thin smile appeared on Moretti's face. "Si, and it will be an honor. I have lived my life by an oath to serve and there is no more fitting way for me to pass than to save others."

The rest of the group stood dumbfounded, unable to speak in the face of such incredible bravery.

Hallett broke the silence. "If we're going to do this, we need to do it quickly." He pointed at several of his men. "Load the bomb back into the Bell. Follow any instructions they give you."

The agents loaded the nuke onto the Bell in less than a minute, then exited the craft as Sam and Moretti stood over the control panel. Michael watched from the entrance, his arm supporting Randall as he waited with him.

"Where are you taking the bomb?" Randall asked.

"Mr. Hallett and I discussed it and he suggested the South

319

Pacific Ocean, here," Moretti said, pointing to a spot on a map he had pulled up on his phone.

"The location is where the South Pacific meets the Southern Ocean, between New Zealand, South America and the Antarctic. In other words, the middle of nowhere. Its where we steer our failing spacecraft when they re-enter Earth's orbit," Hallett answered.

"Are you sure about this?" Sam asked, tears now forming in her eyes.

Moretti nodded.

"How much time left?" Randall asked.

"7 minutes and 14 seconds," Michael replied.

Moretti waved at the control panel. "How did Vogel operate the craft?"

"Think of the controls as a sophisticated GPS system, where you set the coordinates you want to travel," Sam said. "The main difference is that there's a third setting for altitude."

"Bene. A 3-dimensional GPS."

"Right. These are the switches he set before traveling. The problem is, they're in German so I don't know which is latitude, longitude, and altitude."

"My German is good enough to translate," Moretti commented, tapping in the coordinates they had discussed a moment earlier.

"There must be another way," Randall said, his voice barely more than a whisper.

Moretti clasped Randall's shoulder. "This is how it must be."

"Vogel hit these switches before each trip. I'm not sure what they are, but the rest of the controls weren't used."

"Probably pre-set controls and monitoring systems that only need to be adjusted for certain situations," Michael commented adding an aviator's opinion.

Randall shifted his weight. "Let's hope we don't need to adjust them now."

Moretti scanned the switches Sam had indicated, making the appropriate adjustments. "As you Americans say, this should do it."

Michael checked the timer. "5 minutes and 17 seconds."

Randall reached up and grabbed the Knight's arm. "I don't know what to say, except thank you."

Moretti looked into his friend's eyes. "It's time for me to go."

"Everyone clear out!" Hallett announced to his remaining agents as Sam exited the Bell.

"Goodbye, my friends," Moretti hit a switch, causing the door to close with a soft hissing sound.

Hallett and Michael helped Randall hobble out of the room, Sam following behind in case they needed extra help. As they scrambled down the hallway, a loud buzzing noise rose from the hall. They hit the stairs, forcing their way up as quickly as possible, the two men practically carrying Randall now. They arrived on the next floor in short order, pushing the door open and exiting into the corridor. A moment later, the hallway was bathed in bright light as the walls transformed from their normal solid state to an opaque, near-transparent condition.

"We've got to move!" Randall yelled, urging the party forward.

"What happens if we don't get far enough from the Bell?" Sam asked over the ever-loudening din.

"I'm not sure, but I don't want to be here to find out!"

The group pushed their way farther, bursting through several sets of doors, struggling to place as much distance as possible between themselves and the Nazi weapon.

"How much longer until detonation?" Sam hollered over the increasing din.

"About two minutes! We're pushing it awfully close!" Michael replied.

They raced down the hallway toward the exit. The sound was deafening now, a loud piercing whistle, nearly causing each person to drop from the painful buzzing in their heads.

The group burst through the exit door and into the open air, just as technicians from Germany's hazardous materials team poured out of their vehicles, surrounding them with radiation blankets. They hurried the group into a heavily fortified truck to shield them from any damaging effects created by the Bell's departure as the technicians sealed off the building. A moment later, the shrieking sound ended. Moretti and the bomb were gone.

Chapter 54

Randall and Sam waited in the executive suites of the convention center where Hallett had left them after they'd been cleared by the hazardous materials team. Earlier, Randall had been given a local and oral anesthesia when the medical crew had removed the bullet from his leg and bandaged his arm. Initially the medication had made him woozy. Now, as the pain meds began to wear off, his leg hurt like hell again.

Despite the pain, he and Sam had been told that they needed to be debriefed as part of Secret Service operating protocol, so they were forced to wait. Michael on the other hand, had been luckier, having been released to return to Ramstein Airbase. Randall mused that there were certainly benefits to having friends in high places, or in Michael's case, a relative.

Randall's mind drifted as he sank into the rich leather sofa, the cushion contouring to his tired body. Though their ordeal was over, he couldn't help but think about Moretti. His mind replayed the image of a monstrous explosion caused by the detonation of the nuclear bomb beneath the water's surface. Although it was only his imagination, the plume of blue-green sea water launched hundreds of feet into the sky seemed strikingly real. Randall envisioned the torrents of water cascading back to Earth as if he were watching a video in real time. He frowned unconsciously, shaking his head as he massaged his bandaged leg.

"Are you okay?" Sam touched his arm, drawing his gaze

toward her.

He gave her a weak smile. "I think so. I just can't help but think about Moretti sacrificing his life the way he did. I know I offered, but I'm not sure I would have been able to go through with it."

Sam brushed a rogue hair from her face. "Of course you would. Are you forgetting how you charged into the room alone to try and stop Vogel?"

"That was different."

The door swung inward before Sam could correct her father. Two suit clad agents walked into the room and headed straight for them. "Dr. Nicholas Randall?"

"Guilty as charged."

"And are you Dr. Samantha Randall?"

Sam nodded as the second agent swept the room, checking to make sure there was no one else present.

"There's someone who'd like to speak with you." The agent's hand went to his ear as he turned his head and spoke into his wrist microphone. A moment later, the door swung in again and a third agent held it open for another man who entered, flanked by two additional Secret Service members.

The man walked confidently, making direct eye contact with Randall as he glided across the floor toward the waiting scientists. He extended his hand as he arrived by their side. "Drs. Randall, we're deeply indebted to you for preventing a major disaster and saving hundreds of thousands of civilians."

Randall was dumbfounded as the cloud of confusion slowly parted in his mind and he finally recognized the person greeting him. "Thank you, Mr. President."

The President's grasp was firm. "You created quite a commotion when you made your announcement about this attempt on our lives a few days ago." The President turned to shake Sam's hand next, then slid into a chair next to them. "If you don't mind me asking, I'm still unclear about how you learned about all of this."

Randall crinkled his nose. "You mean Assistant Director Hallett didn't tell you?"

The President grinned. "I don't think you were his favorite person when you first arrived on the scene, but if it makes you feel better, I think he's warmed to you."

Randall explained the events that had transpired, beginning with the visit from Grady until Vogel's arrival in the Bell, hitting only the highlights out of respect for the President's time. Although the man was adept at hiding his emotions, ever the politician, Randall noted several times during his tale when a raised eyebrow indicated particular interest on the part of the leader of the free world.

Upon hearing the end of Randall's tale, the President sat back into his seat, his hands folded neatly across his lap. He stared at the ground, deep in thought. "You both understand that the events of the past few days are highly classified and cannot be shared with anyone."

Randall and Sam both nodded.

"However, what you've both done for your country, and, in fact, the world, cannot be overstated." A lazy grin snaked its way across his face. "I would say that I'm surprised that two private citizens had been so intricately involved in an event of this magnitude, but that would be ignoring your past escapades."

Randall and Sam shared a look, then turned back to face the President who now wore a full-fledged smile. "I know people." With that he rose from his chair, shook their hands again, and walked to the door. He stopped before leaving, turning his head to the side. "We could use people with your expertise in the future. When the time comes, I hope you might consider our offer."

Father and daughter watched in awe as the President strode out of the room. A moment later, a familiar face strolled casually into the office. Hallett moved easily, a happy look on his face for the first time since meeting Randall. He pulled up next to them, then dropped into the chair recently vacated by The President. "How did the meeting go?" The look on his face was that of the proverbial cat who ate the canary.

Sam composed herself. "It was amazing. What's this about needing our expertise?"

Hallett feigned shock. "I have no idea what you're referring to." He turned to face Randall his expression suddenly serious. "Nick, I misjudged you. Worse, I completely dismissed your guidance and it nearly cost us the lives of many world leaders and citizens. I hope you can accept my apology."

Randall nodded. "Of course. I can understand how you felt. If I were in your shoes, I probably would have reacted the same way."

Hallett extended his hand to Randall. "Thank you. We've made arrangements to get you both stateside as soon as you're ready."

Father turned to daughter, who rubbed her tired eyes, then turned back to Hallett. "I think we're ready to go."

A short time later, Hallett escorted the pair to a waiting black Chevy Tahoe with tinted windows. Randall moved slowly and carefully over the pavement, using the crutches provided by the medical team. As an agent held the door open for Sam, Randall turned to take one last look at the convention center and surrounding grounds. The air was dry, but a cool breeze caressed his face as he surveyed the area where a near disaster was diverted with only minutes to spare.

About the Author

Robert Rapoza is the award-winning author of THE RUINS, and THE BERMUDA CONNECTION. His action-packed thrillers have been described as a cross between the works of Dan Brown and Indiana Jones, keeping readers riveted from beginning to end. Tommy Howell from Readers Favorite calls protagonist Nick Randall "A statesman and action hero worthy of Pierce Brosnan or Liam Neeson." A member of the Southern California Writers Association, Robert Rapoza resides in the Los Angeles area with this wife and two children.

Learn more about Robert Rapoza and his books on Facebook, Twitter, and at RobertRapoza.com